D0962222

JUDGMENT AT APPOMATTOX

RALPH PETERS' NOVELS PUBLISHED BY FORGE

Cain at Gettysburg (Boyd Award)

Hell or Richmond (Boyd Award)

Valley of the Shadow (Boyd Award)

The Damned of Petersburg

Judgment at Appomattox

The Officers' Club

The War After Armageddon

RALPH PETERS' CIVIL WAR MYSTERIES PUBLISHED UNDER THE PEN NAME "OWEN PARRY"

Faded Coat of Blue (Herodotus Award)

Shadows of Glory

Call Each River Jordan

Honor's Kingdom (Hammett Prize)

Bold Sons of Erin

Rebels of Babylon

Our Simple Gifts: Civil War Christmas Tales

Ralph Peters is also the author of numerous books on strategy, as well as additional novels.

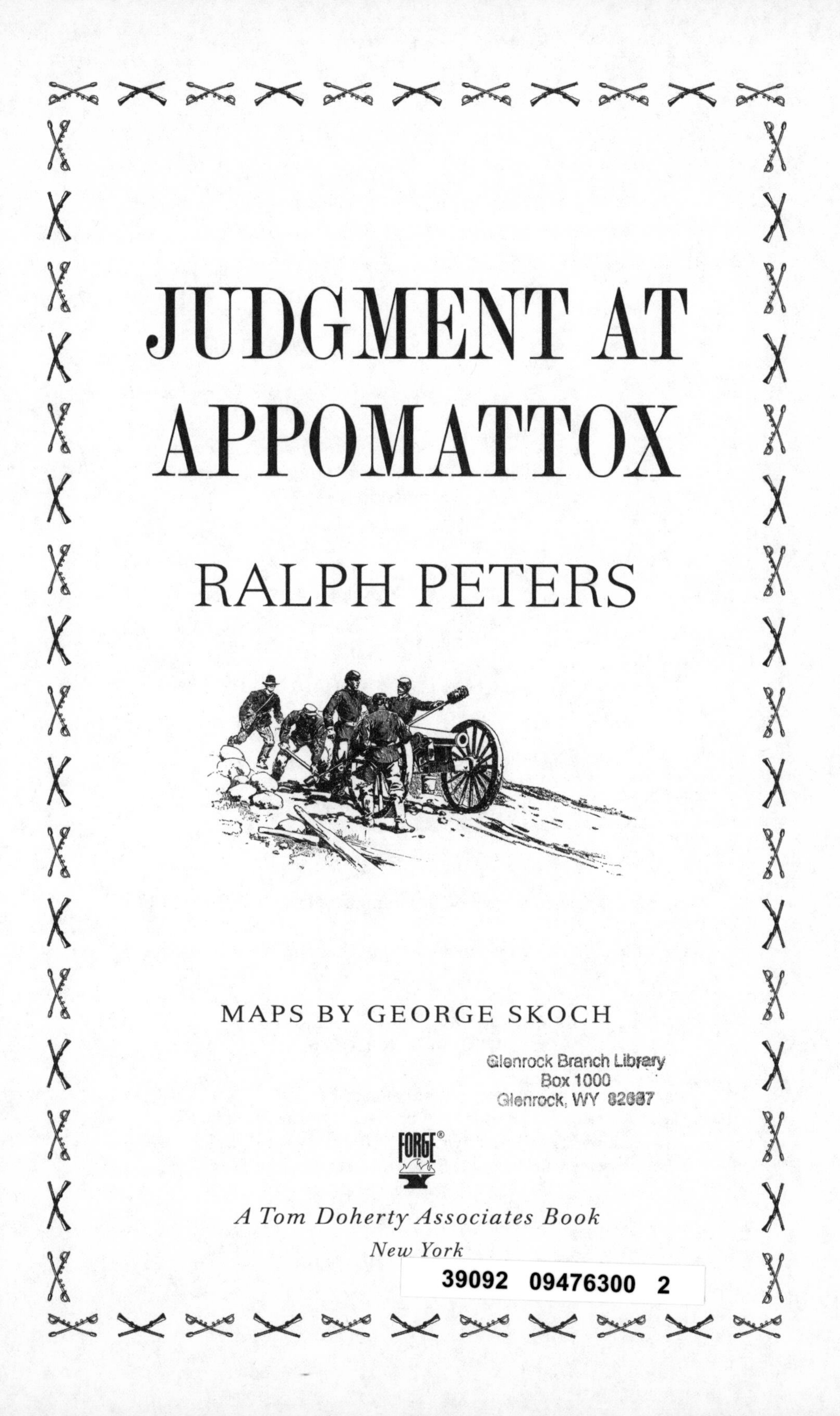

JUDGMENT AT APPOMATTOX

RALPH PETERS

MAPS BY GEORGE SKOCH

FORGE®

A Tom Doherty Associates Book

New York

This is a work of fiction. All of the characters, organizations, and events portrayed in this novel are either products of the author's imagination or are used fictitiously.

JUDGMENT AT APPOMATTOX

Maps by George Skoch

A Forge Book
Published by Tom Doherty Associates
175 Fifth Avenue
New York, NY 10010

www.tor-forge.com

Forge® is a registered trademark of Macmillan Publishing Group, LLC.

The Library of Congress Cataloging-in-Publication Data is available upon request.

ISBN 978-0-7653-8170-5 (hardcover)
ISBN 978-1-4668-8402-1 (ebook)

Our books may be purchased in bulk for promotional, educational, or business use. Please contact your local bookseller or the Macmillan Corporate and Premium Sales Department at 1-800-221-7945, extension 5442, or by email at MacmillanSpecialMarkets@macmillan.com.

First Edition: August 2017

Printed in the United States of America

0 9 8 7 6 5 4 3 2 1

With gratitude,
to my editor,
Robert Gleason,
steelworker, scholar, author, and raconteur,
who caught the vision.

The closer we come to our goal,
the greater the difficulties.

—Goethe,
Die Wahlverwandtschaften

PART I

THE BREAKTHROUGH

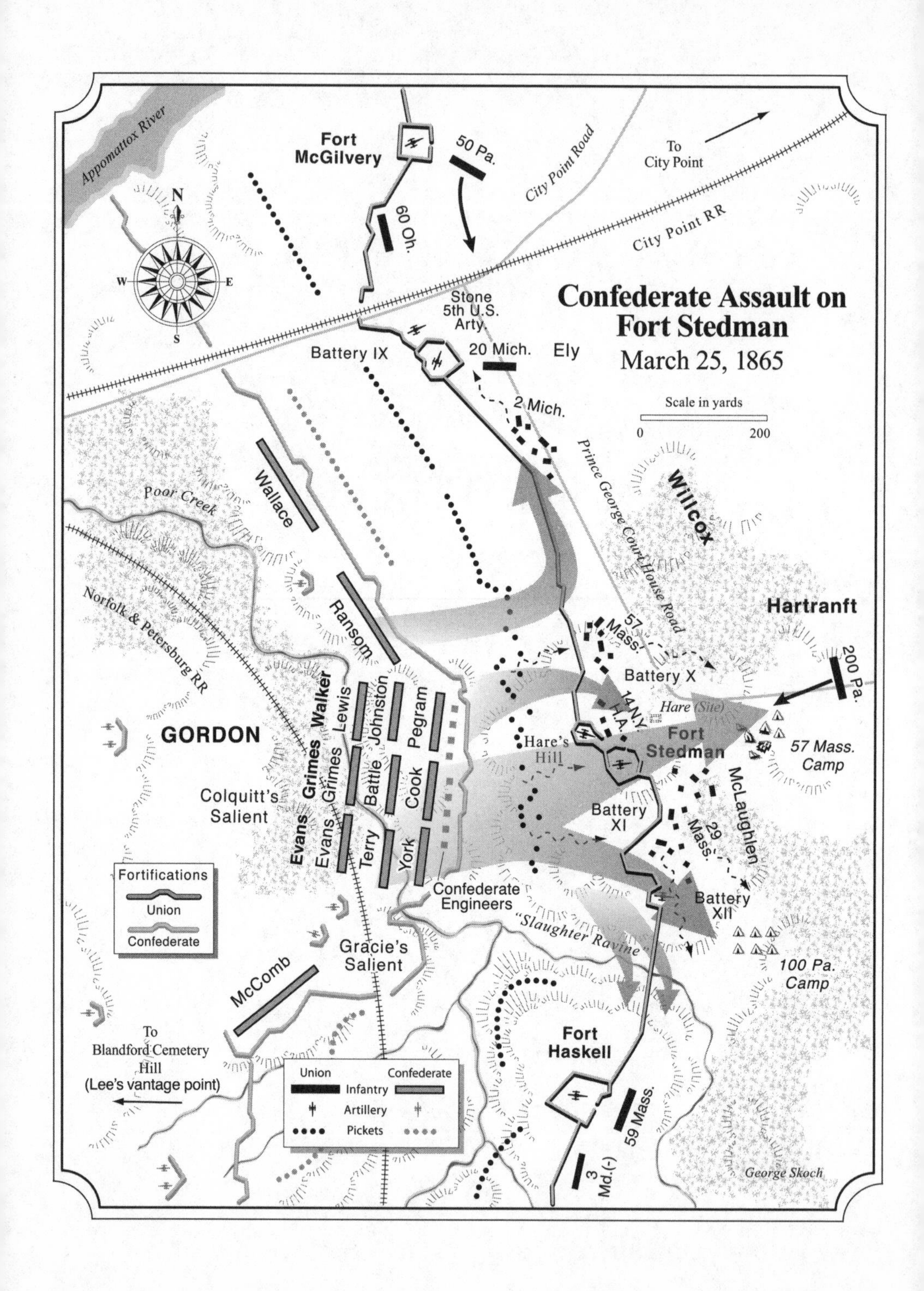

Confederate Assault on Fort Stedman
March 25, 1865
Scale in yards
0
200
Appomattox River
Fort McGilvery
50 Pa.
60 Oh.
City Point Road
To City Point
City Point RR
Stone
5th U.S. Arty.
Battery IX
20 Mich.
Ely
2 Mich.
Prince George Court House Road
Willcox
Hartranft
200 Pa.
Poor Creek
Wallace
Ransom
Norfolk & Petersburg RR
57 Mass.
Battery X
Hare (Site)
14 N.Y. H.A.
Fort Stedman
57 Mass. Camp
Hare's Hill
McLaughlen
29 Mass.
Battery XI
Battery XII
GORDON
Walker
Lewis
Johnston
Pegram
Grimes
Grimes
Battle
Cook
Evans
Evans
Terry
York
Colquitt's Salient
Confederate Engineers
"Slaughter Ravine"
100 Pa. Camp
Fortifications
Union
Confederate
Gracie's Salient
McComb
Fort Haskell
59 Mass.
3 Md.(-)
To
Blandford Cemetery
Hill
(Lee's vantage point)
Union
Confederate
Infantry
Artillery
Pickets
George Skoch
N
S
E
W

ONE

Three fifty a.m., March 25, 1865
Petersburg, Virginia

Gordon stood at the earthen wall, fingers attacked by the cold. Winter still fought rearguard actions before dawn broke. Two days back, a tempest of warm dust had scourged the lines. Now the ill-clad soldiers at his back, fifteen thousand present and more on the way—almost half of Lee's army—shivered as they waited for his signal.

A private knelt beside him, calm in the death-dark. The soldiers who still clung to the Army of Northern Virginia, those who had not deserted to the Yankees or slipped off homeward, breathed the fatalism of Homer's heroes, mythical figures cherished by Gordon and now made real by war. Two hundred yards stretched eastward to the night-draped Yankee fort, ground that might have been the plains of Troy, the waiting multitude *his* bronze-clad Greeks. Fierce, these men would fight. And Major General John Brown Gordon would lead them.

To victory?

Despite the good-tempered confidence he displayed to other men, Gordon was glad of the darkness. Not only would it shield his advancing soldiers, it masked concerns he feared he could not hide. This was *his* plan, his offering, produced at an order from Lee that had been almost plaintive. And the old man had only blessed the scheme for want of better choices: Lee, whose nights were ravaged now, who summoned generals from their beds to talk out the graveyard hours, dreading what might come when he closed his eyes.

The old man expected Gordon to work a miracle, to split the Federal line in two, to roll it up, to slash beyond it, to ravage the Yankee base at City Point, to defy the gods . . .

No longer Agamemnon, but doomed Priam: Poor Lee, grown cantankerous and haunted, complaining of poor lamp oil and bad candles, his fabled self-discipline cracking. By day, he remained a lion to the men, though, all they had left to believe in, the last worth of the Confederacy.

Gordon told himself—insisted—that there *was* a chance this attack would work, bedazzling Grant's hordes sufficiently long for Lee and the army's remnants to slip away, to join Joe Johnston in North Carolina and stretch out the war, combining to beat Sherman and then wheeling to confront Grant. Lee had spoken of Napoleon's strategy of the central position and of Frederick's ultimate victory—despite the fall of his capital—as Gordon listened, nodding but pierced by doubt. At times, Lee seemed unmoored from the army's reality. And all the while Jeff Davis carped and badgered him.

Gordon would not, could not, say no to Lee, that was the gist of it. Not now. Not when the end was near and those who appeared true would retain ascendance over their kind, even in disaster: A victorious people lauded their heroes, but defeated folks *needed* theirs.

The future of the South would fall to those few left untarnished and alive.

A cold gust combed Gordon's beard, which was as carefully groomed as ever. The men behind the rampart rustled, chilled but heeding their orders to keep silent. Aware down deep of how much lay at stake.

Surely word would reach him soon that the last obstacles had been cleared. Then it would all begin at a signal shot.

He had done his best, striving to plan this fight with the guile of Ulysses. He'd studied the Federal lines, selecting the earthen bastion the Yankees called Fort Stedman, along with its flanking batteries, as the attack's first objective. The fort stood where the lines veered close and the road at its back ran straight to the Yankee rear. But the key to ultimate success would be the seizure of a trio of forts half a mile behind the Federal line, masked positions spotted by spies and confirmed, if vaguely, by Union deserters. Take those rear forts and you had that road, and you split Grant's army in two.

They just might pull it off. It wasn't impossible.

Gordon felt he'd done all within human power to craft a victory. And if the attack succeeded, he, John Brown Gordon, stood to be the late hero of the war, an advantage not inconsiderable to a man of high ambition.

Managing defeat would take more skill.

So the plan had been honed in fine detail, key officers taught their tasks. Working in a hush just short of silence, his engineers were clearing lanes through their own side's defenses. When they finished, picked units, relying on bayonets, would rush the Yankee picket line, posing as deserters coming over. With the pickets taken, his best regiments would rush toward Fort Stedman, accompanied by more engineers with axes and grapples to breach the Yankee obstacles. All would be done without firing a shot, for as long as possible. Letting the great blue legions sleep until it was too late.

Following the units tasked to seize the fort and the batteries on its flanks, three columns of one hundred soldiers each, officers and men hand-chosen and led by scouts sent by Lee, would thrust deeper into the Yankee lines to seize those rearward forts and open the road. Gordon's staff had taken pains to learn the names of the Federal officers—Ninth Corps men—along this stretch of line. If challenged, his "Three Hundred" would pass themselves off in the dark as Union soldiers returning from picket duty.

Full divisions, led by his best subordinates, would widen the breach in the meantime, rolling up the Yankee line north to the river and southward as far as possible before dawn.

Once the secondary forts had been taken, more divisions would follow. By first light, a cavalry force would fly down the road to the Union headquarters and depot at City Point.

It *could* work. There really was a chance that it could work.

There had been doubters, of course, not least among Lee's self-appointed guardians, his staff triumvirate of empowered boys. Marshall said bluntly that the plan was too complicated. Taylor reserved judgment, but smirked like a wealthy schoolboy. Worn out by Lee, poor Venable only shrugged.

The thing was, it *had* to work. Or the army was doomed and damned. Along with the Confederacy. It would all end right here, perhaps in weeks, with Grant unleashed by fair weather and the last of them trapped against this played-out city. Not beaten manfully, just beaten down. And *he* might be held responsible.

A voice startled Gordon: a Yankee voice.

"What're you doing over there, Johnny? What's that ruckus?" After a hold-your-breath silence, he added, "You answer real quick, or I'll shoot."

Calm as a front-porch philosopher in August, the soldier beside Gordon rose and drawled, "Ain't no never mind, Yank. Go on back to sleep. Just the boys gathering up the last hard corn, what's left hereabouts. Rations been mighty short."

Cold doubt. Vast night. Waiting thousands.

The Federal called over, "All right, Johnny. Get your corn. Ain't going to shoot a man who's drawing his rations."

Gordon closed his eyes in thanks. But the men clearing off the last obstacles seemed as loud as a stampede.

He flexed raw hands, gloves left behind in his urgency. Why *was* it taking the engineers so long? The attack had been scheduled for four a.m. But he knew without resort to his watch that the hour had passed.

Unbidden, but ever welcome, Fanny swept into his thoughts. Hardly a mile behind him, still in Petersburg, in a lodging just fair and no better, ready to bring their fourth child into the world, a child of war.

Fanny.

Reaching up from the firing stoop, someone tugged his sleeve: his assistant adjutant general, who would lead a brigade this day, at age twenty-six.

Gordon bent down.

"Lanes are clear, General," Major Douglas whispered. "The men are ready."

Gordon straightened. For a moment, he glanced backward, into the complicit darkness, able to make out the nearest troops only because they wore strips of white cloth diagonally over their chests or tied round their upper arms for recognition when the fighting began.

Gordon turned to the soldier waiting beside him.

"Fire your shot."

The signal that would unleash it all.

The soldier delayed. Just long enough to do what he thought fair to a trusting enemy. He called to the Yankee picket, "Halloo there, Yank. Wake up, look out! We're coming."

He shouldered his rifle, aimed high, and pulled the trigger.

Four fifteen a.m.
Hare's Hill

'Twas black as an Englishman's soul, this dark, and bleak as bloody Ireland. Danny Riordan rushed out with the rest, the sweet weight of his rifle in his mitts, a rifle left unloaded on bitter orders, but tipped with a bayonet kept sharp as sin. And every wild-elbowed lad, this wave of scrunty Irishmen swept from Louisiana into the war, every man of them hoped he wouldn't be skewered by a messmate, careful to keep the touch of the stinker next to him as feet felt forward in the dark, all the earth black as the cassock on a priest.

Whole lives passed in the seconds it took to stumble and fumble forward in rough silence. Not a man spoke to warn the Yankees, but small sudden noises there were and enough, the brief cries of blue-bellied pickets surprised and not asked to surrender, and the thunk of axes on winter-worn wood, no shots yet but a terrible tapping of hundreds—nay, thousands—of shoes worn thin as muslin, thin as famine dead.

One shot, two. The grump of a bucko tripped up. Riordan

himself legged wild at a trick of the ground, recovering to leap the berm of a rifle pit, sensing his way uncannily in the dark: a very acrobat he should have been, gone off with the circus, larks! A landing foot found a belly, its man-meat tension recognized from battles and prisons and brawls.

Dead, that one was.

Shouts of struggle tore at the surprise.

"Jaysus," cried the man next to him, a comment on this world and the hereafter.

More shots.

"Help the colonel," cawed a Leinster crow.

Riordan turned from curiosity—a vice more trouble than drink—and lent a mitt to Colonel Waggaman, who commanded what the war had left of them: not much, that was, not many. A hurry of hands pulled the colonel out of the clabber, and hard he snarled, mud-covered in the cold. The high marsh grabbed at Riordan's shredded shoes.

Waggaman cursed, a priest run out of the whiskey.

But why were they running downhill? Their purpose was to attack a fort or the like, but even a fool would not put such on a downslope. Had they mistaken their way in this devil's dark?

In answer, an officer's voice—so different they sounded, you always knew the high lads—called out, "Half-left, *half-left*!" and then came lightning, the bright spew of cannon, a greeting.

By the flash he saw murderous faces. Like his own.

By another gun's flare they spotted the rampart ahead. Sworn to silence still, they raced for the earthen wall, fearful of waking cannon to their front. But there were none, or none tended.

Up and over. A few men howled from habit, but soon were hushed.

Forms dark against darkness. The white bands his kind sported helped, but unreliably. Instinct led his rifle as he blocked a blundering man. One who wore no ribbon.

Too close for the bayonet. Riordan slammed the butt of his rifle into the man's belly, bending him to a gasp. The wood of an ill-managed weapon grazed Riordan's head and clattered down. He gave the doubled-up fellow a knee in the face, then brought the butt down onto the fellow's shoulders or parts similar, beating him to the ground.

When the Yankee had been laid out properly, Riordan smashed down the butt where the bugger's head should be. And he heard the lovely crack of splintering bone, not even a last cry from the fallen Federal.

"That's for Point Lookout, ye bastard," Riordan grunted.

Men packed around him, dangerous, querying each other in hushed brogues.

By the light of a last Yankee musket flash, he saw Daniel Keegan before him, bereft of his tin whistle now but with stripes sewn to his sleeve, promoted while Riordan rotted in Yankee prison pens, one and then another, taken not once in the war, but twice, to his mortification, and worth a fight it was when a man claimed that he'd been swept up *three* times, for third time there had been none, just sickness in a hospital hungry for corpses.

"Cripes, I almost killed ye," Riordan told him.

"Take a bolder one than you, it will."

The donnybrook was done for the moment, though. Officers hissed at them to re-form, still lacking the light to know the east from west.

Whispers ran down the regathered line that the colonel had welcomed a bayonet in his meat. As like from one of their own as one of the Yankees, and damn the confusion. Captain Bresnan took over, unbothered.

"Come on," he called, though still not battle shouting.

They filed out of the fort's rump, most of them in some order, though others went over the walls just for the pleasure. What were they now, this handful of men that remained of the proud Louisiana Brigade, melted into the Consolidated Brigade, with Company E, the old Mercer Guards, as Irish as want and pride, reduced to a mere handful of ragged wraiths?

Forward they went. Or someone believed it was forward.

A rumpus of shooting rose to the left: a tougher time for Grimes' lads in their glory, and let them keep it.

"We should've held back till the Yankees cooked up breakfast," a soldier griped, voice unfamiliar. "I've got the hunger on me, I do."

Riordan snorted. Hardly a man knew hunger as he did. The prison rations at Point Lookout, spare enough, had been a feast compared to the black years in Ireland. Many a man in the army claimed he was starving, but you never heard that word from Irish lips. Hunger, yes. Starvation, no. Starvation was a girl got thin and dried out as a woman of fourscore; starvation was a village abandoned to corpses—those not dead of chewing winter grass gone black with the cholera or flecked blue with typhus, starvation's eager companions.

Yankees. Surprised. Surrendering.

Some fought, though. A ragged volley crackled ahead.

"Load, load!" Bresnan's voice. But the boys were after more than that, for they'd gotten into a white maze of tents, pitched foolishly close to the line. And tents meant treasures.

"Time for that later," the captain pleaded.

When Riordan had been exchanged in January—a surprise to all concerned—he'd grown so thin the Yankees had counted him done. And more than a friend or two had suggested he come along into the byways as winter bit, for they'd had enough, those buckos, and were either going home or going over. It made sense, Riordan allowed. Why fight for an army that wouldn't trouble to feed you? But he'd come back stubborn from the camps, with a mind to kill at least a few Yankees before the fiddler stopped and the jig broke off.

Away they'd gone, all those who'd had enough, but Riordan stayed. A fool, they called him, an idiot. But the army pleased him better than digging ditches, addled with Louisiana's heat and Irishmen valued so low they put them to work next to chained-up niggers. Used to the heat, like animals, the darkies had mocked the misery of white men. Nor were the sons of Africa the worst of it:

Shoveling along the levees, a man learned fast that Pádraic had driven the snakes out of Ireland only to pack them off to Louisiana. Seamus McGintey had reared up sudden with a monstrous gurgle, gripping a great serpent, its fangs so deep in his neck that it couldn't free itself, and Seamus danced out his minutes, swinging the snake back and forth, until he yanked it off and fell over and died.

A rifle was a finer tool than any pick or shovel.

They got themselves into a tangle of trenches, tripping and tumbling. Officers whipped men with the flat of their sabers to drive them on.

Back up on a spit of flatland, the line re-formed, ragged but pressing on. Was there a newborn paleness on that ridge?

Horse hooves clobbered the earth, telling men of the nearness of a road. Yankee prisoners cried, "Don't shoot! Don't shoot me, Johnny!" as they clumsied past, headed rearward into their turn at captivity.

The last sons of Erin and Louisiana exchanged volleys with an enemy who could only be glimpsed by muzzle flash. They'd gotten themselves down another slope. Or perhaps the same one a second time. The earth was dry here, though. Riordan wondered whether a single officer had one sound idea where in the world they were, for he had none himself.

To the left—the north?—artillery grew busy, boding ill.

Their officers stopped the Louisianans, confused and waiting for orders.

Four forty-five a.m.
Union lines

Brigadier General of United States Volunteers Napoleon Bonaparte McLaughlen approached Fort Stedman on horseback, wishing for daylight so he could get things settled. Of course, the Johnnies would probably withdraw long before that, unwilling to be caught in the open on one of their picket raids.

As an enlisted man in the 2nd Dragoons before the war, McLaughlen had learned when to trust a horse. He was glad of that knowledge now, since he couldn't see one damned thing beyond an occasional rifle flash. The dark was so thick you could bite it. The horse knew the roadway well, though, and kept to it even when spurred.

Horse stink, man stink.

McLaughlen had suffered several bad minutes, fearing that the Rebs had struck in force. He'd even sent off his staff to rouse reinforcements. But he'd found Fort Haskell secure in trusted hands, its frontage quiet and no one alarmed, so now he just needed to stiffen up Fort Stedman. Make sure all those sluggards were under arms in obedience to his orders.

His horse shied around shadows.

He thought the sky looked paler. Then it seemed black again.

Somebody had gotten the jumps to the north, up between Batteries IX and X, by the feel of things. The Johnnies might have staged more than one simultaneous picket raid, out of either boldness or desperation.

Grinding his parts against a saddle before the sun came up always reminded him of his frontier days. Damned well hadn't suspected back then that he'd one day become a general. Even sergeant had looked a long way off.

A frontier soldier got his coffee, though. Before he put a horse between his legs.

This Reb disturbance annoyed McLaughlen, not least because he'd been working on his own plan to strike the Johnnies from Fort Stedman. He'd been trying, thus far without success, to interest his superiors. And this didn't help, suggesting that the Rebs remained alert.

He spurred the horse again, spending a bit of the anger he felt at the Johnnies. They were defeated and done with, but too proud to admit it. Anyone could see that Lee was finished. Everything from here on out was a needless waste of blood.

McLaughlen was determined to take charge, to get his lines

under control and end the nonsense before the morning muster. And find some cook fire where the coffee was boiling.

Again the horse swerved to avoid shadows in motion. Shirkers, the general reckoned. Some of Hartranft's green bunch, most like, straying in the dark. Their officers needed to get them under control.

Too near, a cannon discharged and startled his horse. It made no sense. Had his mount grown confused? The direction of that flash seemed all askew.

More noise than there should have been. Yet, not the bang and rumpus of a real fight.

The slope stopped climbing and leveled out. It *felt* like the rear of Stedman. Smelled like it, too, that latrine stench. Matters seemed calmer here. The riflery, which had snapped down the line minutes earlier, had fallen off to isolated shots.

Queer business, though.

The horse took him right into Stedman, where the soldiers sounded disorderly and rambunctious. And seemed excessively plentiful. As if they had been reinforced too heavily, packed together uselessly. Perhaps they really were Hartranft's new volunteers and dregs of the draft. That would explain the indiscipline.

A cluster of man-shapes approached. McLaughlen reined up.

"You there," McLaughlen called, "you're going the wrong way, soldier! Get back to your posts, every one of you."

Laughter.

A voice that was utterly wrong replied, "Well, now, it does seem to *this* body that we're heading just where we'uns want to go. That right, boys?"

"Are you . . . a Rebel?" the general asked, bewildered.

"I do prefer 'Confederate.' But 'Reb' does nice enough. Now you git down off that long-legged cow and surrender."

Outraged—not least by his folly—McLaughlen demanded, "Are you an officer?"

"Don't matter one lick. You dismount right now, or I'll blow your head off."

McLaughlen sensed a pistol rising toward him. A merry, unforgiving crowd had gathered.

The general got down. "I'm General McLaughlen and I demand to be treated with proper respect."

"Your pistol. Give it here."

McLaughlen handed it over, but insisted, "I can only surrender my sword to a fellow officer."

The men crowding close whooped at that.

"Well, I'm Lieutenant Guinn, Thirty-first Georgia. But you hang on to your letter opener. You can give it to General Gordon, he'll be tickled." A big, unpleasant shape, the lieutenant turned. "Bradwell, take this high-flown gent on back to General Gordon, with my compliments." He chuckled again. "Rest of you, let's go. Sportin's over." But he turned once more to warn, "I don't want him picked *too* clean, Bradwell. Hear me?"

The private nudged McLaughlen through a reeking mass of Confederates. The two of them joined a stream of Union prisoners flushed rearward between advancing Rebel columns. McLaughlen let fly with his feelings for the world to hear.

The soldier given charge of him finally said, "Genr'l, I never did hear a man cuss so powerful. Where'd you learn them words?"

McLaughlen grunted. "I was a goddamned private just like you. And lucky if they don't make me one again."

Five ten a.m.
Union Battery IX

First Lieutenant Valentine Stone, 5th U.S. Artillery, leapt from his horse, blouse flapping, and shouted, "Load spherical case!"

Mack MacConnell had already had the men wheel a section of guns to point due south.

In the first gray tease of light, Stone saw them coming: a long, uneven line of Rebs sweeping northward, half inside the Union works, the rest driving up the ground between the lines. Scampering ahead of them, small bands of his kind raced for safety.

Those boys had put up a fight, though. He'd heard it from the innards of Fort McGilvery. Remnants of the 2nd Michigan they'd be.

Within the battery walls and along the traverses, the men of the 20th Michigan, charged to protect the battery, cheered on their fellow Wolverines, urging them to run faster.

There did seem to be a plentitude of Rebs. He wished those Michiganders would go to ground so his guns could fire.

"Under four hundred yards, sir," MacConnell called.

"I see that. Damn me. Open on the Rebs outside the lines."

MacConnell shouted the orders. The gun crews were all but ahead of him. Muzzles shot flame, carriages recoiled, and smoke rose in the half-light.

One round hit perfectly, tearing a gap in the line. The Michigan infantry cheered.

Farther south, toward Stedman, it looked and sounded as though the Rebs had blown a significant hole in the defenses, with episodic encounters flaring and fading. More guns joined the fray, firing in multiple directions

The boys from the 2nd Michigan figured things out. They either scooted off to the east or dove deep into trenches. So Stone's artillerymen could do their work.

"Left thirty degrees. Load spherical case. Ready canister. Fire at will."

There were just more Johnnies than Val Stone needed to see of an early morning. Yipping their high cry now. Flags whipped back and forth in the morning twilight, urging on the graybacks.

To Stone's immediate left, Al Day got his Michiganders ready. Waiting for the Rebs to close within two hundred yards. Not that Stone put much faith in musketry, even in good light. Artillery, that was the thing.

First volley. Johnnies fell. Not enough.

They screeched that ghastly wail. And on they came.

The gun crews slammed in the canister rounds, while infantrymen reloaded with the speed of veterans who meant to live.

A high Reb voice cut the tumult: "Best give up, Yanks. No use now, you're beat. Throw down them rammers."

"Fire!" MacConnell told his gun sections. Before Stone could give the command.

The Michiganders, too, fired another volley.

Through the smoke, Stone saw the Johnnies wavering, some stepping forward still, others hesitating.

First real light coming on. The field looked like hell on a Saturday, as far as Stone could see into the smoke.

Reb officers rallied their men. One grabbed a flag. Urging his Johnnies to resume the attack.

Stone's gun crews fired without need of commands now. Pouring in the canister.

A fuss of grunts, pounding feet, and jangling metal rose behind the battery. Colonel Ely had brought up reinforcements from Fort McGilvery. Stone recognized Captain Brown of the 50th Pennsylvania in the lead. No sword, just a revolver in his paw. Good man, Brown. His raggle-taggle veterans were barely half-dressed, but every man had his rifle, bayonet, and cartridge box.

The Rebs stopped advancing, but appeared determined to hold their ground. Firing in support, artillery opened from the Confederate lines, able to identify targets now. And they knew the ranges, both sides had known them for months.

It looked set to be an ugly morning in godforsaken Virginia. But Valentine Stone barely gave a damn about what might happen elsewhere on the field. This was *his* ground. And he meant to hold it.

Five twenty a.m.
Fort Stedman

Gordon wore a lopsided smile, the right half fuller than the left, a memento of Antietam. He had been pleased enough by the progress thus far to scribble a note to Lee, reporting success beyond all expectations. Stedman had fallen easily, along with its flanking batteries, tearing a great hole in the Union line. His men had bagged hundreds of Yankee prisoners, including one irate brigadier general, whose discomfiture had all but made Gordon laugh.

Now he feared his words had been premature, an effervescence of unmanly excitement, and his smile was a mask to inspirit the troops crowding into the fort, a human churn of intermingled regiments whose officers struggled profanely to sort them out in the dusk before sunrise.

Those men had to believe that *he* believed. But Stedman was only the start. Taking those three rearward forts was crucial. It wasn't enough to break Meade's line, he had to split Grant's army.

He longed for word from his three special columns of picked men, or even from one of them. He had to know that those forts were in his hands and the path to Grant's rear open.

Meanwhile, he had to widen the breach, to push back the Yankee artillery already annoying his efforts, and to make it impossible for one Federal flank to aid the other.

But the advance was slowing, he sensed it. His early success meant nothing unless the attack continued to keep the Federals reeling. A seized half mile of line, even a full mile, would not change the war's outcome.

In half an hour or less, the sun would crack open the sky and the last dividends of surprise would have been squandered. It was already light enough to read his pocket watch.

He *needed* to hear from those special detachments, *needed* to have those forts. Devil it, he'd put one brigadier and two colonels in charge of the elite columns. Surely each man had the rank and skill to lead a mere hundred men? To accomplish a well-defined mission, with every advantage?

He fought down the impulse to go forward himself. He needed to stay at Fort Stedman so couriers could find him and he could report to Lee.

Why weren't *his* men reporting?

The air turned pigeon gray.

On both flanks, the ruckus of battle lacked intensity. The surprise was spent, now they needed to *fight.* Surely his subordinates saw that much. . . .

His aides, who knew Gordon as common soldiers did not, kept a wary distance. The corporal holding his horse watched him the way a fellow eyed a cottonmouth snake.

Damn it, though, he *did* want to go forward and root out the problems. Those columns had guides, prepared maps, clear orders, everything. . . .

The artillery fire from his own lines redoubled. The Yankees answered. Shot shrilled overhead.

Where the devil were they, those three hundred men meant to serve as his Trojan horse?

As if in answer—the wrong answer—Clem Evans emerged from the throng of waiting soldiers, cloak flapping around him. Gordon all but loved the man, whom he'd brought up behind him, first giving Evans "Gordon's Brigade," then command of "Gordon's Division." Clem, who meant to become a Methodist preacher after the war, was a splendid killer and—under other circumstances—good company.

But Evans was one man whom Gordon had *not* expected to see within the fort. He should've been pushing southward, taking the redoubt the Yankees called Fort Haskell.

At his fellow Georgian's approach, Gordon stiffened his regal posture and forced his smile to widen.

"Well, Clem, a goodly part of our prayers are answered. I trust you'll petition the Good Lord for the rest."

"God's labors never stop," Evans said, voice clear amid the bang-jangle. "I find mine own impeded, though."

"What's the problem?"

"The lanes. Through the obstacles. They're just not wide enough, sir, not in my front. We're widening them now, but it's a chore." Clem chawed his lip. "Just got Terry's Brigade through and forming up. Soon as they're ready, we'll make a more vigorous push." Evans absentmindedly touched his side, his Monocacy wound. Then he looked sheepish about it: Gordon never touched *his* wounds when other men could see, not even that long scar where his cheek hollowed. "Thought you should know how things stand, sir."

"Clem, you've got to move *now*. Grab that fort. Before the sun comes over us. Before the Yankees catch their breath."

A man who would have endangered many a female heart, had he not been so devoted to his wife, Evans shook his head. It was meant only to clear his thoughts, not to signal despair. Gordon could tell, he knew the man.

"We'll take the fort, sir. But I'll have to do it just with Terry's men and the Louisianans, many as I can round up. My last brigade won't be ready to go in for another half hour, maybe longer, way things stand. Those narrow lanes. And Yankee prisoners running all over do make things a sight worse."

"I welcome prisoners myself," Gordon said, buttering his voice. "I find their dejection heartening." He cocked an eyebrow. "I wish some other officers showed your alacrity about reporting, Clem." He refreshed his smile. "Go on now. Take that fort."

The Yankee artillery added more guns to the fracas. In ashen light, shells landed near Fort Stedman. Mobs of men crowded toward inadequate cover.

What was going on with those three detachments? Stedman and the batteries on its wings couldn't hold more troops, they had to go forward to make room for others. Or everything would stagger to a halt.

Clem couldn't get enough soldiers through, Grimes seemed to have too many, and Walker's situation was unclear. Ransom was attacking northward, all right, but seemed to have gone off on a war of his own.

A staff man led a messenger to Gordon. Gordon knew the panting lieutenant to see, but couldn't recall his name. He liked to call men by their names, to make them feel appreciated.

The boy saluted. "Lieutenant Wilkins, sir . . ."

"Oh, I know who you are, son. Now take yourself a breath and speak your piece."

"From General Lewis, sir. He says . . . said to tell you . . . he can't find that fort you sent him after. Said all North Carolina couldn't find it."

Great God Almighty.

"What about the guide, the scout? *He* couldn't find it?"

The boy shook his head. With considerably more vehemence than Clem Evans had shaken his. "Just run off, General. Or got separated, maybe, in all the mix-up."

Gordon's smile had disappeared.

"Can you find your way back to General Lewis?"

Nodding unconvincingly, the lieutenant said, "I believe so, sir. I think so. But it's all trenches and bombproofs out there, it's like some crazy run of gopher holes."

In a voice forged into steel, Gordon said:

"Find General Lewis. And tell him I said to find that fort and take it."

Five thirty a.m.

Prince George Court House Road, east of Fort Stedman

Brigadier General "Black John" Hartranft bellowed, "Keep your alignment, boys, and keep on moving!" He held his horse to the rutted road as his men advanced on both sides of it. Damp with mist, his mustache clung to his lip.

Poor situation for a division commander, leading one lone regiment into a fight. All anyone in blue could agree on so far was that the Rebs had serious intentions. This wasn't just a blown-up picket raid, but a major attack. The Johnnies had broken the line and meant to keep going.

Hartranft intended to stop them, or at least to cost them time. After a hardmouthed talk with a fellow general, he'd called up his nearest regiment, the 200th Pennsylvania, which had never been under fire. He'd summoned the rest of his division, too, sending off Captain Dalien and a pack of couriers, but his brigades had been dispersed as reserves behind the Ninth Corps line. It would take time for the regiments to converge to stem the breakthrough, and the entire division, or most of it, was formed of unblooded troops. So the 200th Pennsylvania would have to do, with its pimple-faced boys and calculating draftees.

Blasts and volleys tore the feeble darkness, yet his blind advance went unmolested. For the moment. One thing of which he was certain was that the Rebs he would meet would not be green like his boys, but hard-nut veterans. Somewhere up ahead, they'd be advancing toward this road, or already on it. Ready to slash into anything dressed in a blue coat.

If his men didn't panic at the first encounter . . .

"Steady, boys. Keep the pace, no lagging now. *Nur weiter.*"

Well, he could command one regiment well enough. He'd learned that much the hard way, earning each promotion twice over across the bloody years, ever dogged by the shame of the first regiment he'd raised, the 4th Pennsylvania, ninety-day volunteers who'd rushed to Lincoln. Their term of service had expired on the eve of First Bull Run and, ignoring Hartranft's pleas, the men had insisted on being mustered out. So the regiment of which he'd been so proud had marched away from the battlefield as other men marched toward the war's true beginning. Hartranft had remained behind, a supernumerary on a hapless staff, doing his best to get himself killed and failing at that, too.

It had been a long war after that. *Eine saure Ewigkeit.*

Artillery streaked the sky on the flanks, but the mist to his front was a blindfold. The Rebs were coming on, though, they had to be. They needed this road, if they wanted success to stick.

Hundreds of footfalls slapped the earth around him. Nickering, his horse pranced and calmed again.

You just never knew how men would act when they first came under fire. He'd done his best to prepare these troops, to train them and encourage them. Now he could only display himself on horseback, which would matter far less than how these men felt about their company officers and sergeants.

Don't doubt. Just lead. Don't fail them, and they won't fail you.

The men moved well, if somberly, over the ruined ground, with their rifles at right-shoulder shift and their banners snapping. But that wasn't fighting.

He wanted the sun to pop through the gray, wishing he could drag it up with his hands. There was light enough already for a scrap, but a rising sun, if it burned through the mist, would be in the Johnnies' eyes and at his men's backs. And every last advantage counted now.

Still a quarter hour until sunrise, Hartranft judged. A soldier's eternity.

And there they were: a skirmish line of Rebs, a heavy one. The mood around him tightened. A few startled voices called out, but most of his men kept their silence.

At least these lads gathered up from home wouldn't mock the Pennsy-Dutch accent that possessed him when things grew hot. Or if they mocked, their tone wouldn't be disdainful.

He let the front rank and the regiment's colors pass, then he called out, "Now, Pennsylvania! For your wives and mothers!"

A voice rose from the ranks: "I'll take me a sassy Dutch gal, if you got one."

"Maybe she don't take you, you don't fight good," Hartranft responded, lapsing into dialect.

Men laughed, and it was good—if nervous—laughter.

The Reb skirmishers paused and leveled their rifles.

Hartranft sat up rigidly in the saddle, the only encouragement he could offer now. He pointed ahead with his sword.

Pinpricks of light were followed instantly by the crack of rifles. With a grunt heard above the tramp of shoes, a soldier fell away. The regimental and company officers looked to Hartranft, expecting him to halt and return a volley.

Not yet, not yet. Green troops shot wildly. They needed to be closer.

The Rebs had gotten almost a half mile into the lines. They had to be held here.

Time, it was about time now. The nearest of his other regiments, the 209th Pennsylvania, wouldn't be more than twenty minutes back. He had to hold that long. And the best way to do it was to go at the Rebs, to show some spunk and not wait meekly for a Confederate blow.

The Rebs fired again. Inside of two hundred yards. More men toppled. One pleaded, "Tildy, help me! Help me, Tildy!"

Another thirty paces and he'd halt them. Or forty paces, if he sensed they could stand it.

Plenty of fighting elsewhere now. But none of it mattered as much as control of this road. If the Rebs took it, they'd go straight to City Point.

To his relief, not a single soldier faltered. They really did look as if they were on parade.

They'd soon know better.

The Rebs jammed ramrods down their barrels. Behind them, Hartranft glimpsed collapsed tents, a looted camp.

"Halt!"

His two lines froze, creating a sudden, close-in silence amid the broader uproar. He ordered a volley. It proved sufficient to send the skirmishers back a few dozen paces, toward the ravaged tents. As his men reloaded—well practiced and reassuringly crisp—a small reinforcement came up from behind at the double-quick. He couldn't quite make out their flag.

Nor could he wait. He ordered the 200th forward again.

An officer trotted up, sweating and disheveled. "Fifty-seventh Massachusetts, sir," the captain shouted. He pointed at the Rebs. "Our camp's back there, you can see it, behind those skirmishers. Rebs jumped us. We mean to go back and reclaim it."

"Put your men on my right, Captain. You're welcome and needed."

Instead of a sunburst at his back, Hartranft felt a raindrop.

When the blue lines continued forward, the Rebel skirmishers pulled back again, pausing now and again to fire and sting.

"See that!" Hartranft told the men within hearing. "They're not standing up to you, those *verdammte* Rebs."

It was something of a lie. But the soldiers cheered themselves.

After a brief tease, the raindrops stopped.

The skirmishers faded over a low crest, leaving behind the ruins of the camp, scattered papers and undesired property. Hartranft understood what the withdrawal meant: Their main line would be waiting down the far slope, rifles ready.

He couldn't figure it out, though: If they'd had time to loot that camp and their main line hadn't caught up to them, it meant they'd been ordered to halt. They should have advanced while nothing stood in their way.

Had they grown unsure of themselves? Hartranft knew how easily things went awry on a battlefield, even by daylight. Or was this a trap?

Nothing to do but go forward and find out. Then make them fight for every foot they wanted.

To the north and south, the fighting flared again. The Rebs were attacking in full force now. They'd reorganized in the first light, Hartranft guessed. And there still had not been sufficient time for his brigade commanders or his fellow division commanders to mount proper counterattacks. The Johnnies still had the advantage.

He had no idea how many Confederates waited behind that crest. Dalien *had* to bring up reinforcements.

On rising ground, on the left side of the road, his ranks opened as they worked past the caved-in tents.

Perched in the saddle, he'd see the Johnnies before his soldiers did. Fifteen seconds earlier, maybe more. Time enough to decide and spit out an order.

Stripped of trees and bushes across the winter, the crest stretched barren and ugly, a place of death. Unreasonably, it made him recall the rich, green mountains of northeastern Pennsylvania, where he'd learned survey work as a young man, before his father's businesses consumed him. He loved verdant places. And quiet.

Close now. *Close.*

He saw them. Two regiments. Or, perhaps, a whittled-down brigade. No, two regiments, judged by the flags. Lean ones, the odds not impossible. Down the slope they waited, just where he'd expected them to be.

"Halt."

Again, the blue ranks paused. Still unseeing.

"Fix bayonets!"

The regimental and company officers echoed the command.

When the clang and click of metal on metal ceased, he called out, *"Trail arms!"*

The officers repeated that command, too.

He pointed with his sword again.

"Forward!"

The regiment and its tagalongs passed the crest. He felt as much as heard the gasps as his soldiers saw a Reb battle line for the first time, the flesh-and-blood enemy waiting there in strength, determined to kill them.

Well, he did believe that Sallie would miss and mourn him. Did the dead miss anyone? He'd always had trouble with promises of a cherry-pie hereafter.

Hartranft remained on horseback, between his advancing ranks, a splendid target. These boys—many were boys, indeed—needed to know that someone in authority, someone they might imagine as wise and assured, was with them now.

Leadership demanded such fraud that its practitioners belonged in a penitentiary.

A death sentence for those who would lose this special lottery, the Johnnies lowered their rifles and steadied their aim.

Keep them moving, just keep them moving forward. . . .

The Rebs line flamed and crackled. A dozen men fell. More. Red blood, white bone.

He could see them clearly now, those red flags in the dawn. And he, too, felt the anxiety born of fear that, strangely, drove men to rush ahead when they wanted to flee.

He halted his lines again and had the front rank release a volley in time to disrupt the Johnnies as they reloaded. Then he ordered a charge.

Made animals, his soldiers howled a hurrah. And charge they did, with as much spirit as any regiment Hartranft had seen.

Gore splashed gray air. The Rebels stood their ground, confident veterans. Midway down the slope, the killing became too much. Hartranft waved the men back, ordering a withdrawal, before they could break and run.

Horse bleeding, he led the 200th Pennsylvania in a second charge. And suffered another repulse. They were driven back through the Massachusetts camp again, but he rallied them and the regiment charged a third time. When they fell back, they were fewer.

To his astonishment, Hartranft went unscathed. His horse had been shot at least twice, though, and bled from neck and flank. Choosing his ground, the lip of a ravine, he let his powder-mugged men and boys shelter behind old earthworks commanding the road. He intended to hold that position until the end; he saw no choice.

Where *was* everyone? Where was young Dalien, where was his staff, his division?

The sun had risen behind a somber wall, refusing to blind the Johnnies. Men shivered as sweat chilled. Some vomited. Others realized, at last, that they'd been wounded, some of them badly, and broke down. One man who had made his way back unaided collapsed and died.

The regiment had done nobly, but Hartranft felt spirits ebbing. In plain view, the Rebs aligned themselves to renew their advance. Even he found the sight of those rough ranks daunting, so the display was bound to play havoc with the hearts of young men enduring their first battle.

Cold rain flirted again.

Then Black John Hartranft saw two sights that pleased him as few things in his life had done. First, he grasped that the Johnnies were digging in rather than attacking—it made no sense, but it was surely welcome. Second, he saw the unfurled flags of the 209th Pennsylvania coming up, with Captain Dalien showing the way upon his dancing horse.

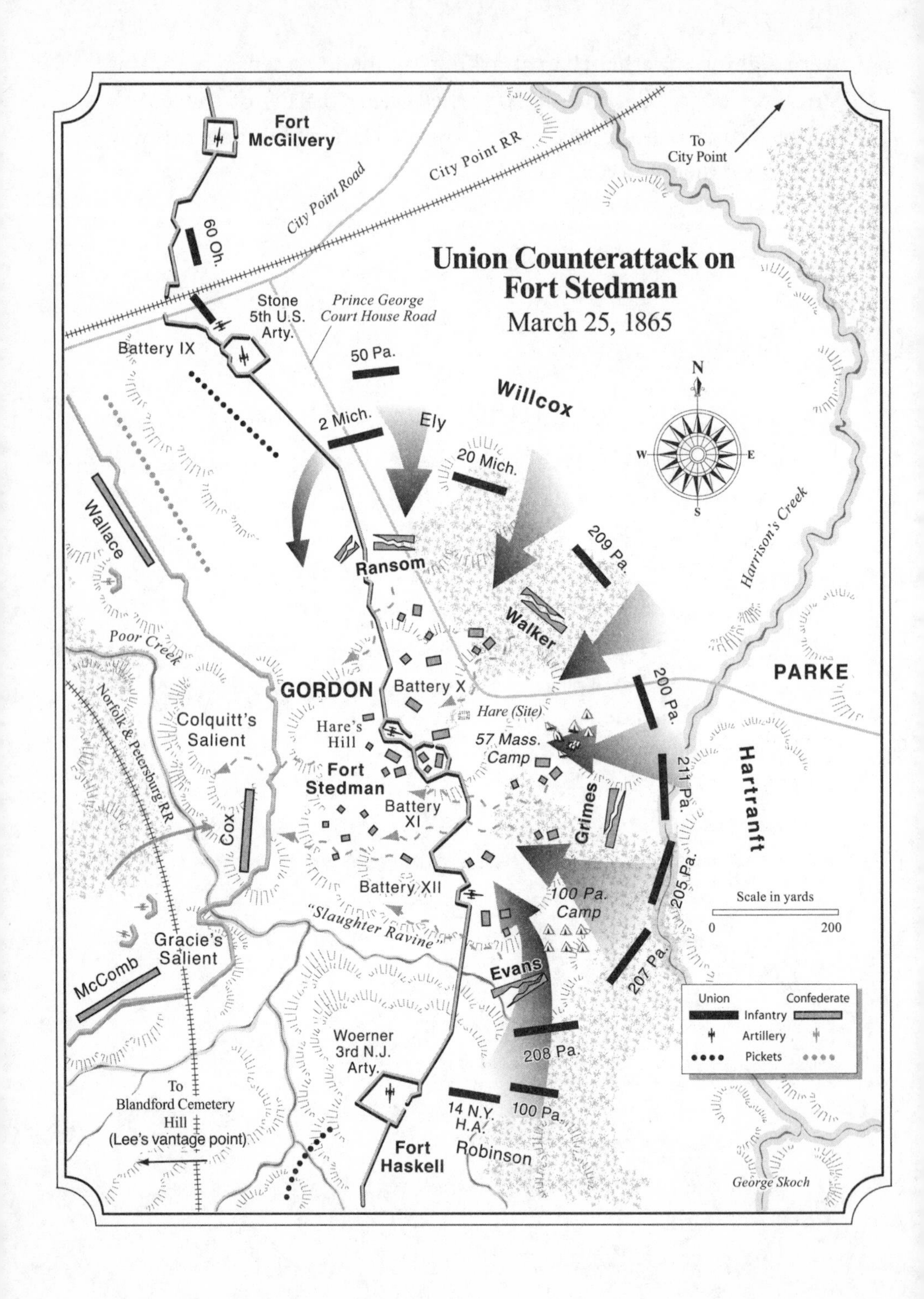

Union Counterattack on Fort Stedman
March 25, 1865
Fort McGilvery
City Point Road
City Point RR
To City Point
60 Oh.
Stone
5th U.S.
Arty.
Prince George
Court House Road
Battery IX
50 Pa.
Willcox
2 Mich.
Ely
20 Mich.
N
W
E
S
Wallace
209 Pa.
Harrison's Creek
Ransom
Walker
Poor Creek
PARKE
200 Pa.
GORDON
Battery X
Hare (Site)
Norfolk & Petersburg RR
Colquitt's
Salient
Hare's
Hill
57 Mass.
Camp
Hartranft
Fort
Stedman
211 Pa.
Battery
XI
Grimes
Cox
205 Pa.
Battery XII
100 Pa.
Camp
Scale in yards
0
200
"Slaughter Ravine"
Gracie's
Salient
207 Pa.
McComb
Evans
Union
Confederate
Infantry
Artillery
Pickets
Woerner
3rd N.J.
Arty.
208 Pa.
To
Blandford Cemetery
Hill
(Lee's vantage point)
14 N.Y.
H.A.
100 Pa.
Fort
Haskell
Robinson
George Skoch

TWO

Six fifteen a.m., March 25, 1865
Slaughter Ravine, Fort Haskell

Riordan ran up the blasted slope, and blasted it was, indeed. Yankee artillery up in the fort took high joy in the killing, as cruel as nuns with a harlot. The last shreds of Louisiana's Irish pride and joy had been crammed into the attack with Terry's Virginians—little good it did, in Riordan's judgment. But up the hill he dashed again, toward the wooden spikes and man-eating ditches, toward the earthen wall that even the sharpshooters could not unpeople, not even by cold daylight. 'Twas as if the bluecoats had packed the legions of Hell inside.

The sky spit on them all.

Riordan shouted and raged at Heaven and earth, bayoneting thin air, his legs hating the climb. Avoiding the squirming wounded and the carcasses of his kind—products of some earlier, unseen slaughter—he kept pace with the boldest, though 'twas folly, as all could see. But a man did things because they were his to do. Or he did them because he did them, with no more sense to living and dying than that.

He did wish to live long enough, though, to eat the lovely rations left by the Yankees, to empty his bulging haversack and stuff his gullet until he burst his belt. But the blue-bellies had grown stubborn over the winter, nor were they merry this morn: Recovered from their surprise, they relished this fight like tenants clubbing a landlord.

All that bloody blundering in the dark . . .

"Come on, boys, come on!" Another kill-me-please officer waved his sword. Out to drape a sweetheart or widow in black, the idiot was.

Well, there'd be no widow for Riordan, no keening Kathleen. The one woman he'd not paid for in his life had put him off with her rotten teeth at last. And the shebeen stink of her.

True to a timeless tale, the officer with the mouth on him caught a ball in his forehead. His hat flew wild and brains fled.

Riordan would've liked to reach those Yankees.

Another lad sprayed blood over Riordan's rags.

Oh, Jesus. Evans again. Welshman and Protestant, tall for a Taffy and cursed with his heathen Bible. But a well-favored sort, the general was, followed by men who couldn't have told you why. Like that high devil Gordon, as greedy for fame as his Scots lot were for money, and yet a fellow not to be resisted.

Riordan believed an *Irish* officer would have taken that fort in the covering dark. Or had the sense to hang back with a bottle, once the light came up.

Evans prancing on horseback, as if the bugger hadn't been shot through enough.

"General, would ye take yourself off?" a voice from the cribs of Cork called. "Ye're only drawin' attention, while we're seekin' to do the work."

Because of his name, every Mickey and Molly assumed Riordan sprang from Cork. And perhaps his forebears had been there, before some undeniable sin drove them northward in a hurry. But Riordan himself was of grimy Galway and her grim stone hills, a hungry land even short of a visiting famine.

A blast of canister swept away a dozen unready souls. The air blurred red.

Evans smiled and preached a murderous sermon: "Go on, boys! You're almost there! Go on, go on!"

But they weren't almost there, and all but Evans knew it. Bullets rained down like a murdering gale from the sea.

Riordan stopped, unready to continue. Unable. But he aimed

his fine captured rifle at the heads bobbing over the rampart. He pulled the trigger and missed.

If curses were bullets . . .

Evans cantered off, bound to bugger up somebody else's brawl, as generals did. Well, say it, then: He liked Evans well enough. For a chapel-poisoned Welshman, he wasn't the worst. But a general, any general, was a terrible curse upon mankind.

Face all blood, a boy collided with Riordan. Running back blindly he'd been, clutching his snout and then flinging out arms to fly, before smacking into Riordan and embracing him. Shoved off, he toppled and thumped the ground, mewing and curling and quaking. Riordan let him wriggle at his ankle, for the Yankees loved to shoot those who stooped to help.

Oh, Jesus, he saw what the others saw, and all of them sighed at once, a gasp almost womanly at the appearance of a fresh line of Yankees sweeping fort-ward, taking firm possession of the high ground and concluding the matter for anyone with sense.

The attack dissolved. Its survivors drifted back into the ravine.

Six twenty a.m.
Fort Haskell

Woerner pushed the wounded man aside. It wasn't a time for mercy or for niceties. A bleeding corporal had blundered into the gun crew, and nothing in the world was more important than serving the Rebs a hard breakfast of doubled canister.

By damp light, Christian Woerner judged the havoc one gun had wrought, the slope strewn with shattered bodies and those still upright reluctant to advance.

Fort Haskell had been fortunate for once, with Charlie Houghton waking the garrison early on the strength of a premonition. So Charlie's defrocked artillerymen and Woerner's own 3rd Battery, 1st New Jersey Artillery, had been grumpily alert on the walls as the first Rebs neared in the darkness, blissfully unsuspecting, with grayback officers hissing boasts to their men of their coming success.

Charlie, in command of the fort, had waited to give the order to fire until he could hear the Johnnies down in the abatis, milling at point-blank range. The slaughter had been sickening.

Now Charlie was down, wounded thrice in three minutes during the second attack, and Woerner had helped his redlegs manhandle a fieldpiece into the fort's rear corner, where its muzzle commanded the slope. His other guns were occupied, dueling with Reb artillery across the lines, but his number four gun had done more destruction than Woerner had seen in any exchange of the war.

The Johnnies still needed encouragement to quit, though. And the men in blue who'd crammed into the fort, with escapees from the Reb onslaught stirred in, made it difficult to bring up the needed charges and rounds of canister. Yet the nuisance was canceled by the effect of the rifles and muskets packing the ramparts, while the wounded below reloaded for men still whole. Whenever a soldier crumpled from the wall, another replaced him.

The soldiers were furious, outraged, at the Rebel surprise. For his part, Woerner had been riled by a bullet that tore through his beard, passing between his chin and neck, ripping out hairs and leaving his jaw scathed and bleeding.

Well, *Gott sei Dank,* that was little enough, given the gore his men tore from the Rebs. The only true crisis had come when, just at dawn, Union batteries shelled the fort, convinced it had been taken by the Rebs. A major who'd escaped from the trap at Stedman had put together a color guard, marched them out the rear of the fort, and halted in plain sight of the misguided batteries. Half the detail had been shot down before the national colors did their work.

His number four gun let off another blast, encouraging Johnnies still on their feet to slip back toward the ravine between Haskell and Stedman. Rebs courageous but moments before cowered down in the low ground, desperate for shelter, demoralized, and broken.

The view across the small valley was remarkable. Despite the smoke that already dirtied the day, Woerner saw thousands of Rebs hiving up around Stedman and the batteries on its flank, with others packing the fallen trenches and stray contingents deep in the Union lines.

"Scheisse!" his begrimed gunner said, shaking an injured hand.

The morning couldn't make up its mind whether to rain or not.

"Raise the elevation," Woerner commanded, accent blighted by Germany. "Three turns, I think. *Dann gib mal* case."

It was time to shift targets, to join the growing number of Union pieces directing their fires on Stedman and that inviting swarm of Rebs.

Sensing a turning of the tide, Charlie's redlegs-made-infantry awarded themselves a hurrah.

But there would be more fighting, Woerner was certain. The Confederates had grabbed so great a piece of the line that further persuasion would be required to convince them to abandon it. Woerner meant to apply his share of the pressure.

Even now, so late in the war, he still heard nativist boors insist that "Germans just can't fight." Well, he had battled the Prussians in freedom's cause in '48, and he and his men had fought through this American war as stalwarts, without losing a gun. Every immigrant on the gun crews, steady Germans all, meant to prove that they were as good as anyone.

Nonetheless, Brevet Major Christian Woerner looked forward to the hour when this latest *Angriff* had been repelled, the casualties counted and crews remanned, guns cleaned and stocks replenished, and routine duties resumed. At which point he planned to return to his bombproof shelter, eager to resume reading, for the third time, *The Life and Opinions of the Tomcat Murr.*

The more that Woerner saw of war, the more he cherished laughter.

Six thirty a.m.
Fort Stedman

Gordon struggled to command his temper.

"It just isn't *there*," the breathless colonel repeated. "There's no fort out there, General.. Not where I was sent." The weary man searched for words. "There's nothing even *looks* like a fort back there."

The colonel was the last detachment leader to report, the last to give up. But each had brought the same news: The three forts to be seized, the vaunted keys to splitting the Union army, didn't exist.

Union shells crashed around the crowded fort, and soldiers cowered. Litters bore off the wounded. The air was a damp rag held against a cheek.

"I'm sorry, General," the colonel said, mortified by a failure not his own.

Forcing himself to be genial, Gordon told the man, "Fault's all mine, if anyone's. You go on now, get your boys ready to trouble a few more Yankees."

A solid shot struck the rampart's berm, prickling the two men with dirt.

He didn't want it *seen* as his fault, of course. And what else could he have done? He'd interviewed Union prisoners and deserters, he'd sent the scouts back and even slithered in spies. And all of them—nearly all—seemed to confirm that the forts were there, commanding the best route to the Union rear.

Or had he heard what he wanted to hear? Had all of them heard only what supported their hopes? Had this last attack of the Army of Northern Virginia, the last that could be mustered on such a scale, been launched in pursuit of a shared hallucination?

He wouldn't give up. Not yet. The Yankees had only launched piecemeal counterattacks, and the swelling bombardment was the preeminent problem. There was still time. If Clem could take that fort a half mile south, and if Ransom could round up his men and move northward again . . . If Grimes and Walker regrouped and pushed deeper before the Yankees got organized . . . If Cad Wilcox's brigades came up, if Pickett arrived . . .

Against his will, Gordon ducked his head at the shriek of a Yankee shell. Straightening promptly, he waved up his staff and couriers. The fight wasn't over yet and there were orders to dispatch. One plan had failed, it was time to try another. They couldn't give up yet, he wouldn't report a failure to Robert E. Lee. Not yet, not yet.

He longed to lash out with a horsewhip, though. To chastise the idling regimental officers and their suddenly feckless soldiers, to force those of rank to take command and show a lick of grit. Instead of waiting like lolly-tongued hounds to be put on the scent by their master.

Well, he had no whip and reckoned that was a good thing. The gods had plagued the Greeks at Troy, as well. So Major General John Brown Gordon conjured knowing Ulysses and told his officers, "Gentlemen, it appears our plan had shortcomings. . . ."

Yankee shells fell closer.

Seven a.m.
Union lines

The Two Hundred Eighth Pennsylvania takes position, *mon Général*," Captain Prosper Dalien reported, saluting with a snap mastered at Saint-Cyr.

Hartranft was fond of the young, resourceful Frenchman. Everyone seemed to be: The fellow had charmed the Pennsylvania governor, and Curtin had presented him, newly commissioned, to President Lincoln himself.

In his former life and in a different uniform, Dalien had been decorated, twice, by Napoleon III for heroism. He'd fought at Solferino. Yet Dalien had chosen a new land and another army. His fellow officers teased him and admired him.

"There are losses," Dalien continued, "but they have made a grand push upon the Rebels, who are thrust back in the *ravin*." The young man drew in his eyebrows under his visor. "The word is the same, I think?"

" 'Ravine,' " Hartranft confirmed.

"They are fine men, my Two Hundred Eighth. *Splendide!* And the Two Hundred Seventh, it crosses the creek bottom now. I think that they will join the line in ten minutes."

Mounted on a fresh horse, Hartranft grimaced. Every minute counted, and ten minutes seemed a lifetime. The Johnnies had been halted; he'd watched their last attack on Fort Haskell disintegrate, an officer leading it shot out of the saddle. But halting them wasn't enough. Nor did he want the Rebs to withdraw unmolested. A counterattack made soon enough had the chance to trap those Johnnies by the thousands.

He yearned to take revenge, at last, for the Crater.

Serving as officer of the day for Hartranft's division, the captain looked both worn and gay as a beau, horse foaming and lathered, but cap atilt to charm invisible ladies. Hartranft had sent him through the maelstrom repeatedly, either with scrawled orders or, when time pressed more fiercely, to deliver shouted commands. And the captain smiled as if no society ball could be more delightful.

Dalien was murdering his mount, though.

C'est la guerre. Hartranft had ruined his share of horseflesh, too. And he hadn't yet encountered a cup of coffee. But he'd soon have two full brigades of his own positioned to advance, with at least one brigade from another division able to join in. He just needed time to complete his last deployments. There would be no more frantic, piecemeal counterattacks, but a sweeping advance this time, trapping the Confederates before they had time to escape.

The Crater, the Crater, the Crater . . . he saw now how it could be.

Yet the morning had piled frustration atop frustration. Parke, his corps commander, had squandered time querying headquarters as to the general situation—only to learn, belatedly, that he, Parke, commanded the Union lines: Meade was off at City Point, joining Grant for a grand parley with Lincoln. No one had notified Parke, of course. In the fray, officers went missing, regiments took inexplicable routes, and batteries shelled the wrong targets. But, somehow, the veterans along the line, officers and men, had pulled themselves together. The defense had found its footing just as the Johnnies began to lose theirs.

Breathing heavily from his own efforts and shivering under old sweat, Hartranft glanced around at the morning's wreckage. McLaughlen's headquarters had been laid waste—not necessarily by the Johnnies, given the criminal sorts the army had now. McLaughlen himself had been swallowed up in the early confusion, but here, upon the heights, Hartranft saw that the Union lines, for all the ground surrendered, had held up well enough. Thanks, that was, to the men in Fort Haskell and those batteries up by McGilvery. And to all the slivers of regiments that had rallied amid the tumult. Dawn had threatened a grave defeat, but daylight presented a chance to punish Lee, even to begin to unravel his army.

The Crater . . . he remembered leaving poor Bartlett behind, cork leg ruined by a mortar shell. The Rebels would pay for that, too.

Hartranft needed the last of his regiments, though. A commander had to distinguish between a prompt response and a rash one; he'd learned that lesson watching others fail. And he didn't want to fight the Rebs to a draw. He meant to crush them.

"*Gut gemacht,* Prosper," he told Captain Dalien. The Frenchman's German grammar was better than Hartranft's Pennsylvania Dutch—it seemed there was nothing Dalien hadn't mastered. "Go to the Two Eleventh now, find out what's taking so long. They're to fill in on the right of the Two Hundred Fifth. Guide them up yourself. *Ich will jetzt keine Dummheiten.*"

The captain saluted and spurred his glistening horse. The elegance of the fellow, even when splotched with mud, amused Hartranft mightily.

Before riding off with his colors and staff, the general let himself savor the awful spectacle. Through ghosts of smoke, he saw much that the Confederates could not: a great semicircle of blue, at least six thousand men, ready to advance when the last tardy regiments closed on the line. And the Johnnies, Lord help them, were dawdling inexcusably, hanging on to now useless gains, as Federal artillery pounded them and ever more clusters of men in gray faded back toward the mob around Fort Stedman.

It was almost as if they wanted to be scooped up.

Seven fifteen a.m.
Blandford Church Hill

Lee watched hope die. Through his field glasses, he had witnessed Gordon's splendid advance stumbling to a halt. Now he detected men falling back from the flanks toward the fort and he worried that his withdrawal order to Gordon might not arrive in time to avoid catastrophe. The attack upon which he'd wagered had come to nothing. The time had come to save all the men they could.

Under him, Traveller quivered.

Lee reached down into his boot, but his fingers could not squeeze in far enough to scratch the bedeviling fleabites on his ankle. The effort only renewed the ache in his back: The morning's dampness worsened his rheumatism.

Bridling his anger, Lee maintained his silence. If the plan had been Gordon's, the impulse had been his own. All too eager for action, he'd demanded a miracle from the Georgian. Something had needed to be done, a last initiative grasped. He had been unwilling to wait for the roads to dry, for Grant to close the noose. He had wanted to *fight*. He always wanted to fight. And so he had approved a plan that stank of desperation, a plan even its author had not quite believed in.

No, this day of rue was not Gordon's fault, but all his own. Like that final, bitter day at Gettysburg. For all his outward discipline, Lee was a headstrong man. He knew it but could not change it. Not always. Not, it seemed, when it mattered.

At a distance of a mile and more, he watched artillery shells arc through the sky to drop among his soldiers, the explosive rounds bright for an instant. The men in the captured fort were suffering now, and morale could be as fragile as the flesh. Gordon had to pull them out immediately—hadn't he gotten the order? Lee had sent multiple couriers.

Those people had such a preponderance of guns and ammunition, it was unjust. The cacophony, too, reminded Lee of Gettysburg, of the great bombardment. Things had not been so unequal then. The South had enjoyed great prospects. They all had believed that, anyway.

Had his fate already been sealed four years before, on the day he crossed the river back to Arlington, the day he drafted his letter resigning from the U.S. Army? He had disappointed grand old Scott, a generous man. Winfield Scott was a Virginian, too, born in Dinwiddie County. But the hero of the War of 1812 had seen his duty in a different light.

Across the valley, beyond the curling ravines, an explosive shell struck in the heart of the fort. Dark objects flew skyward, visible even a mile away, without the aid of field glasses.

Gordon had to get those men out *now*.

But Gordon, too, was proud. His messages, ebullient at first, had declined to measured confidence, then descended to doubt, and, finally, retreated to a barely masked plea for an order to withdraw. Gordon could not bring himself to say outright that he'd been defeated.

Lee understood. "Defeat" was a hard word to mouth.

Well, if the day had not gone well, it was not yet the last day. Grant and Meade, all of them, would not find the way forward easy. There was grip in the army yet.

Lee had stopped reading the tallies of desertions. He could not bear them. The last time Marshall had tried to report the shrinking number of rifles present for duty, Lee had lost his temper, shocking all present.

How many men would be lost today? With no hope of replacement?

Lee promised himself he would not utter a word critical of Gordon. He needed the Georgian, with so many gone. As he needed poor, sick Hill and glum James Longstreet. And more: He needed men to rise up from their graves. Jackson. Above all, Jackson.

The fleabites began to itch again. This time, he restrained his hand.

In the night, in a feeble hour of sleep, he had dreamed of Mexico, when he had been a younger man and flawless.

Seven twenty a.m.
Fort Stedman

"*Go!*" Gordon told the gathered couriers and remaining staff men. "*Just go!*"

He needed them to fly with the wings of Pegasus, but would have to be content with boots in mud. There was no time to lose: Lee's order to withdraw had taken a seeming eternity to arrive. Then two messengers arrived at once. Gordon had leapt to save the men he led, but it would take time, an awful stretch, for the runners and orderlies to reach each last command scattered over the field.

Nor would it be an orderly retreat. Too late for that.

A disconcerting number of soldiers had already made their own choice to retire, too many to be collared and disciplined as they ran the gauntlet between the lines. Worse, Clem Evans had lost two brigade commanders, irreplaceable officers gravely wounded. Then Grimes had ordered a regiment to advance and settle a score with a Federal battery, only to have a captain defy him, insisting a charge would be a useless sacrifice. Grimes had been ready to shoot the boy, but the regiment had got up and gone forward, after all—only to be shattered by shells inside of a hundred yards.

It wasn't the same army. It just was not the same army it had been.

And yet . . . for all his urgency and anger, John Brown Gordon could not avoid the obvious truth of the matter: He should not have waited for Lee's order to reach him. He should have begun to withdraw the men on his own, let other men judge as they would. Not long ago, he would have had the courage to do just that, the common sense and the decency.

He feared that he was not the same man, either.

Well, he would do his duty now. He'd stand his ground until his men were clear. Come what may.

How had it all gone so wrong? Not just this, but all of it?

He would have liked to be with Fanny for the new child's birth, but his presence seemed unlikely.

Seven thirty a.m.
Union lines

Hartranft was ready. Word would soon reach the farthest batteries to shift their fires and concentrate on the ground between the lines, a slaughter pen for any Rebs who ran.

He turned to Captain Dalien, who was gasping to fill his lungs, and pointed at McLaughlen's regrouped brigade, drawn up along the ridge behind Fort Haskell.

"Ride over and find Colonel Robinson. Or whoever's in command. Put it pretty as you like, but convince him to join our attack. Tell him we're set to go in the next five minutes. *Alles klar?*"

Dalien, bless him, grinned and snapped that preposterous salute, as if he were playing a part upon the stage. *Na dann,* Hartranft decided, the fellow was doing just that, as he was himself, on the greatest stage either man would ever see.

Sometimes Hartranft wondered what things would be like after the war. Men imagined a perfect happiness, but what could fill a lifetime after this? Hartranft believed that he hated war, but he feared that he would miss it.

He had never felt as alive as amid this death.

From his vantage point, Hartranft scanned the double and triple lines of blue, nearly continuous, stretching northward into the drifting smoke. Officers rode about, putting the last touches on their alignments, while sergeants to the rear waved arms in anger—and doubtless barked profanities—at the poor devils who'd been allowed a squat in a ditch, sick and soiled but forced to join the ranks.

Black John Hartranft had to smile: The army was no place for a modest man, such as he had been in '61. The public nature of every private matter had been the hardest thing for him to accept.

Now it was time to shit on Robert E. Lee.

Seven thirty-five a.m.
Fort Haskell ridge

Hartranft's pet Frenchman galloped up on a horse about to expire, saluted with a flourish, and asked, "Are you still in command here, Colonel Robinson?"

Robinson grunted. "Who the hell else would be?"

The Frenchman nodded, as if at Robinson's logic. "General Hartranft sends his compliments, sir. His division, it will make the advance in five minutes. It would give him extreme pleasure if your brigade would cooperate."

Robinson looked at the fellow. Just short of astonishment. "Jesus on a fence post, it's been the sole desire of my entire goddamned life to give old Hartranft 'extreme pleasure.' Sounds like I'm running a cathouse." He lifted an arm toward the confusion between his position and Stedman. "You look down there, Captain. I can't hold my boys back, half of them are already chasing Rebs. Black John's the one with the slows."

Unperturbed, the Frenchman said, "The general, he will be pleased you are in accord." He saluted again and turned his nag to the north.

Brevet Colonel Gilbert P. Robinson wasted no more time. He saw what that damned Dutchman Hartranft was up to. Out to grab all the glory for himself, now that the Johnnies were hopping away like jackrabbits. Well, *his* brigade, battered or not, had tipped the scales by Fort Haskell and held the line, while Hartranft, no doubt, had been having himself a leisurely general's breakfast. Bugger that fool of a Dutchman. Robinson intended to beat him into Fort Stedman.

Five minutes? Like hell. *Now.*

Robinson rode out in front of the troops who'd kept their discipline and waited for orders, even as hot-blooded comrades chased the Rebs. Angry as the devil, his men were. Embarrassed at the licking they'd taken in the dark and out to inflict worse on their abusers.

"All right, boys!" Robinson shouted, pointing toward the lost fort with his sword. "Those Pennsylvania Dutchmen over there think they're going to beat us into Stedman and grab those flags. I say to hell with the worthless sonsofbitches! Brigade . . . *forward!*"

Seven forty a.m.
Union lines

Mortified, Hartranft stared at the message the courier from Parke had put in his hands. His superior had ordered him to delay his counterattack until a division from the Sixth Corps came up to reinforce him.

It was madness. Judging things from his headquarters in the rear, Parke had no sense of how swiftly events had moved, how vulnerable the Rebels had become. If they didn't strike now, the Rebs would pull off their retreat. Yet another victory would be lost.

He crumpled the message. Black John Hartranft had never defied an order, it wasn't in him. Hadn't been, anyway.

He just couldn't see it. Throwing this chance away.

Let them court-martial him, then. Let them march him in shame from here to Harrisburg. Hartranft meant to fight.

Before he could give the signal to advance, McLaughlen's patched-up brigade charged down the slope at the double-quick, bayonets fixed. Cheering like children watching the schoolhouse burn. In breathless seconds, he saw Rebs by the dozen rise from the dead with their hands in the air.

And damned if Dalien hadn't turned around to join the attack. Insubordination seemed to be in fashion.

That was it, then. He couldn't let Robinson go it alone. Cheering or not, there weren't enough men in that charge to reach Fort Stedman and make it stick. Or even survive. Dalien, damn him, saw where duty lay.

Hartranft rode out before Harriman's brigade, waving and barking the order to advance. For all the racket, his flanking brigade in the north would have to take their cue from what they saw and hasten to come abreast of the advancing flags.

Thousands of Northern voices loosed a hurrah.

Black John Hartranft rode beside his soldiers. He reckoned the high authorities could wait an hour before stripping him of command.

Seven fifty a.m.
Fort Stedman

With raindrops flirting and blue ranks surging forward, Captain Prosper Dalien couldn't help himself: He had *needed* to join the attack. Shouting encouragement and waving his kepi, he made his horse dance in the interval between the regiments. Those swarming nearby barely kept any order, dashing forward at a pace never taught upon a drill field. Their shells screaming overhead, the artillery fired long to interdict the Rebel retreat as the noose was tightened. Some Johnnies fought stubbornly, proud to the point of madness, but more and more raised their rifles over their heads or threw them down.

The soldiers were no longer individuals, not those in blue, but one great beast with an appetite to devour. Horse shying from the Rebel dead and wounded, Dalien crossed the mire at the bottom of the ravine and started up the slope toward the prize, with scores and then hundreds of soldiers outpacing his mount, all of them eager to be the first to climb those earthen walls, maddened children playing a deadly game.

He peered through the smoke to see if his own regiment was advancing on the right. Better to join them, of course. But the force of the attack carried him forward.

He passed a bareheaded, balding Johnny fallen to his knees, long beard swaying and hands lifted to the sky, eyes hunting salvation as he cried, "Lord, don't let this be, cain't let this be . . . save us, Lord, save your childern!"

A passing sergeant told him, "Call on Satan, you bastard."

But no man molested the disconsolate Reb.

Even Dalien's blown horse caught the fever, racing up the slope toward Battery XII. It was glorious, every bit of it, let those who had never felt this thrill decry it.

The foreign observers, even the French, who'd drifted through the Union command stumped Dalien. All had been dismissive when speaking privately, convinced the Americans didn't know how to make war, that they were hopeless primitives and beneath serious study. Why? Because the Americans didn't wear fine uniforms, but sagging trousers and plain, ill-fitting blouses. Because American generals had not fought one *bataille decisive* and ended things, the way Europeans believed wars should be waged.

Dalien knew they were wrong. This was a new kind of war, in which a single encounter could no longer decide the outcome. This was Napoleon's "nation in arms" made real and supplied by sprawling manufactories, by explosive wealth. It unleashed passions in the soldier's breast as men fought not for a king but for a cause, however confused. The trenches, the killing power, the terrible numbers left upon field after field . . . locomotives, the telegraph, repeating rifles, ironclads plowing the seas . . . *this* was the future of war, and Dalien sensed it would only grow more terrible. The Petersburg trenches, not glittering cavalry stunts, were the stuff of tomorrow.

When peace came, he planned to write a book to warn the smug and oblivious. And maybe he'd marry an heiress, like de Trobriand—

A round tore past his ear with the sound of silk ripped from a dress. Another tore the cap out of his hand.

Order broke down and regiments intermingled. Men in blue stormed over the berms of Stedman's flanking batteries, leading with bayonets or slamming down rifle stocks on skulls and rag-clad shoulders. Red flags fell, and disarmed Johnnies quickstepped into captivity.

Even then, clots of Rebs refused to quit, drawing what last blood they could. Atop one wall, a willowy boy, blond hair streaming back, swung his rifle by the barrel, wielding it as a farmer would a scythe, until a Yankee not five feet away shot him in the chest and the boy lost his grip on his weapon. The Johnny didn't drop at once, despite the punch of the bullet, but stood a few seconds, quaking, before he fell into the ditch.

Screaming, shrieking, curses . . . Rifle fire rattled to deafen a man, and scores of cannon thundered to the rear. Smoke clotted. Dalien could not hear his own hoarse shouts. His battlefield brethren were at the walls of Stedman and going over, some toppling backward, but those unscathed overwhelming the defenders.

The regulated, antiquated wars of Europe were doomed. All he had seen in Italy was nothing compared to this, no matter the casualties of Solferino.

Gaining the high ground and the old muddle of trenches, he saw that for all the surrenders, hundreds of Rebs were chancing the killing ground between the lines, running back toward their waiting comrades, desperate to escape. Explosive shells and solid shot ripped through the frantic mob, flinging men and torn limbs into the air.

Dalien spotted a covey of Johnnies rising from a ditch to make a run for it. He spurred his mount, determined to take them prisoner.

As he neared the men in mismatched uniforms, a Reb wheeled about and shot Dalien in the belly.

Seven fifty a.m.
Fort Stedman

Riordan gave the nearest Yankee a taste of his rifle's butt, smack in the teeth and hunting the back of his gullet. Digging ditches wasn't a high profession, but it did give a man the muscles to do some harm.

In it, they were. Howling like the Banshee and hissing like snakes, with skulls and long bones cracking like walnut shells and bayonets poking into the mush of men. At one point, they were all packed in so tightly that he freed a hand from his rifle and wielded a fist.

Those Yankees learned to keep a respectful distance, those that still lived and stood on their hind legs, but others covered the field and the fort, maggots on a dead dog.

"Form up, form up!" an officer cried. "Form up and withdraw in order!"

But order there was none.

The last time he'd spied General Evans, the sorry Welshman had been afoot like the rest of them, encouraging one pack to stand their ground so another pack could get off. A bloody hooley all of it was, the porridge the old man pissed in.

Surrendering was the catching disease of the day, with ever more flags given up and men disarming themselves in hope of surviving.

Well, that was a plague Riordan didn't mean to catch. He'd never enter another Yankee prison camp, so help him, God or the devil. The officers, the few who remained, could bugger themselves, too.

Riordan bullied his way through a mob that could not decide whether to give up or run. With Yankees propelled among them and at their mercy, the boyos gave in to a laziness queer as could be. Short shells slaughtered blue and gray alike.

He punched his way through the sorry, useless lot of them until he reached the ugly end of the fort. Jesus, though, the sight made a man hesitate. The meager stretch between the lines that he'd passed over in the dark had been transformed. Not more than two hundred yards separated two worlds, but now it seemed as wide as the Atlantic Ocean, with a man as like to drown in shell bursts as in those terrible waters. Yankee guns pounded and swept the ground, erasing men's existence, leaving but shredded meat. The lucky victims—still alive, at least—writhed in agony, flailing the limbs left to them.

And yet, some men made the dash, some made it across, despite the fiery blooms they had to dodge. Canister rounds were the worst: Hit by a cluster, a man's remains might be blown back thirty feet.

Riordan ran for it. Clutching his rifle as if, even now, he had the power to defend himself.

The ground shook under his dissolving shoes. He'd thought to borrow himself a new pair amid the Yankee abundance, but he'd waited too long.

How could two hundred yards be such a distance? The world seemed to slow, all safety to recede.

Before him, a skipping cannonball tore off a soldier's head, spinning it into the face of a fellow who'd turn to bid him on.

Riordan dashed past. Holding on to his rifle as if it were dragging him to safety.

Corpses and cripples lay everywhere and would never more court a colleen. If damned to hell he was, it couldn't be worse. Streaming blood, a riderless horse meandered. As it passed by, Riordan saw guts leaking out, the mass of them only held in place by the girth securing the saddle. The animal's neigh might have been the bleat of a sheep.

Some unknown force, a blast or a body, knocked Riordan into the blood slop. Without a pause, he rose again, rifle still firm in his mitts, and scurried the last few yards to something like safety.

Seven fifty a.m.
Fort Stedman

Major Henry Kyd Douglas yanked Gordon's sleeve.

"Come on, sir. *Now.* General Grimes showed me how to reach that ravine, my men are out. We can still get away."

Gordon stared blankly at the chaos engulfing them. Douglas had never seen the man like that. But he'd already mourned one indispensable general after Chancellorsville. He did not mean to lose another now.

He gripped the general's upper arm. "*Now,* sir. We have to go *now*!"

In an instant, the man before him returned to his masterful self, straightening his back and smoothing his features, a panther crossbred with a greyhound.

"I do believe you're right."

With Douglas leading, Gordon and his much-diminished staff left their position northwest of the fort, hastening through wreckage, confusion, and butchery. Harpy shells shrieked by, and the wounded convulsed. Dying horses quivered and emptied their bowels. But when Douglas tried to increase the pace to a run, Gordon chastised him.

"No need to gallop. Men mustn't think we're spooked."

Well, Douglas thought, I'm pretty well spooked myself.

Recognizing Gordon, strays attached themselves. Even at that hour, men had limitless faith in John Brown Gordon. Douglas had faith aplenty in Gordon, too, but it wasn't limitless.

"I do hope that man got my horse back in good condition," Gordon remarked in that well-trimmed voice of his. As if they were just passing the time of day.

Douglas was tempted to say that he'd be happy just to get their own backsides to safety, but he let the moment pass. Gordon loved to talk, but cared less for discussion.

Their band had grown sufficiently large to draw Yankee artillery, but Douglas—after a moment's fear that he'd lost the way—got them down into the ravine Grimes had used to save his division. Or what remained of it.

The safety wasn't as complete as promised. Corpses lay strewn about in the low ground, too. Gordon ordered his staff and the assembled soldiers to take up some of the wounded, although Douglas couldn't see why Gordon chose some men over others to be saved. It didn't seem to depend on their condition. Gordon was, and would always be, a riddle.

But even then, even on this day of defeat, Gordon was one of the finest soldiers Douglas had ever encountered. Jackson alone had been better. And Gordon was considerably more amenable.

Eight a.m.
Battery IX

With all of them deafened from working the guns for three hours without interruption, the sergeant shouted close to Val Stone's ear, "Sir . . . one of them Rebs what just come in wants a word." The sergeant paused as a gun fired and recoiled. "Rough-looking sort."

"What's he want?"

The sergeant shrugged. "Doubt he's swapping sides, he looks a terror. Hot to talk, though."

Well, why not?

"Bring him over," Stone said. Turning, he told a gun crew, "Swab it again. And scrape that vent. I'll have no fouled guns in this battery, not today."

The men were exhausted, worked half to dropping and bent-shouldered, every one of them. But their work wasn't finished, they couldn't falter now.

He wasn't sure the crew had even heard him, but a few had seen his lips move. For what that was worth.

The sergeant tapped him on the shoulder again. As he faced about, Stone's attention leapt to the Reb who wanted to talk. Far from the scrawny sort of Johnny, the captain looked as though he could wrestle a bear. A black beard framed an angry mouth and his eyes were bitter.

The Reb spoke. Stone couldn't hear him. He pointed to an ear and waved the man closer.

The captain's voice was unexpectedly high in pitch. "Lieutenant . . . if you'd just stop your damned firing, there's good men out there trying to give themselves up." Dropping his voice so that Stone could barely get the words, the Reb added, "Just ran out of choices, they're no cowards."

First Lieutenant Valentine Stone ordered the guns of his battery to cease firing. As soon as the local silence grew convincing, hundreds of Rebs rose from their hides, rifles inverted above their heads in the recognized sign of surrender.

Eight fifteen a.m.
Blandford Church Hill

Without speaking to any man, Lee turned his horse toward Petersburg.

One thirty p.m.
Fort Stedman

Hartranft dismounted amid the wreckage left inside Fort Stedman. Splintered wood, ransacked papers, cartridge boxes, and belts lay scattered about. Captured rifles had been stacked to the left of a bombproof's doorway, while Confederate corpses had been piled to the right. The victory had been complete, but it wasn't handsome to look at.

Two thousand Rebel prisoners. Perhaps more, once they'd been registered properly. It had been a remarkable morning, all to the good in the end. Yet, man of the hour or not, Hartranft found the battle's aftermath sobering.

It was always that way: First came the elation, the exuberance, followed in turn by the flat hours, when casualty lists were prepared and the dead manhandled. For Hartranft, even a triumph seeped regret. War gripped his heart, then betrayed it.

He made his way past a throng of satisfied soldiers and out through the forward sally port, where he found the scene before him even bleaker. Under a gloomy sky, the Rebel dead and wounded sprawled on the damp earth.

They were waiting. For him.

In the ravaged ground between the lines, a Confederate officer stood. Beside him, a gray-clad soldier shouldered a white flag. A hundred yards to the party's rear, Confederates filled their ramparts, watching the spectacle. On the Union side, men in blue had grown incautious, too. Along both lines, that drooping rag held thousands spellbound.

The pair of Confederates had been waiting for hours, though not by Hartranft's choice.

Some of the wounded he strode past could only be told from the dead by the faintest movement, a hint of suspiration that caught the eye. The Rebs could have been drawn from different armies for all their contrasts, some of them ragged as medieval beggars, while others had died in newly issued uniforms.

As he passed the former picket line, he saw Union corpses, too, their death-wounds hideous.

He couldn't say it was raining, but his uniform felt damp: It was an ugly, unseemly day, despite the rewards it had brought him.

As he and his orderly closed on the Rebel pair, the young Confederate officer rallied his shoulders and saluted sharply. The sergeant by his side made less of an effort.

"Major Douglas, sir. Acting brigade commander, Pegram's Brigade, Early's Division, Brigadier General Walker commanding, Second Corps, Major General Gordon commanding, Army of Northern Virginia."

It sounded like the title of a monarch. But what startled Hartranft was the look of the fellow: Even battle-stained, the major was handsome enough to entice a pious beauty to indiscretion. Chestnut hair swept over a good forehead, and warm eyes lit a firm, well-sculpted face. Tall and sturdy, he carried himself easily, an Ivanhoe or a Wallace out of Scott.

The lad brought Prosper Dalien to mind. Whose wound was of the sort from which few recovered.

And that was war: such young men killing each other. No matter the justice of the cause, it seemed a terrible thing, grandeur that collapsed into broken corpses.

Hartranft returned the salute and introduced himself. Extending a folded paper, he told the younger man, "General Gordon's request for a truce to remove the wounded and fallen has been approved. Appointed hours from two o'clock until four this afternoon."

He caught the look of urgency, a flash in the major's eyes.

Hartranft nodded.

The major turned and waved. A runner dashed forward. Only after the note had been passed along did the Johnny say, "Thank you, General."

Both men surveyed the scene. Lifelong captives to separate thoughts and worlds that had converged.

"I regret," Hartranft added, "the delay in our response. There were other matters in play."

"We heard the guns," Major Douglas allowed. "Down the line."

It was quiet now. It had been quiet since noon. But things took time to work their way through the echelons of command, through moods and outright malice.

"Under the circumstances, Major, I don't believe I'd notice if your people moved to recover your wounded and dead a few minutes early."

"That would be a kindness, sir. But protocol . . ."

"Your wounded have no interest in protocol."

"Yes, sir. Of course, sir. Thank you." The major took the white flag from the sergeant and sent him back to hurry things the more.

Hartranft dispatched his orderly to alert his own kind to the change.

And the two men stood alone amid the carnage. Subject to that inexplicable magnetism enemies feel when faced with each other's humanity.

At last, the major said, "General Hartranft? If I recall correctly, you hold a Pennsylvania command?"

"Largely."

"And you're a Pennsylvanian?"

Hartranft nodded. "Don't I sound like it?"

The Johnny looked down at the stripped earth. "Went to college up there."

Unarmed Rebs poured from their ramparts and trenches, some bearing litters.

"Where?" Hartranft asked.

"Franklin and Marshall."

Hartranft brightened. "I went there myself! Took my degree in New York, though. Still not sure why I moved on." He judged the major's face. "Class of '60?"

"Fifty-eight. Started a touch young."

"Long after my time, anyway. Some coincidence, though." Hartranft smiled at a mental picture. "You spending time among the Pennsy Dutch."

"Not the worst times I've seen. Nor the worst people."

"No, I expect not." But Hartranft did not want to let go of their bond. "Virginian? I know we had Virginians in my day."

"Yes and no. Born there. But the family manse—as Father likes to put it—sits over the river, Maryland side. Ferry Hill Place. West of Sharpsburg, nigh on Shepherdstown. Up there on the high ground." He looked away again. "War's been a shade hard on things."

Hartranft understood instantly: Any house on commanding heights overlooking the Potomac would have had its share of unwelcome visitors. And successive uniformed tenants.

Another thought touched him, too:

"You at Antietam?"

The major shook his head, not in denial but remembering. "I was. With General Jackson." The young man's eyes found ghosts. "Oddest feeling, being so close to home. In the middle of all that. Of course, I hadn't a great deal of time to ponder it." He paused, as if unsure of offering more. "I was . . . I felt certain that was going to be my last day, it was so strange. The 'fated homecoming,' how things go in books . . ." He smiled mildly. "Got off a little lighter than I expected."

"It's a strange war."

"I reckon most wars are."

Standing there in parley, among the grisly bustle of battlefield mercy, Hartranft felt a swell of warmth toward his counterpart that passed beyond a shared college and conversation. How on earth had it come to this, that the two of them should be set to kill each other? Were their lives, their hearts, so irreconcilable? Fools and firebrands made the war, leaving better men to fight it.

It had been a good day for John Hartranft. A grand day. Called to the rear and expecting a rebuke for his disobedience, he had been interviewed by an elated Lincoln and promoted on the spot to major general. His corps commander had not shared the president's full enthusiasm for Hartranft's elevation, but Parke, too, was pleased enough with the morning's results.

Later, when Meade offered up Parke's initial report, Lincoln had pointed at a file of prisoners trudging past. "There," he said, "is the best dispatch you could show me from General Parke."

The exhilaration Hartranft had felt had faded completely now. In the presence of this all too human major, who conjured Prosper Dalien. The two bore little resemblance one to the other, apart from youth, attractiveness, and vigor . . . yet they were the same.

Breaking another silence, he asked, "First name, Major? If I may presume?"

"Henry, sir. Henry Kyd Douglas. Generally go by 'Kyd,' though. Just takes on folks."

Hartranft held out his hand. "John Hartranft. May we meet again in better times."

After the briefest hesitation, the major took his hand. He gripped it firmly but did not hold it long.

A litter passed them. The shock-eyed Johnny borne upon it muttered a broken psalm. His legs were splintered, chicken bones left by a glutton.

Hartranft longed to assure Kyd Douglas that things would be all right, that tomorrow would be better. Or, if not tomorrow, then next year. All of this would pass as a terrible dream. Their true lives would resume, inviolate in peace.

But gush didn't serve.

The major, too, looked as if he wished to speak. But the right words fled.

Before either officer found his way to speech again, a cluster of braided Confederates left the ramparts and started toward them, joking and strolling blithely between the dead.

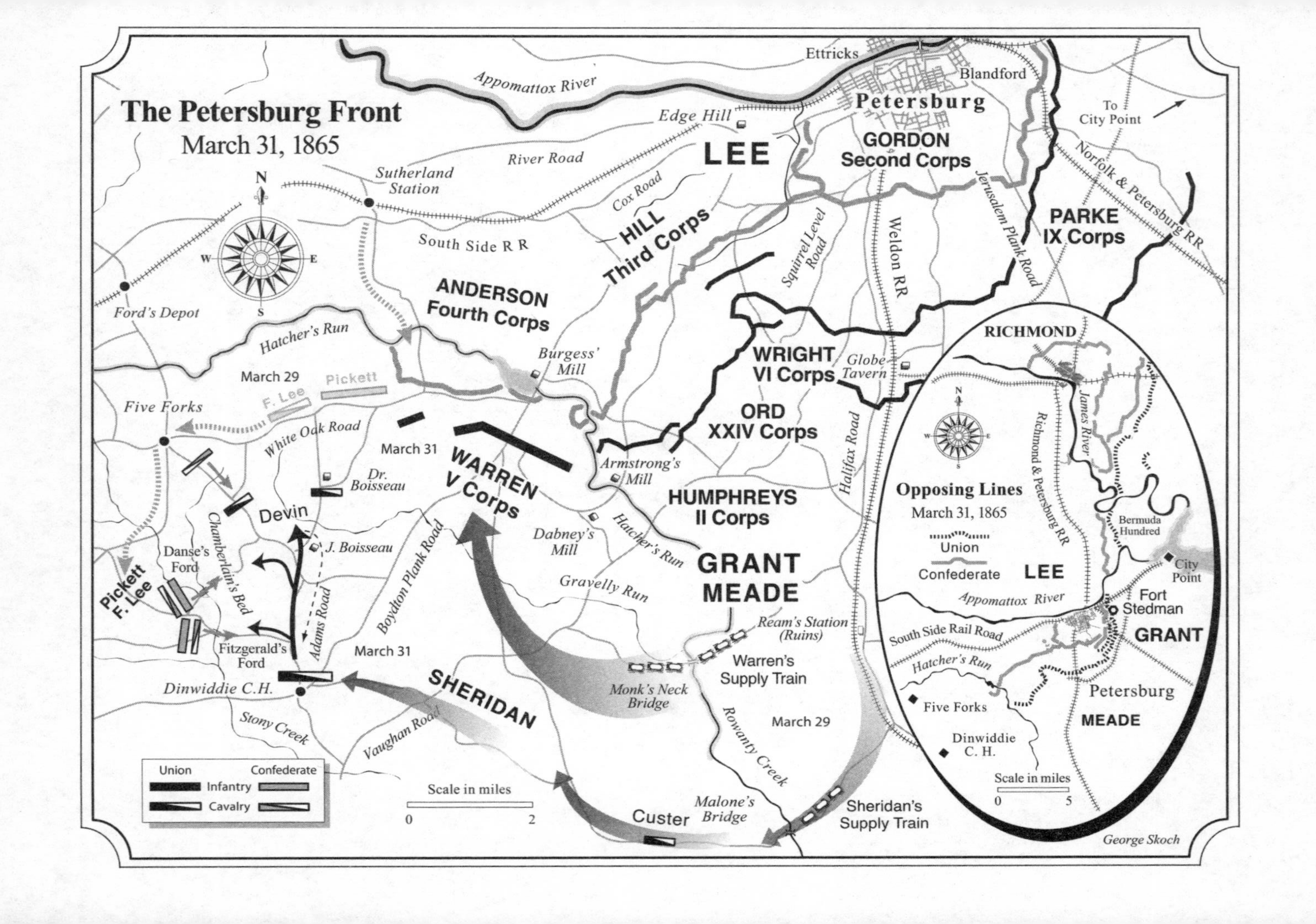
The Petersburg Front
March 31, 1865
N
S
E
W
Appomattox River
Ettricks
Petersburg
Blandford
To
City Point
Edge Hill
LEE
GORDON
Second Corps
River Road
Sutherland
Station
Cox Road
HILL
Third Corps
Norfolk & Petersburg RR
PARKE
IX Corps
South Side R R
Squirrel Level
Road
Weldon RR
Jerusalem Plank Road
Ford's Depot
ANDERSON
Fourth Corps
Hatcher's Run
Burgess'
Mill
WRIGHT
VI Corps
Globe
Tavern
March 29
Pickett
F. Lee
Five Forks
White Oak Road
ORD
XXIV Corps
March 31
WARREN
V Corps
Armstrong's
Mill
Halifax Road
Dr.
Boisseau
HUMPHREYS
II Corps
Devin
Chamberlain's Bed
J. Boisseau
Dabney's
Mill
Hatcher's Run
Danse's
Ford
Boydton Plank Road
Adams Road
Gravelly Run
GRANT
MEADE
Pickett
F. Lee
Fitzgerald's
Ford
March 31
Ream's Station
(Ruins)
Warren's
Supply Train
Dinwiddie C.H.
SHERIDAN
Monk's Neck
Bridge
Stony Creek
Vaughan Road
Rowanty Creek
March 29
Union
Confederate
Infantry
Cavalry
Scale in miles
0
2
Custer
Malone's
Bridge
Sheridan's
Supply Train
RICHMOND
James River
Richmond & Petersburg RR
Opposing Lines
March 31, 1865
Union
Confederate
LEE
Bermuda
Hundred
City
Point
Appomattox River
Fort
Stedman
South Side Rail Road
GRANT
Hatcher's Run
Petersburg
Five Forks
MEADE
Dinwiddie
C. H.
Scale in miles
0
5
George Skoch

THREE

Seven fifty a.m., March 28, 1865
Grant's cabin, City Point, Virginia

Meade stepped into the shanty, wiping his nose. Grant caught his look of surprise.

Glancing at his fellow generals, Meade asked, "President's not here?"

"Calling on Admiral Porter," Grant told him. "Back later." After a moment, he added, "He doesn't want to interfere."

"Bless him for that," Sherman said, rapping the table. "Hang half the damned politicians in this country, if I could. North *and* South." He snorted. "More than half."

Grant nodded toward John Rawlins, a brevet major general, his chief of staff, and his cherished friend.

"John here's tarred with that brush, Cump. Wouldn't hang him now, would you?"

Forehead packed with brains above burning eyes, Sherman told him, "Not unless I had extra rope."

Rawlins coughed. "Like the way you flatter a man."

Grant looked back up at Meade, who still stood in his greatcoat. "Heard you were here earlier. Sit down, George."

"Had a talk with the provost marshal. About the last batch of deserters."

"Ours or theirs?"

"Got on to both." Meade dropped his coat on a bench, wiped his nose again, and scraped out a chair.

"And?"

"Patrick does put the fear of God into them. Line crossers are down. Ours. Since Stedman. Reb numbers are up, though. They sense the game's about over."

"To that end," Grant said, "best get to business. Cump has to get back aboard and on his way. Before Joe Johnston figures out he's gone."

He took out his cigar case and offered it up. Sheridan, who'd remained uncharacteristically silent—merely glaring at Meade—took a Habana but didn't light it. The others declined. Grant lit his smoke as mechanically as a veteran loaded a rifle.

"Phil wants to move tomorrow," Grant said. "So inclined myself."

"I still don't like the weather," Meade told him. "My people think we've got more rain on the way. Teddy Lyman's studied—"

"I don't care what that bookworm studied," Sheridan interrupted. "Dry stretch coming. Any real soldiers can feel it. We've got to move now, to get the jump on Lee."

"Your horses up to a mud march?" Meade snapped. "After your jaunt from the Valley? And I thought you were ordered to North Carolina . . ."

They're like children, Grant thought, the two of them. As soon as they get around one another. George Meade tall and dour, with saddlebags under his eyes, the nose of a Caesar, and a schoolmarm's lips. And Little Phil, queer as a monkey, with that cannonball noggin and gambler's eyes. Sheridan's appearance at Petersburg had not been strictly obedient, but here he was. Grant chose to make the best of things.

Sherman rolled his eyes. Cigar smoke drifted. Rawlins coughed again. Meade sniffled.

"Tell you what I told the president yesterday," Grant resumed. "After Cump tallied up the sins of the South."

Sherman folded his arms across his chest, but kept his silence. The bond between them had grown indestructible, so close that they could laugh over past disagreements. And Sherman *did* laugh. He even told jokes. But only around those he trusted. He'd been scalded by betrayals. They both had.

Grant recalled Sherman, blunt and honest, warning him not to cross the Mississippi below Vicksburg and cut loose. Then, as they closed on poor, abandoned Pemberton, Cump had shown the character to step up and say, "Now I see it, Grant. I see it now." Sherman, who understood war as even Sheridan didn't. Sherman, whom the newspaper fellows had arraigned as a madman. Just as they had belittled Grant as a drunk. Sherman, who never needed a lesson twice.

An army relied on human bonds as much as it did on weapons. Sherman. Sheridan. Meade, who had suffered Grant's command arrangements, but who did his duty ferociously. The men around the table were the men who had won this war. Or all but won it.

Didn't do to say such things out loud, though. End up sounding like McClellan or Hooker.

Grant continued, "Not concerned about the Trans-Mississippi. Sort itself out, once we've fixed our business here. As far as the Deep South goes, Wilson's keeping things lively."

"Wilson? Or Upton?" Sheridan asked, unwilling to share any glory with a cavalryman not under his command.

"Love to see Bedford Forrest drink his own swill," Sherman noted. " 'Wizard of the Skedaddle' would be more like it."

With the stove down to the embers, the cabin began to feel cold. But Grant was not about to call in Bill to coax up the flames. Work first, warmth later.

He stubbed out his cigar and said, "Point is, grand strategy isn't the concern anymore. Cump's seen to that. As Phil has. And you, George. Cump's got Johnston treed, he can't move north to join Lee." Grant scratched his cheek where his beard rose. "Our purpose here is to make certain Lee can't move south to join Johnston."

Heads nodded amid murmurs of assent. Rawlins edged his chair back on its hind legs. Sherman tested the coffee left in his cup, surely cold and sour.

"Stedman affair was a bet Lee couldn't afford," Grant went on, "though I'm not surprised he made it. Man's all fight, give him that. Didn't work, though. Now he has to run." He shook his head, scratching his cheek again. Bedbugs? he wondered. They did thrive in Virginia. "Every morning, I wake up afraid I'll find Lee gone, that he's slipped off. We need to end things here."

"Lee can't win the war," Sheridan said, bile up. "And the old bugger damned well knows it. It's just his high-flown pride that keeps the blood flowing. The man ought to hang, once we take him."

Grant smiled again, but gravely. "Cump wants to hang the politicians, you want to hang Lee. I'd like to be the business fellow who gets the gallows contract." The smile disappeared. "No, Lee can't win the war. But he can stretch it out." Of a sudden, his voice became steel. "We're *not* going to let him escape. Not to North Carolina, not to the mountains. We're going to end this war *here.* Or as close to here as possible. I owe Lincoln that, we all do. We owe the country that. End it. Finish it. We can't let Lee drag it out for another summer, another year." He reached for a fresh cigar but did not repeat his offer to the others. "The president's given us everything we've asked for. Not least, time. He's trusted us. He trusted me, and that did take some fortitude. Now it's time we paid up, cash on the barrelhead."

The silence had bite. Grant rarely spoke in such a tone, or at such length. But for all the literal debts he had owed in his bad years . . . all of those debts wrapped together were nothing compared to what he owed Abraham Lincoln. Who had trusted him as the casualty lists lengthened, who had trusted him as the war refused to end. Lincoln, as good a man as he was plain. A fellow midwesterner.

Maybe the country just needed plain men. Not Southern aristocrats, not New England nabobs. Just plain men, with dirt on their boots. To make a fresh start. Once the horror ended.

Sherman inspected his pocket watch. His red hair burned the morning.

Grant nodded. "Go on, Cump. Your part's settled. I'll see to the rest with George and Phil. And John here."

Pulling on his greatcoat, Sherman insisted, "End it, Sam. Knock Lee into the mud and shove his face in it." He settled the coat's shoulders and drew out his gloves. It made Grant think past the morning's chill to the early blossoms clouding the far riverbank.

"Don't let those sailors drown you," Grant kidded. Or tried to. He'd never been witty, never been good at parlor repartee. Even plainer than Lincoln when it came to society doings.

"Not likely," Sherman said, hard-faced. Looking down at the tin cup before his chair, he added, "Never can figure why the Johnnies are so crazed for Army coffee."

He grabbed the door's latch as if he meant to crush it.

Sherman left a stretch of silence behind him. When the quiet wore out, Sheridan half begged and half demanded:

"Turn me loose, Sam. Right now."

"The roads are *swamps,*" Meade argued. "We can't move wagons and guns in this. Those roads west of Petersburg aren't worthy of the name. They're . . . barbarous." He looked to Grant as the arbiter.

Meade had two moods, Grant reckoned: earnest or angry. And the two did overlap.

"Give it a few more days," Meade suggested. "Lee can't move, either. Unless he wants to leave his trains, his artillery."

"Horseshit," Sheridan said. "We need to get the jump on the old bastard. Give Lee a chance, he'll take it. We need to move first, smash him up."

"I'm all for moving first," Meade told him. "Just not yet. Let the roads dry. So we can actually move when we try to move."

Rawlins cleared his throat. It became another cough. John's consumption had worsened over the winter, alarming Grant. For all the death they had seen, he didn't want Rawlins added to the tally.

He recalled the look of concern he'd caught on the face of John's new wife the night before, when one of John's coughing fits interrupted her chatter with his own wife about their shared distaste for Mrs. Lincoln.

Lincoln had more than one war on his hands. Loved being around the army, like a little boy skipping school. Since Mrs. Lincoln had taken to joining him on his excursions, though, some of the fun was out of it for the poor fellow.

"You're both right," Grant told his generals, looking from Meade to Sheridan and back again. "George, I see your concerns. I share them. To a point. But we're not going to move the whole army. Not yet. If Phil thinks he can push out to the west, though . . . turn Lee's right, or just stretch him . . ."

"He's stretched already," Meade said. "We can beat him right here."

"Well, if Phil cuts the South Side Rail Road . . . that closes off the last escape route Lee still has south of the river."

"I can *do* it, by God," Sheridan declared. He slapped the table. "Turn me loose, Sam. Give me back the Sixth Corps and I'll close the noose on Lee." The little Irishman looked up at Meade with a smirk of triumph, as if he had already done the deeds he promised.

Leading generals was a good sight harder than leading honest soldiers. Grant turned to Meade. "Where's Lee thinnest right now?"

"Opposite Wright, I'd say. Sixth Corps grabbed those Reb rifle pits, a fair stretch of their skirmish line. Lot less ground to cross when we attack. That's the one corps I wouldn't want to move, the Sixth. Even if I could."

"Who's got the Reb division across from Wright?" Grant asked.

"Wilcox. Across from the Sixth Corps' center and right. But it's all A. P. Hill's command over there, on that stretch. Well fortified, but their men look thin on the ground."

Grant forgot his cigar and leaned back in his chair. "Old Cad Wilcox. He and I were messmates down in Mexico. Good old Cad. No meanness to him. Not back then, anyway."

"I remember him," Meade said. "We used to laugh about his name. 'Cadmus Marcellus Wilcox.' Sounds like a Roman senator." He fingered the wet from the tip of his nose. "He did strike me as ambitious."

"Weren't we all?" Grant asked. "Some of us just went about it a little quieter." He sighed, thinking again of what the war had done to friends and old rivalries. "Served at Jefferson Barracks together, too. Cad stood up for me, at my wedding." He remembered their bygone innocence, although they would not have deemed it such in their swaggering days. "Pete Longstreet was my best man. Pete and Cad. . . ."

"Remember," Meade asked, "how we all worshipped Lee? It was naked idolatry."

Grant stopped the cigar just short of his lips. "Cad may have had the name of a Roman senator, but Lee had the look of one. Finest appearance of any man in the Army." He tasted the cigar: Bill hadn't filled his case with the better smokes, one of his servant's petty acts of vengeance. Grant wondered what his fault had been this time. Smacking his lips, he added, "Never looked like much myself. Hated those old high collars, glad they're gone."

"We all wanted to be him," Meade said.

Grant shook his head. "My aspirations never went *that* high." He laughed softly. "Beginning of this war, my highest ambition was to command a regiment. I thought I might make a go of that."

"I was building lighthouses. Doing survey work."

Grant had been waiting for Sheridan, who did not share the memories, to leap in. Phil didn't take to being set aside. He did have a touch of Mrs. Lincoln to him.

"About the Sixth Corps," Sheridan said, reading Grant's expression, "I want *them* on my flank, Sam. They're my boys, from the Valley. They know me, and I know them."

Grant watched Meade's face redden.

"For God's sake, Sheridan! Those roads won't even support your cavalry's movement. I can't leapfrog entire corps back and forth." Meade scraped his handkerchief across his nose. "Warren's on the army's left, ideally placed to support you. He can sidestep, tie in to your flank. *If* you make it out there. It's the only course that makes sense." He glowered. Nobody in Grant's experience could work himself up to the edge of apoplexy like George Gordon Meade. "The Fifth Corps will do to bail you out, if need be."

"Warren's unreliable. And as for the Fifth Corps—" Sheridan caught himself. Remembering, Grant was certain, that the Fifth was

Meade's old corps. There were certain lines that officers didn't cross, not even Phil Sheridan. "It's just," the Irishman amended, "that Wright and I are used to working together. And, frankly, I have no confidence in Warren."

Army politics. That side of the trade had always disgusted Grant. He knew full well that, another time, Meade would have defended Warren vigorously. But Meade and Warren had just had another of their confrontations. Warren had a galling habit of second-guessing superiors. For that matter, Grant's own confidence in him was limited.

Warren was tired. They all were tired. But Warren was fidgety tired, a high-strung man. That wasn't good.

"Well, the Fifth Corps will have to do," Meade insisted. "I'm not about to make a bad situation worse by shuffling this army's corps any more than necessary. Besides, Wright knows the ground he's on, he's already working up plans for an assault. I need to keep him exactly where he is. And Warren knows the terrain out on the flank. Wright doesn't."

Grant had had enough. "Phil, the Fifth Corps will do. It's a good corps." The cabin had grown chilly, even as tempers burned. Strange the way cold brought out different smells than heat summoned. The shanty reeked of ashes, cigars, and tinned sardines. No wonder his wife complained.

Julia was a good soldier, though. Mostly. He just wished she could get on with Mrs. Lincoln.

"All right," Grant said. "Phil, you'll move first thing tomorrow. Cut that railroad. Maintain a position astride it. George, see that Warren cooperates. With none of his fussing. And have your staff work up an assault all along the front, if Phil cuts the South Side."

"I'll cut it, all right," Sheridan said. "I could cut the Richmond and Danville, too."

It was time to rein Phil in. Some generals did too little. Sheridan usually wanted to do too much.

"I'd worry you might get cut off from the rest of the army. Of course, you could just ride down and join Cump in North Carolina, if it came to that."

Sheridan's face paled. "No . . . no, I didn't mean that. I don't intend to lose contact with the army."

Grant forced his mouth to behave. He wanted to laugh out loud, though. Phil wanted to be in on the kill, on Lee's destruction, so badly that no survey tools could measure it. But Grant had to drive home his point, to keep Phil from making up his own rules again. To finish Lee, every man from west of Petersburg to the Richmond lines had to cooperate.

"John," Grant said to his chief of staff, "when you write up the order, state that Sheridan will move to join Sherman, should he lose contact with this army."

"Oh, you don't have to worry about that, Sam," Sheridan insisted.

"You won't get far enough in that mud to lose contact," Meade put in.

With his Chinaman's eyes narrowed fiercely, Sheridan turned on the Philadelphian. "I'll cut the South Side Rail Road long before you get one goddamned soldier into Lee's trenches."

"I reckon you can take that up with Lee," Grant said. "Both of you."

"I can move, then?" Sheridan asked.

"I just said that."

"Well, bully. Bully, Sam. Let me get out of this quartermaster's cathouse and get going."

Runty Sheridan must have been a caution of a schoolboy, Grant concluded. And Lord help the lad who thought that because he was bigger he must be tougher than Phil.

Before Sheridan could hurl himself back toward his command, Rawlins had a coughing fit, a severe one. He rose to go outside, drawing out a handkerchief already pinked with blood. He muttered, "Excuse me," and stumbled toward the fresh air.

Sheridan stood, startled.

"Go on," Grant told him. "Nothing you can do." He remembered that Sheridan hadn't seen Rawlins since the past summer. John had seemed a different man back then, health barely dented.

When Sheridan had gone, Meade said, "Those roads are abysmal, Sam. It'll take him days just to get to Dinwiddie Court House. Without his guns or his trains."

"Let Phil learn." Grant shrugged and felt for his cigars, but dropped his hand away again. "If he makes good, fine. If he doesn't, well, I'd rather have this army doing something than sitting idle."

"We're hardly idle. And his horses are blown. That march must have been brutal. He's going to kill his mounts, if not his men."

"They'll serve. Reb nags are worse off."

Meade gave up. Grant knew that Meade knew that it was unwise to argue horseflesh with him. The only commander of the Army of the Potomac who had survived that responsibility got to his feet. "If there's nothing else, I'll put my staff to work, get the orders down to the corps to plan for a grand assault. They'll be ready, when you give the order." His expression tightened again. "Humphreys made solid gains the other day, but the terrain's broken to his front, I'm not sure how much he can do. My bet's on Wright, he's got himself tight up against them."

"Parke's to attack, as well. And the Twenty-fourth Corps, when it closes. Everybody goes in this time. I don't want Lee able to shift a single soldier, once we hit him."

"We'll be ready, Sam." Meade pulled on a glove. "As soon as the weather cooperates."

Grant almost said, "I'll decide, not the weather," but he didn't want Meade to feel he was drifting to Sheridan's side. The vanity of generals was as delicate as the best plantation china—the sort upon which his Julia had dined, before she cast her lot with a junior officer of uncertain prospects. Well, he'd done all right by her, in the end.

He followed the Philadelphian out into the brisk air. The depot swarmed with soldiers and laborers. Under the bluff, vessels crowded the harbor. Sun glinted on water and metal.

The morning wasn't a bad one. Maybe it wouldn't rain.

"Warming up, all right," Meade said, working his handkerchief clumsily with his riding gloves. "Glad to put winter behind us. Going to have more rain, though. Count on it."

"That cold getting worse, George?"

"Almost gone."

"Look after yourself. Wouldn't want you to miss the end of the show." Grant's brow tightened. "Nearly forgot. Your man Barlow."

"Frank Barlow?"

"Francis Channing Barlow. Another of your society three-namers."

"What about him?"

Down on the river, a steamship hooted, answered in turn by the tugs it had enslaved. The harbor always looked chaotic to Grant, but the sailors and watermen somehow avoided catastrophe.

"He's in New York. At some hotel. Back from his leave in Europe. He's been sending telegrams to headquarters. Making himself available."

"Must be healthy again. That's a pleasant surprise. Miles and Hancock both feared he might die."

"Offered to send him to Hancock, thought he'd like that," Grant said. "Doesn't want any part of it. Wants to come back down here and take a division."

"That's Barlow, all right."

"Harvard fellow, ain't he?"

Humor improved, Meade showed his aging teeth. "Top of his class. Doesn't seem to have done him any harm." Meade's eyes left Grant for a moment, hunting the answer to a private question. "I'd have thought he'd have contacted Lyman. They were classmates, all that."

"Well, he wants to come here, and he wants a division."

Meade folded his arms, sniffling again. "Can't have his old one. Miles has earned it, I couldn't move him now."

"No one you want to be rid of?"

"There'll be openings. When things get going."

"Want him, then?"

"Send him to my headquarters. It'll make every division commander fight twice as hard, knowing Frank Barlow's fishing for a command."

"I'll have John see to it."

The ships and boats maneuvering over the sweep of the James commanded their attention.

"Amazing," Grant said. "Isn't it?"

"War used to be an art, now it's an industry." Meade flicked a hand toward the city of arms that had sprawled around a raw Virginia hamlet, with hundreds of acres covered by warehouses, artillery and wagon parks, smithies, stables and corrals, locomotives and rolling stock, a ramshackle row of bordellos every surgeon wanted closed, and, across the mouth of the Appomattox, the enormous hospital.

"Couldn't have imagined all this back in Mexico," Grant said. The mention of Cad Wilcox had brought back memories. Good ones, mostly.

Meade snorted. "I couldn't have imagined this four years ago." He peered beyond the wharves to the river again. Grant followed his eyes. "Who knew the country had such wealth?"

"Rebs didn't. That's certain." He thought again of Lee, born to command, gaining brevets with ease in Mexico. The envy of them all. Lee had defeated entire armies, but he couldn't whip the *North.*

And here they were.

"It feels as though the country's completely changed," Meade said. "Not just all this."

"It has," Grant told him.

One p.m.

Brevoort House, New York City

"I leave tomorrow," Barlow told his brother.

Around them, knives and forks chimed.

"You're mad," Ed insisted. "You ought to be in an asylum."

Barlow froze. As did his brother, too late.

"Bad form, Ed."

"That was idiotic of me."

"I shan't argue."

Over ravaged beefsteaks, the brothers recalled their father, the minister gone mad, the lost soul, located at last in Philadelphia, only to be murdered. The affair remained unresolved.

"I only meant," Ed tried again, "that it's folly for you to rush back to the war. They've managed well enough without you, it seems to me. God knows, you've done your part."

"It isn't over, though."

"It will be. Even I can see that much." Ed sat back and thumbed his vest. The waistcoat was new and florid. It would not have passed in Boston. Ed's nose had acquired red blotches.

"What will be shall be." Barlow tapped the breast of his coat. "I have my tickets. That's that."

"You love it that much? Belle always said you did."

The mention of his dead wife's name on another's lips, even those of a brother, conjured demons.

"It isn't love. It's duty."

Ed smirked. "Marriage, not lust?"

Barlow leaned over his plate, regarding his newly wealthy, increasingly paunchy brother. The brother who had made certain that he had profited, too, the entire family. Perhaps Ed's was the more responsible role, but Barlow did not feel that he had ever had a choice, not once he'd put on the ill-fitting, unadorned uniform of a private in '61.

"I need to finish the thing. To be there. I need to be part of it, Ed. At the end. If you can't understand it, I can't explain it."

A waiter discreetly pointed out Barlow's table to a messenger. Irish by the look of him, the boy made his way through the crowded room with a mix of bravado and the evident knowledge that he didn't belong among such people as these.

Stopping just short of the table, the lad tried to judge to whom he should address himself.

Ed helped. “I think you want him.”

The boy swiveled. “General Barlow?” He seemed disappointed not to see a uniform.

“Yes?”

The boy held out a telegraph paper. “For you, sir.”

Barlow nodded: *Put it there, on the table.* He fished out a coin.

As the messenger retreated, Barlow slipped the paper into his pocket.

His brother lifted an eyebrow.

“If it’s from Hancock, I daren’t read it,” Barlow said. “Fine old fellow. But he’s not in the fight anymore.” He looked through a smudged window to the ripe display of Fifth Avenue: New York had grown fat. How did war’s destruction make men rich? Ed knew the secret, bless him.

“And if it’s not from Hancock?”

“If it’s from Halleck or Stanton, it’s not worth reading. They’d only bother things.” His mouth twisted up in its sardonic set. “And if it’s from Grant . . . I’ll read it on my way.”

“That’s how the Army does things?”

“It’s how I do things.”

“I wish you’d stayed in Europe. Mother would be crushed to lose you now.”

“Mother would wear it well. The loss of a heroic son.”

“Frank, you know that isn’t true. You should have taken a few days to go to Boston to see her. The war could have spared you that long. She’ll be put out when she hears.”

“No time. There’s just no time now. Ed, I was in Rome, sitting in the Forum . . . and it struck me like a lightning bolt. I *knew* in that moment the war was about to end. I’ve positively scrambled to get back.”

“Mother dotes on you.”

“I’ve sent along a watercolor.” Barlow chose not to mention a second picture.

“And Ellen Shaw? You don’t care to see her, either?”

"Has Mother got you singing harmony now? There's nothing there, Ed."

It was a lie. Barlow rather hoped it was a lie.

"She painted matters as if—"

"Mother's the Titian of the social palette."

"You yourself said—"

"Nellie Shaw is a splendid girl. Does that suffice as a testament?"

"But not as splendid as war?"

"Arabella hasn't been gone a year. It's unseemly even to think . . ."

"Never bothered you before, Frank. Appearing unseemly."

"I have a duty."

"Which one? To whom? To a war that's going perfectly well without you? To a dead wife? To some sort of madcap pride?" Ed panted, as if they'd run a race round the table. "Frank . . . we just want you to *survive*. We feared we'd lost you last year. . . ."

"When I nearly shit myself to death?"

Heads turned at his language. He was glad they were in the men's dining room.

"And after Gettysburg. And Antietam before that."

"Bullets have a certain dignity, you know. The bowels rather not." Barlow showed his crooked front tooth. "It was worse than dysentery, as it turned out. Shall I taint your lunch with details?"

Ed smiled, becoming the playful brother again. From their halcyon days of ignorance, the years of dares and daydreams. "It *would* have been a nasty way to go."

"Not sure how Mother would have dignified it."

"She would've found a way. She always does." Ed smirked. "You just said the same thing yourself."

A waiter approached. Not without trepidation.

Barlow reached for his purse and said, "Don't worry, Ed. Dying now would be tasteless."

His brother stayed Barlow's effort to pay. He signed to the waiter, as if writing his name, and the fellow bowed.

"I have an account here," Ed explained.

"Aren't we grand? 'He hath an argosy bound to Tripolis, another to the Indies.'"

Ed looked wounded. "I've hardly played the Shylock with you."

Barlow laughed, the bray men found unsettling. "Ed, you're a treasure. Don't think I'm not grateful for all you've done, not for a moment. It was the only line I could think of. Literature wasn't my strong suit back in the Yard."

Pride restored, Ed straightened. "Do you realize what remarkable luck we've had? Every single investment showed a profit, every one. That's unheard of. Every ship paid handsomely, every cargo." He tried again: "Really, you needn't go back to the war, there's no point. You're a man of some prosperity, Frank. Take pleasure in it. Go see Mother for a few days, anyway. And Nellie Shaw. Let Boston admire you."

Barlow closed hardened fingers over his brother's wrist to make an end of things.

"You've had a better war than I've had, Ed."

Ten p.m., March 29
Edge Hill, Petersburg
Headquarters of the Army of Northern Virginia

His generals braved the rain at last, leaving Lee with a half-finished glass of Madeira to ponder what an odd assortment they were. A man of immaculate confidence when the eyes of others were on him, Gordon had been at his genial best, at once dignified and warm, leaving it to his subordinate Clement Evans, a rambunctious Methodist, to deploy the worries Gordon had assembled. As for Evans, Lee admired his faith and his talents on the field of battle, but found him gullible. Evans still believed the war could be won. Lee did not.

Nor, Lee suspected, did Gordon or the other two general officers who'd paid a call: Wilcox, aggrieved that his lines had been thinned again to bolster the right, and McGowan, a lawyer with a bardic recall of Shakespeare and Milton, who delighted in entertaining his fellows while masking the cold eye with which he viewed the world.

Earlier, Pickett had complained that even with the promised reinforcements, he would not have men enough on the right flank. Pickett, in whom Longstreet still had faith, but whom Lee struggled to trust. Pickett had the qualities of a regimental colonel, but Lee was not convinced the man possessed a general's judgment. And for all the *eau de toilette* Pickett wore, there was dirt under his fingernails.

But who else did he have?

Hill was expected back, that would be a help. Lee longed for his subordinate's arrival, craved a firm hand over the Third Corps. Lee had long since overcome his distaste for Hill's youthful follies—Hill had paid a hard price for his sins—but the recurring sickness removed him from command at the worst of times.

Lee sipped his Madeira, the last of a treasured keg. He had felt a surge of reluctance to share the wine, so he'd forced himself to order it poured generously for his guests. He did not wish greed or gluttony to count among his sins.

They had drunk to Mrs. Gordon, who expected a child any day. Here, in Petersburg, amid the carnage. Lee could not say whether her stubbornness was to be admired or decried as foolishness.

Who else, indeed, did he have to place in command? The alternatives lay dead, from Yellow Tavern to Cedar Creek. The Year of Our Lord 1864 had been a horrid trial, with a plague of deaths scything the army, robbing him of generals much needed and of the better colonels who might have replaced them. It was not as it had been: These days, he led good men, but not great ones—a view he would, of course, utter to no man.

He drained his glass and forgot to taste the wine.

His wife had sent him another bundle of stockings she and his daughters had knitted to play their part in the war. As was his practice, each pair would pass to a soldier, with none kept back. He did not need more stockings. He needed, yearned for, the mercy of the Lord, for strength and sustenance . . . for a miracle.

How had he sinned? How had they all sinned, these noble spirits, alive or dead, who had risen to fight for their freedom, their laws, their states, their way of life? Had they been wrong? Had they failed to grasp the will of the Lord their God? Why had such tribulations been visited upon them? Surely, it was those people who were godless, not his kind.

He contemplated, yet again, the inadmissible thought that slavery was the transgression that had doomed them. But how would the Negro thrive if granted freedom? Surely, the Lord who had made all things reckoned their inferiority? Lee knew that slavery could be cruel, but might not freedom be crueler?

It was hard to imagine Grant as a tool of the Lord. An agent to humble his pride, perhaps, but not an avenging angel. At times, Lee found it unbearable that he might be defeated by such a man.

Grant. Lee had tried to remember the fellow from Mexico. It was certain that he'd been there with the rest of them. But Lee could not recollect a face or voice, no distinguishing gesture. His image of Grant had been limned by the illustrated papers that crossed the lines.

He had learned to discount the tart stories, though. Grant was no fool. Nor could he be a drunkard, or one no longer. Not given his tenacity, his perseverance.

Often, Lee found himself hating this man he knew only through his willingness to spend blood.

He would never voice such views, of course. Gordon would understand that. Gordon saw that a man had to show front. Only fools paraded their thoughts: The key to a dignified life was discipline. And that included a thoroughly mastered tongue.

He thought, as he so often did, of the cramped house in Alexandria to which his penurious family had been consigned, of the shamed and absent father, of his mother's debilities and near suffocation of him, of summers spent at the plantations of other Lees, the wealthy and respected Lees, and of the shame of a welcome that lacked warmth. West Point had been his escape, the Army, the Engineers, his refuge and fortress.

He thought, too, of his father-in-law, who had opposed his marriage into the Custis line. That Madeira had been one of the old fellow's extravagances. Upon his death, Lee had needed to take a long leave of absence to put Arlington's neglected affairs in order. The labor had been wretched, but satisfying, a testament to his better-managed life.

Why couldn't he remember Grant? Had the fellow been so insubstantial? None of the engravings or periodical sketches triggered memories. In an Army of colorful, notable men, Grant had been . . . nobody. Forced to resign his commission, so the tale went, because he lacked the character to function as a regimental quartermaster.

How could such a man . . .

The intimate members of Lee's staff had left him alone when the generals departed. They knew he was tired, weary. At times, they treated his feelings *too* gingerly, leaving him too much to himself when he needed the tonic of company—above all, the companionship of the young.

The rain renewed its assault upon the roof. The roads had been bad. By morning, they'd be impossible. Grant was on the move with his cavalry: Sheridan, who had displayed neither heart nor scruple in the Valley. The scouts reported shifts of Meade's infantry, too. The blow was coming, but this rain would slow it down.

It also would slow his son, who'd been foddering his horses toward the North Carolina line. Rooney had to rejoin Fitzhugh Lee and his horsemen on Pickett's right to hold open the road and the rail line west, the army's lifelines.

Lee reached down and scratched his ankle above his ancient slippers. The fleabites had not abated.

His back hurt, too. And his knees, his shoulder. For the first time in his life, maintaining an upright posture was a struggle.

He would have liked more Madeira, but he never permitted himself more than one glass. A small glass. Discipline was the surest armor any man could possess.

He was proud of Rooney, of each of his sons, and of his nephew. But he should not have let Hampton go, he saw that now. Hampton had done little good in South Carolina, thanks to the infernal politics of command in the Confederacy. And when, at last, Lee had gained control of all of Richmond's armies, the commission had come too late.

Even the matter of recruiting Negroes to fight had arisen too late.

Well, *he* would fight. It wasn't over yet.

As recently as the autumn, he had toyed with the notion of taking to the hills, should the Army of Northern Virginia be defeated, of fighting on in the fashion of *guerrilleros.* But that would merely call down wrath on the people. The end, when it came, was bound to be bad enough.

As long as the army remained intact, Lee meant to fight on. Honor demanded that. But there would be no resort to useless bushwhacking.

He levered himself to his feet—even rising from a chair had grown more difficult. From other rooms, the pen-scratch of staff work assured him that he had not been deserted. His young fellows were diligent, but the paperwork the Department of War and its many bureaus demanded only grew heavier as the army withered. Richmond's appetite for reports and accounts had become insatiable, as if documentation alone could save the Confederacy. And the requisition forms were submitted in all the copies required, but the bacon didn't arrive, or it turned up rancid. Men hungered in the trenches, but the countersigned papers that wandered from desk to desk proved all was in order.

And President Davis . . . it became ever harder for Lee to practice restraint in the man's presence. He had sought, repeatedly, to warn the president that Grant's power threatened to prove overwhelming, that Petersburg might have to be abandoned and Richmond evacuated on a few hours' notice. But the president refused to credit his warnings. Richmond had become a realm of all the wrong fears, of fables and delusions.

Lee had weighed evacuating his wife and daughters from the Richmond house, but Mary refused to go and signal despair. His family, too, would have to bear his burden.

Should worse come to worst, he did not think those people would mistreat his family. Their ordeal would be humiliating, though.

Paralyzed by his thoughts, Lee stood in the cast of the oil lamp. He had never dreamed it would come to this.

Grant was said to have been fond of poker as a young officer. Perhaps that was why he had made no impression on him: Lee had ever regarded poker as vulgar, had kept away from the games in the musty tents and officers' quarters. His fashion was to be gracious but stand apart.

Where had Grant found his aptitude for war? Playing poker? As a failed farmer? Hawking firewood in the streets of St. Louis? As the simple clerk he was said to have become, employed as a last resort through his family's mercy?

Longstreet, who had known Grant and was fond of him, had remarked, "Well, I guess Sam found a second thing he can do all right. In addition to riding the devil out of a horse."

And Longstreet had told a tale of when Grant, literally ragged, had encountered Longstreet in St. Louis and had insisted that he take a five-dollar gold piece to settle a debt Grant owed him.

"That's just how he was," Longstreet had said. "How he still is, I suppose. Honest to a fault, to an embarrassment."

All that only made Grant a greater enigma. Lee had understood his other opponents, McClellan, Pope, Burnside, Hooker, even George Meade. He'd known them all, he could read their fortunes like a Mexican gypsy. But Grant's palms remained blank.

Weary and lonely, Lee stepped into the parlor that had become Colonel Taylor's domain, the adjutant's redoubt behind ramparts of paper. Colonel Marshall, Lee's military secretary, worked at his own table, while Venable was off on a rain-drenched errand.

Lee had entered softly. Taylor gave a start when he realized that he was being observed. It made Lee smile as indulgently as he did with his own sons. This late, Taylor would be drafting another letter to Miss Saunders, his longtime intended, marooned in Richmond. It was a curious thing to Lee, how Taylor and the young woman for whom he seemed destined had made no move to marry. This had been a war of hasty weddings, of romantic urgency, of terrible dreads and impatience. But Taylor just wrote letters.

Of course, many an impetuous groom had soon been laid in a grave, consigning his young bride to widow's black. Perhaps Taylor had that in mind when he delayed marriage. He was admirably Christian, of course, received into the Episcopal Church, Lee's denomination and, in the view of many Virginians, the *only* denomination.

Jackson had been a Presbyterian. With their hard faith. Lee acknowledged Jackson's loss as the will of the Lord. Jackson himself would have called it "predestined." But Lee had not, even now, reconciled himself to it.

Recovering from his surprise and rising, Taylor said, "May I help you, General?" His voice was raised against the assault of the rain on the roof and windows.

Alerted, Marshall got to his feet as well. Their faces showed that tiredness reserved only for the young, exhaustion without the weariness of age.

Lee could think of nothing to ask. He had wanted, just for a moment, to feel the warmth of youth, of their bright company.

"Rain's bound to slow operations, sir," Marshall said to scratch the silence.

"It will be worse for those people," Lee told him. "Their reliance on heavy trains will embarrass their plans."

"Yes, sir."

Taylor looked toward the ceiling. "It's just pounding down. Half the roads out Dinwiddie way will be under two feet of water."

Lee pictured the Federals' endless columns of limbers, guns and caissons, supply wagons and ambulances, struggling along the quicksand roads of Dinwiddie County.

And his own men out in the trenches? Keeping watch in rifle

pits? On the march in this inundation? After praising the Madeira, Sam McGowan had regaled the audience of generals with one of his famous recitations from Shakespeare, with whose works Lee claimed no intimacy. Now he recalled one insistent line, spoken amid a storm just such as this, when an addled king cried: "I have ta'en too little care of this!"

He had asked so much, continued to ask so much, of the men out there. Had he been just? And righteous? Had he served them well?

The Lord would have to decide.

Looking from one waiting face to the other, Lee said:

"I wish the orders to be unmistakably clear. If the reports of General Sheridan moving on Dinwiddie Court House prove accurate, General Pickett's command and General Lee's cavalry are *not* to await further orders. They must strike at the first opportunity, before those people arrange themselves in good order. We shall not wait until we are attacked, Sheridan must not be allowed to approach Five Forks."

"I believe General Pickett understands that, sir," Taylor offered. "Your orders were clear."

"Tell him again," Lee said.

Two p.m., March 30
Adams Road, north of Dinwiddie Court House

By damn, he was *not* going to let Meade prove him wrong, damned if he would. Goddamned weather. Grant had mortified him, ready to order a halt to the army's movements. He'd had to ride back through the downpour to convince them all that *his* movement should go ahead.

Rain pounded Sheridan's rubber cape. Even Rienzi, as strong a horse as Sheridan had ever ridden, struggled with mud that coated his legs and clung to Sheridan's spurs.

Men who might have cheered as he passed failed to notice him, their heads down and their eyes barely raised beyond withers or wet manes. Even the few who acknowledged him were perfunctory.

They kept moving forward, though. Merritt saw to that. And Sheridan couldn't help being amused at the thought of Georgie Custer. To Custer's chagrin, he'd ordered his division to escort the trains—reasoning that if anyone could move those wagons and guns through the slop, it would be Custer. Young Goldilocks would be wild to get into the fight.

No, Sheridan was *not* going to let George Meade make a fool of him. If he had to drag every horse, gun, and wagon through the flood himself, he'd get on the Rebels' right and take that railroad. There would be no excuse to pack him off to join Sherman, who was able to handle Joe Johnston by himself.

Philip Sheridan meant to be in on the kill. Right in front. And damn George Meade.

He calculated that after the war ended and things shook out, the public would have room in their heads and hearts for three heroes, at most. And two of the places had already been taken by Grant and Sherman. Sheridan meant to be number three in the trinity. And he'd damned sure make certain that number three wasn't George Meade.

Meade, who'd persuaded Grant to leave him reliant on Warren's Fifth Corps, instead of giving him the loyal Sixth—led by Horatio Wright, who knew what was good for him. Wright remained grateful, and rightfully so, that Sheridan had not breathed a word of recrimination over the morning's debacle at Cedar Creek.

He had Wright on a choker. But Warren was a self-important ass. And too damned slow.

His belly acid rose to recall the year-old confrontation south of the Wilderness and Warren's charge that the cavalry had not only failed to fight, but had blocked his march route. The Rebs had won the race to Spotsylvania, and Meade had backed Warren, of course. Thank God Grant had shown sense. Giving him the chance to kill Jeb Stuart.

To hell with Meade and Warren; they'd get their comeuppance.

He caught up with Tom Devin and his staff, hunched over in

their saddles, flags furled and covered in canvas. Water slopped from the rim of Devin's hat.

"Thought you'd be at Five Forks already, Tommy. I could walk faster than your division's moving."

Devin cocked his head toward the mire that had been a road. "Like riding through knee-deep turds." His mick eyes narrowed. "Rebs are out there. I can feel them."

"I don't want you to *feel* the sonsofbitches," Sheridan told him. "I want you to *find* them. And then I want your mob to earn its pay."

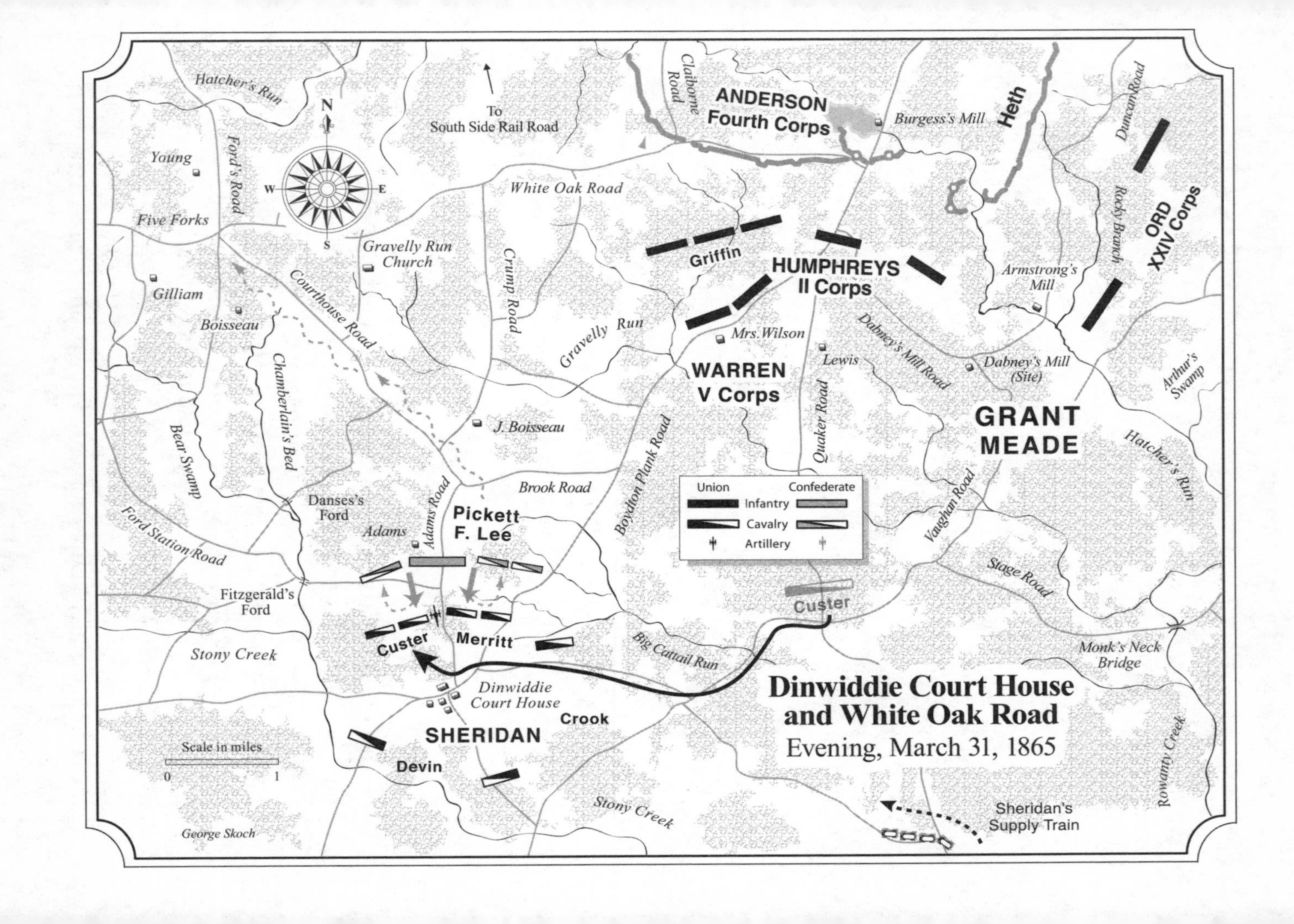
Dinwiddie Court House
and White Oak Road
Evening, March 31, 1865
Hatcher's Run
To
South Side Rail Road
Claiborne Road
ANDERSON
Fourth Corps
Burgess's Mill
Heth
Duncan Road
Young
Ford's Road
N
W
E
S
White Oak Road
Five Forks
Gravelly Run Church
Crump Road
Griffin
HUMPHREYS
II Corps
Rocky Branch
ORD
XXIV Corps
Armstrong's Mill
Gilliam
Boisseau
Courthouse Road
Gravelly Run
Mrs. Wilson
Dabney's Mill Road
Lewis
Dabney's Mill
(Site)
Arthur's Swamp
Chamberlain's Bed
WARREN
V Corps
Quaker Road
GRANT
MEADE
J. Boisseau
Bear Swamp
Boydton Plank Road
Hatcher's Run
Brook Road
Union
Confederate
Infantry
Cavalry
Artillery
Danses's Ford
Adams Road
Pickett
F. Lee
Adams
Vaughan Road
Ford Station Road
Stage Road
Fitzgerald's Ford
Custer
Custer
Merritt
Big Cattail Run
Monk's Neck Bridge
Stony Creek
Dinwiddie Court House
Crook
SHERIDAN
Scale in miles
0
1
Devin
Rowanty Creek
Stony Creek
Sheridan's Supply Train
George Skoch

FOUR

Six p.m., March 31, 1865
Adams Road, north of Dinwiddie Court House

Well, Fitz," Pickett sang, "ain't this delightful?"

Fitzhugh Lee did not share his fellow Virginian's gaiety. It *had* been a good day. Wasn't over, though. More deeds needed doing, a last few. Before the light went.

Rifles cracked sporadically: the lull between attacks.

"Always said Sheridan was a little man hiding behind a big man's reputation," Pickett went on. "Wonder how he likes the feel of a licking? The whupping he just got?"

Sweated, chilled, and tired, Lee said, "Time to finish him."

Whenever he came this close to crushing the Federals, Lee seethed with vengeance. He did not possess his uncle's gift of forbearance.

"Watch now. Down there." Pickett pointed with a gloved hand—like Stuart, he wore yellow gloves, something no Lee ever would have done. "My boys are about to bust up that last line."

Pickett's mount shied at a spook. Lee watched as his fellow major general mastered the horse with an almost womanly gentleness.

"He's put in his last reserves," Pickett resumed, "it's all up now." He pushed his oiled hair behind an ear. "We'll be in that tavern off the courthouse yard, eating Sheridan's supper while it's hot."

Well, many a fine cavalryman wouldn't have supper this night. Nor ever again. The fighting over Fitzgerald's Ford had been long and costly, if decisive in the end. Lee had needed to all but thrash Cousin Rooney and near took a strop to Barringer, but the North Carolina troopers had gone in with a will, with the 1st North Carolina dismounted to wade the chest-high creek under well-aimed fire. Then the 2nd dashed across mounted and ended it, chasing Yankees who just ran out of grit. It had all been gallant and necessary, but those who had fallen could not be replaced. So this was an hour for pride, perhaps, but not for Pickett's jollity.

The rain had quit that morning and the sun had reported for duty. Even the weather gave men cause for hope. But Fitz Lee remained wary.

As he watched, Pickett's infantry rose from a swale and swept over open ground toward a blue line of cavalrymen deployed to fight on foot. A few Union guns showed their rancor, but the source was a light artillery battery positioned too far to the rear.

As Pickett's doubled lines broke into a charge, the Union troopers started to withdraw, working the levers of their Spencers hard but unwilling to stand. A Rebel yell went up, their tribal clamor.

Credit to Pickett, it had been quite a day, Lee had to admit. They'd outflanked Sheridan's dispersed brigades one after the other, driving them fiercely and nearly encircling two of them, keeping them all off balance. Except at that ford, where blood had stained fast water. They'd had to fight for another ford, too, but the price had not been so dear.

Pickett's men overran the knoll the Yankees had not tried very hard to hold, leaving George as merry as a bridegroom, eyes bright and poor teeth showing.

"See that, Fitz? See that? Ain't it the grandest?"

Yes. It was grand. But when he raised his field glasses, Fitz Lee saw that the Federals hadn't dissolved, but had only withdrawn to join a stronger line on a low ridge.

"Still work to do," Lee noted.

George raised his glasses, but his glee persisted.

"Whip them, too," Pickett said.

Six thirty p.m.
Dinwiddie Court House, last Union line

Mud-spattered and happy, Custer steered his horse behind the line of troopers throwing up barricades. His two fresh brigades were tied in now that Pennington had pulled back, with one spread on either side of Adams Road. Remnants from the battered brigades that had fought through the day had rallied on his flanks, refusing the line. It was a fine position, and he did not intend to vacate it for the Confederates.

His spirits had soared when Sheridan's message found him. Leaving one brigade with the trains, he'd ridden forward as hard as he could without blowing the horses. He loved to be summoned to rescue other men, and Phil, when Custer had spotted him in front of the shabby courthouse, had been so glad to see him that he'd failed to conceal it. Custer had never seen Sheridan so relieved, not even at the conclusion of Cedar Creek.

He'd dragged up a light artillery battery, placing the guns himself, and he chose the ground that would form the final line. Fitz Lee was out there, a fellow he'd already thrashed at Opequon Creek, along with Pickett, rumored to be a rival in flamboyance.

"That's it, boys! Sweat now, and kill 'em easy." He delighted in the power of command, the ability to give orders and have them obeyed by violent men. A good fight was the second-best thing on earth.

"They're coming, General!"

"Bless my soul, I feared they *wouldn't* come," Custer announced. His voice was pitched for many a man to hear. "Would've hated for our little ride to be wasted. . . ."

Men laughed: the grim and the nervous, the hard and the doubtful, and, dearest to him, the carefree who *liked* a scrap.

The battery opened again. Custer spurred his horse along, calling, "Any man fires before the Johnnies step inside of two hundred yards, I'll feed his stones to the wild pigs for breakfast."

Dismounted horsemen with Spencer carbines made a fine killing machine, but that machine required a firm hand. Otherwise, men would empty their magazines before they had the least hope of hitting a Johnny.

"Best dismount, sir, don't you think?" a green staff officer asked. Earnest but unsteady, the boy was the son of a helpful politician.

"Wouldn't dream of it," Custer told the lieutenant. "Couldn't see the circus half so well."

He did guide his mount a few dozen yards to the rear, though: time to let his field officers show their mettle.

From the tidbits he'd gleaned off tired, begrimed comrades, it seemed that Phil had indeed had a wretched day. Nearing Five Forks, he'd been ambushed, flanked, and turned out of one position after another. But if he knew Phil Sheridan, the Rebs had better be on the lookout tomorrow. Another man might have slipped off to lick his wounds, but once he'd had a few hours' rest, half a pot of coffee, and a shit, Sheridan's only thought would be revenge.

Probably why Grant liked him so much, Custer reckoned.

A stray round punched the shoulder of a flag-bearer, the corporal entrusted with the national colors. The man twisted out of the saddle. Custer caught the banner.

"It's all right, I've got it," he called, making his horse rear to draw still more attention. He figured he'd hold up the flag for a few minutes, long enough for plenty of men to admire him. Then he'd hand the colors off again. Battle was a peerless stage, and leadership was drama: Men followed him into danger because he performed, in every sense. Rivals accused him of shameless stunts, but men died gladly for less.

Orderlies carried off the bloodied corporal.

Custer watched the Rebs advance, a brigade of them at least, guiding along the road and maintaining their alignment surprisingly well. At three hundred yards, their officers gave the order for a charge and their caterwauling *yip-yip* cut the air.

His officers knew their business. They let the Rebs come on.

Custer didn't believe he heard a single premature shot. Only the light fieldpieces bit the gray ranks.

At two hundred yards, the deadly commands echoed and the Spencers began their work, pouring rapid fire into the Johnnies. The battery shifted to canister.

Rebs dropped like sacks. Others twirled when struck. Colors toppled and rose again. Canister fans turned men into ribbons of flesh and splinters of bone.

The Johnnies broke. They pretended to stand their ground for a few moments. Then they drew back slowly, pausing defiantly to return the fire. Next, some trotted off. And then men ran.

As cheers went up from Custer's line, skirmishers pursued the withdrawing Rebs. Blood-happy veterans paused to aim their shots, but most men fired on the move, ramming fresh magazines into their carbines.

"Sound the recall," Custer ordered. As the bugle rose, he said, more quietly, "They'll try us once more, at least." He imagined a grimace on Fitz Lee's mug and a crestfallen look on Pickett's. "Thought they'd won, poor devils. Now they'll be cross as can be and they'll foul it up."

Nine forty p.m.
Mrs. Wilson's house
Headquarters, Fifth Corps

How long will it take?" Warren begged.

"Three hours," Captain Benyaurd, his staff engineer, told him. "*If* we tear down that house and use the boards."

The room smelled of mildew, unwashed feet, and coffee. Fresh rain stung the roof.

"Tear it down, man! Get it done. Sheridan needs help."

The weary, mud-slapped officer said, "Have to work by torchlight, risk the Rebs looking in. It's pitch black down there. Now the rain, too. It's going to take a forty-foot span, at least. Gravelly Run's flooded over, worst I've seen it."

"And there's no place it can be forded? None? You're certain?"

"General, it's running ten feet deep."

"Well, get going. Tear down the house, I don't care who it belongs to. Tear down *ten* houses. Use all the torches you need. Just get that bridge up."

Benyaurd saluted and took himself off, a good man.

Major General Gouverneur K. Warren did find the prospect of rescuing Sheridan tasty. After all of that blarney-boy's insults and lies.

He planned to be gracious, though.

Warren's corps, too, had been roughly handled that day, along White Oak Road. And Grant had witnessed the worst of it, sad to say. But Charlie Griffin had put things right, as usual, with Chamberlain heading his lead brigade—despite his latest wound—and knocking the Johnnies right back into their ditches.

Little Phil had not fared so well. Warren had interviewed various officers of Merritt's command who'd been cut off and had needed to work their way east to the Fifth Corps lines before they could dogleg back to Dinwiddie Court House. It sounded as though Phil had made a proper mess of it.

It was only as darkness fell that Warren had realized how great an opportunity lay before them: The Rebs' success against Sheridan would undo them. It bewildered him that no one else seemed to see it.

All evening, the telegraph lines had blazed with messages between Grant and Meade, between Meade and Warren and the Lord knew who else. Shock at Sheridan's reverse had excited no end of confusion. Warren didn't know precisely what Sheridan had reported, since the telegraph lines didn't stretch as far as Dinwiddie, but spirits seemed to have fallen all around, the loss of heart made manifest by a torrent of hasty orders crossing each other. At times, modern communications seemed a plague to Warren, with everyone meddling from a distance, certain they had the facts.

Ever methodical, Warren had taken pains to verify what he saw before submitting his recommendation. Meade had grown sensitive to his suggestions about the army's management, but this . . . this was the chance they'd been waiting for.

The planks underfoot groaned like a tormented prisoner, and his ever-clean-shaven brother-in-law appeared. Roebling was empty-handed.

"No response?" Warren asked. He heard the plea in his voice, but couldn't help it.

"Just the same back-and-forth, sir. Looks like Grant still means to pull Sheridan out. And us."

Warren all but wanted to weep in frustration. "It's the *worst* thing we could do. I wouldn't have expected Grant to panic." He clasped his hands, but his long fingers still writhed. "I should send another message."

Roebling looked doubtful. "Wait a few more minutes?"

"Wash . . . this is the best chance I've seen since Sheridan fouled up royally at Todd's Tavern. We can cut off a shank of Lee's army and eat it up." He unclasped his hands, made fists, and punched his knuckles together. "That gap, it's fatal. *If* we show some fight. It's not Sheridan who's exposed, it's Pickett. He's chased Sheridan so far that he's lost contact with Lee's army. We could gobble up every man he's got in his ranks. Cut the railroad, too."

"Maybe wait a few more minutes, though," Washington Roebling counseled. "Meade has to present it to Grant, sir. You know how that can go, the debating society."

Warren hid his hands behind his back. "There just isn't *time*, Grant must be made to see reason. I need the authorization to move this corps." His hands reappeared and fingered the air at his belt. "One division to Sheridan, the other two smack behind Pickett. There'd be no escape. The Rebs opened the door themselves, and they don't even feel the draft. Bartlett went out as far as the Boisseau house without a challenge. We could *stroll* into their rear."

The prospects for the morrow were so grand, Warren couldn't still himself.

"If Pickett has any wits, he'll pull back tonight," Roebling said. "Far as Five Forks, anyway."

Warren lifted his paws as if giving a sermon. "Five Forks won't be far enough, he'd *still* be too far out for Lee to save him. That's the beauty of it. Even if we can't surround him completely, we can envelop him. Withdrawing now won't help, unless he leaves Five Forks, too. And he can't, they'd lose the rail line. They needed to smash Sheridan, then scoot back to their lines. But they only did half the work, now Pickett's stuck. And, whatever he does, that gap's still there. We only need to step into it."

A clerk delivered a new telegraphic message, but it only modified a minor order.

G. K. Warren yearned to end the war at a high point. They'd all lose their brevet ranks, of course, and suffer reductions in grade in the Regular Army, but as a corps commander who'd fought to the end, he might at least expect a decent posting. Something in Washington, perhaps. Or even in New York City, the harbor works. Given the Roebling family's endeavors, an appointment to New York would be more than welcome.

He and Em had never had a home. The war that had brought them to marriage had kept them apart. At times, his longing for her felt unbearable. Oh, he felt nostalgia, now and then, for the prairie or for the fineness of the Black Hills, where he'd had such adventures, but the time had come for a quieter life with his darling, with sensible hours and engineering problems to fill his days.

He ached to hear from Meade, to receive the order that would let him finish the war as a hero.

The telegraph fell silent.

Ten p.m.

Field headquarters, Army of the Potomac

Meade looked up at his waiting chief of staff. He extended the corrected draft, then hesitated.

Rain slapped the tent. It was a bad time to be under canvas again, given the persistence of his cold.

Letting Webb take the paper at last, he told him, "Before you send it, scratch out the bit about Warren putting this up. Grant's sour on him. Partly my fault. Just never took to the man, though. And I don't want Grant or Rawlins to scorn the idea just because it originated with Warren. I believe G.K.'s right this time."

"Anything else?" Al Webb asked. Meade understood that the prospect of yet another night of issuing and revising orders appealed to the chief of staff as little as it did to the rest of the headquarters. Or to the corps commanders, who would receive their orders even later and curse the powers that issued them. Or to the couriers blundering through the dark and all the thousands of hard-sleeping men who would feel the boot of a sergeant to get them stirring. That was as much a part of war as giving battle itself.

Meade wiped his nose with the back of his hand. He still missed Humphreys, that was the long and the short of it. As chief of staff, Humph always grasped the politics of the matter. But Humph had his corps now, and well deserved it was. Meade had valued their late-night conversations: a couple of old Philadelphians and Regular plugs, they could finish each other's sentences. Webb was a solid soldier, but a New Yorker. A hero of the third day at Gettysburg, he'd proven an able staff officer as well. Nor did Webb complain of the wounds that pained him. Webb was a very good man. He just wasn't Humphreys.

Still, Humph had built a staff so crisp that Webb only had to avoid doing any damage. Not that this evening had seen the staff at its best, as scribbling majors struggled to respond to Grant's changeable moods.

"No, nothing else," Meade said. "Send it."

The chief of staff tightened his rain cape and strode off toward the telegraphers. Meade sat back. He was weary not just to the bone, but to the marrow. And the damned cold wouldn't quit; he felt as though he had needles stuck in his sinuses. When he lay down on his cot, he gasped for air.

He just wanted the war to be over. So he could rest. Sleep for a week, if Margaret allowed it.

He had to credit Warren for clear thinking. They'd all been so engaged by Sheridan's troubles that they'd nearly stumbled past this opportunity. Pickett and Fitz Lee were cut off as surely as Robinson Crusoe and Friday. It wasn't Phil who was threatened: By getting himself knocked back to Dinwiddie Court House, he'd drawn his enemies fatally far from their lines. It was yet another of war's endless ironies.

If only Grant issued the order, April Fools' Day would break Robert E. Lee.

Ten p.m.

Adams farmstead, north of Dinwiddie Court House

We don't have a choice," Pickett told Fitz Lee. "Damn, though. Damn Warren. Anderson was supposed to knock him back on his heels. Damn Anderson, too."

"Fortunes of war," Lee said.

His tone miffed Pickett. "That's taking things lightly. I feel as though I've been robbed. Both pockets."

"We had a good day. Just not good enough."

"He's gotten behind our left."

"You've told me. Twice."

"They came out as far as Boisseau's place. At least a brigade of them. And where there's a brigade, there's a division. Warren doesn't take chances like Sheridan does. Old Bird-face is set to cut us off." Pickett lipped his tin cup. "Ain't there any *hot* coffee in this army?"

No one replied. Eyes averted, staff officers kept a-bustle, scrawling reports or scraping mud from high boots. Pickett let it go. They knew him, he knew them. He'd just felt the need to holler.

As for Fitz Lee, it didn't do to quarrel with him. Or with anybody name of Lee. But it did seem to Pickett that guarding their flanks had been the cavalry's job. And that job had been neglected.

But no Lee ever apologized. Not really. Not the younger ones. Or if they said the words, they didn't mean them. Fellow might take them for royalty, way they behaved.

Pickett looked at the larger man, a proper bear, with his uncle's manly form somehow degraded. Despite the veneer of manners, Fitz always seemed the most brutish of the Lee clan. And all of the Lees were as closed and unforgiving as they were proud. Robert E. Lee had never pardoned him for Lee's own mistake on that third day at Gettysburg. So it wouldn't do to sour things any worse. Better to be as friendly as cream on pie.

It did go hard, though. In Pickett's view, the Confederacy had far too many generals named Lee, five blood-kin at last count.

Rooney was the most tolerable. At least he could squeeze out a laugh. Didn't even pain him to tell a joke. Unlike Fitz, who was a thing of darkness, way McGowan put it.

"No choice I can see," Pickett repeated. "Have to slip past Warren, fall back to Five Forks. Get into the entrenchments, build them up. Sheridan won't attack an entrenched line, not after all we put him through today. He burned his fingers right back to the knuckles."

"General Lee hoped for more."

Pickett kept his temper, sighed, and said: "I can whip Sheridan, Fitz. Or I can whip Warren. But I can't whip Sheridan *and* Warren. Not out in the open and half-surrounded."

"Five Forks doesn't leave much distance between us and the railroad."

"Sheridan and Warren won't assault entrenchments. They know what that would cost them."

"I'd rather stay here and attack. First thing in the morning. Pull back after, if it doesn't work out."

Exasperated by the entire world, Pickett struggled to remain a gentleman. "All I know is that General Lee wants us to hold Five Forks. That's the strategic point, Fitz. Nothing more important to him than that." He summoned his amiability, but that dog just wouldn't come. "We'll see what tomorrow brings. Sheridan's played out, and Warren wouldn't dare step off by himself. Give the men a couple of hours and Five Forks will be a fortress." He conjured a smile at last. "Tell you the truth, I expect a quiet day."

Ten forty p.m.
Dabney's Mill
Grant's headquarters

He'll be all right come morning," Grant said. "Phil's just rattled. Not used to taking a whipping."

"I'd say we were all a bit rattled," Rawlins noted.

Grant crushed out the stub of his cigar. "Be the death of me, these things. Never could afford a decent cigar, now they send me crates of them. Courier get off?"

"Two couriers, with duplicates. Best riders we've got, they'll get to Sheridan. Did catch them in time to hold back that note of yours. Which, apparently, even an old friend and chief of staff's not trusted to read." He cleared his throat, a ghost cough. "Damn this rain."

"Thought the matter over," Grant said. "No need to have it in writing. Babcock can ride out there in the morning, talk to Phil in person. Or maybe I'll write it down, after all. Don't want Sheridan mulling it over tonight, though. I just need him to get his Irish up."

"Well, you've got me wondering. Oh, I got the order off for Mackenzie, too," Rawlins reported, used to Grant's ways and untroubled. "The one reinforcing Phil. Fresh cavalry division ought to lift his spirits."

Grant knew his body had been awake long enough, but the day's events had left him too quickened to sleep. Julia would scold him, and Bill would rebuke him with silence. He said:

"All credit to George Meade. For spotting an odds-on chance. When we were all set to hang crepe."

"Really expect much to come of it?"

Grant rubbed his beard, then fingered a persistent itch. "I'd bet a box of my best cigars that Phil will be up on his hind legs, come first light. He'll be embarrassed by those messages he sent, he'll want to clear things. If something can be done, I believe he'll do it."

"And if not?"

"We'll try something else." Grant looked down at his unpolished boots. "Just can't let this drag on much longer."

Rawlins coughed again. "And Warren? He's not going to like being put under Sheridan."

"I don't care what Warren likes," Grant said with unusual harshness. "That message for Phil? I'm authorizing him to relieve Warren of command, if he don't measure up."

Eleven p.m.
Mrs. Wilson's house
Headquarters, Fifth Corps

Didn't they know that Gravelly Run was impassable? That he had to build a bridge? He'd sent messages. . . .

Warren stood bewildered at Meade's orders. There would be no retreat, Warren's views had been accepted to that degree. And he would join Sheridan for a broad assault. All that was fine. It annoyed him to be placed under Sheridan, but he had to admit that he'd expected as much. Sheridan was Grant's pet, and Grant would want to protect his protégé. That was all right, too, although it galled more than a bit.

But the order of march and timetable Webb had designed and Meade had approved was a mess. Hadn't they bothered reading his reports? He'd been moving brigades all evening, readying his three divisions, but even if Gravelly Run could be bridged by one—which was optimistic—it would be dawn before a division reached Sheridan. And that was if his soldiers got no sleep.

"Good God," he said to Roebling, "they're asking the impossible of me."

He wondered what promises had been made to Sheridan. He hoped they were sane and that Little Phil would have rational expectations. He didn't want to get off on the wrong foot again.

"You should get some rest," Lieutenant Colonel Roebling recommended. "Could be a rough day tomorrow."

"Order up my horse."

Four a.m., April 1
Edge Hill
Headquarters, Army of Northern Virginia

Lee woke reluctantly and bitterly.

"What is it *now*?"

Taylor stood by the bed. Holding a candle and a dispatch.

"General Pickett has ordered a withdrawal. To Five Forks."

Lee was flummoxed. "I . . . thought he had Sheridan on the run . . . had every advantage . . ." Lee forced himself to sit up.

"The message states that his left flank was under threat. By infantry, well to his rear. He felt that his position was untenable."

Lee pawed his face, rubbing awareness into his flesh.

"And he's withdrawing to Five Forks?"

"I believe he's already withdrawn, sir. Given the time of the message."

"My spectacles . . ."

Taylor found them on the bedside table.

His adjutant held the candle close. When Lee finished reading, he closed his eyes.

"I regret that. I regret that exceedingly."

"Shall I reply, sir?"

A number of intemperate responses filled Lee's mind. But he only said:

"He *must* hold Five Forks at all hazards. Tell him that." Then he gathered himself. "Wait, Colonel Taylor. I'll write to him myself."

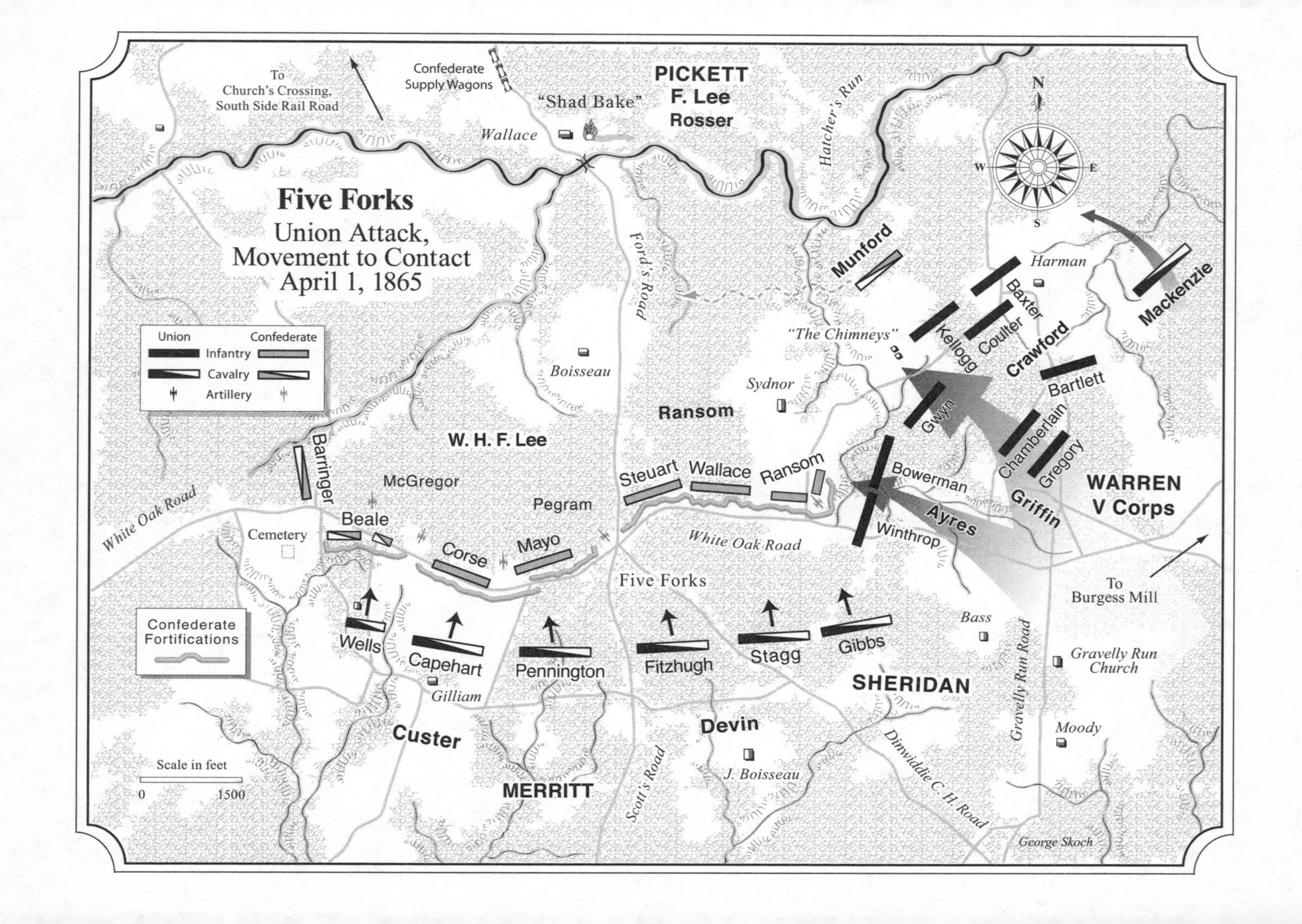

Five Forks
Union Attack,
Movement to Contact
April 1, 1865
To
Church's Crossing,
South Side Rail Road
Confederate
Supply Wagons
"Shad Bake"
PICKETT
F. Lee
Rosser
Wallace
Hatcher's Run
Union
Confederate
Infantry
Cavalry
Artillery
Boisseau
Ford's Road
Munford
Harman
Baxter
Mackenzie
"The Chimneys"
Kellogg
Coulter
Crawford
Sydnor
Bartlett
Ransom
W. H. F. Lee
Gwyn
Chamberlain
Gregory
WARREN
V Corps
Barringer
McGregor
Steuart
Wallace
Ransom
Bowerman
Griffin
Ayres
White Oak Road
Pegram
Beale
Cemetery
Corse
Mayo
White Oak Road
Winthrop
Five Forks
To
Burgess Mill
Bass
Confederate
Fortifications
Wells
Capehart
Pennington
Fitzhugh
Stagg
Gibbs
Gravelly Run
Church
SHERIDAN
Gravelly Run Road
Gilliam
Custer
Devin
Moody
Scale in feet
0
1500
J. Boisseau
Dinwiddie C. H. Road
MERRITT
Scott's Road
George Skoch

FIVE

Seven fifteen a.m., April 1, 1865
J. Boisseau field

The brigade commander's eyes closed as his horse plodded along, only to open sharply at a barrage of pounding hooves. Mounted on a beast that evoked a medieval charger, Sheridan, unmistakable, spurred ahead of his flags and pennants, as if he were out for blood. Anybody's blood.

The brigadier general straightened his posture and fought off an insistent yawn. Perhaps a mile to the north, someone's pickets sparred.

Sheridan reined in so late that their horses nearly collided. In moments, his staff swirled around them, driving foot soldiers out of their way, kicking back mud, and, inexplicably, raising dust despite the nighttime downpour.

"Who the hell are you?" Sheridan demanded.

The brigadier saluted. "Chamberlain, sir. First Brigade, First Division, Fifth Corps."

"Griffin's bunch?"

"Yes, sir."

"You're *late*. Why weren't you here earlier? Where the devil's Warren?"

"He's at the rear of the column, sir. Bringing up Crawford's division."

"At the rear, is he? That's where I'd expect to find Warren, all right. What's he doing back there?"

"General Sheridan, we fought the Rebs all day yesterday. General Warren's been handling our disengagement."

Sheridan grunted. His horse pawed mud. "Probably sleeping in some farmhouse bed, if I know Warren."

Chamberlain opened his mouth to defend his corps commander but thought better of it. Warren had never lacked for courage or vigor. He didn't merit such insults. Especially not charges mouthed to a subordinate—that wasn't done. Sheridan had a reputation, though, and seemed unlikely to forgive a rebuke from a junior brigadier. Said to be Grant's favorite, he could block a man's promotion with a word. And Chamberlain rather wanted a second star before the war ended.

He said nothing.

Charlie Griffin, his division commander, came to his rescue. Aggressive, gruff, and kind to those below him, Griffin had a knack for sizing up matters.

Griffin's staff added their own mud and dust to the rumpus. The soldiers trudging along gave them plenty of room.

"Well, Griffin," Sheridan called, "maybe *you* can tell me what's buggered things up? You're late, by my watch."

"Not by mine," Griffin said flatly. "Men fought all day, marched all night, and here we are." Unspoken, a challenge hung in the air before Sheridan.

And that was all it took to back Sheridan down. Chamberlain did feel a bit ashamed of himself. Warren had been quite good to him, after all.

He found it so much easier to find courage on a battlefield.

Drawing his reins taut and troubling his horse, Sheridan told Griffin, "Hold your men here, just stop. Until I have a talk with your corps commander."

And off he went.

When things settled down again, Chamberlain said, "He was rather brusque about General Warren, sir. Before you arrived."

"You mean he was rude and insulting and broadly a shit?"

"You might put it that way, sir."

"I *do* put it that way, Professor. Listen, you keep your mouth shut around Phil. I can handle him, you can't. Try it and you'll find yourself fucked for beans." Griffin wore an expression suited to a Celtic Attila the Hun. "You handle the Johnnies, I'll handle Sheridan."

Chamberlain welcomed the offer.

Nine a.m.
Field headquarters, Army of the Potomac

Frank, old fellow!" Lyman cried the instant he spotted Barlow. "You look positively robust! Just look at you, though!"

He dropped the tent flap behind him and dashed up like a child. Out on the road, horsemen sloshed along and wagons churned mud. Men strung fresh telegraph wire. The earth sucked shoes. But Teddy beamed as if it were summer at Newport.

"Hello, Teddy." Barlow looked for a dry spot along the row of sodden tentage. None to be seen, the sun had more work to do. He shifted his valise to his left hand and grasped Lyman's paw.

"You know, Frank," Lyman said more quietly, "I do wish you'd call me 'Ted.' I've weaned most of them off of 'Teddy.' " Lyman's trimmed beard and bald pate framed a hopelessly innocent face. Smudged spectacles glinted. "You wouldn't want them calling you 'Frankie,' would you? We're not at Harvard now."

"But I don't seem at all like a Frankie. No one's ever called me that, they wouldn't dare. While you seem like a Teddy through and through. How's Mimi, anyway?"

"She just wants the war to end." Lyman's look turned quizzical. "Didn't you stop by Boston?"

"No time. Boston can wait."

"I thought . . . Ellen Shaw . . ."

"Good God, Teddy. Not you, too? Listen, I've got a small trunk on that wagon. Where might I put it? And this?" He held up the valise.

"Oh, in my tent for now. I'm allotted one of my own."

"Good performance? Or foul digestion? Listen, Teddy. Does Meade have a division for me, or doesn't he?"

"Well, he *wants* to give you one, I know that much."

"That's not what I asked."

"Not now, not yet. He can't very well relieve Miles, he's done too well."

"I suppose it's too much to ask Nellie to take a tumble? Break his neck or the like?"

"He'll be glad to see you."

"I wouldn't be too sure. Things went a bit badly, as I recall."

"All forgotten. Frank, you were *ill*."

"A mild description of an infernal malady. Sound enough now, though."

Two passing staff men greeted Barlow, expressions shifting quickly from welcome to wariness.

Lyman made to take the bag, but Barlow just said, "Lead the way, Teddy, and I shall humbly follow."

In the tent, which smelled of mildew, drying wool, and lamp oil, Lyman said, "Really, Frank, I think you're just in time. Things are starting to move, we may see an end to it." He bent to unlock his field trunk.

"They'd move a bit quicker, if I had a division."

"Well, wait and see. Brandy? To celebrate your return?"

Barlow patted his stomach. "Still a bit sensitive. This early in the morning."

"At least you're alive."

"For which I'm indebted to an unwashed Scotchman. Old fellow knew his stuff, though. Indian service."

Lyman returned the bottle to his trunk and locked it again. "Could be a grand fight today. Over on the left. We've pushed out several miles since you took ill. Lee's stretched to breaking."

"And?"

"Grant's ordered general assaults twice now. Canceled them both times, at the last minute. I think we'll finally go, though, if Sheridan does a bit better than he did yesterday. From what I gather, our Southern friends made an error they may regret."

"Let's hope they see it that way. And cooperate."

Ever good-hearted—although a wicked gossip—Lyman smiled. "Really, Frank . . . the change in you, it's remarkable. Meade will be delighted."

Barlow guffawed. "Old Meade isn't 'delighted' to see anyone. The man's utterly incapable of delight. All that Philadelphia dignity . . ."

Hurt-faced, Lyman said, "No worse than our Boston crowd. Meade's really quite the fellow, once you know him."

"I suppose it's too late to put him up for the Pudding? Ever the loyal aide-de-camp. . . . Teddy, you're an example to us all."

"Really, Frank. He quite likes you. He speaks of you very highly."

"Teddy, I don't care what George Meade *says*. I just want him to give me a division."

Ten thirty a.m.
Five Forks

Pickett found Fitz Lee talking with Willie Pegram behind his gun line. Commanding the intersection of vital roads, the clearing was one of the few spots near Five Forks where artillery might be of even short-range use. Tangled scrub and trees too poor for timbering blighted the landscape, hard ground even for infantry, and the few open fields were cropped with stumps and briars and poison ivy. Ugly country, but blessedly hard to attack, in George Pickett's opinion.

Had to split off Fitz from Pegram, who had not been invited.

Halting his mount, Pickett lifted his damp cap and said, "Morning, gents! Ain't the weather gone handsome, though?" And turning to Fitz Lee: "A word, if I may?"

Fitz looked hard-used. It had been a long, wet night for everybody. But the sun had conquered the last rear guard of clouds as drying uniforms loosed themselves from raw skin.

Lee nudged his horse and followed Pickett to the edge of the clearing. Skirmishers pecked and pocked off to the south, but there wasn't much to it beyond a howdy-do.

Pickett turned his mount and they stopped, bridles to saddles.

"Well?"

"Well what?"

"You joining the party?"

"Not sure I'm so minded."

Amused, Pickett said, "Don't wait for coaxing from me. Eat up your share, too. And call myself lucky."

"It's still early, George. I just don't trust things."

"Rosser's planning on two o'clock. We'll surely know by then."

"Maybe." Lee's horse stamped, then calmed again.

"Sheridan ain't coming, Fitz. Nor Warren. And even . . . well, say they did. We won't be but a mile back from the line. We'd hear any ruckus start up."

"Never did care for shad myself. Too bony."

"My, but the gent's partic'ler. Nottoway shad's fine eating, if you do it right." Pickett winked. "And I hear Tom foraged up liquid refreshments of note."

Fitz Lee nodded, but the gesture said nothing. "I'll give you this much, George. Sheridan would be a damned fool to attack in this briar patch. Have to dismount his men. And he couldn't hold a line together, not in this."

"And Warren hasn't been heard from again. Probably spooked himself, went bump in the night." Pickett smiled broadly. "Shad bake on a sunny April day? Better than a table at the Spottswood, in my opinion. Come on now, Fitz. You truly pondering the gravity of the matter, or playing the coy *demoiselle*?"

Two soldiers laden with canteens walked past to rejoin their comrades laboring on the entrenchments.

"Have to see what happens," Fitz said.

"Nothing's going to happen," Pickett insisted. "Fetch you a tad before two, we'll ride up together. And don't tell nobody where you're going, either. Can't repeat the miracle of loaves and fishes."

Eleven a.m.
Adams field

Warren sat down on the log. Reclined on a blanket, Sheridan rubbed his eyes open. Nearby, staff men crowded around field tables set in a glade, pointing at maps, scribbling, and calling for messengers. In haste, the boot tips of couriers sought stirrups. Where the landscape opened toward a farmstead, horses and dismounted cavalry trampled a meadow. The air reeked of a poorly managed stable.

"Took you long enough. Where've you been?" Sheridan's tone was hardly welcoming.

"Bringing up my corps, Phil. We've closed, just awaiting your orders."

"You'll get my orders when I'm ready to give them." Sheridan cleared his throat and spit at a bush. "Meantime, keep your men centered on the Boisseau place. Let 'em feed. Rest in place. But be ready to move, as soon as I tell you."

"They'll be glad to eat something. The corps had rather a field day since yesterday morning, quite a—"

"You call it a 'field day'? You were in a goddamned *fight*. Men died. And you call it a 'field day'?"

Abashed, Warren explained: "I was being ironic. I meant—"

"Just report what happened, when you report to me. Spare me the intellect."

Warren was tempted to ask a pointed question about Sheridan's reverse the day before. But he warned himself away from it. They had to get along to make things work, to annihilate George Pickett and Fitzhugh Lee.

"What I meant to communicate, Phil, is that the Johnnies gave us a nasty morning yesterday. And then we gave them a very bad afternoon. I hope we can repeat the latter part."

A cavalry captain strode toward them and stopped. Sheridan waved him on, ignoring Warren.

"What news, Bob?"

"General Mackenzie's up, sir. His full division."

Sheridan got to his feet, mood changed in an instant. "Grand. Perfect. Now we'll see what's what." He marched off on his dwarf's legs, as if Warren had disappeared.

Make the best of it, Warren counseled himself. *Just make the best of it.*

Two p.m.
Five Forks

For all his earlier eagerness, Pickett was late. It grated on Fitz Lee. He'd talked himself into an appetite for shad, bones or no bones. He put on a good show in front of others, but the truth was that he was highly fond of his vittles, and the feeding of late, even for generals, had not abounded in delicacies. A big man, he did take a high degree of filling. And half-cooked ash cakes grew tiresome.

He could almost smell the fish baking.

A rider worked through the back-tangle of trees. Wasn't Pickett, but Tom Munford, the colonel to whom Fitz Lee had given his old cavalry division.

Damn it, Lee thought, if Munford thinks he's going to jump into that shad bake . . . couldn't anybody in the Army of Northern Virginia keep a secret?

Glistening with a horseman's sweat and grand mustachios dripping, the colonel saluted. Up close, his expression didn't say *Shad bake!* after all.

"What is it, Tom?" Lee asked. Not without a hint of impatience.

"Yankees. Got a dispatch here. From a lieutenant in the Eighth Virginia. Says Union cavalry embarrassed Roberts, sprang his boys every which way."

"Roberts isn't my responsibility," Lee said. "Not today."

Munford held out the dispatch. Lee took it, but didn't unfold it.

"That means," the colonel went on, "that there's Yankee cavalry in between us and Petersburg."

"And whose bunch might that be? Oh, Sheridan may be nipping a little. Got to be plain ashamed of how he fared yesterday. Nothing to worry about, though. Nothing in the wind."

Munford didn't look convinced. He aired his hat, wiped the sweat from his forehead, and said, "Wasn't Sheridan's men. Dispatch said they were from Mackenzie's division."

Lee looked askance, plain irritated. "Somebody's seeing hants, then. Mackenzie's thirty, forty miles away, north of Richmond. No reports of him moving. Longstreet would've warned us."

The colonel replaced his hat, but it couldn't find a comfortable sit. "Just passing on what that message says, General." He pointed. "If Yankees are on White Oak Road, they could cut us off."

"No pack of blue-bellied bushwhackers is going to cut us off." Behind his beard, Lee's mouth curled. "You said it was from a lieutenant, this message here?"

"Wythe Graham. Eighth Virginia."

"Explains things. I know Wythe. Good boy, but he's excitable."

"General Lee—"

"Listen to me, Tom. We're dug in here just fine. Yankee horse may be prowling here and there—I'd be surprised if they weren't—but I won't be concerned until we see infantry come up. Even then, it's unlikely we'd have a real scrap. Federals don't commit infantry without artillery backing them up, they're not like us. And Hannibal himself couldn't bring up more than a pair of popguns through that snap pine. Nor use 'em, if they got here. No fields of fire worth a lick, Willie Pegram's busting his head about it." Lee thought again of shad done right and added, "Afternoon's well along. Most I'd expect might be a touch of skirmishing."

"Sir . . ."

"*Damn* it, Tom . . . if you're so itchy, see to it yourself. You've got a division under your haunches now. You want to send out a reconnaissance, you just do it. I'm not your ma nor your auntie, hear?"

"Yes, sir. I take the correction." Munford did sound resentful, though. And, Lee suspected, Tom wasn't truly the one who was in the wrong. He was letting himself be led by thoughts of a picnic the way some men swooned at a woman's stink.

"Reckon we all need sleep and a feed," Lee said by way of apology. "You do what you think's right."

He was about to read the note, after all, when he saw George Pickett approaching, clotted locks on the bounce.

"Go on now," Lee told the colonel. "General Pickett and I have matters to attend to."

Three thirty p.m.
Gravelly Run Church Road

The atmosphere had gone queer. Warren had encountered the phenomenon a few times in the war, but usually the cloud cover was heavier. The science of it intrigued him, but he had no time to ponder the natural world. He could only accept that, for whatever reason, sound did not carry. According to Sheridan's plan for the attack, Phil's dismounted cavalrymen would be working forward by now, harassing the Rebs with their Spencers, positioning themselves to attack in the front while Warren's Fifth Corps outflanked the Johnnies and turned their position. But Warren heard only faint ghosts of shots, reports so vague they might have been imagined. The birds nearby were louder.

"Hurry along there," he called to the passing troops, the first of Ayres' division coming up. "We've got the Johnnies this time, just keep moving."

And the men did move, as best their bodies could. Exhausted and rendered shabby by the weather, their feet moved on by habit, not from enthusiasm. Warren had not slept himself and functioned on his last reserves of energy, quickened by the prospect of a battle. It was ever thus: Somehow, the body managed when it had to.

Charlie Wainwright, his chief of artillery, trotted up. Saluting, the redleg said:

"There's no way I can get any guns up, sir. Even the few I

brought are miles back. Road's all clogged with troops. And the woods are impassable."

"Doesn't matter, Charlie. No place to site them, anyway. Hardly artillery country." Warren squeezed crusts of weariness from his eyes. "Bears an unholy resemblance to the Wilderness, does it not?"

"Not my fondest memory," Wainwright said.

"Nobody's fondest memory. Charlie, would you mind playing the underclassman? Ride back and make sure Griffin's formed and ready."

"Griffin's always ready." The artilleryman considered Warren, making his scrutiny several degrees too obvious. "Anything wrong, sir?"

"Nothing of grand import. Sheridan's impatient."

"Well, Christ on a cuckoo, this corps's been moving as well as I've seen it march. Road wouldn't pass as a farm track, where I come from. And the damned terrain—"

"Keep up there, move along. It's not far now," Warren called out to a lagging soldier. He turned back to Wainwright, of whom he'd grown quite fond. They'd passed through a great deal together . . . the North Anna, when Charlie's guns had rattled up just in time to put things right, or his splendid short-range work when the Rebs popped out of the woods at Globe Tavern. There were so many memories.

"Well, I can't drive the men any harder," Warren said. "Even Sheridan can't overrule physics and biology."

A great commotion down the road announced an imposing arrival. Warren half expected to see Meade or even Grant, but it was Sheridan. His posture warned of unpleasantness.

"I think I'll move along," Wainwright said. "Little bugger's never been to my taste."

"You're fortunate, Charlie," Warren told him. "I'm afraid I'm planted."

Immediately, he regretted the hint of disparagement. Discord helped no one. And one did not complain to one's subordinates.

He made an exception only for his brother-in-law, who never seemed quite a soldier.

With his usual lack of preliminaries, Sheridan no sooner reached barking distance than he demanded, "Are you or aren't you ready to attack? Your corps's dragging up like whores to Sunday breakfast."

Warren restrained his temper and drew out his watch. It was three forty-three.

"By four o'clock, Phil. Perhaps a few minutes after."

Drawing close and panting like a bulldog, the cavalryman continued: "What in damnation's taking you so long? Waiting for sunset? My boys will run out of bullets before you're in, they've been at it for over an hour."

"Phil, the men are giving you their best. They've had to move cross-country, it's been difficult."

"Excuses never licked a single Reb." Sheridan drew closer still. "Deployed the way I told you?"

"Yes, Phil. Two divisions up, *en echelon*. Crawford leads, on the right. Ayres trails on the left. Griffin follows Crawford, in reserve. And I've ordered the divisions to advance in three lines of battle. My prerogative, I trust?"

"And then?"

"If the Rebs are where you depict them—"

"If?"

"*When* we strike the Rebs, Crawford's division centers on the return of their refused flank. His right envelops them. Ayres then assaults frontally to immobilize the Confederate line and establish contact with your dismounted cavalry. Griffin reinforces Crawford or Ayres, as the situation requires."

A bird swooped near, as if it had meant to snatch Sheridan's hat but changed its mind in a blink.

"You've got that much straight, I suppose," the little cavalryman allowed. "Just get them moving. I won't have more excuses."

Sheridan took off down a trail no better than an Indian path, followed by dipped flags and his staff riding single file.

Wash Roebling, who had hung back, nudged his horse forward. "It's almost as if he wants to see you fail, sir."

"Nonsense. That's just Phil's way."

Three forty p.m.
Wallace farm, north of Hatcher's Run

And then Pete Longstreet comes back hours early, tired as old Job and in one of his tempers. Won't be delayed by any man, just heads straight for that bedroom and the one fine featherbed in the county." Face flushed, Pickett barely harnessed his mirth. "And right on in he goes, clomping along with those big boots of his, no idea what's been going on . . . and that country quail Rob flushed out of her shack is snoring like Methuselah, and Rob's just got to pulling up his drawers, back to the door . . . and poor Rob doesn't even look around at those footsteps of doom, just hollers, 'Nigger, I told you not to come in without knocking!' "

Pickett howled. Struggling to match mind and tongue, he added, "Gentlemen . . . I leave Longstreet's response . . . to your imagination . . ."

All present laughed long and mightily. Tom Rosser, their ever-amiable host, had taken off his uniform coat and draped it over a bush. He held up a nearly empty bottle of applejack. "Any bones still twixt your teeth, boys, this here'll melt 'em right out."

"Any more of that fine whiskey, Tom?" Pickett asked. "Not that apple brandy would not suffice . . ."

Rosser turned, not fully steady, and called, "Shep? We run ourselves out of that Virginia tonic?"

"Seein' to it, General. Seein' right to it. Not sayin' either way, though. All this frolicking."

"Tom, you're a devil of a fellow," Pickett declared. He patted Rosser, inaccurately, on the shoulder.

"Here, here," Fitz Lee agreed. But he frowned. Belly full, and not merely of shad, he'd been listening for any indication of trouble to the south. But the afternoon remained silent beyond the fiddle and banjo of Rosser's two-man band.

One tune, "Camptown Races," had summoned Stuart to mind, stirring up a welter of difficult feelings. But the day was fine, for all that.

How many more afternoons might there be like this? Lee wondered. How many more reprieves? Grant all but blocked out the sun, he loomed so terribly.

Well, no need to be morbid. Appreciate this one God-given day. And Rosser's overripe shad.

Fitz Lee accepted another pour of applejack, promising himself that it would be his last.

The banjo player had drifted off, but the fiddler struck up "Dixie" to stir things up again. Pickett seized Rosser's arm and began to dance.

Four p.m.
Sheridan's left flank

George Armstrong Custer did hope he'd come up against his West Point chum Tom Rosser. He'd bedeviled poor Tom wonderfully the autumn before, at the "Woodstock Races," driving him and his ragamuffins for over twenty miles. Now Tom would be itching for revenge and rash, and that would make him easier to whip.

He did hope things would get properly under way. It was high time. Warren seemed to have a case of the slows, though. Nor had his own subordinates distinguished themselves thus far—the ground was impossible, requiring even dismounted men to slash their way forward, with proper formations impossible to maintain. But once Phil turned the Rebs out of their position and he could get a mounted force over the road . . . wouldn't it be splendid, though, if he took Tom Rosser prisoner? He'd treat him royally, of course. Only rub it in a little. Oh, wouldn't Tom be crimson-pussed and seething?

Nearby Spencers drove lead nails into the afternoon, but Custer couldn't hear much of anything else.

Four twenty p.m.
Intersection of Gravelly Run Church Road
and White Oak Road

Trained as a surgeon and now in command of an infantry division, Major General Samuel Wylie Crawford rode abreast of his front ranks, surprised and increasingly troubled.

The Rebs weren't there.

Immediately upon receiving Warren's order, he'd led his men forward, with soldiers bashing and thrashing through the undergrowth while his own horse shied at a length of fleeing black snake. He'd stepped off ready to pitch into the Reb works along White Oak Road, expecting his center—where he had positioned himself with his staff—to hit them where their flank was supposed to bend back. Sheridan had been certain of the Confederate dispositions, according to Warren's man.

Now here he was, in the middle of the road and passing over, with his men moving on unbothered. The only foe putting up a fight was an early batch of blackflies.

He heard the *tap-tap* of carbine fire, barely audible, well off to the left where Sheridan's lads were at work. In front of his division, Crawford saw nothing but a broken field, derelict earth of the sort that afflicted so much of Virginia south of the James, with more scrub forest beyond.

"Orders, sir?" his adjutant asked.

A few hundred yards ahead, three Reb horsemen bolted from a wood line like flushed birds. They soon disappeared again.

Crawford fingered his muttonchop whiskers. "Keep going. Rebs must have pulled back to another position."

"Or withdrawn entirely?"

"They'd lose the railroad. They're out there."

Well, Sheridan had made at least one mistake. Sam Crawford

reckoned that Warren would fix things, though. Say what you like about Warren—and he'd said plenty himself—the fellow kept his head when things got hot. Warren's problems were in between the battles, not in the fighting.

On both sides of him, thousands of soldiers brushed trouser legs across the overgrown field, collecting nettles and ticks. Their flags hung dully in dead air, stirred only by the motion of their bearers.

That wood line ahead. Were they in there? Waiting? Know soon enough. Had they managed to get any fieldpieces in there, too?

Along his blue lines, veteran officers mirrored his concerns, keeping their soldiers steady, compact, and alert.

Right about now, Crawford thought. They'll fire now, if they're in there.

Nothing happened. Advancing at steady quick time, his soldiers reached the tangles of the grove and pushed into its shadows.

Miserable ground. Appalling that any fellow, North or South, should have to bleed for it.

He almost barked, "Keep the men together," just to *do* something, to achieve the illusion of action, but he shut his mouth again before he'd gotten it properly open. The officers knew what had to be done, there was no point in being an ass.

A surgeon, trained at Penn, he'd confounded family and friends by accepting a commission as an Army doctor in the deepening twilight of peace. His work, mostly lancing abscesses and tormenting clapped-up corporals, had deposited him in Fort Sumter in time to hear the first shots of the war. By then, he'd seen enough of military life to believe he might do more good on a battle line than in a hospital tent. Just short of four years later, he felt he'd been right.

"March much more and we'll be at the river," a high-strung captain muttered.

"Hatcher's Run," Crawford corrected him.

"Sir?"

"Hatcher's Run. It winds around out here, mile north of Five Forks. At least, it does on the map. We'll hit that long before we reach the river."

"Think that's where the Rebs are?" his adjutant asked.

"Good a place as any. Still be flooded and hard to get across, we do know that much. Rebs dug in on the north bank could give us a nasty time. And they've been fond of the Hatcher's Run line elsewhere, too damned fond." He grimaced, remembering. "Just as soon never see that creek again, nor any stretch of it."

Even as he spoke, he believed he heard rifle fire. Not carbines this time. Rifles. Two artillery thumps followed. Not in front, but well behind his division and to the left. If the heavy air wasn't playing tricks.

Members of the staff had heard the sounds, too. It wasn't his imagination.

"So much for the plan," Sam Crawford said.

Four thirty p.m.
Five Forks, Confederate left

Fire!" Ransom shouted. "Give it to them, boys!"

He tried to sound confident, but it did look like a significant passel of Yankees passing by a thousand feet to the east, just plunging ahead and merry as Holiday Henry. Bound to overlap his refused flank, if he didn't fix their attention right away.

Only two artillery pieces were set in to do any good, and both shot their first rounds long. Going to be another infantry fight. His North Carolina boys were set to give a good account of themselves, with volleys crackling. Needed reinforcement, though. A lot of reinforcement. Right quick.

Left in uneasy command of a division, he wasn't sure which other brigades he should draw on, where to thin the line back along the road. He needed Pickett's blessing before putting another stretch of the works at risk.

But Pickett could not be found. As soon as Matt Ransom's outposts had pulled back, the soldiers leaping in like hares pursued by a horde of hounds, he'd sent riders from his staff to warn George Pickett. But no one had any idea where the man was. The most that could be gotten out of anyone was that Pickett had gone off with Fitzhugh Lee. But nobody knew where Lee had gotten to, either.

Through the first rags of smoke, Ransom saw the Union ranks swinging to face him, wheeling crisply, an alarming sight. There were even more of them, many more, than he'd feared. He needed help.

Where the devil was Pickett?

"Here they come now, Tar Heels!" Ransom shouted. "Here they come!"

Four thirty p.m.
Wallace farm, north of Hatcher's Run

Hear that?" Fitz Lee asked, sitting up.

Lounging against a tree trunk all his own, Pickett looked over. "Hear what?"

"Thought I heard firing." Lee's big face tightened. "Don't hear it now, though."

Pickett grinned, happily showing the world his much-worn teeth. "Not like you to get the Ginny-jumps, Fitz. Not like you at all."

Lee growled mildly, retreating back into his drowse. Pickett was ready to take another stretch of rest himself when Rosser's boy came back with another bottle. He stopped at a proper distance from the generals.

"No suh," he told his master. "Ain't no more of that drinking whiskey nowheres. Nothing but this here bottle, be the last."

In a generous spirit, Pickett told Rosser, "Leave him be, Tom. Sorry I dropped my manners and raised the subject. Applejack's fine."

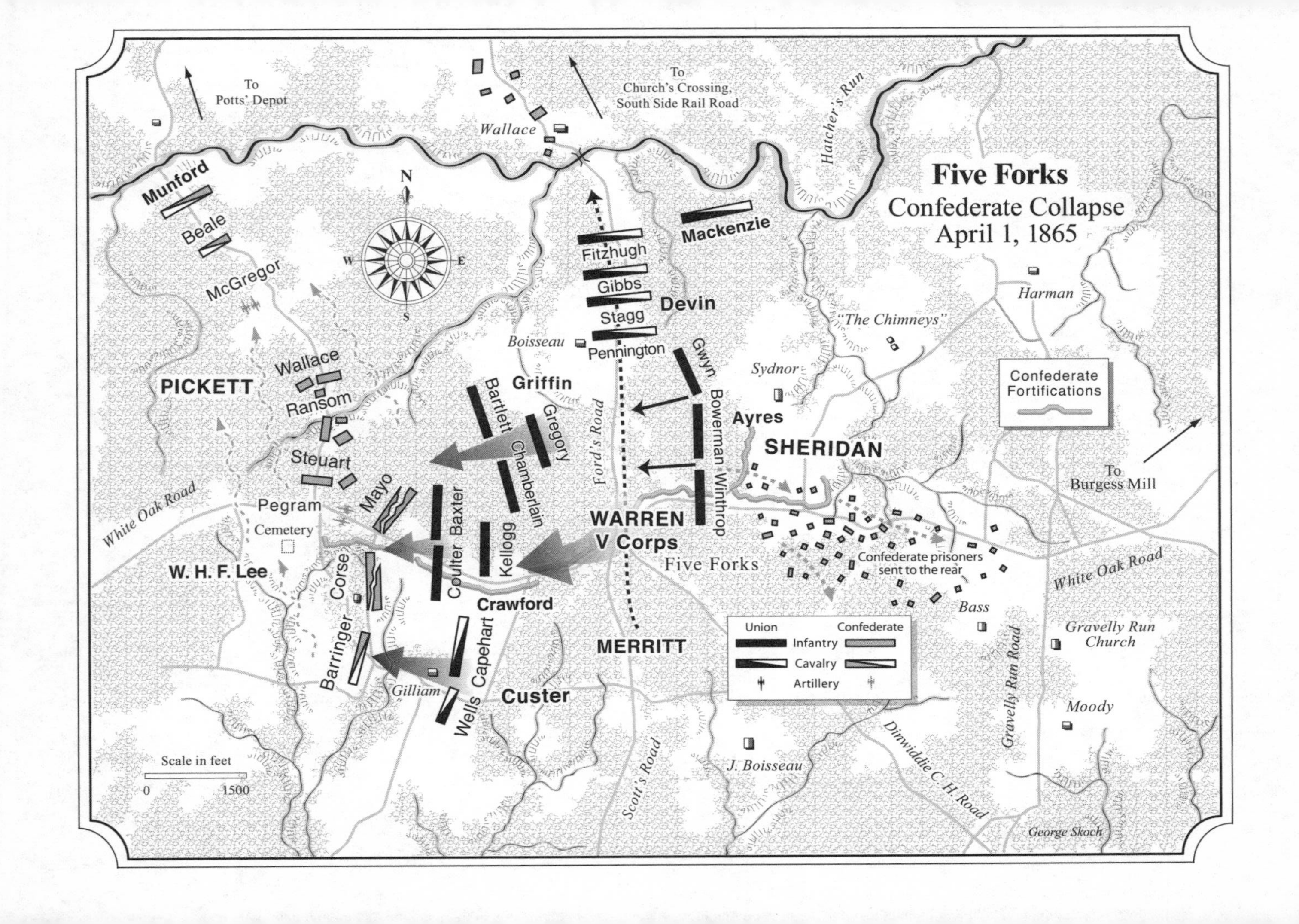

Five Forks
Confederate Collapse
April 1, 1865
To
Potts' Depot
To
Church's Crossing,
South Side Rail Road
Hatcher's Run
Wallace
Munford
Beale
McGregor
PICKETT
Wallace
Ransom
Steuart
Pegram
Cemetery
W. H. F. Lee
White Oak Road
Mayo
Corse
Barringer
Gilliam
Wells
Capehart
Custer
Coulter
Baxter
Kellogg
Crawford
Bartlett
Chamberlain
Gregory
Griffin
Boisseau
Ford's Road
Fitzhugh
Gibbs
Stagg
Pennington
Devin
Mackenzie
WARREN
V Corps
MERRITT
Scott's Road
Five Forks
Gwyn
Bowerman
Winthrop
Ayres
SHERIDAN
Sydnor
"The Chimneys"
Harman
Confederate
Fortifications
To
Burgess Mill
Union
Confederate
Infantry
Cavalry
Artillery
Confederate prisoners
sent to the rear
J. Boisseau
Dinwiddie C. H. Road
Bass
Gravelly Run Road
Gravelly Run
Church
White Oak Road
Moody
George Skoch
Scale in feet
0
1500
N
S
E
W

SIX

Four thirty p.m., April 1, 1865
Five Forks

As bullets hunted past and soldiers faltered, Sheridan grabbed his command flag from the color-sergeant. Seconds later, the sergeant jerked backward and blood spurted from his neck.

Damned mess. Rebs a quarter mile west of where they were meant to be. After wheeling smartly to face the Johnnies, Ayres' brigades had begun to buckle after the second volley.

Men toppled around Sheridan. A hundred yards to the right, Rome Ayres rode forward, waving his sword and urging on his division, but the fellow lacked the touch to grip soldiers' hearts.

Sheridan kicked Rienzi to rearing vigor. Ignoring the torrent of lead, he turned the great horse out in front of the troops.

"Come *on,* you sonsofbitches! They're ready to run, they've got no spunk at all. Come on, goddamnit. They'll get away again, if we don't go after them now. Follow me, boys, and we'll give those buggers the whipping they came here for."

He cantered along the fickle line, lofting his red-and-white banner. His mounted staff followed without hesitation—although he suspected a shade of inner reluctance.

As good an Irishman as ever had been born, Captain McGonnigle cried out in amazement and clutched his middle.

To hell with McGonnigle, too. All that mattered was getting these brigades moving.

"I'll go after the Rebs my goddamned self," Sheridan bellowed at the still hesitant troops. "They're ready to break, you can smell it like shit in an oven. Come on, you buggers, let's go for them!"

With a sudden howl that swelled toward a cheer, the men started forward again. The fakers dropped away, and the unlucky splashed red on their comrades, but on the others went. Bayonets glinting, imperfect blue lines plopped through a mucky field. As they neared the tree line and its speckles of fire, formations loosened further, but the soldiers had made their choice to kill and stuck to it.

A courier reaching Sheridan yanked his horse about and opened his mouth, only to have an eye burst from his skull. Sheridan felt a tug on his banner. A round had ripped through the cloth just above his head.

God, there was nothing like it, though. A lovely business it was, say what men would.

The boldest soldiers had just reached the breastworks when the Rebs began to break and bolt like jackrabbits. They'd been properly flanked and they knew it. On the left, near the elbow of the return, Reb artillerymen hastily chained their guns to their limbers and fled down a fresh-cut trail.

"Get 'em, boys! They're running, the low sonsofbitches, get every one of them!"

Ayres' men leapt the entrenchments in packs, screaming and bloody-minded now. Fired at short range, bullets found bellies. Men went at each other with bayonets and rifle butts, as the Johnnies who hadn't escaped fought on for spite.

Remaining behind to wave fresh regiments forward, Sheridan saw Reb hands climb in the air and inverted muskets rise above men's heads. It wasn't another minute before the first grayback prisoners staggered out of the works.

Giving Rienzi a kick, Sheridan leapt an earthen wall topped with head logs, his mount bursting from the sodden ground and landing amid an untamed passel of Rebs.

"Lay down your guns, boys," Sheridan ordered the astonished Johnnies. "Just drop 'em on the ground and get along, you're all safe now."

"Where'n y'all want us'uns to go?"

The speaker wore the beard of a patriarch. With no stripes on his sleeve, he nonetheless seemed to speak for dozens of Rebs. Officers there were none.

Sheridan pointed to the rear. "Just go off that way. Best get moving, the boys are in a temper. Go on, you'll be safe back there."

And the ragged men who'd fought his own kind to a standstill time and again obeyed him and went slump-shouldered into captivity.

By God, Sheridan thought, if this isn't the end, it's damned close to it.

But the fighting wasn't over, not by a hard mile. He teased Rienzi to life again, and the beast wove between thin trees and nets of thorns. He found Ayres at the edge of the grove, missing his hat but giving orders crisply. Fellow hadn't the best division, but he'd done all right.

In the low, wet field, Ayres' bluecoats mingled confusedly with dejected men in gray and rags of brown.

"Ayres!" Sheridan barked. "Get your shit-pail sonsofbitches reorganized. Push on westward. Roll the buggers up, don't waste any time. We've got them, don't let up."

"Trying, sir. I've lost two brigade commanders. And we must have a thousand prisoners on our hands. I have to—"

"You have to do what I goddamned say, and I say shove it down their goddamned throats. Get organized and get moving, or I'll find somebody who can."

"Yes, sir."

Sheridan turned to judge more of the match, but paused for a moment.

"And Ayres?"

"General?"

"Damned fine job. Now finish it."

As Sheridan took himself northward, weaving through the dead, wounded, and captive, his chief of staff, Jimmy Forsyth, joined him again.

"Ha!" Sheridan said. "Heard you were dead. Told 'em you weren't. Find Warren?"

"No, sir. He's off somewhere."

"The sonofabitch."

Four forty p.m.
"The Chimneys"

Warren found Charlie Griffin and his division. After riding through enemy fire, blundering in the woods, and giving new orders to Kellogg's errant brigade, he'd come upon Charlie well north of his intended place in the corps order of battle, but—typical for Griffin—already doing the right thing and wheeling westward.

"Ayres is on them," Warren called. "He's going to need help, though."

Charlie's lopsided old-soldier smile came and went. "When doesn't Rome need help?" There was no meanness intended, it was just Griffin being himself.

"If you push due west, toward Ford's Road, you'll come in behind the Rebs. They hadn't refused the flank but a few hundred yards, their rear's wide open." Warren pawed away sweat. "We got it wrong, but it's coming out better than if we'd gotten it right. Fortunes of war. Move fast and we'll bag 'em."

"Already moving. Cope found me, gave me your orders."

"Cope had better luck than I've had today."

"I've been forward, had me a look. Maps are right, for once. Broad field just past this one, you can see down to White Oak Road. Rebs are jumping like grasshoppers, they know they're in the shitter."

"Go at them, Charlie. You know what to do."

Griffin nodded.

"I've got to get Crawford back in line," Warren continued. "God knows where he's off to."

"He's got one brigade just north of me," Griffin told him. "Muddled up, as usual."

"I'll see to it." Warren leaned from the saddle, extending his hand. "Counting on you, Charlie."

Four forty-five p.m.
White Oak Road

Matt Ransom made the decisions that couldn't wait for Pickett. Somebody had to. He swung Wallace's Brigade about to refuse the flank anew, reassembled his own men as best he could, and put Steuart on warning that he needed to be ready to curl back and extend the line to the north. Terrible shambles, terrible. But the Yankees had paused to get themselves fixed up for another thrust, which spared him some minutes.

Where the devil was George Pickett, anyway? Or Fitz Lee? His own authority was limited. Couldn't order a single cavalryman to displace, and Rooney Lee was looking for Pickett, too. Nor had he authority over Pegram's guns, reliant on Willie's good sense and taste for a fight. But Pegram was hell-busy, with Sheridan's troopers pressing him from the front.

He watched a shriveled regiment hasten to extend the line again, their numbers paltry, uniforms patched, and eyes grim. Not enough of anything these days. Even looking at those men ran bitter.

And shameful. Not sure he'd ever get over it, live it down. Seeing his own men surrender by the company, almost by the regiment, his good old division just quitting. Men he'd praised as having "lice in their hair and fire in their hearts," men as brave as any who'd ever saluted. So many hadn't bothered to run off, merely gave themselves up. Just like that.

"Ignominious." That was the fancied-up word.

Had to hold the new line, keep the Federals off Ford's Road and stop them from closing the trap. Redeem what could be redeemed, save what could be saved. Wasn't going to be a blue-ribbon day, though.

Billy Wallace cantered up on his gray. Billy'd had a rough year in '64, with four companies of his old 18th South Carolina blown to hell at the Crater and his promotion to brigadier coming late enough to hurt.

"Matt, they're on the far side of Sydnor's Field. My boys can't stretch. And the cavalry up that way couldn't hold up their own pants."

"Doing what I can, Billy. If you should see George Pickett . . ."

"I'm like to see Yankees first."

"See what I can do, but you've got to hold them."

Just to the east, a fresh ripple of shots announced that the Yankees had finished re-forming. They were coming on again.

Hadn't wasted much time, give the scoundrels credit.

As the pair of gray-clad generals scanned the field, blue lines burst from the grove Ransom's men had lost.

"Could use some artillery now," Billy Wallace said.

"Can't find those boys, either."

Four fifty p.m.
Sydnor's Field

After they left the canebrake, things went fast. Chamberlain gave the order and his men rushed across the field, with Bartlett's brigade lagging slightly to their right. In the muddle back in the tangles and groves, their brigades had swapped positions in the line.

The Johnnies hadn't been able to throw up earthworks or do more than scratch the ground for rifle pits. No time. The Rebs had won the race to the long meadow, but they were going to lose the fight to hold it.

Fewer of his men fell than such a charge normally cost. The Rebs just were not ready, out of breath and surprised out of their senses. Their firing was ragged, hurried.

As always, the New York Irishmen in his ranks blasphemed with grandeur. Roman Catholics seemed to have a knack for it.

Under a fine spring sky, men slaughtered each other. Chamberlain reckoned that it had been so for the Romans and the Greeks, the Assyrians and Persians. For all soldiers, at one time or another. This carnage amid beauty.

If fury were beauty, his men surpassed Diana and Aphrodite. They tore into the Confederate line, such as it was, and the Johnnies who didn't flee promptly surrendered. It was worrisomely easy, but Glenn's Pennsylvanians had ruptured that line for good, with those profane New Yorkers by their side. Two of his other regiments remained locked in battle's embrace, but he still had men uncommitted and feared none of it.

His moral lapse that morning remained with him, though. His failure to defend Warren against Sheridan. He had said nothing dishonorable, of course. But his silence had not been honorable, either. He had fallen far short of his philosopher-heroes.

Eddie Glenn sent a runner: His own situation was good, but Bartlett had run into trouble on the right, his men were running back to the half-dug rifle pits Glenn had seized.

Couldn't let things bog down now. Once men stopped advancing and took shelter, it was devilish hard to get them moving again. Chamberlain tugged the right rein and rode for his two trailing regiments. He ordered them to Bartlett's support at the double-quick, making a hash of his brigade's prescribed order, but it had to be done.

The men of the 185th and 188th New York responded handsomely. Dogtrotting over the field, they hollered at Bartlett's hesitant men, mocking them, and that was all it took. Embarrassed, Bartlett's boys pulled themselves together and pushed on.

Soldiers he recognized from the 198th Pennsylvania escorted hundreds of Reb prisoners rearward. The Johnnies looked as relieved as they did glum.

All too easy, too easy. Had they finally broken? Would it all be over soon, this monstrous war?

His latest wound pained him severely and his arm remained uncooperative, but Chamberlain took counsel, as ever, from Epictetus, as cited by Marcus Aurelius, that a man was but a little soul dragging a corpse.

The war had changed him, and not only because of his wounds. His body was the least changed part of him, for all the scars. He'd graduated from Bangor Theological Seminary armed with the words of Jesus Christ and now found sustenance in pagan philosophers.

He still believed in Christianity but found it unreliable on a battlefield.

Joe Bartlett rode up, grinning. "Owe you for the help, Josh. Good of you, old fellow."

"A friend in need . . ."

"Damn me, look at those shirkers, though." Barlett pointed at a copse of trees behind Chamberlain's back: A sorry number of soldiers had taken refuge. "Shall we roust 'em?"

"Time enough, I suppose."

The two brigadiers rode for the brambles where soldiers in blue coats loitered. None of them attempted to run off, not now that they'd been caught out. And Chamberlain believed he understood: They weren't cowards, not exactly. They only sensed that the war was nearing its end and didn't see much point in dying now.

Well, he didn't, either. But the work had to be done.

Bartlett cajoled them with a hint of menace. "Come on, boys. Get out here and form back up. *Now.* You missed the fight, but you don't want to miss the victory."

Chamberlain's tone was colder. "Form up. Right here. *You.*" He pointed at a boy who looked half-weaned—the draft had grown less than discriminate. "Stand right there. All of you form on him."

Marcus Aurelius offered a splendid quote for these hesitant warriors: "Look within thyself and you shall find reserves of strength spring forth, if only you bid them." But Chamberlain knew it would go unappreciated.

The firing moved westward, toward White Oak Road. The Rebs would fight for that, surely, their best line of retreat. But they wouldn't hold it, Chamberlain didn't think. Momentum, that was the thing. It was really a question for the physical sciences, was it not? Once matters accelerated past the irrevocable? The positive force of inertia superseded the negative force, or, in rhetorical terms, the objective subdued the subjective. Events transpired as if predetermined. Of course, Epictetus would have countered . . .

Abruptly, he recalled his wife's red face—angry, not tearful—

when he told her he would return to command again. He half suspected that she dreaded widowhood more than his specific loss.

The Stoics taught allowance, not forgiveness. That worked rather better in certain human affairs.

About to return to his line—if a proper line still existed—he spotted Jim Gwyn's headquarters' banners plunked down in a field. Waving up an aide, Chamberlain said, "Fisher, go ask Colonel Gwyn to come up to our support. Tell him we've got the Rebs on the run but could use some help with the chase."

The lieutenant saluted and spurred his horse to a gallop, although a man could have walked the stretch in a minute.

When he got back into the fighting, Chamberlain found that his advance had slowed, though it hadn't stopped. Briars proved more of a hindrance than the Rebs.

"Push on, men, get to the road. We need that road, get to the road."

With a grand thrashing of greenery, Charlie Griffin and his staff materialized behind Chamberlain.

"Good work, Professor," his division commander said. "Keep driving them. Your boys *and* the Rebs. Just drive them hard."

"I shall, sir."

Griffin's crooked smile appeared. Below wry, glinting eyes. "I suppose you feel like Julius Caesar himself. *Veni, vidi, vici* and all that Latin."

Brigadier General Joshua Chamberlain answered, "Better Caesar than Vercingetorix, sir," but the allusion was lost on Charlie Griffin.

Four fifty p.m.
Wallace farm, Ford's Road

No, I *do* hear something. That's gunfire," Pickett said, nerves vanquishing the effects of drink in an instant. He turned to Rosser.

"Tom, send a man down to Five Forks, find out if it's anything serious."

Rosser drew himself together, shaking off the remains of their mild debauch. "Prefer to send two. One man a hundred yards ahead of the other. Just in case."

"I hear it myself," Fitz Lee muttered.

"Best find out what's doing," Pickett repeated. A headache grazed the backs of his eyes, worsening the tremors of alarm.

It didn't take long for Rosser to get a pair of men in the saddle. And off they went, toward the wooden bridge over Hatcher's Run and the far field that led to a copse. The riders covered ground swiftly, a credit to Rosser's manner of doing things. One, then another, they hammered over the planks and thumped the road again.

The lead rider neared the far trees. Pickett was about to turn back to the campfire when he saw the worst sight that he'd seen since Gettysburg.

Yankee infantry dashed from the grove and took the first messenger prisoner, dragging him from the saddle under threat from rifle and bayonet. The second rider whipped around, chased by rifle fire. As the generals watched, amazed, more bluecoats appeared across Hatcher's Run.

"Lord Jesus," Pickett said.

Five p.m.

Just skirmishers, looks like," Rosser said. "I'll clear those boys right off."

Stunned slow, Pickett said, "I've got to get through, Tom. I've got to get down to Five Forks. . . ."

"I'll clear the way, sir. We'll sort this out right quick."

"You do that," Fitz Lee ordered. "I'll gather up your division. We'll soon put a stop to whatever this is."

To Pickett, Lee's tone of confidence sounded forced. A shared sense of guilt had enveloped them, plain as stink, a foreboding that their indulgence would prove costly.

Rosser's headquarters guards pounded over the bridge, howling.

A mere handful, after all, the Yankees fired and faded into the trees. Pickett followed Rosser as quickly as he could get his horse saddled again. He'd meant to give the poor beast a bit of rest.

No time for thanking Tom Rosser, Pickett galloped through the protective gauntlet formed by his horsemen. He certainly heard firing now. Plenty of it. Too much of it. A full-pitch battle was under way, no doubting it.

How had it happened? Why hadn't he heard a thing?

His mount caught his excitement and splashed down the puddled road. Ahead, Pickett saw a battle line of gray-jacketed cavalry. They were drawn up facing eastward and didn't look as if they expected good news.

Pulling up briefly, Pickett demanded, "Who do you boys belong to?"

Colonel Tom Munford rode out of the brush, face hard but eyes distraught.

"Fitz Lee's old division, General. Seen him, by any chance?" The colonel's head swiveled. "Christ, here they come!"

Beyond a fringe of trees, a Yankee battle line strode across a field. The blue ranks were less than three hundred yards off. Union skirmishers were closer.

"Colonel, hold them back, give me three minutes. I need to pass on to Five Forks."

Without waiting for orders, a youthful captain who retained a dash of the cavalier kicked his horse to life and shouted, "Third Virginia! After me! Come on!"

A too-small band of horsemen broke from the line and charged toward what appeared to be an entire Union brigade, if not a division. The captain was going to fall, but that was war. He and his men existed for this purpose. Pickett felt no least regret, only anxiety over the fate of the rest of his little army, the force entrusted to him by Robert E. Lee, the man who had already doomed him once.

Why did he always seem to have bad luck?

Yankee voices issued swift commands and rifles cracked. Pickett galloped onward, spurring his mount bloody and leaving Munford's horsemen to their fate. When fresh shots sought him, he tucked his head down on the right side of the animal's neck.

Riding like that, as the Indians did, made him think of the squaw and the child he'd left behind in the Oregon Territory, his place of exile from civilization back when he'd worn blue. But he didn't think of them long.

He never did.

Five thirty p.m.
Hatcher's Run

Bringing to bear most of Rosser's division of cavalry, Fitz Lee still could not reopen Ford's Road and join the fight. Couldn't even assert a position south of Hatcher's Run. At least a division of Yankee horse barred the way southward and parried every thrust. With masses of Federal infantry behind them.

And damn it to blazes, it *was* Mackenzie's division, after all. How the devil had it slipped away, under Longstreet's nose, and marched forty miles? Without a soul in gray pantaloons noticing they were gone?

Fitz Lee was more convinced than ever that Longstreet's best days were behind him. Of course, that might be said of many an officer now. For all he knew, folks might have said it of him. And more of them might say it after this day.

His old Comanche wound pained him of a sudden.

Damn George Pickett, though. And his own greedy appetite. Idiocy, sheer idiocy. The very idea of a shad bake, with Sheridan out there drooling over man-flesh. Biggest damned mistake of his entire life. For the sake of fish he didn't even care for.

Begrimed and specked with other men's blood, Rosser returned from another futile effort.

"Can't do it, sir. All the cavalry . . . their infantry . . ."

Fitz Lee felt caged and poked. Growling as much as speaking, he said, "Have to move cross-country."

"And then what, sir?"

"Cover the retreat."

The sounds of combat were clear and ugly now. Shifting westward at a walking pace. Some boys were fighting still, but Lee didn't have to see the struggle to know how it would end. He'd been on battlefields enough, though never in such shame.

"We have to cover the retreat," he repeated.

Five thirty p.m.
Five Forks

Yankees were everywhere. Enclosing them on three sides and doing all they could to complete the encirclement.

Mayo's defense had collapsed. Ransom's men were finished. Steuart couldn't hold. Regiments and brigades had intermingled, their lines of command all but useless. No one brought good news.

Pickett searched for an inspiration, for any way to turn the fight to advantage even now. He knew what defeat would mean. For the defense of Petersburg. For Lee. Not least, for his reputation.

They'd have to keep things quiet about the shad bake. Nobody could know.

But soldiers talked. Couldn't keep their mouths shut.

Why had he been such a fool?

Exposing himself to the ceaseless Yankee firing, Pickett rode out into a field to rally his fleeing soldiers.

How many men had already been made prisoner? How many were left?

The wounded and merely worn shambled off, some using rifles for crutches, others borne upon a comrade's back, a few on litters. Most of those still whole had kept their rifles, but not all of them. Nor were many inclined to heed his call.

Matt Ransom came up. Pickett felt an urge to lash out, to blame Ransom for the quick collapse of his line. All of the trouble had started over there, at the return. Everybody said so. But George Pickett also realized he'd need every friend he could muster.

What would Sallie think when she heard? Next thing, they'd tell her about the squaw-woman, too. And the newspapers . . .

"General, we've got to withdraw right now. Save what we can while there's time."

"Boys still got fight," Pickett said. His tone didn't even begin to convince himself.

"Maybe enough to make good a retreat, that's about it."

"Pegram's still got his guns in play. Yankees ain't licked us yet."

Ransom's face grew still more stricken. "I assumed . . . I figured you'd heard . . ."

"What now?"

"Willie Pegram. He's been carried off. McCabe suspects it's mortal."

Pickett turned to another band of soldiers that had just abandoned the fight. Fixing on the only officer in their midst, he shouted to be heard above the cacophony, "You there! Lieutenant! Turn these men around. Or I'll rip that rank off your collar with my own hands."

The lieutenant edged away and quickened his pace. The soldiers with him eyed Pickett as if tempted to do him harm.

What had happened to his fine division? This was worse, far worse, than Gettysburg.

A Yankee hurrah announced another breakthrough.

Gripping himself anew, Pickett began to do what had to be done.

"All right, Matt. Hold them another ten minutes, just ten more minutes. I'll swing back Corse's Brigade astride White Oak Road, keep it open westward as long as possible. You and the others, you get your men off. No running, I won't allow it. But you're in charge here, see to the retreat, save your command. I'll get up a fresh line, handle the rear guard."

Ransom nodded. "Last I heard, Rooney Lee's holding on the right. If he can keep off their cavalry . . ."

Pickett kicked up his horse. Two flag-bearers and a shred of his staff followed after, survivors who had found him in the melee, half of them bleeding and every one of them crushed. He did not turn to look at them, unable to bear the reproach in their eyes.

More Yankee cheers.

Had to save what he could. Not least, of his reputation.

For a few luxurious moments, he pondered leading a forlorn hope himself. Charging headlong into the mass of Yankees. A brave death would redeem him. . . .

The problem was that he didn't care to die.

Five thirty p.m.
Five Forks

Reb prisoners streamed past. They'd been taken by the thousands.

Sheridan was thrilled and furious. The Rebs were collapsing like a slut's excuses, with Warren's men sweeping through the fields and woods, unstoppable. A bit more to do and this would count among the great victories of the war.

And therein lay the part that left him irate: Warren's men had achieved this. His own cavalrymen had done little more than pester the Johnnies' line. Only in the past fifteen minutes had Devin's lads gotten over the barricades, their Spencers snapping. And Custer, on the left, had been unable to outflank Rooney Lee. The situation was exasperating, intolerable.

His men were in the thick of it now, but something had to be done. The credit for this victory would *not* go to that mediocrity Warren, not any part of it.

God bless Sam Grant.

Six p.m.
Gilliam's field, White Oak Road

Warren had rushed from one of his divisions to the next, doing all he could to impose order and keep the corps moving. For over an hour he'd not paused long enough to drink from his canteen.

Everything had to be seen to, the lines of advance sorted out in confounding woodlands and sullen marshes, fallen leaders replaced, weak points reinforced, and, above all, the fight pressed to the Confederates' destruction.

He sensed that his beloved Fifth Corps was on the verge of its greatest triumph ever, perhaps the decisive battle of a campaign that had dragged on for nine months—the campaign that was bound to decide the fate of the nation.

He rode up to Crawford's division. Disordered and weary, the soldiers had simply stopped. Facing yet another Confederate line. Across a last field, he could see Reb infantry throwing up breastworks, grasping any material at hand—fence rails, fallen limbs, a few tipped-over wagons, and plenty of dirt. Every moment that the attack remained stalled made it deadlier for those who would have to cross that open space.

Company and regimental officers called on their men to advance, to make one more push, but the soldiers seemed to have reached a collective agreement that they were done. Whether pleading or raging, the captains and majors had no effect at all.

With Captain Benyaurd back at his side and his color guard trailing after, Warren rode along the line, ordering officers to re-form their units and reestablish order.

One step at a time, Warren thought. He'd dealt with soldiers long enough to know that they could be stubborn as mules. It was at such times that generals had to lead and take their chances.

The Johnnies kept piling up logs and rocks and muck, hurrying to construct a poor-man's fortress. To block the road westward and save what was left of their force.

Why hadn't Sheridan's cavalry flanked them by now?

Well, he'd see to his own responsibilities. Let Sheridan rally his own men, Warren's fight was here.

The soldiers remained unwilling. He could feel it. But this last charge had to be made, the *coup de grâce* delivered.

Where was Crawford himself? Nowhere to be seen. Warren

hoped the fellow had not been shot. He couldn't even see a division flag.

Now, or never.

Warren took his Fifth Corps flag from the corporal who carried it. Holding the banner as high as its weight allowed, Warren rode into the field before his men.

"One last push, lads! Come along! They're making their last stand, they know they're whipped. Come on, for the good old Fifth Corps!"

He never had possessed the gift of rhetoric. But he meant to go on alone, if it came to that. He would not falter.

Sorry for Emily, of course. And sorry for himself that he'd nevermore see her.

"Come on, boys! I'll go with you, let's go together!"

Fixing on the cluster of horsemen, the Rebs began to fire at long range.

But some among his soldiers began to move. Field officers came forward and flags advanced.

Still, the mass of soldiers hesitated.

Forearm muscles straining, Warren thrust the flag higher, reversing his course along the reluctant line.

"Follow me, men. Let's put an end to this war, God bless the Fifth Corps. . . ."

By an act of will immeasurable, he turned his horse toward the Confederate line, estimating the Rebel strength at a reinforced brigade. The last intact brigade that Pickett had, Warren suspected.

He had not ridden twenty feet when a great hurrah arose, the roar that he would recall to the end of his days.

Crawford's division followed him, the thousands of footfalls audible above the increase in rifle fire, above the war cries and dry-throated commands. Warren felt a child's impulse to draw his sword and ride ahead, but he kept his mount to a walk, staying with his soldiers.

His soldiers. Dear God, they were magnificent.

On all sides, men cried out. Wounded. Surprised by the sudden change wrought in their flesh, astounded by splintered bone and spurting blood, by limbs made abruptly undutiful and balance lost to a maelstrom of sensations. Or driven to fury by a good friend's death, men made fierce by the gore of comrades splashed on their faces like the paint of Indians.

He rode erectly, fully expecting a bullet. He had asked this of these men so many times. Now he would go with them to the end.

Nearing the Rebel line, men screamed like savages. It was an unnerving phenomenon, a chilling sound rarely heard. Bayonets fixed, his soldiers began to run straight for their enemies.

Warren's horse buckled under him, spewing blood from its neck and chest. Warren hit the ground hard, just yards from the Rebel breastworks. Rifles, several of them, pointed straight at him as he struggled to rise.

Richardson, lieutenant colonel of the 7th Wisconsin, threw his horse and himself in front of Warren. Just in time to catch the flurry of bullets. An orderly fell, too, and his head struck Warren's thigh.

Then it was over. Johnnies stood with their hands in the air, eyes terrified for awful, uncertain moments, not yet sure their surrender would be accepted.

Crawford's men chased other Rebs through the trees.

Still a bit dazed from his fall, Warren called out, "Push on! Keep going! Go on, boys!"

Then he bent over Hollon Richardson. To everyone's astonishment, the lieutenant colonel still showed signs of life.

Six fifteen p.m.
Vicinity of White Oak Road, west of Five Forks

Rufe Barringer's day had not been pleasant. But his North Carolina cavalry had done its part, if few others had done theirs. Well, Rooney Lee had done his, give that man credit. But other men of rank—of greater rank—had failed the South. And it was bitter.

The cavalry had held, though. *His* men were still holding.

Custer's gussied-up toughs were out there, feeling his flanks again. With their magazine carbines that never seemed to go empty. He'd held them off, despite their gross advantages in weapons, horseflesh, and numbers. While the shattered remnants of Pickett's command made a run for the South Side Rail Road.

Damned well have to fight for that as well, come tomorrow morning. Yankees would be too tuckered out tonight, they never did much after dark. But morning would bring a challenge. Not content with the prize pig, they'd want the prize steer, too.

Brigadier General Rufus Barringer, Confederate States of America, couldn't shake the feeling that judgment was coming.

Bad, bad day. Just awful. But Curly Custer had seen a rough day, too. They could write *that* down when they got around to chronicling.

A courier pounded up, one of Rooney Lee's men. Barringer waited for the rider to catch his breath and speak his piece. There was no time for written orders now. Nor, apparently, for even the quickest salute.

"General Barringer, sir. You're to fall back at once. To the northwest, not more than five hundred yards. Otherwise, at your discretion."

"Not much discretion."

Ignoring the retort, the courier added, "General Lee asks that you entertain the enemy as long as possible. New orders will follow."

"Oh, I reckon I'll entertain him some," Barringer said.

Six forty-five p.m.
Five Forks

Jimmy Forsyth dismounted and strode up with a whorehouse grin.

"You look like you just went a round with the Queen of Sheba," Sheridan teased his chief of staff.

"Next best thing, General. Rough count has it we bagged two thousand prisoners, maybe three." He rubbed an eye and added, "Warren's men took most of them, of course. Nature of the fight."

"Speaking of General Warren," Sheridan said, "I want you to carry a note to him."

Seven p.m.
West of Five Forks

Warren unfolded the message and read it with disbelief that decayed into shock.

It was from Sheridan:

> *Major-General Warren, commanding Fifth Army Corps, is relieved of duty and will report at once for orders to General Grant, commanding Armies of the United States.*

Charlie Griffin was to have his command.

Seven thirty p.m.
Five Forks

I wish I could have seen the look on his face," Sheridan said. "Should have delivered the goddamned order myself."

"He certainly didn't expect it," Forsyth said.

That triggered one of Sheridan's gunshot laughs. "Well, fuck him. He's slow and he's a coward and he's a fool."

Beyond them, detailed soldiers gleaned discarded equipment from the field. Litter bearers sorted the Union wounded from the dead. They'd tend to the Johnnies later. Then there were the slinking ghouls picking the pockets of dead and wounded alike, Union or Confederate, united in victimhood. It was ever the same.

"Looks like General Warren's coming to see you, sir," Forsyth announced, nodding toward the road. "Believe I'll absent myself. With your permission."

"My permission, hell. You stay right here. This should be memorable."

Nine p.m.
Petersburg, Lee's headquarters

My God," Lee said.

Nine fifty p.m.
Petersburg

John Brown Gordon cradled his newborn son in his left arm and gently touched the infant's cheek with a finger.

"Just can't fix on whether he's more a Hercules or Adonis," he said, delighted. "Don't he look fine, though?"

"Better than your wife looks at the moment," Fanny told him.

Gordon handed the newborn to one of the inevitable attendants.

"Fanny, you look finer than an apron full of perfect Georgia peaches. And you're twice—no, thrice—as sweet, I swear on the Good Book."

He swooped down over the unchanged sheets and kissed her, inaccurately, on the side of her nose.

"More likely on a bad book, knowing you."

"If we weren't in company . . . ," he whispered.

"You hush. There's respectable people in this house."

Fanny lay there, exhausted and pale, raccoon-eyed from the labor and hair askew, not yet tidied one jot . . . and yet, immeasurably beautiful. His Fanny. More woman than most men could handle, that was certain. And he was glad of it.

"What are we going to call this young lion of ours?" He gestured for the busybody to bring him the baby again.

"You can call him whatever you like," Fanny declared, "but I've already named him 'John Brown Gordon.' "

That put another smile on Gordon's lips. Ever so gently, he jollied the tiny creature. "Hope the poor fellow can live that moniker down. And here I was set on 'Telemachus.' Thought it might give him a measure of gravity, just about guarantee he'd make county judge." He tickled the infant's cheek again, wanting the fragile gift to reopen its eyes. The child had Fanny's eyes, Gordon was sure of it. But the infant would not be prodded, every bit as stubborn as his mother.

Well, let him rest. After his struggle to enter this dubious world.

"That's right," Gordon cooed, voice barely there. "You just be quiet and let your mama rest. She's going to need every last ounce of her wickedness to keep *you* penned." He put his right hand under the infant's rump and began to rock.

Let this one live, let him join the three who'd survived. He didn't want Fanny to lose another child. She was strong as iron, but iron could be brittle.

The room smelled of sweat, waste, and woman. He wished that his wife were ready for him, right there, at that moment. Just chase these hanger-on women out of the room and get right to it.

Well, there'd be time enough, the Good Lord and the Yankee bullets willing. All but sinful, to love a woman so much. Worse than sinful, maybe. To want her so.

Of a sudden, the world roared. *Artillery.* A hundred guns, at least. The floorboards quaked. Glass chimed.

What the devil?

The baby began to cry. Gordon felt wet seep through to his right hand. This little man, announcing his physicality. Once more, he gave up the baby.

"Best see to things, I reckon."

Fanny lifted a hand to touch him but couldn't reach. "Are they coming, John? Now?"

The cannonade's power grew. Speech had to rise to be heard.

"Not till morning, at least. If then. Might be nothing. You know how they are."

"You'd tell me, though?"

"If I knew myself. Fanny, I have to—"

"I know. Go on."

He bent over his wife, kissing her full on the lips, uncaring of what others thought.

"'If ever any beauty I did see . . . and got, 'twas but a dream of thee.' Fanny-gal, I love you like a catfish loves cool water. . . ."

A breathless courier waited for him downstairs.

"General Gordon, sir . . ."

"That's me, son. What is it?"

"General Pickett. He got whipped right bad. Out by Five Forks. Major Douglas said you'd best come back, that things are fussing."

"How badly was he defeated? Do you know?"

"Can't say truly, General. But the riders who come in with the news was crying."

Well, that was it, the scales had tipped. Grant would hit them now. With every man he could muster. This was the reckoning.

Gordon wanted to go back up to his wife, to cradle her in his arms. One last time. But he decided it was best to leave things as is, they'd enjoyed a handsome parting. Something pretty for her to remember.

Eleven p.m.
Church's Crossing

Four Confederate generals stood by a campfire, divided, two and two, by what each had done or left undone that day. To the east, Union artillery bombarded the Petersburg lines, thunder that promised a storm would strike in the morning, if not sooner.

"Held Custer, anyway," Rooney Lee said. His voice had an edge. "Long enough for anybody who meant to get away to take themselves off. Thanks, not least, to Rufe here." Looking directly at Barringer, he added, "You set in?"

Newly arrived at the conclave, Rufus Barringer said, "Yes, sir. Brigade's all gathered up. Just below Potts' Depot." He took off his hat and smoothed a hand over his baldness. "Not the finest day North Carolina's seen. But not the worst."

Fitz Lee said nothing. Beside him, Tom Rosser, too, was newly subdued. No man had pointed a finger, not one slighting word had been spoken, but everyone had heard by now the reason their leaders had not been on the field.

Rosser's shad bake had been folly enough by itself, but Fitz Lee's participation, his self-indulgence, a damned-fool caprice, had been the worst mistake he'd made in the war. Perhaps the worst of his life. Damned-fool business. He'd tried to blame Rosser and Pickett in his heart, but he knew the guilt was his own. He should have been the one with common sense.

Somber and rueful, Fitz Lee bared his soul for the cat-o'-nine tails. It was not a condition to which he was accustomed. He had been admired all his life. Resented, perhaps. But admired. And now this.

He had not uttered one word of apology, not to any man. And he would not. He wasn't made that way. Lees did not apologize. He might express regret for a minor discourtesy, but not for losing a battle. A Lee might be mistaken, but never wrong.

He dreaded seeing his uncle. Who would not breathe a syllable of admonishment but would bring to bear a look of disdain more potent than a shouted public rebuke.

Miles off, the Yankee batteries pounded unseen lines. It wouldn't be just a victory celebration, not this time. The barrage was relentless and massive. And back in the Petersburg trenches there were stretches where his uncle could only post a soldier every ten feet, relying on fortified batteries to make good the weakness in numbers. The lines had been stripped to give Pickett his force. And now that force was gone or left incapable.

An aide brought him coffee. Fitz Lee took the hot tin cup in hand but did not drink. There was no consolation to be had, only the hope that on the morrow he might begin to redeem himself. The cavalry had gotten off fairly intact, it was still a force to be reckoned with.

Tomorrow . . .

They would have to fight for the railroad now, a last stand to be made with inadequate forces. Trotting about to gather up the soldiers who'd escaped, Pickett had been all but unintelligible, as distraught as a bonded madman, but George had managed to communicate that whatever troops he could concentrate would defend the South Side Rail Road.

Perhaps, Fitz Lee told himself, his uncle might send reinforcements, after all. He could bring down another brigade of Mahone's from Bermuda Hundred, or even pull out the whole division to fill in the Petersburg lines and free up men from the right. Anderson's boys were close enough, they could fight through, if necessary. And the Yankees would be tired, they had to be. His men and Pickett's remnants might just hold the South Side, with some help. Hadn't they been in tighter spots?

Fitz Lee yawned. The show of weakness embarrassed him.

Gone hard of eye and unkind, Cousin Rooney watched him. Good-natured Rooney was in a foul mood now, an obviously insubordinate mood. Allowing a glimpse of his father's regal temper, that mastered and measured ferocity. But he, too, was a Lee and held himself in, seething in silence.

Rooney's pawn, poor Rufus Barringer, managed to look exhausted and plain stumped. But he edged away from Rooney, inch by inch.

Had Barringer seen a hidden side of Rooney, his division commander? One that Fitz Lee himself had never seen? Did he take his temper from some old blood in the family? Whatever it was, Cousin Rooney would have to get over it.

How bad had their losses really been, though? Bad enough, of course. But there might be hope. More of Pickett's men might come in by morning. Perhaps fewer had been captured than first thought. . . .

"Does sound like the Yankees mean business this time," Rosser said. "I don't figure they intend us a peaceful Sunday."

Barringer nodded along with the remark. It didn't signal agreement, necessarily. It was just Rufe's ease of manner.

Without so much as the grace of a rattlesnake's warning, Rooney Lee struck. His blow hit harder for being unexpected:

"I was Grant, I'd send in every man I had tomorrow morning, come first light. Finish up our whipping, just get it over with. Put us out of our misery." He did not shout, but his rage was of biblical force. "And we deserve every stroke, every lash we get. We didn't lose that battle today, we threw it away, just pissed down our own legs." It felt as though he had finished, but Rooney added, "Men who surrendered had more sense than any one of us. And a sight more goddamned decency."

Despite the cannonade battering Petersburg, their smaller world fell silent. No man's eyes met another's.

After a time, Rufe Barringer said: "I believe I ought to get back to my brigade."

Midnight

Grant's field headquarters, Dabney's Mill

Calmed down, are you?" Grant asked, smiling. Painted ginger by firelight, he leaned forward in his camp chair and held out a message. "Pass this to the clerks, they can log it in."

But just as Horace Porter reached for the note, Grant withdrew it—a curious habit the general had developed.

As his aide waited empty-handed, Grant leaned even closer to the fire, unfolding the paper and squinting to scan it again. Porter listened to the bombardment: a fine serenade for the Johnnies. The ground rolled beneath his riding boots.

Despite the late hour, the entire headquarters pulsed. Even the dullest lieutenant sensed great things ahead, and weary men discovered reserves of vigor. Multiple telegraphs clicked, their lamp-lit operators silhouetted against the canvas of tents or signal wagons.

"Glad Meade forwarded this," Grant said, surrendering the paper at last. "Wright's got the idea. Listen here. 'The corps will go in solid, and I am sure will make the fur fly.' Says once he lets loose, Sixth Corps will crack their lines in fifteen minutes." Jaw set, Grant nodded. "That's the spirit I want."

Porter hesitated. There was another matter. "I believe General Warren desires to see you, sir."

"Not tonight."

Porter understood. Grant did not want to talk to Warren at all, not tonight, not tomorrow. Grant disliked confrontations. The aide added:

"I believe he had an unsatisfactory interview with Meade."

Grant hunched his shoulders and looked down, sealing Warren's fate. Everything Porter had come to know about Grant, every bit of private knowledge, told him that the general would not intervene. Once empowered, Sheridan had made the decision, and Phil's decision would stand. Phil's private dispatch claimed that Warren had very nearly cost them the battle, implying that only he had turned it into a glorious victory. That was Phil, of course—an utterly unforgiving man, except when forgiveness was to his advantage. Porter just said:

"Meade's still sick as can be, sir. And I do believe Warren's situation unsettled him."

"He's no sicker than John Rawlins." Grant stopped abruptly as sorrow touched his face, an emotion quickly vanquished. "He'll have to buck up. We all do. And I'd rather have unsettled generals than complacent ones." He looked Porter dead in the eyes, the effect of which could be sudden and frightening, a side of Grant few saw—men saw the cigar, not the soul, the smoke, but not the will. "All that fuss straightened out now, the confusion?"

"Yes, sir. Everybody understands. Assault all across the front. At four a.m."

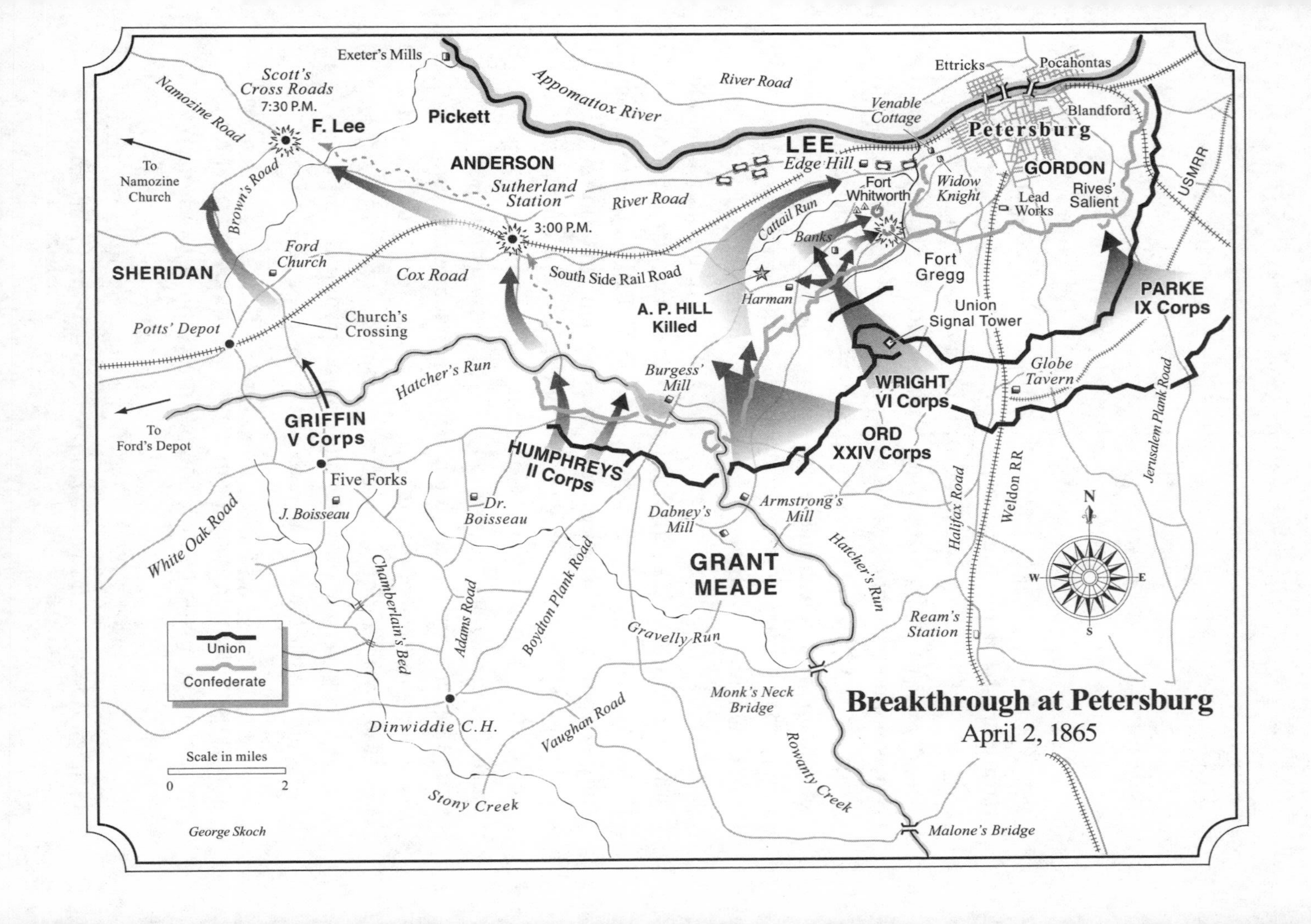
Breakthrough at Petersburg
April 2, 1865
Exeter's Mills
Scott's Cross Roads 7:30 P.M.
Namozine Road
F. Lee
Pickett
Appomattox River
River Road
Ettricks
Pocahontas
Venable Cottage
Blandford
Petersburg
LEE
Edge Hill
GORDON
ANDERSON
To Namozine Church
Brown's Road
Sutherland Station
River Road
Fort Whitworth
Widow Knight
Lead Works
Rives' Salient
USMRR
Cattail Run
3:00 P.M.
Banks
Fort Gregg
Ford Church
SHERIDAN
Cox Road
South Side Rail Road
Harman
A. P. HILL Killed
PARKE IX Corps
Union Signal Tower
Potts' Depot
Church's Crossing
Hatcher's Run
Burgess' Mill
WRIGHT VI Corps
Globe Tavern
Jerusalem Plank Road
To Ford's Depot
GRIFFIN V Corps
HUMPHREYS II Corps
ORD XXIV Corps
Five Forks
J. Boisseau
Dr. Boisseau
Dabney's Mill
Armstrong's Mill
Halifax Road
Weldon RR
White Oak Road
Chamberlain's Bed
Adams Road
Boydton Plank Road
GRANT MEADE
Hatcher's Run
N
W
E
S
Union
Confederate
Gravelly Run
Ream's Station
Monk's Neck Bridge
Dinwiddie C.H.
Vaughan Road
Scale in miles
0
2
Rowanty Creek
Stony Creek
George Skoch
Malone's Bridge

SEVEN

Three forty a.m., April 2, 1865
Union Sixth Corps lines

Cargo clanging and banging, the renegade mule almost ran over Rhodes in the fog. A man couldn't see twenty paces, but everyone heard the racket. Including the Reb pickets, who opened fire again in the heavy dark.

The Rebs were jumpy. With good reason.

Soldiers from the pioneers dashed after the beast, bumbling through Rhodes' regimental lines, a pantomime of shadows, with everyone striving mightily to be quiet. Any other time, men so riled would have been blaspheming, with punches thrown after hard, hapless collisions.

This night was different. Everyone knew that silence was a matter of life and death. Everyone but that mule.

Forced to his knees, Rhodes dropped flat beside his color guard as blind Reb shots sought targets. His uniform coat gained another coating of mud, but it hardly mattered—they hadn't assembled for a dress parade. Toward the Confederate lines, to which the mule had been inclined to desert, the creature's bray-and-whinny turned to a groan. After a last crash and clatter of dropping tools, silence asked to be recognized again. The Reb pickets eased off.

Frank Halliday, the 2nd Rhode Island's acting adjutant, whispered, "Never trust a mule. First time I've ever been grateful for Reb marksmanship."

"Quiet," Lieutenant Colonel Elisha Hunt Rhodes told him.

He didn't dare strike a match to check his watch, but the signal for the attack had to be near. It had been a grueling night, beginning with a four-mile march to Fort Fisher during the grand bombardment, followed by a walk-on-eggshells deployment in front of their lines, nakedly exposed to enemy fire. The soldiers had been admonished to be quiet on pain of court-martial, but the threat of death from jittery Reb batteries proved far more effective at stilling tongues in the dark.

The Sixth Corps had slithered forward, with the 2nd Rhode Island Volunteer Infantry placed in the rear assault line, following the 5th Wisconsin, on the left flank of Edwards' brigade of Wheaton's division. And Wheaton's ranks butted up against Getty's division, the entire corps disposed for maximum force, as Rhodes understood the plan. His men were tucked in soundly amid the many, yet the position seemed lonely enough.

He blamed the fog. It was heavy as wet canvas.

He'd need to write a letter to Corporal Mills' mother, the sort of duty that pained him worse than battle. It grew harder, not easier, to find the words as the casualty lists lengthened.

Rhodes smiled at himself. He'd assumed, as men did, as they had to, that *he'd* be alive to write the letter at the end of this day.

Poor Mills, so proud of his role in the color guard, had been killed by a chance shot from a Johnny on picket post. It had occurred just after midnight, as the bombardment tapered off. The corporal had been the victim of a nervous shot triggered by someone else's disturbance, when the men were still standing in ranks, waiting for the command to go forward at once, before the order came down for the soldiers to lie on the sodden earth and wait again. The attack had been rescheduled for four a.m.

Young Mills had been a good soldier. Even struck by that bad-luck ball, he'd kept silent as he died, merely gasping, surrounded by mute comrades trying to save him.

Again, Rhodes smirked at himself. "Young Mills" indeed. Here he was, a twenty-three-year-old lieutenant colonel playing the hoary father to his men. War overturned odds—and much else. Not four years before, his suitability to serve even as a private had been questioned. Even after gaining his widowed mother's permission to enlist, his slight frame and narrow shoulders had led the examining doctor to warn that he wasn't fit, that he'd be in a hospital in a week.

Well, he still wasn't tall or much brawnier, but he'd proved that doctor wrong. Chosen for clerical duties in Washington, he'd learned the phenomenal intricacies of military bureaucracy and could have had a safe berth for the duration. But he'd fought to go back to his regiment, to do what he saw as his duty, with his father's ghost, the spirit of the dutiful Rhode Island sea captain lost in a storm, reluctant to nod his approval from the grave until his son showed grit and worth and courage.

And now? In the clotting mud of a ravaged field in Virginia, with soldiers by the ten thousand waiting for miles along the line, Rhodes could only hope that his good fortune would hold a bit longer. The war would be over, perhaps that day or the next, surely in a matter of weeks. It seemed to him that every soldier sensed it, these long lines shrouded by fog and night and fear, waiting for the bugle call that would launch them forward to their personal fates.

And if *he* fell? A descendant of Roger Williams, coursing with the old New England blood, he was confident enough of his salvation, for he had striven to live a Christian life, as best a fellow could amid a war. And while he hoped that Carrie Hunt might miss him, he knew his mother would. But she would have the consolation of his brothers and his sisters. Never quite impoverished but long faintly imperiled, the family would go on, perhaps to better things. Those who wore the name of Rhodes worked hard and traded honestly.

Still, he much preferred remaining alive. It just didn't pay to think too much about it. You had to get up when it was time, go forward when it was time, and do what had to be done. His Maker would decide all other things.

Not a bad business, though, to be positioned in the brigade's second line. Perhaps it would go so well that they'd hardly engage.

For more than a week, the plan of attack had been refined and polished, as one assault after another was scheduled, then called off. Men knew what they had to do, they'd essentially practiced it. And General Wright had taken unusual pains, approaches to the Reb lines had been scouted in detail, frontages had been paced off after dark, and the corps' three divisions echeloned right and left in formations narrow and deep for maximum power. Of course, that made them perfect targets for the Reb artillery. . . .

The Johnnies wouldn't see much in this fog, though. They'd have to guess at targets and ranges. That much was a blessing. On the other hand, Rhodes could not see the rear line of the 5th Wisconsin. Nor could he see all of his own regiment with clarity.

His orders were plain enough, though: Go straight forward. If the attack proved a success, his regiment would advance to the Boydton Plank Road and there await further orders.

Quietly, Rhodes got up on his hind legs. Lieutenant Halliday rose beside him.

"This fog . . . ," Rhodes whispered. "You take the right, I'll handle the left. Have the men uncap their rifles. Officers will have to be out front in this, and I don't want them killed by their own men by mistake."

"Or on purpose," Halliday joked.

The wit did not play well with Rhodes. "Just do it quietly."

"If I don't get lost in ten yards."

That was just the way Frank Halliday was: When he felt dread, he joked. All men handled their fear in their own way. But every man felt it who wasn't fit for the madhouse.

Rhodes worked along his regiment's two lines, bending and whispering. It was the oddest business, how leadership worked. You learned to sense things that weren't in any book. Men rendered nearly invisible by night and gun-cotton fog responded to his presence, to authority, to assurance, however false, with childlike warmth.

He saw nothing and felt everything.

A nimbler man, Halliday knelt waiting as Rhodes returned.

"Colors up," Rhodes ordered, voice still hushed. He'd grown impatient, on edge. You just never got used to this, the waiting.

The flag-bearers had been lying on their backs to protect the rolled banners. They rose awkwardly, clumsy phantoms. Their movements remained stiff as they unfurled the colors. With reverent care, in silence.

"It's *got* to be four thirty, at least," Halliday whispered, voicing Rhodes' own thoughts.

Summoned, the bugle responded. The few notes pierced the darkness with fearsome clarity.

Although they'd been enjoined to silence until they reached the Rebel rifle pits, the men—the many thousands of them all across the front—could hold back no longer. They got to their feet with a roar, howling still as they hurried to dress their ranks, receive their orders, and step off through the fog.

Placing himself five paces in front of the colors, Rhodes tried to judge where "straight ahead" might lie. He still saw no shadow or shred of the 5th Wisconsin. He heard shots now, but none were close. His habit—pointed out long before by his men—was to favor his left side as he advanced, so he tried to correct any drift by inclining rightward. Hoping he'd come out where he was meant to be.

His men moved swiftly across the uneven ground, stumbling with little gasps of surprise but maintaining their order. The fog was so thick that he could not see the blinking of the shots rising to the left.

Flashes appeared to the front, just yards away.

The report of rifles fired close stung his ears after the silence. His men cheered and rushed forward. Rhodes nearly tumbled into a rifle pit, where a Johnny raised ghostly arms and cried out, "Don't shoot, Yanks. I surrender."

More Confederate wraiths appeared, their fighting over. The advance threatened to break up, surprised by the flushed-out prisoners.

"You Johnnies. Just make for our rear, you know the way," Rhodes ordered. "Get going."

He wasn't certain he knew the way himself, but he couldn't let the assault founder so soon, his men had to press on.

Where the devil was the 5th Wisconsin? *They* should have hit the Rebel outposts first.

Cannon hammered away now. The light of their blasts diffused into the fog to become shrouded lightning.

"Second Rhode Island, forward! Maintain your alignment. Officers, guide on me, guide on my voice."

His unmistakable voice Irish as blarney, Corporal O'Hearn idiotically cried out, "Three cheers for Colonel Rhodes!"

The cheers that followed were heartening but deadly, quickly attracting more Confederate fire.

Still couldn't see a doggone thing.

"Forward!"

Artillery fire shimmered in the fog to their right and left, revealing battery positions, but there didn't seem to be any guns straight to their front. Another blessing.

Rhodes tripped and promptly corrected himself but had to withdraw the blade of his sword from the muck.

"Lieutenant Halliday . . . post to the front of the colors." Rhodes needed to see to the regiment's right companies, which seemed to lag.

Halliday rushed up and took Rhodes' position.

Rhodes feared they'd inclined too far to the right. Were that so, the 37th Massachusetts would have to be somewhere to their front. He trotted along before his advancing lines, hoping that all of the rifles had been uncapped. The newer men would be nervous, quick to yank triggers before they'd even aimed.

Instead of the Massachusetts boys, he and the soldiers near him came up on the Reb abatis, banging right into it. Good Lord, where were the pioneers who were supposed to open paths through the obstacles? Surely they hadn't *all* gone after that mule. . . .

To their front—too close—Reb rifle fire sparked. They were already at the Rebs' main line. With no one in front of them. And no inkling of how it happened.

Men cried out, but he could not tell whether they were of his kind or the enemy.

The fog was thinner, though. On a mild upslope.

"Colonel! Over here!"

As his men wrestled with the obstacles, Rhodes followed the voice of Lieutenant Dorrance.

"What is it?"

"There's a road. A trail. Something. Through the obstacles. Look. It's faint, but—"

"Quiet, they'll hear us. John," he addressed Dorrance, "run back along the line. Tell Halliday to bring the regiment this way. Guide him. Tell him to put the regiment through by the flank and re-form in line on the other side of the gap. Then go right over the works." And to the dozens of soldiers closing around him, Rhodes said, "You men, follow me!"

He drew his pistol with his left hand and cocked it with his thumb.

Rushing through the break in the obstacles, men pressed up around him, smell close, making a perfect target for even the blindest shots. Or for canister, if the Rebs turned a single gun to enfilade them.

It wasn't Reb fires that stopped them. Rhodes toppled headlong into an unseen ditch, splashing into cold, stinking water up to his thighs and striking wet earth with his chest so hard it beat the breath right out of him. Another man landed atop him. More piled in.

Several exclamations were unchristian.

They were right at the Reb earthworks. Southern voices called out in confusion. Flames streaked above their heads, but for all the commotion it wasn't clear that the Rebs knew they were there.

"Sir, there's ropes here. Two of them."

Another stroke of luck.

Grimy knotted ropes lay down the wall's steep angle, meant to help pickets slip back over the breastworks or for men to slip out and relieve themselves in the ditch . . . a prospect Rhodes preferred not to ponder, given the bath he'd just taken.

The first men scrambled up the wall without awaiting orders. Others, waiting their turns, recapped their rifles. Sword sheathed, Rhodes was the third man climbing the left rope, feet slipping on the steep grade of the wall.

They leapt in among the Johnnies, howling, a complete surprise to all of the defenders. Few resisted. Many just ran, some dropping their rifles to speed away, while others surrendered. A gun crew tried to save their piece by manhandling it off, but the members were shot down until those remaining surrendered.

The fog seemed to have confined itself to the low ground they'd passed over. In the redoubt they'd just stormed—almost by accident—the night had begun to thin.

His men kept piling in. Halliday's grin was visible yards away now.

"Thought you'd gone back to Providence, sir," the lieutenant said.

"Wouldn't mind being there just now," Rhodes told him. It was all right to kid each other again. Just not too much.

"They're forming back up, Colonel," a sergeant reported. "By them there huts."

Rhodes squinted to distinguish shadow from shadow and ordered the company officers to man the fort's rear parapet, turning it against the unvanquished Johnnies.

"Put a volley into those huts."

Rebs returned the fire.

On the right, Halliday improvised a gun crew to wield a fieldpiece against the adjacent Reb line. The lieutenant seemed to be having the time of his life.

"They're getting set to come back at us," Dorrance called.

"Halliday . . . roll that gun over here. Aim at the huts. Any canister handy?"

"I got something better than canister," Corporal Railton insisted.

The men were downright giddy. For nine months the army had sought to crack this line, and they'd been present for almost half of the contest, the rest spent out in the Valley chasing Early. And now, with astonishing ease, they'd found themselves masters of the forbidden world, or at least one part of it. They were . . . almost . . . children in Fairyland.

But a deadly fantasy it was. Railton and his chums shoved stones down the cannon's muzzle until it was too full to take much of the ramrod. Before Rhodes could warn them not to attempt to fire it, the Rebs came back at them from amid the huts, wailing their skin-a-man screech.

Rifles snapped and bit. Railton yanked the lanyard.

The barrel burst near the muzzle and men flew backward. But the improvised canister stopped the Reb rush cold.

Corporal Railton regained his feet, wearing a look of wonder and some blood streaks. Men laughed and teased him about joining the artillery.

The darkness had softened enough to see movement a hundred yards off and more. But Rhodes could not spot another Union regiment, not in any direction.

Around them, battle crackled, thundered, and screamed.

After assigning a detail to plant the national flag on the fort's banked wall and guard it, Rhodes had the bulk of his men file out the rear of the fort, form back into two lines, and advance behind the regimental colors, rifles at trail arms and bayonets pointed. They passed over wounded Rebs, some badly disfigured. One corpse had a stone embedded deep in a ruptured face.

No, it wasn't Fairyland.

Confederate stragglers approached with their arms high.

How could it be this easy? After all the death? His regiment hardly seemed to have suffered casualties.

His orders were to advance to the Boydton Plank Road. And if he got there alone, well, someone had to be first.

Rhodes repeated his order: "Forward!"

There was no resistance at all.

Five a.m.
Venable cottage, Confederate lines, Petersburg

A. P. Hill woke in pain. He lived with pain. Weeks earlier, his ailment had struck him so fiercely that he had needed to take leave, again, from the army. One mistake on a Saturday night away from West Point in his youth, a single indiscretion in New York City, and he'd paid for it all his life.

This morning, though, something else was wrong. He could feel it.

Hill rose as gently as he could. Letting his wife sleep. The bombardment had kept her awake until well after midnight. Dolly wasn't as strong that way as some of the other wives. He could not see the fineness of her features in the dark, only strands of hair on a white cheek, but he knew the look of her by heart and loved her.

He had thought it ill-judged for her to return to Petersburg, especially given the late stage of her pregnancy, but Dolly had insisted. And he craved her presence, any form of nearness to her, adoring the prim set of her face turned to the day's affairs and the lush, familiar scent of her at night.

He drew his nightshirt over his head and tossed it toward the outline of a chair. From a hook, he took down the paleness of his new shirt, sewn by his wife of linen of a quality now rare. His instinct had been to pull on his calico battle shirt, his lucky charm, given the unsettled temper that had woken him. But Dolly had been wonderfully proud as she'd presented her gift the day before. She would expect to see it on him today.

He waited until he stepped outside, into the ebbing darkness, before he turned to urinate on a bush. He didn't want his groans to wake his wife, to worry her further. The doctor's latest inspection had not been encouraging.

Finished, he closed his eyes and breathed, letting the pain ghost off as he buttoned his trousers. He did not know how much more he could bear.

In the distance, the usual morning exchanges rang out, sentinels spooked by hants as the dark receded, cannon annoying the enemy as the picket lines were refreshed. But was it something more? Or was he succumbing to worry, hearing phantoms?

Certainly, there was much to worry about. He had returned to duty the day before to find his lines plundered of men, the soldiers defending his stretch of the front spread as thinly as a skirmish line. The last batch of soldiers had been sent to the right, in a shift to allow the reinforcement of Pickett, who had behaved far worse in his private life than Hill had done, but who never seemed to suffer any consequences.

Before lying down by his wife the night before—hoping the bed would ease the misery caused by riding long to inspect his lines—Hill had been warned that Pickett had just suffered a reverse, perhaps a severe defeat, out by Five Forks. But Hill's flesh had been too aggrieved to allow him to wait up for more reports.

He crossed the road to the Widow Knight's. Billy Palmer was already up, standing by a parlor lamp, borrowed china cup steaming in his hand. The corps chief of staff looked tense. Palmer never did sport a poker face.

"Was just about to rouse you, General. You saved me the worrying."

"Looks like you've got other worries, Billy. Something doing?"

Palmer held up his drink. Hill shook his head. What passed for coffee made things worse.

No, matters didn't feel right. Didn't feel right at all.

"Sent Norrie Starke to have a look at things," the colonel told him. "Hours ago. He just got back. Federals seem to have gotten into our lines down around Rives' salient. There's been an assault on Gordon's lines, as well. And that bombardment last night. May be a major push, just my opinion."

"Any more details?"

"None. Ground fog on top of the darkness. Norrie pieced things together best he could."

"Not many pieces."

"No, sir. Not yet."

"Nothing from Harry Heth? Or Cad? Wilcox would report, if he had trouble."

"Nothing."

Hill sighed, dreading the thought of dropping his groin back onto a saddle. The pain would shoot up to his shoulder blades. It was like that first morning at Gettysburg, only worse.

"Everybody up? Out in the tent?"

"Mostly. Rest are rising. They had a late night, General."

"Let's hope it's not a long day. Billy, you stay here. You keep a watch on things. I'll ride over to Edge Hill, see General Lee."

"Should I go with you, sir? In case he has orders?"

"You stay here. Just get the staff up and cracking. Have the headquarters ready to move, if it comes to that."

"Shouldn't be that bad," Palmer said. "Norrie didn't report a major breakthrough."

"Major breakthroughs start with minor breakthroughs. Send out a few more riders, I want complete reports. See that Heth and Wilcox are alerted. I'd rather plug a small hole than a big one."

And he stepped out, aching, to call for his horse. His servant, bless him, already had it saddled.

"Sergeant Tucker? Tucker, where are you?"

"Him be grooming that big ol' gelding he ride."

The sergeant came around the side of the house in the first tease of light.

"Have your couriers ready, Tucker?"

"Day and night, General. Ain't let you down yet."

"Who's on duty?"

"Jenkins and Kirkpatrick."

"They'll come with me. To army headquarters. See that all of your other men are up and jumping. Then you ride after me."

Tucker saluted. "Yes, sir." The sergeant turned sharply, barking, "Jenkins! Kirkpatrick! Muster up now, or you'll see me in the corncrib."

By a mighty act of will, Powell Hill stirruped his left foot and levered himself high onto Champ's broad back. He tried to land softly, but the pain was still such that it bent him over the horse's mane.

The couriers appeared, leading their mounts. Hill didn't bother with further commands. He just turned Champ's head and nudged up the animal's power, encompassed once more by the reek of horse and the smell of sweat-burnished leather. Hill rode with his rump in the air, jockey style, hardly caring if he looked a fool. Helped the pain a little.

What was he going to do if it got so bad he couldn't command at all? The interruptions in service were sorry enough. What would men think of him, if he slunk off home?

It wasn't much over a mile to the house Lee's staff had chosen as headquarters—a finer place than Lee would have picked himself—but the brief ride was alarming. Individual stragglers and clusters of soldiers wandered from the direction of Wilcox's lines. Then there were more. Hill didn't need to question the runaways to recognize trouble in a glutton's portion.

Sergeant Tucker caught up at a gallop, and Hill ordered Kirkpatrick back to corps headquarters: Colonel Palmer should send out the staff to halt the fleeing troops, to re-form them and send them back into the fight.

With his new shirt already sweated through under his uniform coat, he reined up before Edge Hill, old man Turnbull's place and, temporarily, Lee's abode. Pale with tents, the yard hosted a commotion.

Lee was still upstairs, half-dressed and hair disheveled. Longstreet was with him, the two of them burly enough to fill the bedroom. Space enough for a scarecrow, though, Hill thought as he slipped in. And that's what I've become, bones under rags.

But that was unjust. Given the handsome shirt he wore this

day. Bones, then, under linen smooth and supple, if a bit damp now.

It was odd, a downright rarity, to see Robert E. Lee unkempt and slumping, eyes wishing they had been allowed to sleep.

Lee wasted no time with niceties. He demanded, "What do you have to tell me, General Hill?"

"Matter's unclear, sir, but it looks like Wilcox has gotten into trouble. Had one report of Yankees passed over Rives' salient. I hoped you might know—"

Lee's eyes flashed anger. "I expect intelligence from *you* regarding events in the Third Corps lines."

Pete Longstreet just looked on. He appeared weary, too. Long night traveling from Richmond, Hill suspected.

"Yes, sir," Hill agreed. "It's being looked into. We'll put things right."

"First," Lee said, still annoyed, "we must know what is wrong. Before we can put it right."

Before Hill could reply, boots pounded the stairs.

Venable of Lee's staff came in without knocking, behavior ever forbidden in Lee's circle.

"General, the Yankees . . . their skirmishers are less than a mile away. Hardly more than a half mile. River Road's madcap with wagons, teamsters fleeing every which way."

Controlling his temper—but still formidable—Lee asked, "Where, precisely, are those people, Colonel?"

"My apologies, sir. They're last reported down by Harris' winter shacks."

The statement made Lee wince. He wasn't yet master of his daytime mask.

Lee rose, reaching for a shirt. "We must see to this. Colonel Venable, you will send out scouts immediately. And go back out yourself. I want to know exactly where those people are, how many, and who they belong to. We cannot delay." His eyes hardened. "Do not *linger,* Colonel."

Venable took himself off, but Hill said, "I need to look to this myself, sir. Problem's in my corps' area. I'm responsible."

"I do not detain you, General." Lee's voice was cold.

But as Hill touched the door latch to overtake Venable, Lee added in a softer tone, "Look to your safety, General Hill. I shall need you."

When Hill strode out of the house, Sergeant Tucker and Private Jenkins leapt into their saddles. His bearing and haste were all the command they needed.

"Colonel Venable," Hill called, "wait, we'll go together."

And they did. As the four men rode along, pausing briefly at Cattail Run to let their mounts lap a drink, Hill tried to read the battle sounds. Along his own stretch of line, he couldn't be certain whether the noise had increased or faded off, but it certainly sounded as though a full-up fight was in progress a few miles to the east, in Gordon's lines around Petersburg. Not much fuss to the west, not at the moment. Just some sparring.

As the riders crested a low ridge, a pair of Yankees strolled out of a copse, as easy of manner as if on a holiday lark, careless of their rifles. When they spotted the horsemen, they tried to flee, but the party quickly surrounded them.

If Yankees had already made it this far . . .

Hill looked at the tops of their caps. "Sixth Corps?" he asked.

One man nodded, the other grunted something near to a yes.

"You, Jenkins. Take them back to General Lee's headquarters, let them tell their tales. Run 'em. And if they won't run worth a lick, you can just shoot them."

Jenkins would do no such thing, of course. Prisoners were prisoners. But the charge did liven up the brace of Federals.

Disheartened Confederates appeared. Venable tried to organize them, but many were visibly heart-quit, reliable only as long as they were watched.

What was happening to his corps?

A courier caught up with news that an element of the Second Corps artillery had been overrun. So it wasn't just his stretch that was in trouble.

A soldier, hewn spare by war and perhaps ashamed of his flight, looked up at Hill and said, "Yankees are thick as termites on an old log thataway. Best you look out, General."

Sidling up on his well-bred mount, Venable seconded the advice. "Turn back, sir? Try another route?"

"I've got to see what's happening on my right," Hill said, spurring Champ.

Pain made him groan again.

The others followed him through a swale and up another rise. This time, it was Sergeant Tucker who mouthed his concern:

"General, where the devil are we going? Seems to me we're heading straight for the Yankees."

"I've got to get to the *right*. I know this ground, Sergeant. We can reach General Heth's headquarters in a few minutes."

But he did agree to follow the bed of Cattail Run, where the party on horseback would be shielded from view for a stretch. Then, topping a slope, Hill spotted artillery—Confederate guns—drawn up in a field, doing nothing.

"Venable, whose guns might they be? Any idea?" Hill called over the hoofbeats and various snorts.

"Should be Poague's Battalion, sir. Just down from Mahone's front, from Dutch Gap."

"Colonel, you ride over there and tell them I said they're to deploy to guard your headquarters. Show them the way." He turned to look at the courier who'd joined them, a young fellow named Hawes. "Go with the colonel, son. The fewer we are, the less attention we'll get from our Yankee brethren."

That left only Tucker riding beside him.

"Should we cut by your headquarters, sir?" Tucker asked. "Wouldn't be so far. See to the doings? You might be needed."

Hill almost snapped that he didn't require a nursemaid.

"No time for that. I must speak with General Heth."

The sergeant was clearly worried, though. About his charge, not himself. Well, Hill was hardly delighted with the situation, or what he understood of it. But he needed to know that Heth was standing firm, if he could spare a brigade to plug any hole. Then he'd ride back to see Wilcox and take charge, if Cad was struggling.

He did acknowledge the sergeant's concern sufficiently to tell him, "If anything should happen to me, you get off quick and tell General Lee. Understand?"

Tucker nodded.

They halted in a high field with a view of the Boydton Plank Road. The middle distance was crowded with troops. Hill uncased his field glasses.

"Dear God," he said. "Must be a full brigade of them."

"Which way now, sir?"

Hill nodded toward a wood line. "We get down there, we're covered. Time to ride hard, Tucker."

Even now, the pain from his male parts up along both sides of his spine would not grant a reprieve. But he brought Champ to a gallop, pain be damned. Sergeant Tucker kept up on his left, doing his best to put himself between Hill and the enemy.

But the Federals were already in the grove. As the horsemen neared, a passel of Yankees bolted, but two dashed out to a lone oak and leveled their muskets.

"Turn back, sir," Tucker called. "We can't outshoot rifles."

But Hill had drawn his pistol. "We have to take them."

"Stay here! I'll do it!"

Tucker rode for the Yankees, calling, "Pull those triggers and you'll be swept to hell. Our boys are all around you, best surrender."

Hill drew up beside the sergeant, pistol extended.

One of the Yankees eased his rifle from his shoulder, thinking better of his impulsive challenge. It was going to be all right, it was going to be fine.

But the other Yankee snapped out words Hill couldn't hear, and the doubtful one raised his rifle again.

They both fired.

Six thirty a.m.
Captured Confederate lines

His men were exhausted. And hungry. And exuberant.

No payday had ever rivaled the delight the troops felt as they marched across the fields so long denied them. Now and again, Rebs rose from a hide to surrender, but mostly the bristling lines passed deserted camps, abandoned wagons, and the occasional body.

Rhodes felt as elated as any private. A bit bewildered, he was kept wide-awake by the thrill of the morning. They'd been recalled from the Plank Road, an order that made little sense to Rhodes, only to receive a command still more surprising. He'd thought they might have been gathered back up to advance on Petersburg, to force their way through any inner defenses and take the city. Instead, General Wheaton had ordered them to face west, to roll up any Confederates separated from Lee's army. Rhodes could only trust in his superiors and rely upon the mercy of the Lord.

General Wheaton had been marvelous, though, praising the actions of the 2nd Rhode Island. By the fortunes of war, they'd somehow become the first regiment in his division to plant a banner on the Reb entrenchments.

And his men had caught a stray Reb horse to substitute for the mount left behind when they moved to the attack. The beast was a bit gaunt, but its saddle and blanket were of the finest sort. He rode at the head of his regiment, with only flankers and skirmishers to the fore, one proud man among a victorious army, an army of conquerors.

He did wish Carrie Hunt could see him now, powder smears, mud, and all.

Seven a.m.
Edge Hill

Tears crowded Lee's eyes as he looked up at the sergeant, but there was discipline in his quiet speech.

"Well, he is at rest now. We . . . we who are left behind are the ones to suffer."

"There was nothing I could do, General. Nothing. . . ."

Lee nodded. He was glad he had spoken kindly to Hill at the last. Often, he had chastised him, perhaps with more severity than he brought to bear on others of similar rank. If so, the reasons were not to be pondered now. The loss was immense, the death of Ambrose Powell Hill counted at least as much as—nay, more than—the disaster Pickett had called upon himself the day before.

War was unjust. Pickett lived, while Hill lay dead, his body left to the foe.

He turned to Colonel Palmer, who had intercepted the sergeant and had accompanied him to Lee's headquarters. As Hill's chief of staff, Palmer would have more than enough to do in the growing crisis. Yet the personal had its place. Even today.

"Colonel, I must ask that you inform Mrs. Hill, if you would." He added, "Break the news to her gently."

Palmer's eyes, too, had grown wet. A hard and ready man, the colonel stood helpless for a terrible moment. Then he said:

"Come along, Tucker."

Mouth slack and features glum, the sergeant coaxed his horse back onto the road, careful of the staff men jostling around him.

The man would blame himself, Lee saw. For the rest of his life. But there was nothing to be done.

He drew out his clean handkerchief—chosen that morning—and dabbed his eyes.

"Well, gentlemen," he said, "we shall honor General Hill by fighting well."

Those people would have a bitter time of it yet.

Lee stepped toward his headquarters tent. He had put on a fine uniform, belted and sashed, and wore a newly presented, gilt-handled sword. Hair smoothed, he'd knotted his black cravat precisely. A good appearance bred confidence; it was an article of faith with him that went back beyond West Point. And his soldiers would need much confidence today.

Yet, as he trod the ruined lawn, he felt as though he had dressed up for a funeral.

Eight a.m.
Gordon's lines, Petersburg

A hooley in Hell, it was. With the Banshee's bitch for a partner. You shot the buggers down, and still they came at you. You gave them steel, and they danced a jig with their guts drawn out like sausages, but the next one wanted a rifle butt to his snout to learn his manners. And just when you thought the reel had played out, the hard tune started over.

They'd come across the dead ground in the darkness, hollering to annoy the dear departed, piling on by the Crater again, as if they'd taken no lessons, and as the heavens lifted their skirts to let the daylight in, Riordan and his fellow Louisianans, the few of them standing up on two legs still, had been ordered up from the pitiful reserve by Colonel Waggaman, whose wound from the Stedman fuss should have sent him home, but no, not he, and up they rushed in time for a gay to-do, with Yankees everywhere. Evans the Prayer and Gordon the Glory had ridden up themselves, stupidly careless of bullets, scratching their throats dry with orders until they'd spoiled any singing they had in them.

They'd beaten back the Yankees twice and thrice, only to be recalled and shifted to another gouge in the line. At one point, the Federals pushed in deep enough to create opportunities for a man of enterprise, and Riordan had parried a captain's sword, then bashed him in the eye with the point of his rifle's butt. Oh, blood there had been and cries, and when he had the boy kneeling, perhaps thinking to surrender, Riordan had put a quick stop to the prospect, bringing the butt down on the sweetness of his neck until his head lolled like a rock loose in a sack. A beautiful watch the boy had carried, blessedly protected in a pocket. 'Twas a small reward for a morning of hard work.

Jesus and Mary, though.

"I'm out of bleeding bullets," a comrade called, one of the handful who, like Riordan, had been too foolish to see the wisdom in leaving the army while the leaving was good. Riordan cursed his pigheadedness, pledging his envy of wiser men who'd gone, even as he realized that he'd never go, not as long as it lasted. After all, they'd hang a man for killing a boy and taking his watch in peacetime, when now it led only to praise: "Riordan there yonder, that bucko's a fiend in a fight."

Little Paddy Murphy came up, swishing the blood from his mug. His eyes were as wild as the women deep in the hills, where the law of the priests went not.

"We licked 'em, we did. Did ye see that, Daniel Riordan?"

"You're in the wrong company, boyo."

"What of it? I am where I am. And who's to say you're not in the wrong place yourself, for the ballyhooley?"

"Get any goods worth the mention?"

Murphy shook his head. "Must not have been paid of late. Empty pockets, the most of them."

"Ah, they're growing too wise. Seen Keegan, have ye? And standing up?"

"The last I saw. I liked him better, I did, when he was a whistling man. Before he took up his stripes."

"Well, he's none the worse nor better. I'd miss the great fool, though."

Someone shouted, "They're coming back! They're coming."

"Damned fools," Riordan declared, "the dirty buggers."

And come on they did, flags flying, storming up to the parapets, creatures of vicious tenacity, like the manor agent come to collect the rents.

Nine a.m.
Gordon's lines, Petersburg

It's bad, Clem." Gordon looked up from the message just received. "Hill's dead. His front has collapsed. Anderson's cut off, along with the cavalry. Longstreet's hurrying reinforcements from Richmond, but . . ." He felt a smirk harden his face. "*Our* front's the only stretch that's hanging on. Wilcox is making a stand west of the city—trying to, anyway—but Lee needs us to hold, at least until nightfall."

"Which means . . ."

"We're leaving. End of this particular cotillion. We have to keep the Yankees out of the streets until the others get over the bridges, get north of the river, run west. Here. Read it yourself. You don't have to worry about restoring lost lines. Just hold them off wherever you can and keep them out of Petersburg till dark."

Bullets hissed and shells fired long shrieked madly. Federal hurrahs resounded. The Yankees had gotten a taste of Southern blood, they wouldn't quit.

Evans looked downcast. Poor Clem had believed in victory to the end. Perhaps he still did, even now. Mild Clem, of the Methodist Church militant.

Evans sighed like a circuit preacher with a hard ride ahead of him.

"Like to be a long day, John."

" 'Many are called, but few are chosen.' I reckon we've been chosen. Go on back now, see to your division. I'll ride over to Grimes and make sure he hasn't gone off on a holiday."

Before he swung his horse about, Evans asked, "Fanny?"

"Challenge to keep that gal in her bed, she'll be calling for a musket."

"A boy, I hear. Congratulations."

"Probably hooting and hollering for a pistol to guard his mama."

The humor was hollow, inept, untrue. Neither man managed a smile worth a penny.

"I truly hate this," Gordon said. "I hate it to my core."

"The war?"

"No. Getting whipped."

Ten a.m.
Edge Hill

As the headquarters packed up around him, Walter Taylor carried Lee's message to the telegrapher's tent, whose occupants had been forbidden to dismantle their apparatus. It was his last military task of the day before he set out for Richmond. Startled at first by the timing of Taylor's request, Lee had grasped the import in moments and granted him twenty-four hours' leave from the army to marry his Bettie. But first it was his duty to transmit the darkest message yet sent in the war.

To ensure no word was mistaken, Taylor read the text aloud to the sergeant tapping the key:

> *I see no prospect of doing more than holding our position here till night. I am not certain that I can do that. If I can I shall withdraw tonight north of the Appomattox, and, if possible, it will be better to withdraw the whole line tonight from James River. The brigades on Hatcher's Run are cut off from us. Enemy have broken through our lines. I advise that all preparation be made for leaving Richmond tonight.*

EIGHT

Eleven twenty a.m., April 2, 1865
St. Paul's Church, Richmond

President Jefferson Davis sat rigidly in his pew, incensed at God for His treatment of the Confederacy. From the pulpit, Dr. Minnigerode read an irrelevant chapter from Zechariah as worshippers judged each other's faded finery. Davis revealed no sign of his agitation, but he could not help feeling that everyone, in Heaven and on earth, had let the South down. His countrymen and their harping wives were more concerned with promotions or touched-up silks than with their duties.

How had it come to this desperation? Would the Lord overturn the order he had decreed? Slavery was ordained and beneficial—not least for the Negro. To "free" the coloreds would be akin to loosing helpless pets into the wild: Those who did not turn feral would go hungry, a burden to all and benefit to none.

At times, he felt himself another Job. He had striven to serve the purposes of his kind, only to be assailed by greed and venality. Governors cheated, legislators quarreled, generals failed, and speculators lobbied. While Lincoln, the great ape, gloated from afar.

And then his toddler son had died, leaving Varina bereft and hollow of heart.

That very morning, before Davis could reach Richmond's one acceptable church, Reagan, the postmaster general, had waylaid him with an incoherent report of trouble at Petersburg. With behavior short of a gentleman's, the fellow had shown alarm in a public street.

Lee was failing him, too, of course. Still, he couldn't credit Reagan's hand-wringing. Lee was forever warning of catastrophe, and

Davis had learned to brush the fears aside. Lee was simply protecting his reputation, in case things did go badly.

The army had held off Grant for almost a year. No doubt it would hold longer. Despite Lee's playing Cassandra.

Davis had already nursed suspicions about Lee down in Mexico, when the latecomer's achievements had garnered excessive praise, while his own decisive action at Buena Vista was noted, but soon eclipsed. Much of that could be credited to Army jealousy, of course: His Mississippi Rifles had outdone the Regulars, but Robert E. Lee had become the man *à la mode.*

Reagan's stricken eyes leapt back to mind. What if the crisis *had* come? And why? Why should Great Jehovah permit such a thing? Had Southron lack of fervor angered the Lord? Had they failed in rigor, in righteousness? How could they be so judged, when it was the North that embraced the Golden Calf?

Was this but a test of God's people? Would he finally emerge, like Job, in blessed raiment?

Minnigerode closed the Book. Davis wished the old Hessian would hurry Communion along. He needed to return to his office and find out whether the trouble Reagan had blabbered about had any substance to it.

A hand tapped his shoulder. Davis turned a cold look on the offender. He did not like to be touched.

It was the sexton, Irving, who allowed himself imperial pretensions. With a gesture more pompous than discreet, he offered Davis a note.

Davis felt an impulse to wave the man off, but given the morning's unsettled tenor, he took the folded paper.

It was a copied telegraphic message from Lee to Breckinridge, the secretary of war. Lee had, as always, been careful to go through the proper chain of command. This day, Davis wished he had not. But Lee was as sly as the rest of them, wrapping himself in the armor of formalities.

Davis read the message. It burned his soul.

What had Lee done? Betrayed him, betrayed the South. How

dared he presume to order Richmond's evacuation? Davis could read the message as nothing less than that, a brazen usurpation of his authority, no matter how artfully Robert E. Lee had couched it. Lee cared more about his army than he did about the capital. It was . . . barely short of treason.

With no change of expression, Davis rose. Careful to maintain a commanding posture, he walked back up the aisle to the entrance.

He had known it from the start, he'd known Lee would give up Richmond, the signs had always been there. He regretted that he had ever trusted the man. He'd been warned that Lee's side of the family had bad blood.

Jefferson Davis emerged into a perfect April day, an unappreciated gift from God.

Twelve fifteen p.m.
Harmon house

Grant was a queer old bird, in Lyman's view. There the fellow stood, conferring with Meade and a passing array of generals, besieged by colonels eager to be noticed, and cheered by any troops passing through the scene, but the fellow hardly seemed moved by the day's events. Smoking, or at least chomping, a cigar, Grant alternated between a sort of attentive blankness and intermittent smiles worthy of the Sphinx. Now and then he scribbled a message. One would never have taken him for a general deciding a great nation's fate.

Yet, there Grant was, victorious, after nine months of grappling for Petersburg. At best, he might have passed for a middling farmer awaiting his wife on their Saturday trip to town. Men whooped and jabbered around him, but Grant just gave an ear to Meade or calmly took in a report, nodding almost vacantly and shifting his posture only to grind a cigar stub to its death.

Grant was a genius, Lyman supposed. In his way. Not of the mental fireworks sort, no Professor Agassiz, of course. Yet the fellow had seen what others could not, what war required of men in modern times. The oddity made Lyman wonder if he shouldn't throw over his work in marine biology to study the human mind, that ultimate riddle. Generals truly were a breed apart, begging for microscopic examination.

Theodore Lyman smiled to himself: Wouldn't that be a change of specialty, though? From starfish to the men with stars on their shoulders.

In their defense, starfish were more manageable.

A mile off, blue lines hurrahed and rushed to keep up with their flags.

What a delight the morning had been! The good news had resurrected dear old Meade, who had cast aside his sickness to lead his staff on a ride up the Boydton Plank Road, a route forbidden them all until this day. Everywhere they met cheering soldiers, dejected prisoners, abandoned wagons, and all the waste of war. With the sun benign and the sky blue overhead, it seemed as if the heavens themselves had gone for the Union at last.

From Lyman's vantage point—chosen by Grant's staff—the panorama was splendid. All the world teemed and blazed, from the dizzying signal tower to the southeast, from whence the attack had advanced, to the lead works' chimneys to the northeast, around which the Johnnies scrambled, doing their best to form a new line of defense.

Well, the jig was up. One almost felt sorry for those in gray, though not for their odious cause.

Babcock, one of Grant's acolytes, sauntered over.

"Well, Lyman, what's the Harvard view on matters?"

"I should think much the same as yours."

"Grant brought it off, though, didn't he?"

"General Meade had a part in the play, I believe."

Babcock laughed. "Not how Sheridan's bound to tell it. Lucky if he leaves any credit for Grant."

"Glory enough for all. Don't you think so, Babcock?"

Grant's man snickered, as if told a nasty joke. "There's *never* glory enough for all. Old Meade had best look to it."

Without further explanation, Babcock took himself back to Grant's coterie. Grinning, he slapped Badeau on the shoulder and nodded back toward Lyman—who did not believe that Grant was a fine judge of character.

What a curious man Grant was, with his famed aversion to the sight of blood, even on a beefsteak, and his matter-of-fact acceptance of the casualty lists. At times, he seemed almost childlike, a simple man of the West. Then, on the next occasion, the man's depths seemed incalculable. Grant's contradictions would have befuddled Aristotle.

Lyman recalled that incident in the Wilderness—so very long ago, it seemed, although it was less than a year—when Meade had needed to step over and straighten Grant's coat, patting down the lapels to draw him back into the battle's reality.

Newly positioned Reb batteries hurled shells, but their targets were the soldiers forming up for a fresh assault, not this outing of generals and staff men. Gibbon had come up with his corps to push into Petersburg, but it seemed a pair of small forts stood in his way. From Lyman's position, the Reb defenses didn't look like much, but he'd learned to keep such opinions to himself.

Webb, Meade's chief of staff, approached at a strut.

"I suppose your friend Barlow doesn't much care for being left back today."

"Oh, Frank's a good sport," Lyman said staunchly and dishonestly.

"Someone has to reckon out the march tables. Have to move fast, if Lee gets off with any part of his force. Run the old fellow down, get the business done."

A repositioned Federal battery opened, forbidding speech.

After the number six gun had fired, Webb added, "Barlow should have waited for his orders. Like any other officer. Before dropping in like some Boston social call."

Lyman doubted that Webb knew much about Boston social calls, but his response was confined by good manners: "Frank's always been precocious. Patience never counted among his virtues."

"Well, he's not as special as he thinks, I'll tell you that. He's lucky Meade didn't send him back to Baltimore. Where he was supposed to settle his ass until his orders came through."

Lyman finally caught the note of jealousy—unexpected from Webb, who wasn't a bad fellow. Barlow did bring out the green-eyed monster, especially among the Regulars. Whom he'd quite outdone on one field after another.

"Well, Frank's atoning for all his sins today," Lyman said as amicably as he could. "Mathematics was never his happiest study."

Webb snorted. "He'd better not make a mess of moving this Army."

"He does have your staff's assistance, of course." Lyman smiled, hoping to imitate Grant's inscrutability. "Frank shan't fail."

Just then, Meade beckoned. For a moment, it was unclear which man was wanted. It turned out to be Webb.

So Lyman went back to the spectacle, watching Gibbon's legions move up to brush those forts aside.

Really, though, he couldn't help feeling a bit of secret glee at Frank's discomfiture. When a Fifth Corps division had come open, Barlow had let it be known—beyond the bounds of good taste—that he'd welcome the command, even if it wasn't in his old Second Corps. But that same hour it had emerged that Frank had bullied his way to Petersburg without the War Department's authorization. The purveyors of boundless bureaucracy in Washington thought him still in Baltimore. Frank was lucky that Meade—who really wasn't the crab he was often painted—had taken an indulgent view of things. But there'd be no division for Frank until the proper orders were in place.

Barlow had been the same fellow at Harvard, presuming to stand a step above the common run of his uncommon classmates. The faculty pashas and emirs had forgiven his infidelity for his brilliance.

Theodore Lyman had to admit the truth: Frank's besting of him for the title of valedictorian grated still. Just a bit.

The cannonade intensified, but Lyman was certain the Johnnies were getting the worst of it. Seen from a distance, they looked few and disorderly. They'd collapsed everywhere except right in front of Petersburg, where Parke's Ninth Corps pushed forward at a crawl.

Teddy Lyman felt a wave of shame: He mustn't take pleasure in Frank Barlow's predicament. Poor Frank had lost so much, a wife, his health, his command. And they were Harvard men and classmates, too. Even fellow Bostonians, although Frank's pedigree had a stain or two. And Frank wasn't always nice.

Mimi had always found Barlow greatly amusing, which baffled Lyman. Couldn't see that side of him at all. But his wife had a mind and tastes of her own, quite pleasant ones. Most of the time.

That winter, he'd been tempted to resign his commission to join Agassiz on his great journey to Brazil. He'd decided against it, though, partly because, having come to the war late, he felt it would be bad form to leave it early, but primarily because he didn't wish to be separated from Mimi for one more year. As soon as peace triumphed, he meant to go high-tail for Boston and his old life: studies in the fresh of the day, late afternoons at the club, and dinners at home with delicious chat among the very best people and Mimi reigning handsomely over the table.

That would be the life he resumed, but what would become of Barlow? Against character, breeding, and reason, he'd become enraptured with war. Could he simply return to his law books and decent society?

Lyman expected the war to end within days after such a triumph, but he did hope it would last long enough for his old friend to get a division command again.

Barlow seemed as unsuited to peace as Grant.

One p.m.
Edge Hill

With Longstreet somber beside him and Venable standing off, Lee read the return message from President Davis. When he finished it, he tore the paper in two, crumpled the shreds, and threw the wad on the ground.

Longstreet's heavy face froze, and Venable stood drop-jawed. Lee had surprised himself, too, and regretted the action immediately. Never in his career had he done anything so coarsely insubordinate.

But he did not stoop to take up the message again. Nor did he share its contents. There was no need. Those around him understood too well the festering differences between his views and Richmond's. He was struggling to save the army, the Confederacy's last hope, and the president's message had chastised him because Richmond's loss meant abandoning government stores and "valuables." Davis insinuated—no, all but announced—that he had been negligent.

Lee would reply as a gentleman, with appropriate respect for the president's office, but he could not recall feeling such outrage. At least, not since those childhood taunts from cousins of greater privilege.

"I didn't want to interrupt . . . ," Longstreet said, voice subdued against battle's snap and roar.

"No, no. What is it?"

"I should have more of Field's men up by three."

By three? Could Wilcox hold out so long? Those two slight forts, Gregg and Whitworth . . . how much time could they purchase?

"How many?" Lee asked.

"Five hundred. More later."

Not enough. Where was his splendid Army of Northern Virginia? Dead, like Powell Hill.

He had been told that Hill's widow had borne up bravely, but Lee did not doubt that with her door shut behind her, Mrs. Hill had bent to embrace her grief. He knew the cost of restraint before the world, each moment of false composure compounding the torment.

"Well, we must make do." Lee turned to Venable. "Did Colonel Taylor get off?"

"Yes, sir. Dashed for the ambulance train to Richmond."

Lee had been appalled by Taylor's unexpected request—at such a juncture—for a day's leave to wed his sweetheart. He had almost lost his temper then, too, but had paused long enough to see with the young man's eyes: the army bound to retreat and Taylor's beloved Miss Saunders abandoned in Richmond. Taylor had asked for nothing over his years of dutiful service. And so, that horrid morning, Lee bade him go.

And then he thought of his own wife in her rolling chair, and of his spinster daughters, all of them trapped in Richmond because of his pride.

General Wilcox rode up, his retinue reduced to one flag-bearer and a two-man staff. Wilcox was ashamed of the morning's debacle and eager to make it up.

Lee's face grew stern, assuming the visage Wilcox needed to see.

"Beg to report, sir." The division commander's whiskers dangled.

"What is it, General Wilcox?"

"Fort Gregg's filled to bursting, all the men I can fit along the walls." He took off his hat, as if come upon a burial. His hair was uncombed and matted. "Hotchpotch, I'm afraid. Mississippians, Georgians, a few North Carolinians. All splintered off from their proper commands, just rounded 'em up. Say three hundred in all. And two guns. Louisiana and Maryland crews. Best I could cobble together, but they'll fight."

"They *must* fight. They must purchase us two hours. Cost what it may."

"Yes, sir. I told 'em. Rode in there myself. They promised they'll hold, they're pledged to it. Looks like the Yankees are lining up two divisions, though. At least two. Just against Gregg. More against Battery Whitworth. And maybe another corps closing on the river." Wilcox looked toward Longstreet, as if for support. Longstreet said nothing, so Wilcox added, "It's all about Fort Gregg, though. Whitworth's weak, can't be defended if Gregg goes."

Coldly, Lee told him, "I am not disposed, General Wilcox, to be told what cannot be done."

One fifteen p.m.
Petersburg, Gordon's front

"Doing all right, Kyd?" Gordon asked, looking down from the saddle.

Masked by sweat and powder, the major called, "Middling, General. Not so good as I'd like." His voice was loud, his hearing numbed by battle. "Getting by, though. Getting by."

"About sums up the day, I'd say."

The two men glanced beyond the caps and shoulders of their men, beyond their weapons, beyond this final rampart, to the new Yankee position, gained with corpses.

"I do believe I could retake that line, sir. Hit them while they're getting ready to hit us again, surprise them."

It was precisely what Gordon would have done on another field. Major Henry Kyd Douglas was a good student. But Gordon shook his head. "No point now. Waste of lives. Just hold the inner line, right where you are."

"Yankees been giving a fair account of themselves," the younger man credited. "Feeling some hurt, though."

"Well, make them feel some more."

Gordon had ridden up intending to pull Kyd Douglas from command, to set his erstwhile adjutant to work to plan the best order of march and routes for withdrawal to join the retreat that had become inevitable. It was evident to Gordon that his men would be the last to cross the bridges, becoming, by default, the army's rear guard. The movement would be a challenge, to put it lightly, disengaging from a vigilant enemy. Clear thinking was wanted, experience, guile, and firmness, all of which young Douglas had in excess. But seeing the major in the thick of the fight, leading a brigade as if he'd been born to it, Gordon decided that other officers possessed sufficient skill to plot the movement.

The corps was a great deal smaller than it had been, a leaner instrument. He felt as if he'd returned to division command.

To the west, on the other side of Petersburg, the firing swelled again.

"Just hold right here, Kyd," Gordon told his adjutant. "And I'd view it as a personal affront, were you to get yourself killed short of necessity."

"Hadn't planned on it, sir."

"Don't."

Struggling to beat down thoughts of his wife and baby, Gordon turned back to convince other men of miracles.

One thirty p.m.
Fort Gregg

Weren't fair, weren't right, not hardly. Private Frank Edwards shot down Yankees like they was hogs in a pen, aimed truly and shot them down as they crossed the field—those that weren't turned into puffs of blood and scraps by canister—and then he shot them down as they fought through the abatis, all but holding still for him to aim for a chest or belly, and once he crawled out onto the top of the rampart to shoot down at them teeming like worms in the water ditch, at least ten feet below, Yankees at his mercy. He killed them, exulting, and yet they kept on coming, ants got onto a pie, and then more of them came on and it just weren't right.

Hot as summer on that wall, with the best shots standing on the firing step, potting the Yankees like crippled deer, that easy, and other men, less bold, loading gathered rifles and handing them up, until the field yonder was clumped with blue-wrapped bodies the way stones blighted a meadow high and poor, and once, his eyes met those of the man he shot, just as he fired, and he watched the amazed fellow fall backward into the tangle of the abatis, suspended and displayed there like a nigger strung up for a wrongness, maybe just for carrying himself too high.

Yankees carried themselves too high, every one of them.

What did the blue-bellies want here, anyway? Weren't none of their business, no doings of theirs to attend to, none of their holdings. Not here in Virginia, nor home in Georgia, where they had conducted themselves like Pharaoh's army tormenting the Children of Israel. Sherman was the beast from Revelation, although he had spared the Edwards homestead, land too poor to draw such high attention, not even worth the extra miles of marching it would have cost to clean out the smokehouse and hayloft.

Would've liked to be there now, back in his springtime Georgia, near enough to the Alabama line to end up there if you strayed past the outhouse on a full-dark night. He claimed LaGrange as home, but truth was that the family's old bed-down, the place his kin were drawn to, lay across the river, above the bend where the flow was still all Georgia.

Yankees came on like rabid dogs. And damned fools. Making it clear they wanted the fort that didn't even have a name Edwards knew. Just a high-walled, wet-ditched place where he and many another had taken a spell of rest after the Yankees swarmed over their lines, some treachery there. The fort had filled up with gaggles of soldiers cut off from their regiments, or just plain gone off, discouraged and bitter, imagining in their fool-headedness that such high walls meant safety, or anyway a respite, that fond word of his mother's.

Respite. None here.

Officers had crowded in, too, at least at first. Only to go off again after making speeches about how the men with no rank on their collars and not much on their sleeves had to stay behind to save the army, rescue the entire Confederacy, excepting that they didn't find it helpful to stay themselves.

Well, some did. But Georgians, such as his handful of dirt friends from the 35th, plain Company D Troup County men, the most of them, they weren't much inclined to take orders from North Carolina captains, with their worrisome reputations, or from different-talking majors from Mississippi. Just didn't work that way, not now, not here, not after the wreck of the morning. But somehow folks just sorted themselves out, took over a section of wall with the men from their companies, regiments, and states, and then the

Yankees came on, goddamn-them-beg-pardon, and you shot them and more came, anyway.

Too dangerous to get atop the rampart now. Man went up there, and if he came back, he came tumbling, with his brains retreating first, brains, blood, and bone. For all the racket to every side, you still could hear the Yankees, masses of them now, splashing about in the ditch or slopping up the high-slant, packed-earth walls, commands given in voices flinty and foreign to Georgia ears, and whenever one dared show his rifle and snout above the rampart, he got a bullet in maybe his forehead, maybe his mouth, and went over backward to add to the writhing snake nest of venomous Yankees below.

They could kill the Yankees as they came over the field, wave after wave. They could kill them when they bunched up and slowed in the abatis. They could even catch a few at the edge of the ditch. But once they slopped or swam or walked over the water like Jesus Christ himself, beg pardon, they were safe enough. They couldn't climb the wall and get in, but the men inside couldn't crawl out far enough to shoot down into the blue mass and survive.

Yankees didn't quit, just caught their breath—Lord willing, their last. They clawed up the outer wall and planted their flags on the far side of the rampart. And got bullets for their trouble. One officer waving his butter knife topped the wall and Edwards shot him up so close the sparks from his muzzle set fire to the blue-belly captain's coat.

Men screamed, cursed, elbowed, grabbed, and got crazy-eyed so it frighted a man to recognize a blanket-mate so transformed, mad as a Baptist drunk on hallelujahs. Not saved by church doings now, though, each man become a devil in his pit.

Edwards' rifle barrel grew so hot he could not touch it, so hot he had to fear ramming down a cartridge. But he had the scent of Northern blood up his nose, like a bad-tempered hound, a biter. The ramrod clanged, steel burned his hand, and he didn't give one damn.

Yankees stubborn as back-stall mules. All you could do was kill 'em.

Two ten p.m.
Harmon house

Grant watched as waves of blue-clad soldiers swept toward the troublesome Reb fort. It was a clumsy attack, no credit to Gibbon's skill as a corps commander. Clumsy and costly. A dozen regimental flags had piled up along the fort's outer wall, where a ribbon of blue ringed the rampart like a hatband. Didn't take glasses to see it was a mess.

Wasn't inclined to interfere, though. Gibbon was going to take that fort, no matter how high the price, and that was what mattered. Grant reckoned that every life spent this day saved a dozen, perhaps a hundred, by tomorrow. Or for as many days as Lee had left.

Couldn't think about the cost. You just had to fix on winning. Get it done.

Lincoln back at City Point, waiting for each telegram from the front, too decent to come forward and be a burden. Grant had learned to hold the president dear. Even hoped he might continue to serve him, once the war was done. Stay a general, anyway.

Of course, John Rawlins—dispatched to City Point to attend to Lincoln and his own health—had a head full of politics, more ambitious for Grant than even Washburne. All sorts of talk.

But Grant was a Lincoln man.

Grant wondered how Robert E. Lee was feeling just then, with his army crumbling. Lee, who had seemed like a god of war to eager, itchy lieutenants back in Mexico. Lee, who had been the perfect officer, always. Grant didn't wish to be mean of heart, but he couldn't help feeling a measure of satisfaction.

Just sent a message to Sheridan, who was pressing the Rebs who'd been cut off to the west. Offering to send him the army's pontoon train, get him across the Appomattox, establish a blocking position to head off Lee, should he try to flee by the city bridges that night. End it right there, if not right here.

Standing close, George Meade gestured toward the fort a mile off and muttered, "Brave to a fault, but hardly well-conceived. I expected better of Gibbon. It's a slaughter."

"Don't matter," Grant said.

Two forty p.m.
Fort Gregg

Woeful. Weren't no other word for it. They'd manured that field with Yankees and they'd filled in the water ditch with their wicked bodies. They'd killed them when they topped the rampart and wrestled for their flags. Whole war through, Edwards had not seen him so much killing in so small a space.

He ran out of cartridges. Others did, too. They threw rocks over the wall separating them from the blue-bellies. With only one gun left in service, they took what remaining bombs there were from the other, lit the fuses, and hurled them over the wall. Cursing the Yankees, cursing them to their souls. Men who still had rounds to fire kept at it. Edwards poked blue-bellies with his bayonet until a skewered Yankee wrenched the socket free, a startling event and that man's prize in death.

Awful, plain awful. Yankees kept gaining. More and more of them got atop the wall, their hateful flags just out of a man's reach. Company remnants got called from one spot of trouble to another, until the men from each state were all mixed together and the officers gave up hope of sorting them out. Just fought as one-man armies from then on, using what they had to hand, doing what they could do.

A Yankee cannon, maybe even a Reb one—aiming for them Yankee flags, most like—dropped an explosive round in the depths of the fort. Men went flying, followed by shrapnel. Right beside Edwards, a stranger who'd been ramrodding his rifle thumped against the wall, gasping as his opened chest revealed his beating heart. He puked blood and fell, bedazzled.

Terrible thing to see.

A Yankee topped the wall and stood looming over him. Edwards swung his reversed rifle at the blue-belly's ankle. The big fellow toppled with a cry and Edwards gave him the butt against hip and thigh, wherever he could strike. But more Yankees came swarming, they couldn't be stopped, pouring over that wall all screaming and mad-eyed, gone beyond all church law and Christ's mercy.

Noise was such a man couldn't make no sense out of all the shouting, but it somehow got through that the Yankees had run in the back gate, too, the weakest point, storming the wooden wall that rumped the fort—as if there hadn't been dirt enough in Virginia to finish the job.

A blow knocked Edwards from the firing step. He fell among struggling men. Yankees was hollering out that the fort was theirs, but it weren't, not yet.

Edwards got up. Wished he hadn't lost his bayonet, though there was hardly enough room to use it. Men fought close.

"Frank, over here!" a messmate called. Survivors from the 35th Georgia had claimed a corner to make their last stand.

Yankees were gone blood crazy. Bayoneting men already dead. Stomping them. Edwards took another knocking that like to broke his arm. Didn't, though, thank Jesus.

He'd made some mighty plans for after the war. He meant to learn better reading and writing, to become respectable, wear him a collar and cuffs. But the Yankees didn't seem in a sparing mood. Wounded twice before, the closest he'd come to dying had been when the measles near took him, early on in the war. But the butchery on this day did pass the measles.

Men grappled, biting ears and gouging eyes, chewing into necks, growling like beasts. Rifle butts came down on the heads of men who'd tried to quit, who'd laid themselves down like sick dogs. A Yankee ran straight for Edwards, leading with a dripping bayonet, but another Reb, a man Edwards did not know, put his own bayonet through the back of the blue-belly's neck. The blade burst from the Yankee's mouth like a steel tongue, splashing blood over Edwards' face and stinging his eyes. Agog, the Yankee gasped and choked and pawed at the blade stuck through him, gripping it with fingers soon red with his lifeblood. The Reb who'd speared him was trying to yank his bayonet free again, but it got bone-stuck. A Yankee shot Edwards' savior in the back. Meat peeled from his breast.

Edwards didn't want to die. But he reckoned he was about to.

Go down fighting, though. *Hating.*

Out of bullets, rifles broken, fingers mashed, men began attempting to surrender. If they still had weapons, they threw them down.

The Yankees killed them anyway.

Still, the men around Edwards either raised their rifles, butts skyward, or dropped them and lifted their hands.

Yankees gutted men whose hands were high.

Edwards no longer knew what he was doing, no longer commanded himself. He threw his weapon into the blood-slop, too.

Yankee officers fired their pistols in the air, threatening their own men. Ordering them not to harm any Johnnies surrendering. Some blue-bellies heeded them. Others didn't.

A captain shoved his pistol into a maddened sergeant's cheek.

Somehow, the killing stopped. Mostly. But there was still a roughness, a sharpness, in men. A Yankee private built to shoulder barrels of salt pork grabbed Edwards by the coat sleeve, ripping the garment.

"What you got in them pockets of yours, Johnny?"

Edwards produced a half plug of tobacco. Mean-eyed and greedy, the Yankee bit off a chaw and stashed the remainder.

"What else?" his captor asked through the unworked chaw.

Edwards surrendered his pocketknife, a treasure guarded since he'd put on the gray.

"And what else?"

Money from his last pay, forty Confederate dollars. The blue-belly sneered at the bills, but took them, too.

"Still ain't all you got, is it now?" The Northerner pawed his rifle, as if it had an unruly life of its own. Then he shot out a hand to grasp a peeping stem and snatch the friend-carved pipe from Edwards' pocket.

Grinning, the Yankee gripped Edwards' shoulder to force him to the ground.

But the ground was a fearful place for an unarmed man. Edwards leapt aside in time to escape a trip-a-man kick. The Yank almost lost his own balance.

Then their officers got to doing officer things, telling sergeants to do sergeant things, and the prisoners who could walk were herded together, the first step toward captivity, leaving the wounded to groan and fear the Lord. There were far more bleeding men than those left whole.

Beyond the walls of the fort, shells continued to shriek and volleys rippled. Distant Yankees cheered. Edwards reckoned they were giving the other fort a turn.

At first, he'd felt relief, an open-my-mouth-wide wonder, that he looked set to survive. But that gave way to anger quick enough, a spread-out anger at all things in creation. Then he felt like he wanted to cry in shame.

Wasn't going to do that, though. Not in front of no Yankees.

Three fifteen p.m.
Edge Hill

A solid shot crashed through the house, tore down the telegrapher's tent, and sheared off the leg of a horse standing in harness.

That, Lee feared, was merely the start of what the house would suffer for harboring him.

Fighting his way out from under collapsed canvas, the telegraph operator emerged flailing his arms and shouting, "Can't do this no more, I can't do this no more."

He ran.

"Collar him!" Venable shouted. "Stop him!"

"He will need some minutes," Lee warned, "to regain a steady hand. There can be no errors now."

He had issued orders constantly for hours, directing General Ewell to withdraw the troops from the Richmond front after dark, to abandon the city, cross the James to the south bank, burn the bridges, and march to join the remainder of the army. Messages went to the Danville depot to forward rations to Amelia Court House by the railroad. The pieces left of the army would rendezvous there—by which time the soldiers would be hungry indeed.

He sent multiple couriers westward with verbal commands for those cut off, wary that written orders were subject to capture. More orders would follow, relayed on horseback or by wire, as Marshall and his staff worked out the details of the withdrawal, specifying march times, designating routes and assigning bridges, clarifying priorities and revising missions, identifying the stores to be evacuated and those to be destroyed, the guns to be rendered useless and left behind, strict limits on officers' baggage and on the number of ambulances, all the details that kept an army from chaos, all decisions made with an eye to rapid marching and racing away from Grant.

At Amelia Court House, with the army reunited, he'd make his decision as to the best route to North Carolina and General Johnston's army. It was not yet time to despair.

Another round screamed past, sparing the house this time. The dwelling had been a fine haven and deserved a better fate. Until that winter, Lee had lived in his tent, no matter the weather, aware of how the Yankees might punish the families and walls that took him in. But as the cold had come down this last time, he had allowed his staff to lead him to comfort. He was ailing, and they knew it. There were days when he feared he could not continue to lead, when even prayer failed him.

The shelling presaged a renewed attack, of course. Ill-sited and poorly laid out, the second fort would fall more easily. And to the north, toward the river, the Union Sixth Corps had reappeared, pressing forward again.

Yet Lee believed that it would be all right. Gordon had denied those people the city, working a wonder. And Fort Gregg had astonished even him by its resistance, delaying Grant and Meade as surely as those Spartans at the pass had stymied the Persians, winning the time for Field to help Wilcox ready the inner line and for Longstreet to see things done right. And the Federals' Sixth Corps would be exhausted—it had led the breakthrough, then marched and countermarched, he had firm evidence. Those men would be even wearier than his own soldiers.

Lee's battlefield instincts told him that those people were nearly finished for the day; the inner line had to hold just a few more hours. A strong array of batteries had been organized, a substitute for the much-thinned infantry ranks. Artillery ammunition, at least, was plentiful. And the ground was favorable.

Venable stepped closer and said, hush-voiced, "Perhaps the headquarters should withdraw now, sir? They're coming our way."

Yes, those people were coming on again. But Lee did not believe they'd come far enough.

Not this day.

Four p.m.
Brown's Road

Sheridan ate in the saddle, balancing a tin plate of ham, beans, and cornbread. The meal came courtesy of Georgie Custer, who applied a liberal notion of the term *contraband*. Sheridan wasn't fussy about his vittles during a fight, but the ham, salty and rich, suggested that Virginia wasn't worthless.

"What now, Jimmy?" he asked his approaching chief of staff. "Keep that damned horse from spitting on my grub, would you?"

"About those pontoons . . ."

"To hell with the pontoons."

"Grant wants us to—"

"Grant's there, I'm here. I know what we need better than he does. We're not going to lay a bridge that takes us nowhere." He lowered a piece of cornbread that had failed to reach his mouth. "Lee's not going anywhere. He's trapped in the city, he can't get off. He'll surrender tomorrow." Sheridan snorted. Crumbs shook from his mustaches. "If he doesn't quit today."

Forsyth looked doubtful. The chief of staff had been a pest about the pontoons for hours, determined to follow Grant's wishes and shift to the north bank of the Appomattox, to block an escape by

Lee. But there were some things Sheridan couldn't explain even to Forsyth, aspects of affairs that were best not shared. Jimmy also wanted to pound the Rebs harder. And they'd pressed them, the Johnnies had felt it. But Sheridan didn't want to drive them too far west. That would take him westward, too, and farther from any surrender featuring Robert E. Lee. As it was, he had half a mind to ride back to "consult" with Grant. He hated the thought of a ceremony at which Meade might be present—while he was off catching stragglers. The newspapermen would immortalize Lee's surrender—and the Union generals present when it was signed.

For their part, the Rebs had fought tenaciously. Their cavalry wasn't quitting, he had to admit. Fitz Lee, Rooney Lee, Barringer . . . they still needed their heads knocked. Reb infantry was another matter. Poor leadership. Pickett's ragtags couldn't muster the spit to blow a trumpet, what was left of them. Nor was Anderson a worry now; that thorn had been pulled. Miles had come up from the Second Corps and, after a stumble or two, his division had shredded the Johnnies at Sutherland Station. They were running like monkeys let loose from the circus, shitting themselves as they went.

As for the Rebel cavalry, the map robbed them of choices. They'd do all they could to hold the successive crossroads along the way to Namozine Church. And the last crossroads was the key. He already had Devin moving against their first position, with Crawford's infantry following, plenty of force.

Take those crossroads and hold up for the night. See how things looked in the morning. War was over, a fool could see it. What mattered now was who got ahead in the peace.

He chewed and swallowed and looked at Jimmy Forsyth.

"Damned fine ham."

Seven thirty p.m.
Scott's Cross Roads

Knocked them back again. Fitz Lee had come forward to make certain the battered infantry did its duty, ready to summon more of his riders, if Johnson's boys showed signs of breaking. Instead he felt his first lick of satisfaction in two days. Sheridan's men had tried twice to seize the crossroads, and dead and wounded Yankees lay in the soft light, struck down by soldiers rallied from Pickett's command and by cavalry dismounts placed on the flanks to stiffen them. Confederate casualties had been few. Desertion was a bigger problem than bullets now.

The men needed a victory. Even a small one. So did he. That ever-to-be-regretted, never-to-be-lived-down, infernal shad bake gnawed him.

Awful pair of days. Worst of the war.

Rufus Barringer trotted up from the rear. Without Rooney Lee or an escort.

"Told you to dismount and go afoot," Fitz Lee snapped, "this close to the line. I'm weary of losing subordinates."

"Right close to the fight yourself, General."

"I'm not on a damned horse." Lee grimaced. "White one, too. Sharpshooter could see you a mile off."

Reluctantly, Barringer dismounted. Rufe never did care to walk. Fairness would have judged his mount a dapple-gray, but Lee had a point to make. Felt about as surly as he was like to. His satisfaction at watching the Yankees get slapped back hadn't stretched.

The North Carolinian asked, "Think they'll come on again?"

Outburst over, Lee nodded. "One more time, I expect. Before full dark."

"Well, then we'll hold them one more time."

"Surely."

Barringer scratched behind an ear. Lice, Lee had no doubt. Every man had them on and off, even his uncle. Poor Rufe had barely a fringe of hair left to him, but lice had an old soldier's knack for foraging anywhere.

The brigadier frowned, but with a thoughtful look. As if the itch had nothing to do with it.

"Thought they'd press us harder today, to be honest."

"Hard enough," Lee said. "Dogs are tuckered out, would be my guess. We're just more lasting, we cozied on up to misery long ago." He gestured toward the Yankees off in the gloaming. "Tired men, sloppy tactics. Seen it time and again."

After a shade more hesitation, Barringer said what Lee figured he'd come to say. To ask, really.

"Sounds like things turned ugly back at Petersburg."

Lee nodded.

"And you expect . . ."

"I expect to be fighting for some time yet," Lee told the brigadier. "We'll put this army back together." He spit. "Seen worse times, Rufe."

He couldn't remember any worse times, though.

"Think General Lee will look to join up with Johnston?"

"Couldn't call that a secret."

"Well, ain't that a queer thing now?" Barringer wondered in a changed voice. "Hooty owl, this time of the evening. Mid a fight."

Fitz Lee shrugged. "Not the wisest owl in the Confederacy." He smirked. "Typical Southsider."

Rufe failed to get the joke.

The brigadier removed his hat and smoothed his baldness, sparing the lice behind his ears this time. "Must admit to feeling a trifle downcast."

Voice hardened, Lee told him, "Then I suggest you cast the Yankees down. Isn't over, Rufe. Not by a sight."

Then the Yankees returned, repeaters snapping and sparking through the twilight.

Eight p.m.

Banks house yard

He'd come outside at Orville Babcock's bidding. Petersburg was burning. Part of it. Grant judged the small, false dawn to be near the river.

"Lee's running," his aide declared. "They're burning their stores."

"Won't get far, if he does. Told Sheridan to shift north of the river, in case Lee tried to slip off. Told him he could have the army's pontoons." A battery fired at spooks. "Probably already across, knowing Phil."

John Rawlins joined the pair. He'd made his way forward from City Point, ignoring orders meant for his own good. Soon, the commandeered house had emptied completely. All of the officers studied the eastern horizon, while the sergeants and corporals expressed the desire to see the whole city burn.

Rawlins coughed in the chill air and asked, "Send Wright in? Make Lee fight his way out, if he means to go?"

Grant shook his head. "Order stands. Bombardment at five a.m. General assault follows. Send out patrols first, though, see if Lee's really running. I want reports by four thirty." He felt for a fresh cigar. "Don't want to shell the place, if we're going to have to clean up the mess ourselves." He paused. "I suspect the citizenry's had enough war for a while."

"Hard-heart Secesh," Babcock snarled. "Every one of them."

"Lee leaves, they'll come around." Grant's voice had taken on a hint of annoyance. He was tired, too. The world was tired. And he was weary of explaining things that couldn't be explained, things he understood down deep that stopped making sense when he forced them into words. He bit off the cigar's end and spit it out.

Rawlins turned on the officers and all the clerks in uniform. "Every one of you, back to work. Any man here lacks an occupation, I can find him one."

The officers and men stepped away, but did not rush back to their labors. The glow from Petersburg enchanted them: They'd waited so long for this.

Rawlins gave Babcock a look that cut through the darkness: *Private talk now, you're not needed, either.*

As the aide drifted off, Grant smiled. "You're hard on those boys, John."

"War's not over yet."

"Will be. This part, anyway."

"Not like you to ease up, Sam."

"Not easing up. Just thinking."

"Giving Lee a free hand to slip off?"

"He doesn't have a free hand. Far from it." Grant looked down. "Watched an assault today. On a fort blocking our way. Had to take it, but it was a mess. Not inclined to repeat the performance, if we can help it. Get Lee out in the open, that makes it easier." He lofted the unlit cigar. "He's not going to reach Joe Johnston. Or Danville. Or any place that's going to make a difference. And he knows it. It's just about his pride now."

"I don't trust Robert E. Lee. The man's a trickster."

Grant smiled in the purple darkness. "Well, trust *me,* then." He changed the subject; he'd had enough Lee for one day. "Saw Lincoln, did you? I told him it was all right to come up tomorrow, he'd be no bother."

"The man's transported, Sam. Halfway to Heaven. Read every telegram two, three times. Doesn't have any gloat in him, though." Rawlins folded his arms. "Passeth my understanding."

Grant struck a match on his riding boot and worried the flame in front of the Habana. "All we had to do was break the South. He's got to put the whole thing back together."

"Wouldn't want the job, speaking for myself."

"Not sure he does, either," Grant said. "But he'll do it."

"Union's been lucky to have him, I suppose."

Grant puffed and thickened the night. "South's lucky, that's who. Congress is in a vengeful mood. And Stanton. Hard men to appease, the stay-at-homes. Then there's the nigger question. But he'll do it, all right. Knows what has to be done, bring the South back in. You heard him. He doesn't want persecutions, no vindictiveness. He's not a hating man."

"Neither are you, Sam. Which is almost enough to restore my faith in mankind. All you've been through."

"Never saw the point in it. Hating a fellow never made things better. Just sickens you, eats you up."

"Plenty of men hate you, though. Not just Southrons. McClellan's gang, for a start. Copperheads . . ."

Grant laughed his quiet laugh. The cigar's tip faded. "Not enough of me to hate. Best I can excite in a man is dislike. But they do hate Lincoln. Trumped them left and right." He laughed again: childlike, mischievous. "Thought you told me they'd all rush out to vote for me? If I ran for office? Which is unlikely."

"I said that 'plenty' of men hate you. But plenty more see what you've done, the public's grateful. You'll see."

Bemused, Grant said, "Weren't grateful after last summer's casualty lists came out."

"Sam, if you wanted it, you could run for—"

"I *don't* want it. Leave it, John."

To the northeast, the pink light flared higher.

Rawlins sniffed the air. "Smells like they're burning tobacco bales."

"It's just my cigar," Grant said.

Nine p.m.
Petersburg

The infant squalled as if it knew.

"You stay in bed," Gordon told his wife. "Have the girl identify you to the first officers she spots. They'll see that you're protected, they're not beasts." He staged a grin, forcing his mouth to cooperate. "Not all of them."

"I hate this, being like this. I swear I do."

"Have a swearing wife now, do I?"

"I'd fight them myself, if I could. . . ."

"My Diana, my Amazon."

"I thought I was your Penelope?"

"Well, *your* Ulysses won't be delayed ten years. I promise."

Her sheets had been changed, but Gordon could not help noticing new spots of blood. Leaving her here was the hardest thing he'd ever had to do.

Their minds were so attuned that she said, "You go on, General Gordon. Go back and see to your men. Your wife's doing just fine, thank you." She tilted her head toward the borrowed cradle, which had seen much use, and their calming, eavesdropping son. "Him, too."

"Fanny . . ."

"Just go."

"I—"

Abruptly, she raised herself on her elbows. "Just tell me the truth, John. You tell me now. Have we lost? Have we lost the war?"

"Not yet," he said, voice grim.

"But we're going to lose it. Aren't we?"

She had begun to cry. And Fanny was not a tearful woman by nature.

When he didn't speak—when he couldn't speak—she smeared an eye dry with the fat of her palm and said, "After all this . . ."

The room wanted airing. That old saw about fresh air killing new mothers. Just added stench to the suffering.

"You'll be all right, Fan. They'll respect you. As my wife, you've got position." He forced another smile. "Some of them might almost pass for gentlemen. You'll have whatever you need."

"I need *you*! I need *you*, John Gordon. . . ."

Her outburst shamed her, he saw that instantly. Last thing the woman wanted was to bedevil him.

"You'll *have* me, Fanny. For many years to come. And I do expect to be a wicked old man, best look to your skirts, girl."

"If you . . . if you get yourself killed . . . I'll . . . I'll dig up your bones and grind them for the hogs."

He smiled genuinely. "I not only married a beauty, but a peerless lady of a most delicate mien. . . ."

A flare lit the windowpane.

"They're not burning the city, are they?" Fanny asked.

He shook his head. "Tobacco. Cotton. Army supplies."

An unwelcome hand knocked on the door downstairs, followed by an unwelcome voice that called out, "General Gordon?"

"Go," Fanny said. "I'm John Brown Gordon's wife, I don't need pampering."

He bent and kissed her, hard and hot and wet, a near smash of lips and tongues. She clung furiously to his upper arms, but just for a moment.

His own eyes had become a difficulty.

"I love you more than a Christian ought," he told her. And he went.

Halfway down the stairs, he realized that he lacked a last glimpse of his son, but it was too late.

Eleven p.m.
Richmond

By argument, bribery, and luck, Walter Taylor, much delayed, secured the last mount from the government livery stable. It wasn't a lot of horse. The stalls had been picked clean. Like the looted shops he'd passed on his way from the Richmond & Petersburg Depot.

On foot, in the fog created by a flaming tobacco warehouse, he'd swung around the basin and up through Shockoe, headed for the stable, and he'd found the city's worst citizens helping themselves to the best remaining goods. Warehouses had been thrown open, and women—mostly women—rolled barrels of flour or shouldered great slabs of bacon kept back from the army, cackling through alleys lit by fires got up in midstreet. The gasworks had been shuttered well before, throwing the city back into a medieval darkness challenged only by lanterns and torches, but now fires crackled through roofs here and there with no sign of the fire brigade.

Near lower Cary Street, he'd been bewildered by the sight of men and women, belly down, lapping from the gutters. Only when he caught the scent of whiskey behind the smoke reek did he decipher things. The order would have come down to destroy the liquor supplies. And this was the result: gutters running with whiskey.

Men staggered, sang, and fought, not all of them white. Women whisked dirty skirts in invitation, their tongues and teeth a horror.

It was Sodom and Gomorrah come to Dixie.

Other streets were crammed with burdened wagons and household carriages striving to reach Mayo's Bridge. Lone men and families less fortunate wove between the excited teams, shouldering valuables as they joined the exodus to the Richmond & Danville Depot. Gray-haired gentlemen displayed ancient pistols thrust into their belts, protecting daughters and their terrified children. Unleashed, the lower orders bellowed obscenities and made suggestions to ladies passing in terror.

A dozen times, Taylor felt he should interfere. But he kept to his purpose.

Then he got that last unclaimed nag in all of Richmond, along with well-worn tack. The acquisition had only demanded the name of Robert E. Lee, a twenty-dollar gold piece he'd been hoarding, and a hand rested on the holster of his pistol.

Back in the streets on horseback, he rode without hindrance. Too many easier victims offered themselves.

One block from the Capitol, he encountered a man and woman in shameful embrace. Their flesh shone pale and shocking against a brick wall.

Stray detachments of soldiers straggled along, men withdrawn from the outlying defenses. Not frontline troops, but bewildered cadets officiously led, and militiamen, sailors, and seedy detachments of cavalry, they were all concerned with going, not with doing. More than one horseman nursed a bottle and listed as he rode.

Negroes ran free, helping themselves to the spoils and scraps after whites had what they wanted from the shops. Bucks wore millinery and danced in skirts, while the aunties bundled up all they could and slipped off.

It seemed to Taylor the end of civilization, his wedding day.

Midnight loomed before he gained the calmer reach of Main Street and the Crenshaw house, where Bettie had been allowed a wartime home. He'd feared that all might have given up on him, but one of the family niggers waited on lookout, posted on the front porch with a lantern. And the mansion's first floor was illuminated.

He wished he'd had time for a bath and change of linens.

Then there was Bettie, his Bettie, with her immortal smile. There were cries of delight all around, and the boldness with which she rushed to him found no censors. When they kissed—too briefly—even prim old biddies applauded the forwardness.

The Reverend Dr. Minnigerode had come to perform the ceremony himself and greeted the tardy groom with a handshake and yawn. Taylor found himself carried on a tide, almost as overwhelming as in battle. He later recalled a quick drink—no more than a stirrup cup—and a water closet that needed a bucket to prime it. He dusted himself and borrowed a brush for his hair as the minutes raced. Then he and Bettie stood side by side in the parlor, just shy of midnight.

"Elizabeth Selden Saunders, do you take . . ."

"Walter Herron Taylor, do you take . . ."

I do, I do, I do!

There were slight refreshments, the best that could be assembled. More than a few of the guests betrayed rude appetites. And these were the very best people. Taylor thought wryly that he might have brought along some of those looted provisions from down in Shockoe.

They did not go upstairs: Their bliss would be postponed. The hour already leaned heavily, a new day already begun. Time only for Bettie's tears in the sewing room, where they were afforded a few minutes of privacy. She wept and said she was happy. He did not cry, but ached. He held her close.

And then that time was gone. The bridges would be fired at any moment and he had to fulfill his promise to Robert E. Lee. To join the gray columns converging from the Richmond front and the Howlett Line, from Petersburg and the fractured western lines, meeting, if the plan prevailed, on the long tongue of land between the Appomattox and the James, then to dash westward and southward, to North Carolina and Johnston . . . to win the war that he knew could no longer be won.

For one treacherous moment, Walter Taylor wondered whether he should not remain behind with his new bride.

But no, he could not fail Lee.

At the front door, Bettie clutched his hand in both of hers, unable to let him go. He realized with a shock that she was afraid. Not only of the prospect of his death, but of the Yankees, the city, the end of the world.

He lifted her hands and kissed them. Then he broke off.

Turning away on the high porch, he saw that a great light had risen in the east.

It wasn't yet dawn. Richmond was on fire.

PART II

THE PURSUIT

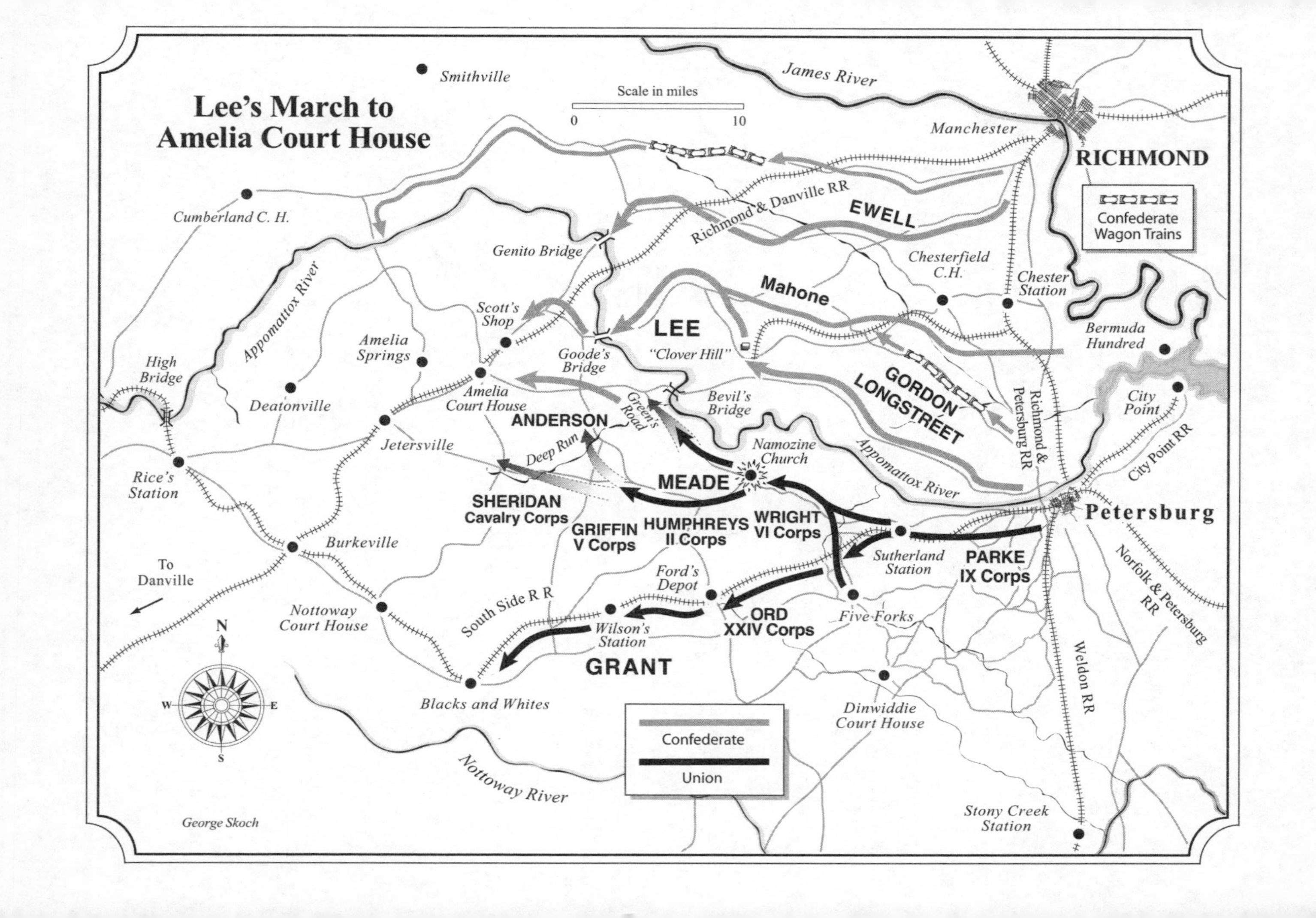
Lee's March to Amelia Court House
Smithville
Scale in miles
0
10
James River
Manchester
RICHMOND
Confederate Wagon Trains
Cumberland C. H.
Richmond & Danville RR
EWELL
Genito Bridge
Appomattox River
Chesterfield C.H.
Chester Station
Mahone
Scott's Shop
LEE
Bermuda Hundred
Amelia Springs
Goode's Bridge
"Clover Hill"
High Bridge
Amelia Court House
GORDON
LONGSTREET
Deatonville
Green's Road
Bevil's Bridge
City Point
ANDERSON
Richmond & Petersburg RR
Jetersville
Namozine Church
Deep Run
City Point RR
Rice's Station
Appomattox River
MEADE
SHERIDAN Cavalry Corps
WRIGHT VI Corps
Petersburg
GRIFFIN V Corps
HUMPHREYS II Corps
Burkeville
Sutherland Station
PARKE IX Corps
To Danville
Ford's Depot
Norfolk & Petersburg RR
South Side R R
ORD XXIV Corps
Five Forks
Nottoway Court House
Wilson's Station
N
GRANT
W
E
S
Blacks and Whites
Dinwiddie Court House
Weldon RR
Confederate
Union
Nottoway River
Stony Creek Station
George Skoch

NINE

Ten a.m., April 3, 1865
Wallace house, Petersburg

Grant smiled.

"To hear the local worthies tell it," he said, "every last man of business in Petersburg has been hiding Union sympathies all these years."

The grief left Lincoln's face, replaced by his veil of humor. On his way into the city, the president had paused over the uncollected dead from the past day's fighting. But Grant's remark brought light back to his eyes. Long-legged, the president tipped back his chair. The front porch creaked.

"It *has* been my experience," Lincoln told him, "that whenever a business fellow insists on his patriotic devotion, he's got something patriotic he wants to sell me." He looked at Grant directly. "You know, General, I don't believe I've ever heard you speak of patriotism? Not once. You just went out and did what had to be done."

"Not much of a talker, Mr. President."

Lincoln let his smile bloom into a grin. "Now there's the difference twixt us. Talking's what I do for my living, puts the meat on the table and coal in the stove. Sew a politician's lips together, he'd swell up and float away." He rocked on a chair not meant for the purpose. "If the good burghers of this city want to do business, I'm all for letting them. Fellow makes a dollar off you, it's hard for him to stay mad."

"Women seem to be a different story."

"I've noticed. All my life." The president laughed.

"These in particular. Sullen, every one of them. Hard-faced. Their men may have given up, but they haven't."

Lincoln pondered that. Their mingled staffs kept a carefully judged distance, feigning attention to duty but agog at the who and the where of this fine spring morning. Provost guards restrained excited darkies.

The president scratched his knee and said, "Once their husbands and sons come home—the ones who do come back—they'll settle down. Trick of the thing is to let them spy out a future, not just mope about what they think they've lost. Man or woman, folks need to see some advantage coming their way." Lincoln's long fingers dug through cloth again, seeking that elusive knee. "I long for this war to be over. Truly over."

"We're close, Mr. President."

Again, Lincoln mastered his sorrow. He slapped the bothersome knee and said, "You know, General, I had a sneaking idea all along that you intended this, taking Petersburg now. And Richmond, God be thanked. But I thought you'd bring Sherman up here to finish things, have him cooperate with you."

"Believed it just might run that way myself," Grant told him. "Thought Sherman might finish Joe Johnston and come up here in time for the spring campaign. But Cump went a little slower, and Lee went a little faster." He shook his head. "Truth be told, it wouldn't have done to have the western troops here. Would've caused no end of sectional feeling, politicians arguing over which troops from which states really won the war, westerners claiming the easterners couldn't beat Lee without their help." He cleared his throat, yearning for a cigar but waiting for Lincoln to invite him to smoke. The president was ever good of heart, but increasingly forgetful of lesser matters. Plenty else on his mind, Grant accepted that. But he would have liked a cigar. "Thing is, Mr. President, the Army of the Potomac and the Army of the James earned the right to whip Robert E. Lee themselves. And they're doing it."

"How . . . long now?"

"Days, a few weeks. Can't say exactly, but we'll end it soon."

Grant thought, with resurgent anger, of Sheridan's refusal to cross the Appomattox and block Lee's route. Phil might have cut off a good part of Lee's army. But Phil had been stubborn, and Lee had been quick. Now it was a chase. Multiple corps had set off in pursuit, but Lee had gotten a head start, after all.

No point dwelling on it. In the light of day, Phil could see his error. He'd be mad as Satan on Easter Sunday, he'd tear after the Confederates.

"The city," Lincoln said, waving a hand at the street of handsome homes, "seems to have suffered a good deal less than I'd feared."

Grant snorted. "More broken hearts than broken windows, this part of town. Looks a sight worse down in the commercial quarter, toward the river."

In the lower reach of the street, ever more Negroes gathered, wondrously alerted to Lincoln's presence. The provost guards kept them under firm control, but their singing and merry hollering resounded.

"Richmond may be another matter," Grant continued. "Waiting to hear from Weitzel. Report last night said fires looked to be spreading. Burning their military stores, I expect. Might have gotten a little out of hand. Hard to believe they'd torch the city on purpose." He gave a rough-lunged sigh. "Weitzel may face a chore, though. Beyond any fighting required."

"When do you think we'll know? If Richmond *has* fallen?"

"Hoped to hear by now, Mr. President. Wanted to give you the news myself. Fall today, though. If it hasn't already. With Lee running, I don't see their government staying."

Lincoln shook his shoulders, as if at a sudden chill. Flakes of dandruff flew. "I don't wish to interfere with military operations, but . . . if Richmond's ours . . . I'd like to go up there tomorrow, have a look before I return to Washington. If General Weitzel wouldn't object."

"He won't," Grant said.

Ten a.m.
Namozine Church

Custer drank down the spring air.

"Fine day for killing Johnnies," he told his brother.

Tom drew his kepi lower on his forehead. He struck George Custer as a knight of old lowering his visor.

"Expect some good sport myself," Tom said. He nodded rearward. "Not a bad start back there, sir."

They'd driven the Reb rear guard from the position that had stopped Tom Devin cold the evening before. Devin hadn't been able to take it even with infantry backing him, but Custer's division had worked jolly havoc first thing in the morning. Brilliant day all around: peach blossoms on the trees and Rebs dead in the bushes.

Didn't want to make too much of a glorified skirmish, of course. Just a bit of Rebel blood for breakfast and a dish of tattered prisoners. He'd suspected that the Johnnies had only meant to delay him a bit, little more than a gesture. Last night, they'd needed to hold off Devin so their army could escape, but their main defense would be closer to that church now, defending the westward roads Lee's army still needed.

As the two officers and Custer's retinue neared Namozine Church, it looked as though his assessment had been right: There they were, just up ahead, firing and giving their position away, sleepless and nervous, bound to a country church like Baptists on Sunday.

Custer halted his escort in the middle of the road, caring nothing for Rebel marksmanship. His leading regiments were already deploying to right and left, they didn't need orders. Those men and their commanders knew what he wanted: The terrain appeared perfect for his favored tactic, a fixing attack on the Rebels' front, while a flanking force turned their position. He'd done it time and again, yet the Johnnies never seemed to cotton to it.

One more time today, then.

His only regret was that most fighting was done dismounted now. Custer adored a good saber charge, the glory and romance, the delicious violence. He even had fond memories of his first, flawed effort at Gettysburg, that foolhardy charge with just a handful of men. He'd made up for that within days.

There simply was nothing like bringing a blade down on an enemy and feeling it bite. No pull of a trigger offered the same thrill. On the other hand, any killing a man could do was better than none. In its way, it was every bit the equal of lovemaking. And considerably more sporting.

Well, if the war's end meant he couldn't kill other men, they'd probably let him kill Indians and buffalo.

Wasn't it what a man was meant to do? That, and taking a woman?

He'd woken that morn with his cock as stiff as an oak log. After dreaming vividly of Libbie. He wished he could give her a good poking that minute. And how that woman loved it! In their first intimate encounter, he'd been delighted and then a little alarmed at her enthusiasm. Except for whores, the young women he'd known had rationed their cunnies, strict as Army quartermasters. Then Libbie, demure in public to the point of sternness, had ravished him when he'd thought to ravish her.

Good woman waiting at home, good horse under his rump, and a good fight just ahead. And a major general's stars on his shoulders, a division at his command. What more could a fellow want?

God, he yearned to give Libbie a tumble, though. He loved the way she laughed when she went wild. Calling out, "Autie, oh, Autie!"

Wouldn't he just make her holler the next time they met?

Peering through his field glasses, George Custer saw all that he needed to see. He turned to his brother, the privileged lieutenant, and to his senior staff men.

"What do you say? Shall we give those poor devils a thrashing?"

Ten fifteen a.m.
Namozine Church

Brigadier General Rufus Barringer knew what was coming. Nothing he could do about it, except stretch matters out as long as possible. He was about to get whipped. And it felt like getting slapped on one cheek, then the other. In public.

Those red scarves and kerchiefs announced Custer's division, plain even at a distance. A full Yankee division coming up, and Barringer had his bled-hard North Carolina Brigade, three shrunken regiments present for duty, maybe eight hundred men this morning, depending on how many had slipped away in the night. And one in five of his "cavalrymen" had no horse to ride. They either doubled up on a mare's back with a messmate or got along on foot to jeers from the infantry. Add in the single gun surviving from McGregor's battery, and that was all he could offer against Custer's thousands.

Birds made shrill comments from branches budding green. Horses nickered as they were led by the holders. The men left on the firing line were as grim-faced as the day was soft and lovely.

Rufe Barringer would just as soon have been home in Cabarrus County, North Carolina, doing his lawyering. Never had wanted this war, not like his brothers. Knew what was bound to come of it, as surely as he knew George Custer would play his two-dog trick.

Well, he wasn't going to quit. Every man who wasn't the damnedest fool knew the war was lost. Didn't take a lawyer to draw up the writ. But he'd come this far and figured he'd go to the last. There'd be no stain on his conscience, nothing a friend or neighbor could say against him.

Would the Yankees let him practice law again? Would lawyers who'd served in uniform be disbarred? Would a hard justice prevail? What kind of life would be left to the man who survived but lost his vocation? Middle-aged, bald, and broke, a subject for ridicule? How would he support a wife wed on the war's eve, a woman married not out of passionate, young-man's love, but because his children needed a mother with his first wife dead?

At that moment, the obligations waiting on him at home almost seemed harsher than those he faced in battle. Almost. . . .

And today it came down to this: just him and that scoundrel Custer.

He'd burned to hear the order passed down in his presence from Fitz Lee to Rooney Lee on that fine, bitter morning: ". . . and hold this position to the last." While the rest of the once great cavalry of the Army of Northern Virginia showed its tail.

Barringer knew exactly how Custer would play it. The man's bag of tricks was shallow. He'd studied Two-Dogs Custer on many a field, and he of the golden locks was as predictable as he was brave—no gainsaying the latter. One dog comes right at you and locks on to your leg. And while you're busy thrashing at the first dog, the other dog takes you from the side or jumps you from behind. But knowing didn't help. All Barringer could do against the horde of bluecoats headed his way was to spread his men as broadly as he dared and make it as hard as possible to outflank him. So he'd positioned the 1st North Carolina on his left, by White's Store, with the 2nd in his center, north of the crossroads, and the 5th tucked in by the church—it appeared to be Presbyterian, which Barringer found ironic. The day's outcome did seem predestined.

Well, he'd buy that passel of Lees appointed over him as much time as his band of Tar Heels could.

Rufus Barringer turned his eyes to Heaven and, irreverent for one bitter moment, said, "Judge, I rest my case."

Ten thirty a.m.
Namozine Church

Lieutenant Tom Custer had no authority to lead a charge, but he galloped ahead of the 8th New York Cavalry anyway, passing the regiment's officers and hollering like a little boy chasing a cat.

Autie loved sabers, but Tom preferred a pistol and rode with his Colt half-extended and already cocked. What a magnificent thing it was to ride straight at the Johnnies, hundreds of hooves pounding and a horse one great throbbing muscle under a man.

The sweeping, separating lines of horsemen hurrahed and spurred their mounts.

The Rebs had put up a good fight against attacks mounted and dismounted, but Autie had only been teasing them, testing them, tricking them. And the foolish Johnnies had tried a counterattack—swiftly defeated and weakening their line. All just shuffling the deck so the 8th New York could throw down the aces.

Mere seconds away, the Reb line sparkled with rifle fire. Rounds ripped past. But "Custer's Luck" did seem to run in the family.

Some of the Johnnies began to run before the riders reached their flimsy barricades. Others reloaded as swiftly as they could, jamming down ramrods, full of grit but hopeless just the same.

"Come on!" Tom Custer told his horse, although it was galloping to burst its heart. He gave it another spurring.

His mount gained still more speed and easily cleared the unfinished Reb defenses. He came down amid his enemies, nearly a dozen of them. Alone.

Grabbing the red flag from a color-sergeant, he threatened the rest with his pistol. His horse threw sweat. It took a few seconds to catch his wind before he could make his demand:

"Surrender!"

And they did. Just like that. Dropped their weapons and put up their hands. As if all the fight had gone out of them, quick as snuffing a candle.

With blue troopers by the dozen swarming around him now—some casting envious eyes on the tattered flag—Tom Custer turned his horse and trotted off to rejoin his brother. The field over which the attack had passed had been churned and trampled, but few were the corpses or wounded men in blue. Two riderless horses moped about, but that was the extent of the butcher's bill. Amazing.

To the south, closer to the church, a last artillery blast annoyed the morning and rifle fire snapped, stubborn but slight. The scrap was done, though, any man could feel it. The rest was just cleaning up.

Hundreds of disarmed prisoners came trudging out of the woods.

Approaching his elder brother, Tom grinned and flaunted the flag.

Autie smiled back. “That’s good for a Medal of Honor, Tom.”

“You tell Mama I got one before you did,” Tom teased.

Autie leaned from the saddle and clapped his brother on the shoulder. “Spread those colors out, you let me see.”

Tom Custer dipped the flag toward his brother, who stretched out the ragged cloth.

“Second North Carolina,” Autie said. “Just whipped Rufus Barringer again.” He nodded toward the lively pursuit that was under way. “Hope we catch the bald-headed bastard this time.”

Eleven a.m.
Green’s Road

Barringer had gathered up all the survivors he could, but there weren’t many. A hundred, perhaps, remained from the 5th North Carolina, and they were on foot, their horses captured. He’d led them through the scrub, where the Yankee cavalry couldn’t follow easily, then he’d gotten them back on a byroad, hoping that other men from the brigade might find them.

None did. It all seemed as futile a thing as he’d ever done. The only bother that had slowed the Yankees was rounding up the prisoners they’d taken.

Bitter end for a fine brigade. His soldiers had deserved better than to be sacrificed—abandoned—by the high and mighty Virginia compact of Lees.

He *still* wouldn’t give up, though. Not a chance in damnation he’d quit. No more than he’d quit a court case halfway through. Juries did surprise you.

Noon
Richmond

Mrs. Elizabeth Saunders Taylor hardly felt herself a gay new bride. Her little sleep had been spoiled by a dream of rats—creatures of which she had a particular dread. It was not the way she'd imagined her wedding night as she'd waited forever for Walter to propose. Nor had Auntie Ruth saved her any breakfast. Positively insolent—so unexpected from her—the tubby old Negress had muttered into her layers of chin, "Things changin' round here, times changin'."

The younger house servants had disappeared, while their elders performed their chores at a pace much slowed. A body felt trapped, unable even to take a turn in the garden, given the soot in the air and the stench of smoke.

Dear Richmond, what would become of it? The darkies, with their queer ways of knowing things, claimed that the Yankees had taken over the city, that they were everywhere, "the Jubilee done come." Would spiteful Northerners let the city burn? Or put a torch themselves to what remained? She wished she could see what was happening for herself, but she dared not go out, envisioning lurid crimes visited on ladies left to the mercy of uncouth Federals. Her thoughts made the new bride shudder—what was the French word for what she felt? A *frisson*? Or did that suggest the wrong meaning? She wished she'd paid more attention to Mademoiselle Henriette.

And she wished that Walter hadn't gone off, that he'd stayed here to protect her. His sense of honor seemed less appealing by daylight.

She didn't know what she'd do when she first met a Yankee—one who wasn't a prisoner of war. Just snub him, that might be best. Let him feel the degree of her disdain. Pass by without a word, without a glance.

But what if he . . . behaved badly?

She sat down at the piano in the parlor. Where had everyone gone? It struck her that she had not seen another resident of the house for hours upon hours.

Well, it seemed like hours. . . .

What if the Yankees broke in through the front door?

In that case, she resolved to behave with dignity and defy them. If she was to be martyred, Walter would be forced to mourn her memory.

She did hope that any Yankees who broke in weren't Irish, though. *That* would be intolerable.

Walter had *abandoned* her. That was the truth of it. She poised her fingers over the keys, ready to pound the instrument—perhaps play "The Bonnie Blue Flag" as an act of defiance? Loud enough for any stray Yankee to hear?

She dropped her hands into her lap again.

Surely the servants would come to their senses by dinnertime? She was getting awfully hungry.

That morning, she had not even had assistance with her corset. Forced to lace it herself, she had needed to leave it loose enough to shimmy it front to back. The war had brought privations, but this was unbearable.

She'd thought that glorified pickaninny was loyal. You really couldn't trust any of them, could you?

Of a sudden, she heard cheers. Shouts. Singing. Faint at first, the jubilation swelled, as if it were marching toward her, straight up West Main Street.

The cheers became a roar. And the voices unified in delight were . . . colored.

Howls of glee vied with hallelujahs. Voices broke out in that odious Federal song, as if their eyes really had "seen the glory," a song she had only heard sung by defiant prisoners. It was like . . . like a great ocean wave rushing her way.

Bettie Taylor dashed to the front door but found it bolted, with no servant to assist her. She chafed her hands on the rude iron, hurrying to let herself onto the porch.

A horrid scene awaited her.

Flanked by crowding, jostling Negroes, a Union cavalry regiment paraded up the street in a column of fours. Perfectly uniformed and disciplined, with sabers gleaming at rest against their shoulders, the troopers rode handsome horses, the mounts of the privates as fine as those ridden by Confederate officers.

It was a brilliant spectacle, irresistible to the eye, made terrible only by a single fact: Except for the officers riding at the front, every one of the cavalrymen was a nigger.

Four p.m.
Chesterfield County

He wasn't a wicked one for complaint, he didn't think, but how much weariness could they pile on a man without so much as giving him a feed? Riordan had stabbed an extra hole in the belt he'd had of a Yankee, and he felt that he'd need a new hole soon enough. Rations there had been none to issue before they'd slipped off in the dark and crossed the bridge, making a grand torch of the wood in their wake. They'd gotten a start on the Yankees, all right, but at the price of no sleep at all and thread-flavored crumbs picked from the seams of haversacks. Even water came in miserly portions, the roadside wells drunk down to mud by the army that went before them—oh, wasn't it high and noble and fine to serve as the rear guard?

Colonel Waggaman had announced that it was a glorious honor and the army had no better men for the purpose, but the time for speeches had come and gone, and more than one boyo complained that the Yankee who'd wounded the colonel at Stedman hadn't demonstrated sufficient skill.

'Twasn't hot, thank God and the holy saints, and Riordan could still put one foot in front of the other, though there was but a walking corpse's life in it. Along a man plodded, grateful that the roads had dried a bit and the going wasn't all mud and muck and clabber. But hard it was, hard, to remember sleep and a belly that was at least a quarter full.

Caw, the shabbiness of the business, though. To march at the army's ass end was to learn how much even poor men had to discard. The officers high on their horses didn't need maps to follow the grays gone ahead, no, all they had to do was to mark the trail of coats and blankets dropped by the roadside, of broken-wheeled wagons abandoned by frightened teamsters and the carcasses of horses and mules that had given their last and got, at most, a bullet to end their misery.

Well, many a man got less.

Books, even Bibles, newspapers and journals, letters, playing cards, pictures of women and children, spare shoes worn hard yet hoarded, a chess set spilled black and white, here and there a bandsman's dented instrument, all these and—more and more—rifles lay strewn about, announcing the passage of an army as surely as the death bell told of the cholera. Men lay there, too, like plague dead, until the appointed bastards woke them with bayonets from the slumber that had captured them on the march. And multitudinous turds there were, of marvelous variety, the calling cards of sick and well alike, though Riordan couldn't figure how men so hungry could make so bold an offering.

Now and then a pair of men wandered off. At first, such like had met with glum derision, but only silence accused them after a time, a quiet that verged on envy and connivance. Rare was the lieutenant who troubled to chase them, and rarer the captain who turned his horse their way.

'Twas only April, but the army was melting.

At least the Yankees had not yet come upon them, left to their riots and revels in Petersburg. Up they'd come when ready, of course, but a man had to be grateful for what life yielded.

The column stopped for the hundredth time, a squeezebox shut with a wheeze. Had they struck the rear of the wagons again, the train that cursing officers insisted was on the wrong road, damn them? Oh, but standing still was a terrible thing when a man was wearied. Better to stumble on.

Tired men rode tired horses up and down the column. Earlier, he'd heard officers rattling about what lay ahead of them—they'd crossed the river to the north, but soon they were to cross to the south again. There had been no mention of food, merely of routes and bridges and water levels.

Impatient of orders, men sat down in the dust to wait out the pause. But would they rise again? Steps away, one fellow mick shoved another, declaring, "I'll not be put upon by the likes of you!" But neither bucko had the fire for fisticuffs.

His own anger came in bursts—that tired anger that makes a man rude and rough-mouthed. But what had he to say? Who was left to curse? With a throat as dry as chaff? More than once he was minded to stalk off himself, officers be damned, and to walk until he found something to eat. Instead, he shuffled forward as the column came back to life, only to stop again and stump forward again . . . barely mocking when he decided he understood the Irish who'd eaten their children.

"It's not so bad as the famine years, not yet, ye wimpering bugger," he said aloud, imposing correction. Strict-hearted a man had to be, and square of shoulder. Whispering to himself, he added, "Mind yourself now, boyo. They'll feed ye when they feed ye, not before."

But cautions were wasted on his bile-bitten belly, and Daniel Riordan felt the violence in him.

Four thirty p.m.
Clover Hill Plantation

Lee had eaten moderately, but with pleasure, and he'd found it refreshing to chat for a brace of minutes with the Cox girl, Kate, who was a gentle flirt. As Lee's party passed on the road, Judge Cox had invited them in for juleps, then dinner. Lee had abstained from the juleps, though Longstreet accepted a second, but the meal had been startlingly fine, as if long in preparation. Miss Kate had behaved handsomely, cutting up Longstreet's chop for him when it became all too obvious that his Wilderness wound still hampered his use of utensils. Lee then dared a flirtation of his own, "demanding" her attention by virtue of his rank, even appealing his case to her father, the judge. All present had thought it merry, but Lee had felt the passage of the years, smartingly aware of the span between his own age and that of the winsome Miss Cox.

Women had adored him once, those chaste and those less steady. He had always behaved as a gentleman, of course. Always. But he had reveled in their attention at balls or receptions or ceremonies, his blue jacket perfectly fitted and buttons blinding. He had enjoyed the admiration of fellow officers, too, but nothing surpassed a warm glance from soft eyes or the tap of a fan on his wrist.

He had been proud. In so many ways. And vain. Pride and vanity had ever been his nemeses, masked by polite reserve and attention to duty. He had built his life gesture by gesture, one courtesy at a time. Only to come to this.

In his darkest moments, he feared that a triumphant Union might prosecute him as a traitor and hang him in public. He would end in an ignominy worse than his father's, the long endeavor of his life to revive his family's reputation ruined.

Well, he could bear even that, he believed, if the Good Lord willed it. As long as those people spared his sons and his nephew. The young did not bear the responsibility. They had been unwitting and passionate, and he had led them to this.

As for the splendid meal Judge Cox's servants had put on the table, Lee consoled himself that he needed his strength. His soldiers had not eaten, he knew it well, but starving himself hardly seemed a useful response. He was careful, though, as he chose among the delicacies. He could not afford a return of his digestive ailments, not with his heart already a bother again. And his back ached severely and constantly, a punishment decreed by a higher judge.

He had to be strong for the men now. In mind and body alike. At least, he had to appear strong. And confident. Invulnerable.

Oh, what a terrible lie it was to be a leader of men.

When the judge invited them into the parlor for a round of coffee, Marshall, Venable, and the haggard, just returned Taylor had looked at Lee in such perfect unison that the effect was one of comedy: three schoolboys afraid the hour of play was up.

Let them have their coffee. Who knew when they might rest like this again?

Longstreet and his aide beat them all to the parlor.

Matters then verged on indelicacy. Lee's first taste of the coffee struck him a blow. Miss Kate had served them *real* coffee, rich and powerful. Lee could not drink it. In moments, he read identical reactions on the faces of all who were clothed in dusty gray. Except for boiled chicory or watery brews made from captured beans stingily rationed, none of them had tasted coffee for years, its scent as alluring as a beauty's perfume and its bite that of a wolf.

He chose not to question how Judge Cox might have come by such a treasure. Whatever the coffee's source, pouring it so freely showed generosity.

Venable, quick and clever, saw the solution.

"Miss Cox," the aide began, "might we impose upon you for cream or milk? I don't believe any man here has enjoyed such marvelous coffee for years on end, and a small pour of cream would stretch out the general pleasure."

Longstreet grunted. "Just say you want some cream, Colonel."

Sprightly and fair, as light as the girls with whom Lee once had danced, the daughter of the house smiled and disappeared.

The cream was as soothing as it was delicious, the disarmed coffee restorative.

But soon, too soon, a silence as dark as the coffee prevailed in the room. The day's worries had grown insistent again, thoughts of the soldiers left to the roads intrusive, imagined commands from bleary captains accusatory, and their full stomachs guilty.

Miss Kate spoke out. Almost brazen. "General Lee, I do believe we're going to win this war. I believe it with all my heart. We *have* to win."

All present looked to Lee.

"Miss Cox . . . whatever the future may hold, let me assure you that no men have been braver than those who have served our cause." Lee gestured, gently, toward the velvet drapes and the triangles of light that shone between them. "Those men out there . . .

have never failed you. I wish you to know that. They have never failed any of us."

The poor girl's attempt at valor ended in one tear, then a second. She brushed her cheeks with the back of a white hand.

Lee rose and turned to his host. Despite his patriotic generosity, the judge appeared to Lee as a man who would thrive whatever might come.

"Our thanks, sir," Lee said. "Your kindness has counted for much."

"An honor to this house, General."

"And now . . ." He gestured toward the front door.

"Yes," the judge said. "Your duty."

"Indeed."

The party went into the yard, into the sunlight. In the middle distance, dust rose from the endless column of soldiers. Taylor and Venable excused themselves, following Longstreet toward the privy concealed behind the house. Colonel Marshall, who'd been waylaid by a courier, approached Lee.

"Bad news, sir. Bevil's Bridge is underwater, can't be crossed."

"The pontoons?"

"Current's too quick that far downstream."

Lee wished he might think more clearly. With the quickness he once had brought to bear so easily. In Mexico, even earlier in this war.

"Colonel Marshall, you have brought me a problem. You must bring me a solution."

"We'll have to turn the columns, sir. General Longstreet's men and Gordon's. They'll have to use Goode's Bridge, too. With everyone else."

"That will slow us. Considerably."

"Yes, sir. But the engineers are already shifting the pontoons, they'll do up there. We won't have just one span."

Lee nodded. It was the best that could be done.

Longstreet returned, settling his belt. "Long faces, I see. Didn't like your dinner, Marshall?"

The military secretary explained about the bridges.

"Goddamn," was all Longstreet offered.

Lee chose not to chide him for the profanity. Not even with a look. He feared they were beyond gentility now.

"General," Lee told his favored, quarrelsome subordinate, "we shall surmount this, too."

"Slow us to a crawl. I've already got men set to gnaw their belts and shoes."

"Tomorrow, General Longstreet. They have only to endure it until tomorrow. I've ordered up a hundred thousand rations. They'll be waiting for us at Amelia Court House, on the boxcars."

Longstreet nodded. "I know. But I'd like to keep some distance 'tween us and the Yankees. Distributing those rations will take time. And while we're not yet being pestered up here, I suspect it's a different story south of the river. Fitz Lee and Anderson, they've got to hold back a flood of blue. And Pickett—"

"We will not speak of General Pickett now," Lee interrupted.

Longstreet sensed his temper. The lieutenant general's posture eased and he gentled his deep voice. "Can't cross one place, we'll cross at another. Make it work, either way." He turned his great bearded face and thick brows to Lee. "Embarrassing, to have to have some young filly carve up my dinner for me. Next thing some little gal might try to tie a bib to my neck."

The image struck Lee and he smiled. He couldn't help it.

"I should like to see that very much, General," he said, treasuring the moment. "I should like to see that, indeed."

Five thirty p.m.
Petersburg

With his company relieved from duty, Captain Charles Brown and three of his sergeants slipped off to visit Petersburg. It was the queerest feeling simply to walk across that dead stretch between the lines, with not a Reb or a hostile rifle in sight, then to clamber over fortifications that still stank of the Johnnies who had abandoned them. Before them the city waited in easing light, with only a few trails of smoke to tell of war.

Parties from sister regiments had set off to have their own look, and Negroes lay in wait along the road behind the entrenchments, offering to sell Confederate money or jars of suspect whiskey. Whatever joy had filled the coons in the morning had since collapsed into greed and speculation.

Brown and the sergeants waved them off.

"Lookee here, Marse. Here a hunnert dollar. Give to you for one green dollar, jus' one."

"Ain't worth a nickel, that ain't," Levi Eckert told him.

"It a hunnert dollar! Look!"

"Hau ab, du Negerschwein," First Sergeant Losch said. He never did have time for the colored race.

Sergeant Henry Hill kept his usual quiet.

"Womens for you, too, boss," a young Negro persisted.

He went ignored and, finally, fell away.

"What do you think it's like with a colored gal?" Levi asked all and none.

"You poke that, your *Schwanz* fall off," Losch said.

Brown stopped. Pointing. "Look at that. Just look."

"Must see something I don't see," Levi told him.

"The flag. Atop the courthouse. Or church, or whatever that is."

"Been there all day," Levi said. "Saw it from back in McGilvery."

"But you can *really* see it now," Brown tried to explain. He couldn't even explain it to himself, though. He was better with his hands than he was with words. Frances would have understood, though. Without words.

How long would it be now? Before he saw her?

As if all of them were thinking similar thoughts, Levi asked, "Well, now, Captain Brownie . . . think it's true? That we'll hang back? Just look after things, tidy up? And let the rest of them chase old Bobby Lee?"

Brown shrugged. He'd heard the rumor, too. That the Ninth Corps would remain in the rear—their division, at least—to garrison the city. He *hoped* it was true. He'd had enough of war. More than enough. He hoped that not a single man more from Company C of the 50th Pennsylvania would suffer so much as a dog bite. Just take them all home, those still alive and whole. March them up Main Street and down again. And call out a final, "Dismissed!"

Would it be like that? Could it really be over?

Inspecting the city's eastern lanes, Levi, who never could shut that mouth of his, declared, "Makes the Irish Flats back home look like some high-flown plantation."

"*Ja, ja,*" the first sergeant said, "*und* on Eckert Hill all houses is big mansions, *nit*?"

"Not an outhouse on Eckert Hill as shabby as these heaps. And the Rebs were fighting for *this*? So they could go on living like dirt people?"

"For God's sake, Levi," Brown interrupted, "it's the Negro part of town. What do you expect?"

"And Honest Abe got *us* fighting for *this*? Let the Rebs keep it, I say. Every damn inch of it. Their niggers, too."

"I'd let the Rebs keep *you*," Henry Hill told him. In one of his rare and incontestable statements.

The fact was that Brown would have much preferred to step into town with only Henry Hill, his wartime brother, beside him: Henry, who'd filled the space left by his blood-kin brother, dead of a Southern fever outside of Vicksburg. But all four of them had begun the war together, as privates, green as spring grass, and the group had just come together that afternoon, the way the four of them always did when they weren't stuck at their duties. It just happened that way, men grew together in war.

Disdaining the neglected streets, they aimed for the courthouse and found a New York regiment lolling about. Nor were their officers demonstrating much rigor.

Brown was not fully churched, though he went to services and read the Bible for Frances, but he prayed, inside himself, *Lord God, let it truly be over. Please, God. Let me and mine never hear another shot.* He didn't have anything else to add, so he just concluded, *Thy will be done. Amen.*

"What're you so serious over, Brownie?" Levi asked. "Camp trots coming on again?"

"He still is Captain Brown to you, Sergeant Eckert," Losch corrected, a Dutchman to the core and a fine first sergeant.

"Not for long, he ain't. We'll both be on the canal by summer, I bet." Levi grinned with yellowed, uneven teeth. "Then we'll see who's who." His grin broadened further. "And you, Sam, you'll be shoveling cow shit and giving your orders to billy goats."

"As long as we go home," Brown said, relaxing the hold of his captaincy for that moment.

He still found cause for wonderment that the flag really flew above that steeple. After all the bloody, disheartening months.

In the central streets, Negroes bantered and bartered with soldiers who teased them back and a few of those doubtful jars of liquor changed hands. Plugs of tobacco were plentiful, too, but not cigars. Officers and messengers rode about, their attitudes of importance no longer matched by urgency. Cautious white civilians—men only—saw to their doings, regarding every blue-coated soul as if the feared rampage had just been delayed and might start any moment. Solid brick buildings had taken a licking from artillery fire, but most of the damage looked like it could be patched up. Replace the windows, slap on some paint or whitewash. Didn't look ever to have been tidy, anyway. Nothing like Schuylkill Haven. But he supposed it did for Southern folk.

Faintly disappointed, the four of them turned back toward their company billets.

First Sergeant Losch said, "It wonders me, how we fight so long for such a no-good place. The generals say we fight, so we fight. But for *so einen Scheisshaufen*?"

"It's called 'strategy,'" Levi explained. "When generals decide one place is better for killing their men than another."

In a yard, a white woman in a coat made of burlap worked a pump handle, eyes fixed on her task. Brown felt the impulse to offer her help, a pure urge, a plunge toward decency and home, but before he could take a step in her direction the woman looked up with such hatred on her face that it chilled his heart.

"You git inside," the woman told an openmouthed child Brown had missed. "They's who killed your pa. You git inside."

None of them spoke for a while after that. They just walked. And Captain Charles Brown felt as though he might weep, for no reason at all.

He didn't, of course. Levi would not have left that tale untold, once they got home. But he pondered things, with his Medal of Honor forgotten.

Seven thirty p.m.
Cousin's Road

Sure we picked the right road, Fred?" Barringer asked his aide.

"Seemed like the right one, sir. Colored gal back there said so." But there was evident doubt in Lieutenant Foard's voice.

"Been riding too long. Should've come to that bridge by now, should be seeing soldiers."

Earlier, they had met assorted stragglers, along with escapees from Namozine Church. Barringer had organized them, then sent them off on the direct route to the army. But he'd veered off himself, seeking Rooney Lee, with only his aide and three couriers for an escort. They'd ridden a good six miles on the byroad, and that was some miles too far. Now the light threatened to fail.

He heard the voice the moment he spotted the rider on picket duty. To his relief, it belonged to a Southerner.

Barringer halted his little party. "Go see who that boy belongs to," he told a sergeant.

The sergeant nudged his horse back to a walk, right hand held in the air: *Don't shoot.* It was a nervous business. With the army busted up and on the move, no new signs and countersigns had been issued.

"Y'all identify yourselves," the picket called.

Raising the hand that held his reins as well, the sergeant replied, "North Carolina Brigade. Who you boys with?"

The picket allowed his own horse to clop forward. A half-dozen other riders clad in short gray jackets and an assortment of hats emerged from the shadows.

"Ninth Virginia," the picket announced. "Weren't expecting y'all, thought you looked like Yankees. Glad I didn't shoot."

"Glad of that myself," the sergeant told him. "Seem to have gotten ourselves a touch astray, we could use some help."

"Surely." The picket's voice darkened slightly. "Why're those other fellers hanging back? Who you say you're with?" He settled a hand on his holster.

"First North Carolina Brigade." The sergeant gestured back over his saddle. "That there's General Barringer himself."

"Well, I'll be!" the picket gasped. His tone mixed awe and penitence. He and his companions rode forward, slowly, to join Barringer's party. The lead picket headed straight for Barringer, extending his paw and grinning to pass for a simpleton. "Don't mind, sir, I'd be honored to shake your hand, right honored. Tell the folks back home I shook that hand."

It was something of a novelty to have a Virginian fuss over him, whatever the picket's rank. Even Virginian privates tended to haughtiness. Barringer gave the paw a handsome shake.

"Would you happen to know, son, where General Lee might be? Rooney Lee?"

The picket seemed to have trouble controlling his horse. It danced around Barringer's mount, making a half circle and coming back up on his left side.

"Can't rightly say where General Lee's gone off to," the man said. "Might say we been looking for him ourselves. But you'll do." He drew his revolver with a bandit's skill and grabbed Barringer's bridle. The entire picket party had drawn their pistols. They'd positioned themselves to encircle Barringer's men.

"Can't bring you to Rooney Lee, I'm afraid," Barringer's captor said in a voice much changed, a Yankee voice. "But I'll gladly introduce you to General Sheridan. You'll find him most hospitable."

Barringer's aide and the couriers had reached for their own weapons, only to find revolvers aimed at their heads.

"Go ahead," the lead Yankee told them, tone gone fierce. "Draw. And your general's war ends here."

Another Yankee added, "You lift them pistols out gently now, by the end of the butts. And drop 'em in the road. *Do it.*"

His subordinates looked to Barringer. He nodded. Revolvers thudded on the ground.

"You're violating the rules of war," Barringer protested. "You're disgracing yourselves and your flag." He had never felt so upended in his life. "Only spies change uniforms. And they hang."

"Well now, why don't you tell that to your own scouts?" a Yankee who'd held back a few yards asked. Stepping lazily, his mount approached. "They've been masquerading as our boys for years. And murdering, while they were at it. Cutting throats."

The Federal had the assurance and tone of an officer. He edged his horse closer to Barringer and doffed the feathered hat he wore for his fraud. "Major Henry Young, sir, United States Volunteers. At your service."

"You're all damned spies," Barringer snapped.

"Well, General . . . allowing that your fellow Confederates might hold a similar view . . . I suppose we'd ought to be getting on our way." He turned to Barringer's couriers. "Don't want you boys. You just get out of here. And I recommend you go back the way you came. Unless you want to get shot. Go on now."

That surprised Barringer. His men would sound the alarm. Why let them go? It struck him that he must have strayed far from any great prospect of rescue. Or the Yankees meant to move fast.

"You go on," Barringer told his men.

"Not *you,* Lieutenant," the Yankee major said to Barringer's aide.

"This is . . . ," Barringer began, reaching for the right word. "It's . . . it's ungentlemanly!"

The major nodded. "Myself, I've always felt that way about horse thieves." He pointed at Barringer's dapple-gray. "Wouldn't happen to be the horse some Southern gentleman took from Colonel Cooke at Black and White's Depot last June, would it? I don't pretend to great expertise in equine matters, but there is a striking resemblance." He offered a mock shrug. "The colonel will know. You'll see him before you see Sheridan."

"You all deserve to be hanged," Brigadier General Rufus Barringer declared.

The Yankees laughed.

Eleven p.m.
707 East Franklin Street
Richmond

Mary Custis Lee lay on her bed, crippled in body but capable of mind. It was all right now. She and her daughters were safe, thanks to the Federals. Their general, a man with an unfamiliar German name, had sent his compliments and posted a sentry at her front door to protect the house: She intended to see that her daughters served the boy breakfast, even if they had to do without. Rushing to be considerate, even courtly, the Federals also had stationed an ambulance nearby to evacuate her, should the fire reach her home.

Soldiers in blue—in the blue that Robert had worn for so many years—had fought the flames, containing them one block away, just past the blackened Presbyterian church. The air remained acrid and dirty, cruel to the lungs even with the windows shut, but the heat had faded and what remained of the city would survive.

How could she hate these men? She had burned with anger when told that Arlington House was lost beyond recovery. She had scorned the vandals who torched White House Plantation. She had known outrage and bitterness. But not hate. Hate was not Christian. Hate was not in her. Nor was it, she believed, in her husband, either.

How could she hate them when she'd shared their sentiments? She had recognized secession as a tragedy, her feelings about it stronger still than Robert's. But he had gone with Virginia, and she had gone with her husband.

How could she hate them, when to do so would be to deny the best times of her life? Those first years of marriage, when she, accustomed to servants, had been all but helpless at housekeeping, doing her best to bear up as she left behind Arlington House for a pair of rooms with dirt floors at Fortress Monroe . . . what would she have done without the sisterhood of Army wives, their shared tricks of making do and the endless generosities of which husbands were unaware, each catty remark wiped away by a dozen kindnesses? The states from which they hailed had been matters of curiosity, not of enmity. In the ramshackle quarters allotted to junior officers, they had made lives incomparably rich.

There she had been, a frail, quick-minded girl, still bewildered that Robert had chosen her, persistent against her father's initial refusal, determined, although she lacked the beauty to match his own. She *had* been a clever thing—and mad Sam Houston had courted her—but she knew the sought-after belles in her set had dubbed her "the little fox" for her small, sharp features. Nor had she ever enjoyed the best of health.

Yet Robert had taken her for his wife out of all of them. And she, a spoiled creature, had disappointed him more than once. Yet they had loved one another and still did. Robert had always been a terrible flirt, but he had been true, she knew it. Robert just needed admiration, as she needed his love.

He had called her "Molly" back then and had pressed his strong body against her.

They had danced well together, always. She always remembered the dances, whether homespun affairs got up by bored young officers or regimental balls with ticklish protocols. And Robert had been proud of her, "Lieutenant Lee's Southern belle," her dance card always filled by his fellow officers. Oh, they had all sought to dance with her then, in the golden days. And later, when she was the colonel's lady, they had danced with her out of duty. But they had *danced*.

And now there were days when she could not rise from her bed, not even with the assistance of her daughters—still unmarried—days when she could not bear to sit in her wheelchair and be pushed through her shrunken world of parlor and sewing room. She had let Robert down that way. He had needed a stronger wife, stronger in body, and that was the truth.

She only wished to live with him in peace again.

His pride would need much soothing when it ended. And the future was opaque. Once, it had seemed a life-altering tragedy when their furniture had been lost in a steamboat fire, and she recalled a time as a young wife when she'd been short-tempered for days because she'd left Arlington House with a Greek dictionary, although she'd meant to take along a Latin one. Now she worried over the fate of her husband and sons, over possible retribution, over . . .

Thank God that Robert had come to Christ at last. All who knew him only in middle age assumed that he had always been devout. But her greatest worry early in their marriage had been for his soul. He had gone dutifully to Communion, but had not been convinced. And then, in the decade before the war, perhaps at a premonition, he had found a faith that matched and exceeded her own.

She feared they would need much prayer in the days to come.

Mary Custis Lee did not hate anyone. But the closest she came to that sin was in her feelings toward the firebrands who'd made the war, this terrible, unnecessary war.

The chimes at midnight jarred her. It took her a moment to recognize what had changed: The bells were hushed, they were distant. Her own kind had burned down the churches that tolled through her nights. As they had burned down her life.

TEN

Nine a.m., April 4, 1865
17th Street dock, Richmond

Abraham Lincoln never did have sea legs. He teetered a bit as he tried to gain the dock. In his slight experience with naval affairs, it was the short fellows who leapt about like monkeys. Perhaps the cartoonists were right: He was too much of an elongated ape.

Some of those drawings did pass muster as comedy. Just a tad wounded, he had to laugh himself when Hay or Nicolay failed to hide the newspapers. Mary took the illustrations hard, though. His wife was a great one for dignity.

Admiral Porter reached out to steady the president. Lincoln got one foot and then the other on dry land. On the planks of the old pier, anyway.

Surveying the hard-used city, the admiral muttered, "I don't know, Mr. President . . . might be best to wait here for the escort."

"They'll be along. A little walk won't hurt any."

And Lincoln set off. Porter formed a bodyguard from the sailors who'd rowed his barge, then hurried across the wharf to catch the president. Amused by Porter's shortness of breath, Lincoln decided that while he might not possess sea legs, the admiral wasn't much for land legs, either.

Porter had organized quite a procession up the James, worthy of an emperor. From City Point on, the river had been lined with ships of war and cheering sailors, right up to Richmond's harbor, where scuttled Confederate vessels forced them to leave Porter's flagship for the barge. And while the admiral worried about "torpedoes" his clearing crews might have overlooked, Lincoln had sorrowed over the blackened waterfront, the scorched brick walls of warehouses and factories left roofless and still smoking, while nothing remained of lesser structures but chimneys and piles of rubble. The devastation stopped just below the august Capitol, where the Stars and Stripes stirred mildly after four years.

Crows circled the flag. He had never wanted any of this.

The promised Army escort either had been misdirected or had been given the wrong time for his arrival. Complicating matters, the choice of dock had been no choice at all as the plan broke down. Sailors had needed to jump into the current to pry the barge loose when it ran aground. After that, the admiral ordered them to put in alongside the first surviving pier. None of it troubled Lincoln. Too many things had gone right, and a few loose ends could be overlooked in the wake of great events. He'd had his fill of ceremonies, anyway. Made him feel like a combination of potentate and fraud.

He had hardly gotten beyond the wharf when a Negro on a work crew took a second look and cried, "Glory hallelujah! That the Messiah, that Marse Lincoln!"

And to the chagrin of one alarmed admiral and his bewildered sailors, the joyous crowding began.

Negroes simply materialized, conjured from alleys and ashes, crying, "Glory, glory!" and asking, "Him really Lincoln? That *him*?" They called him "Moses," they thanked the Lord, and they cried, "I done lived to see this day, done lived to see this day!" Only a few dared shake his hand, conditioned by a lifetime of servitude. Instead, they gathered around in their bright rags or household liveries, in frock coats out at the elbow and workingmen's stiff cloth, in sweat and splendiferous odors, straining just to touch his sleeve but never, never pushing him, warning each other to show respect, and thrice Lincoln had to lift up those who tried to kiss his boots.

"Hallelujah, hallelujah, black folk got they freedom!"

"Glory to Jesus Lord, Kingdom done come!"

"Freedom!"

But were they free? The demands and horrors of war had left him uncertain of what freedom meant even for white men, let alone for these exultant creatures. In their delight, he saw hopes bound to falter, not despite, but because of, their humanity. They were neither the holy martyrs proposed by the abolitionists nor the two-legged beasts damned by the slaver party. They were born to imperfection, as all men were, and he knew that some would be good and others bad, bound to disappoint advocates and detractors. Worse, they were destined to disappoint themselves. They expected Heaven but would awaken on earth.

He smiled as gently, as warmly, as he could at their caresses. So much remained to be done, so many wounds had to be healed on every side, and some of the gashes would never be made whole. It would demand a full generation and more before the Negro, educated and formed to modern society, discovered a fitting role and a fresh utility. And it would be that long, at least, before white Americans, South and North, agreed upon how much living space to cede.

A hard road stretched before all of them, black or white. But it would not be as hard as the war, he told himself. Nothing could ever be as hard as that.

Tears bejeweled faces brown and black, and features twisted in joy. Formidable women gone weak petted his sleeves and men touched the hem of his coat, expecting miracles.

"Admiral," Lincoln said to his flustered companion, "do you have any idea where we're going? I don't."

"Don't know the city myself, Mr. President. Never set foot . . ."

Lincoln turned to a colored man who had an intelligent face. "Know the way to Jefferson Davis' house?" He had almost said, "President Davis."

"Sure do, sure do. Every last soul know *that* house. You already going right, it just a stretch on."

A dozen and more voices insisted they'd lead him to Davis' house, as buoyant of spirit as if they were off to the Promised Land.

Edging in, Porter said, "Mr. President, I must fear for your safety. . . ."

The crowd had swelled to hundreds.

Lincoln smiled. "Reckon I'm safer here than in Washington." He strode on.

The fuss increased. They had left the last burned blocks behind, and white faces, summoned by the celebration, appeared at second-floor windows to show disdain.

Fear, too.

The climb up the streets had set the admiral wheezing, but Lincoln's problem was not with lungs or leg muscles. It was what to do next with this riven, expectant, stained, and striving country.

This was *it*. The end, or pretty near. Of an immense and agonizing effort. He thanked God for it as fervently as these Negroes thanked him. But with the wondrous relief came the suppressed worries, the nightmare doubts. There had been times when he wondered whether he might not be the monster the Southerners made of him, times when he felt drenched in gore, bathed in other men's blood. How far did his guilt go for all of the suffering?

He had ably mouthed the arguments for refusing to let the country divide in two, from the need to defend those Southerners whose allegiance remained with the Union, through the wantonness of extending slavery to states whose populations did not want it, to the hypocrisy of bondage in a land that proclaimed freedom for all men. But none of the earnest arguments added up, not to a sum that justified such bloodletting. A logical man, a wiser man, in his position might have allowed secession to proceed, striving to limit the damage and pain of parting.

But logic had little to do with the stand he'd taken. He had acted on a mystic belief in the Union's sanctity, a conviction he could not justify with law books, one that relied on a sense of justice, of the *necessity* of justice, above the common run. Even the word *justice* did not suffice. His belief in the United States was as blind as the faith of a Christian in salvation.

He had acted as he did, *he* had made this war, because he could not do otherwise. He had not been fitted for the choice forced upon him.

"Freedom! Hallelujah! *Freedom!*"

The Negroes did not walk, but danced beside him.

The city's uncharred streets wanted paint and tidying, but peace would see to that. It stumped him, though, how folks took pride in very different things, some in a fine property, others in achievement, Mary in new curtains and good china—how the newspapermen had attacked her for trivial things amid war! He meant to make it up to her, after they left the White House, which was far too big for such a little woman. Too big for him, too. And too haunted.

He had meant to bring his son along on the day's excursion, but had decided at the last minute to leave him back on the *Malvern,* watched over by the sailors. Mary could not bear another loss.

Pride, though. Pride, not slavery, had led a haughty South to clamor for war. That was what men did not understand: This struggle hadn't been about black bondage, not at the start. Arguments over slavery served as the trigger, and the abolitionists had done their share to provoke friend and foe alike, but it was the *pride* of the South, not the Negro question, that stirred millions to violence. The war had sprouted from the planter class, whose members believed they were not only better than the Negro, but better than other whites, especially Northern "shopkeepers." They had imported notions of aristocracy, of honor worn on the sleeve, better left behind. They valued indolence above honest work, wealth above rectitude, position above justice, and the horsewhip above the apology. The war had been made by "gentlemen" who had never chopped their own wood.

Those proud men had watched as the North passed them by, with Northern bankers holding their notes and Northern businessmen setting the price of cotton. They had let their fates slip from their hands and found they could not bear it.

They would have to bear it now.

The singing, weeping crowd surged past finer establishments, proud dwellings with heavy curtains and forbidding doors. The jubilation quieted a measure, as if dark-hued humanity still feared disturbing the master.

Well, he would do what he could for them while he remained in office, but he had no magic solutions, that was the truth. Nor would he drive the South to another war. It was going to take time, but everyone, on every side, would be impatient, he knew. Victory would unleash demands no president could honor, no wounded country sustain. And the South would be sullen and stubborn in defeat.

He wished he had a convincing plan. He'd learned to respect plans. Grant had had one, based on a clear-eyed vision. But Lincoln saw that his own decisions would have to be taken one after another, day by day, the stumbling improvisations of a blind man feeling his way.

And who would replace him, when it was time to leave Washington, time to go home and let others take up the burden? He wasn't about to say it aloud—make too many enemies of men he was going to need—but he'd bet on Grant. The veterans would carry him in, they wouldn't give him a choice. And while Grant didn't seem to have much interest, it was obvious that his circle had ambitions.

Well, Grant would do as well as any other and better than most. If he wasn't skilled at hoodwinking Congress—the primary job of a president—he possessed decency, even goodness. And Grant could lead men.

Lincoln only hoped that Grant's supposed friends, those of his intimate circle, would not mislead him. Rawlins was fine, but the man was sick with consumption. And others . . . Babcock, Grant's other pets . . . they were not all men to be trusted.

Leading his grand parade up the boulevard, Lincoln noted an elderly black man ahead, standing alone on a corner, erect and of serious mien, dressed in what Lincoln took for his Sunday clothing. The man's rigor calmed Lincoln's smile.

As the throng approached, the old man's eyes sought Lincoln's. There was no subservience in his gaze, only one upright man meeting another. The old fellow did not say a word, but removed his hat and placed it over his heart. Only then did tears escape him.

The president of the United States tipped his hat to a Negro.

A detail of cavalry clattered down the street toward the procession. The captain leading the horsemen stopped them short and leapt to the ground. He rushed toward Lincoln, saluting and almost tripping.

"President Lincoln, sir! We expected you down at Rocketts . . . General Weitzel's apologies, sir. He'll be along shortly, I'm sure."

"No better way to see a city than walking, Captain. And you would be?"

"Graves, sir. Aide to General Weitzel." The young man looked bewildered still. "You must've walked two miles, at least."

Lincoln smiled. "I had good company."

The sheath of the captain's saber tapped the cobblestones. He seemed overwhelmed by his circumstances.

"We anywhere near the Confederate White House, Captain? Or have I been on a wild-goose chase with all of my new friends?"

"You're almost there, sir. It's just ahead. General Weitzel's taken it for his headquarters."

Lincoln thought about that for a moment.

"Good."

The president wasn't at all what Thomas Thatcher Graves had expected. He'd turned out of Clay Street to find Lincoln looking like the Reverend Dr. Scarecrow, leading the Children of Ham on a picnic outing. Then, in Jefferson Davis' house, he'd sat down in the arch-rebel's office chair, delighted as a child and grinning foolishly. Next, Lincoln had leapt up and run through the house, upstairs and down, opening closets and drawers and asking questions that seemed impossibly trivial. All in all, he'd had the air of a little boy on a lark—and not a well-bred one.

When General Weitzel arrived, the playfulness stopped. There were serious matters to discuss and—as if notified by a wizard's telegraph—high-ranking Confederates begged for an audience. And the president had repeatedly to step outside and show himself to the multitude. Lunch was got up, after which the president asked to visit, of all places, Libby Prison and Castle Thunder. The general had taken him by carriage, with a proper cavalry escort this time, and Graves had been allowed to sit with his back to the driver.

He'd rather expected the president to be pleased that the vile prisons, which had been dens of torment for Union captives, now teemed with Richmond's scrofulous sorts caught in acts of destruction and looting, intermingled with Confederate soldiers who'd been scooped up tardy, drunk, or just plain quits.

But Lincoln had grown somber. Inspecting Libby Prison—a filthy tobacco warehouse with bars added—he had stopped asking questions and done no more than putter about and nod to himself repeatedly.

Back in the carriage—and the fresh air—General Weitzel had asked the president for guidance about how to treat the vanquished population. In a voice that seemed not entirely present, Lincoln had told him, "I don't have particular orders for you, I don't want to interfere. Do what seems best."

General Weitzel's expression told Graves he had not found the president helpful.

But after pondering the matter, Lincoln added, "If I were in your place, General, I'd let 'em up easy, let 'em up easy."

Eleven a.m.
Amelia Court House

Robert E. Lee could not credit his commissary's report. He needed to judge the truth of it for himself. Leaving his staff behind at the edge of the hamlet, where Marshall had selected a headquarters site, Lee rode straight for the water tower that announced the rail line. Only Lieutenant Colonel Cole, his abashed commissary chief, and two couriers trailed him.

At the rustic depot, seven freight cars sat behind a slumbering locomotive. Longstreet stood beside the tracks, alone, looking as somber as Lee had ever seen him.

Lee dismounted, his action aped by the empty-handed Cole.

Longstreet said nothing. Nor did he salute. He only shook his head slowly, as if the barest movement caused him pain.

"Well, General?" Lee asked.

"Best look for yourself, sir."

Lee walked to the first car and peered in the door. There were no rations. The car had been crammed with harnesses and saddles. He walked the gravel roadbed to the next car. It held artillery charges and shells, of which the army already had a surfeit. The next two cars carried identical loads. But Lee did not give up. He had to believe the mistake had not been complete.

The fifth car was filled with blankets, with perfectly new blankets that could have warmed his soldiers in the winter. The next car held enough pantaloons to outfit a division. The last carried more artillery shells.

It took all of Lee's discipline not to weep. Beside him, the chief of commissary said nothing.

Strict of posture and stern of face, Lee returned to his First Corps commander. Longstreet looked stricken, even more so now than upon Lee's arrival. As if the lieutenant general had hoped that Lee would see something other than he had himself, that Lee's presence would work a wonder.

"A disappointment," Lee said.

Lee read Marshall's draft of the proclamation:

Amelia C. H., April 4, 1865

To the citizens of Amelia County, Va.

The Army of Northern Virginia arrived here today, expecting to find plenty of provisions, which had been ordered to be placed here by the railroad several days since, but to my surprise and regret I find not a pound of subsistence for man or horse. I must therefore appeal to your generosity and charity to supply as far as each one is able the wants of the brave soldiers who have battled for your liberty for four years. We require meat, beef, cattle, sheep, hogs, flour, meal, corn, and provender in any quantity that can be spared. The quartermaster of the army will visit you and make arrangements to pay for what he receives or give the proper vouchers or certificates. I feel assured that all will give to the extent of their means.

R. E. Lee, General

"That will do," he told his military secretary. "But it must be copied swiftly and put in the hands of couriers. It must be carried in advance of the wagons."

"Yes, sir."

"The people will not let their army down."

"No, sir."

But the mood in the tent was glum. Lee turned to his chief quartermaster, summoned from his duty to help distribute the rations the commissary had failed to provide for the army.

"Colonel Corley, I must ask two things of you. First, you will empty additional wagons, all wagons not bearing essentials. You will send them to Colonel Cole, to join those assigned to the commissary detail. We must reach every farm and settlement. We must bring in all that the people may provide, and do it in haste."

"Yes, sir. And the second matter?"

"Pare down the trains. Any wagons not critical to this army's battle-worthiness must be dispatched on more northerly routes. They cannot further impede the army's movements. Nor can we spare such lavish detachments of guards. Am I understood?"

Corley nodded.

"The artillery, too, will be reduced," Lee added. "But that is not your concern."

Still, there would be a thousand wagons, at least. Lee knew it and rued it. Even an army lean and lithe could not carry all on its backs or in its saddlebags.

When the quartermaster had gone, Lee addressed Marshall,

Venable, and Taylor, whose labors let him administer the army. "I need to know *precisely* where General Ewell is now, if he has finished his crossing. He must not be dilatory. And I must know General Mahone's present situation. Has his rear guard crossed? Has the bridge been burned, the pontoons broken up? Have those people pressed him yet?" He looked specifically at Venable. "Any more reports from our cavalry?"

"Nothing since the earlier message. Still sparring with Sheridan."

"I can hear the 'sparring' as well as you, Colonel. I must have reports, *coherent* reports. Where are Grant's forward elements? When will they close? Where are we likely to meet them? We are not at sport, gentlemen."

No one dared speak.

Applying his cold fire to Marshall, Lee continued: "Communicate with Lynchburg. Before their scouts cut the wires. We *must* have two hundred thousand rations delivered by rail to Burkeville, they must be there in twenty-four hours. It *must* be done. I will not sacrifice this army to the leisure of supply clerks and railroad men. This inefficiency, this . . . this irresponsibility, is intolerable. And Colonel . . ." Lee could feel the force of his own glare. "There must be no confusion this time. Do you understand me?" He scanned the blanched faces, the sleepless eyes. "Does everyone here understand me?"

He left the tent. He was wrong, he knew, to chide them so. All had been used without respite, each of them did his best. But since he had walked that terrible line of railcars . . .

Longstreet rode up, a big man on a big horse. He dismounted heavily, hampered by his bad arm.

"Just heard Corley whipping up the teamsters. Thought I'd see if I should believe my ears."

"And what have your ears told you, General Longstreet?"

"Corley's sending out wagons, hither, thither, and yon."

"That is correct."

Longstreet's eyebrows climbed beneath his hat brim. "Going to take time. Foraging. How long—"

"The good citizens will support us. They will provide what is needful."

"Yes, sir. No doubt. But even if they do . . . we can't expect those wagons, most of them, to come in before morning, not with anything in them. You know these roads. Grant will be all over us by then."

Lee turned on him. "Do you believe I'm not cognizant of the risk? Is that what you suggest to me, General Longstreet?" He struggled to rein in his temper again, to discipline his voice. "What would you have me do? The men must eat. They must be fed, if we expect them to fight. If . . . we expect them to stay with this army."

On the road, another increment of soldiers began its passage through the hamlet. Heth's Division, in fair order. But they seemed so few. Even in the autumn, their strength would have been double what Lee saw. Spring was supposed to bring increase, flowering. . . .

"There's a consolation, I suppose," Longstreet said. His voice had no more argument in it, just weary acquiescence. "We can concentrate this army, catch everyone up. Become a proper force again. If Dick Ewell convinces his ragtags to step along."

The men plodding past saw Lee and Longstreet, but they did not cheer them.

They know, Lee thought. They've already heard: No rations.

He said, "I'm certain General Ewell is doing his best . . . sailors, militiamen, cadets . . . they are not used to marching, not as our men are." He thought of his eldest son, Custis, who commanded that makeshift division under Ewell. Custis, who had made his contributions in Richmond, not on the battlefield. "We must make allowances."

"Grant won't."

Lee did not choose to think about Grant at that moment. He would have enough of Grant, he did not doubt. Nor would he indulge in special concerns for Custis. Or Rooney, for that matter.

"That may be correct, General Longstreet. But we must find advantage where we can. When next we move, we shall move as one body, not as remnants in flight. We shall go forward as an *army*. You said so yourself."

"And . . . when *do* you foresee us moving, sir?"

"As soon as possible. Let us say noon tomorrow."

"That late?"

"We cannot expect the foragers before morning. I believe you said that, too."

"We'll lose our lead. We're giving the Federals a gift."

"The men must eat," Lee repeated.

Four p.m.
Amelia County

Eat he would, whether the high and mighty fed him or no. What kind of army was it, then, that asked a man to bleed and gave him no bread? A great comedown it had been for this poor-bellied lot, this Army of Northern Virginia, and what had that to do with Louisiana? And what had he to seek, after all, so far from New Orleans? Ah, glory, wasn't that it? Not at all, for he'd never believed in such moonshine, in all that gentleman's folderol, no, he'd seen that the going was better than staying would be, because he had soured on pick and shovel and fever, so he'd traded a spade for a bayonet, and now he had neither shovel nor spade, only bare hands and a tin cup to scrape up the loveless soil of Virginia.

No digging today, though, it had not been asked of them, the position would not be fortified. That was a comedown, too, a drop in the trusty discipline, but even the officers had grown haggard with hunger. March they had, hard from the rear, handing off the work, ta-ta, to Billy Mahone and his billy goats, oh, let them scrape along and suffer in turn. But hard it was, hard, to come to the village where all said they would eat their fill and stuff their haversacks, only to pass empty wagons on the road and then to be hurried past houses that gave no welcome, past strips and straps of the army already resting, but no, *they* must go on, another five miles.

And here they were.

His horn-hard feet ached and every muscle pained him, but his body would have to carry him a little farther. As men dropped on every side of him, complaining their way into slumber instantly iron, Riordan resolved to eat before he slept, and if Robert E. Lee could not put on a feed, he'd see to the business himself.

Off he went, alone, bleary-eyed through the beauty of the day, past rumpled officers snoring in their saddles and halfhearted sentinels terrified by the look of him, unwilling to quarrel or think beyond their misery.

He passed a lad who'd fallen asleep as he squatted to empty his guts. With privacy and shame reduced to a snore, the boy lay bared and still in his own filth.

There were toughs on the wharves of New Orleans who would have seen to the lad's ugly awakening. He knew suchlike, men with such tastes, but never had been one of them.

And into the brush and bush he went, into the briars and nettles, and through that trial and onto a road, still bearing his rifle to show he wasn't quitting—for quit he would not, unless forced by circumstance—and the road wasn't fit to be given a name, a back lane unworthy even of barren Galway, unworthy even of Mayo, a track untraveled by men of polish and pride, a poor man's way to nowhere.

That lane came to nothing, but beyond there lay another slashout, and he wondered whether he shouldn't turn back, whether he might not lose his way, with the old fear of the deserter's fate come over him . . . but the whole sorry lot of them were far past that now, they'd have to hang half the army and lacked the rope.

Desert he would not, but eat he would, and let no man stand in his way.

Birds mocked him. A black snake slithered off in haste, as if it feared he would gobble it still squirming.

He heard the screams before he saw the house.

'Twas more than a black snake making that missy howl. Against all reason, against all sense, he set off at a run, insulting his feet and tormenting every muscle.

The house was but a clappy affair, more than a shanty but falling far short of grand. Lived in, it looked, but neglected.

The screams were interrupted, as if smothered, but came again.

He leapt to the porch and through the open door. Nor had he to look far.

A great pimpled rump thrust in between a skinny pair of legs, a big man atop a convulsing girl on a parlor floor, and her screaming with her country dress thrown up above her waist.

There was no thought to his action. His left hand held his rifle tight and his right found the collar of the bully's uniform. He gave it a savage yank.

The fabric tore and the big lad woke to his presence. He growled, "Wait your goddamned turn."

"Get off her, ye bastard," Riordan snarled.

Frightened the more, the girl left off her scream to sob like a madwoman.

The fellow would not stop his doings, his ugly thrusts. Riordan grabbed him by his long hair, yanking him back with a sharpness that would have snapped a lesser man's neck.

With a howl, the fellow let go the girl, pulled off, and swung toward Riordan. Skilled, he was, for he came up to his full size with a knife ready in his hand. Or perhaps the blade had been there, used on the girl. His manhood hardly drooped.

He slashed the knife toward Riordan's face, a knowing move. But the big lad's trousers chained his ankles together. He all but toppled.

Riordan double-gripped his rifle and slammed it, upended, into the fellow's ear. But a strong one, the bastard was. He did not go down but fought to keep his balance, cursing the while.

This time, Riordan gave him the butt-plate full and fair in the mouth.

The big soldier toppled backward with an animal's fierce lament.

Quaking and mewling, the girl lacked the sense to cover the bloody mess of herself, let alone take herself off.

"Out of me way." He kicked her meat.

The big lad still held the knife and had just about steadied himself for another frolic. Riordan noted a sergeant's stripes red on an artillery jacket. Rank had not been foremost in his thoughts.

Deft and glad of it, he just had time to cap his rifle and cock it. When the man who had made him his enemy threw himself toward Riordan, he was met with a blast to the chest that hurled him backward, spraying blood and meat across the parlor.

The girl had bunched herself up by a chair, shivering as with a fever, unable to look the world or any man of it in the eyes. She rolled onto her knees and vomited.

Riordan could not explain the rage that had taken him up and possessed him. What had he to do with a half-starved piece of baggage that passed for a woman? She was none of his, nor any of his kind.

He stood there, gasping, amid the poor room's wreckage.

He lacked the least idea of what to do, his brain as empty as his haversack. Just leave? With the work here done? He'd owed the girl nothing, and now he owed her less.

Disappointing himself, he could not go. Not yet. And though he felt sick—sick in a way that reached beyond ready words—he thought he might at least have a look through the kitchen. He'd earned a feed.

But he could not start himself to do that, either.

"Missy, get up." He took her by the arm.

She shrieked, rebellious, and fled through the puddle of vomit, crawling and cringing.

And no sooner had she quieted back to sobs than the sergeant's corpse jerked, as fresh corpses sometimes did to fright the living. She screamed again, though once only.

His mind began to work again, if slowly. The corpse had to go, at least out into the brush. For they'd hang a private for killing a sergeant, no matter the sergeant's shame. Riordan was sure of it. And the missy was gone off mad and could not be trusted. Who knew what tales she'd tell?

Instead of grasping her arm, he reached out a hand. It was dirty and rough and it shamed him. For all her travails, the girl looked an orderly sort, no hayloft slattern.

"Missy, I know it's a trouble on you, but I need your help, there's things that want the doing."

He knelt before her, hand still extended, the way a man made friends with another man's dog.

Timidly, she offered a paw. 'Twas reddened by work, but fine. The instant she felt his touch, she pulled back again. Shuddering.

"You must help me, girl. Or there's trouble and worse for the two of us."

She steeled herself, took his broken-veined hand, and managed herself to her feet.

Standing there before him, though, she gave him a terrible moment. For tall she was, slender and fair. As he looked at her, he knew that he would never have such a woman in his power again, never know what such a one was like. . . .

Dread lit her eyes. As if she read his thoughts.

He broke off. The danger passed. He cursed his decency.

To work he went, and he made her do her part. He propped his rifle by the door, had a peek to be sure they had not summoned an audience, and made her lift the dead man by the ankles as he gripped the corpse by the armpits. There was no grace in the doings, but they lugged and dragged him into the nearest grove and out of sight. The corpse left a trail of blood, but it could not be helped.

The girl took turns staring off to the land of the fairies and glancing at the waggling, bloodied bit that had harmed her so. A bold one, the sergeant had worn no undergarments.

When she could go no farther, Riordan dragged the body another thirty yards into the undergrowth. He considered going through the fellow's pockets, but soon realized the folly of such a deed. For it might well come about that he'd have to explain a possession he could not explain. He even left the wedding band on the dead man's finger.

When he came back, the girl was bent over, retching again, but with nothing to bring up.

"Well, you needn't thank me," he said, embittered now by his foray into nobility. No good would come of it that he could see.

She wiped her mouth and brushed off a strand of drool.

"Missy . . . have ye a thing to eat in the house? I'd be grateful for the least bit ye could spare."

She stood, still bent, with her eyes closed. And he waited, hating the tone that had entered his voice. He'd sounded like a beggar, like a roving tinker come to the back door with his hand stretched out.

He gave up. "Come back and bury him, if ye have the strength," he told her. "Ye'll find the labor easier than explaining. Then keep to the house till the armies pass."

He stepped off, sick in a thousand ways, to fetch his rifle and be on his way.

Halfway to the house, the girl caught up to him. Her dress was torn and he hoped she had another. The women he'd known would have shrugged away what she'd suffered, as soon as the whiskey wore off. This girl would not.

"There's food," she said.

He nodded. Conversation between them was unwelcome. On both sides. One of life's mysteries, a mystery unlike those praised by priests.

In the house, he took up his rifle to reload it. As if the sergeant's corpse might come round to call. The parlor might have been orderly once, but the doings of the day had left it a shambles. He cautioned her to scrub up the blood and no nonsense, to put things right. She didn't answer, but passed along a hallway.

Before he followed, he noted a picture displayed upon the mantel, the image of a fresh-faced lad in a still-fresher uniform. It was wreathed in black crepe.

Brother or sweetheart, it made no difference to him. No husband, though, for she wore no ring. He always noticed gold, wherever he saw it.

He trailed her into the kitchen. She stood at a cupboard, back turned. The girl was slender, all but starved herself.

I've earned whatever she puts in front of me, Riordan assured himself.

She gave him a pretty china plate, with lads and maids at play. It was chipped, but precious, he sensed. Upon it, she put a meager square of cornbread and set a jar of sorghum molasses by. Then, after unmistakable hesitation, she brought out a folded rag and opened it up. Four strips of bacon, cooked but cold, were the treasure of the house.

She gave him water.

"There's no more," she said. "Government took everything, gave us scrip. When Ma died, they took the cow, too."

He barely heard her. He poured the molasses over the cornbread, broke off chunks with a filthy hand, and shoved the sticky marvel in his mouth.

He was done almost before he had begun. Somehow, he found the strength to leave her two strips of the bacon.

She'd stood there while he gobbled. Staring but not seeing. Dripping private woman-blood on the floor.

Women had ways with such matter, he was certain. She'd care for herself. Anyway, there was no more he could do, 'twas no business now of anyone but her kin. And he had to get back to the army, to know how it ended.

"I'm away," he told her, rising. "Keep to the house, do. Bury him, if you're able. But otherwise keep to the house. And see to the parlor." He wanted to say something more, but words were difficult. At last, he told her, " 'Twas nothing, missy. Just put it from your mind."

She slid down by the cold stove, wrapped her arms around her knees, and sobbed again.

He left her that way.

Nine thirty p.m.
Deep Run

Major General George Gordon Meade felt put-upon. Of all times to be ill, this was the worst. His Army, the great, oft beleaguered Army of the Potomac, was on the move, pressing after Lee, filling the wretched roads and worse byways of Southside Virginia, the way forward marked by cavalry skirmishes, extended marches, and quarrels over priority at crossroads . . . and he was so sick he had needed to take to bed after arriving at Humphreys' headquarters. Good old Humph had managed a supper for Meade's staff and his own, simple and welcome, but Meade had hardly been able to get a bite down.

He didn't know if he faced pneumonia as a consequence of presuming his cold had passed, or if his Florida fever was back upon him. He only knew that he yearned to stay in bed—even at the risk of Virginia bedbugs—and could not do so.

Nor had he slackened. He'd spent the day in the saddle, following the Namozine Road at first, driving his army forward, and frustrated by a thousand and one delays. Grant had ordered that Sheridan's cavalry take priority whenever columns collided along a route. That made sense, of course. Sheridan had the means to press ahead, to determine Lee's next objective, the obvious choice of Danville, or Lynchburg as an alternative. Phil had to get to Burkeville, where the railroads crossed, and cut off the Rebels, if possible.

Despite the logic, the practice was exasperating. Cavalry columns dallied like society matrons at a flower show. Humphreys' hard-marching corps had been held up for hours, Wright's for much of the day, and everyone needed rations. The trains got stuck in the mud even with no rain, and Humph had needed to put his men to work corduroying roads crucial to the army.

And yet they were moving. Ranging the countryside, free of fear of ambush on any great scale. Robert E. Lee was running for his life. Meade didn't underestimate the sting left in that viper, but he had a big enough stick.

The men wanted rations, the men wanted sleep, their generals wanted clear orders, and Grant, already at Wilson's Station, wanted intelligence of Lee's whereabouts.

So did George Meade.

He had to pay homage to the Confederate cavalry. For all their losses, they screened Lee's movements with skill. It was all but certain that Lee would have to pass through Amelia Court House, doubtless as swiftly as his army could go, yet no scout had been able to report his order of march, his remaining strength, or his headquarters location. What information came in was gleaned from deserters, of which there was a hungry, dejected surfeit. But their utterings were confused, their insights overtaken by marching armies, and the tales of deprivation they told inflated to cover their shame.

And Lee had always been at his best when cornered. A viper indeed. If one masquerading as a flawless gentleman.

Meade groaned and turned on his side. He'd already soaked the bedclothes with his sweat. And his guts churned. He did not know if he could ride again tomorrow.

No, that was nonsense. He *would* ride. And he would command. And his army would get its due.

A knock on the door. His chief of staff. Webb held a hurricane lamp reeking of poor oil.

"General . . . my apologies . . . you need to read this yourself."

"From whom?"

"From General Sheridan. A courier just delivered it."

What was that devious Irishman up to now? Trying to steal all the glory yet again? Poor Warren, shamed, had been consigned to the empty command of Petersburg, now that there was nothing left to command. Meade knew all too well that Sheridan had schemed against him, too.

He took the scrawled message. Webb brought the lamp close.

It was marked as having been sent at seven p.m.

"What time is it, Webb?"

"Just after nine thirty, sir."

Meade's eyes focused more sharply; he'd read the time, but not the preceding place name.

"Good Lord," he said. "He's at Jetersville! Bully for Sheridan. That's moving as cavalry should."

"Read it all, sir."

"GENERAL: The rebel army is in my front, three miles distant, with all its trains. If the Sixth Corps can hurry up we will have sufficient strength. I will hold my ground unless I am driven from it. My men are out of rations. Please notify General Grant."

Meade rose from his sickbed and reached for his uniform coat. "The Sixth Corps won't be enough, not even with the Fifth right behind Phil. Not if Lee determines to break through. Humph is going to have to march tonight. All night. With the entire Second Corps."

"I've already warned him."

"Good." Unwilling to waste the time to summon his orderly, Meade pulled on his own boots. Even that taxed his strength. "And fetch Batchelder. I want a train of rations moving up right behind Griffin. Start on the formal order, I'll answer Phil myself."

"You know, sir . . . Ted Lyman's right," Webb said.

"About what? The mating habits of starfish? What's Teddy up to now?"

"About Sheridan. That he's doing all he can to cut you out."

Meade chose not to think about that now. He was as jealous as any man. More. But he had been a soldier too long and loved the profession too much to let it rule him. They just might have Lee cornered. Nothing else mattered.

"I'll worry about that later. Here." He extended Sheridan's message. "Have it copied, send Grant the original. Move sharply, man."

Meade strode out into the commandeered parlor, where Humphreys' staff matched his own in slouching exhaustion: That part would get worse, they'd just have to bear it. If he could, they could.

"Somebody give me a damned piece of paper," he bellowed, fevered and sweating and ablaze with hope.

This just might be the end.

He wrote:

Major-General Sheridan:

The Second and Sixth Corps shall be with you as soon as possible. In the meantime your wishes or suggestions as to any movement other than the simple one of overtaking you will be promptly acceded to by me, regardless of any other consideration than the vital one of destroying the Army of Northern Virginia, which I judge from your dispatch you consider as practicable.

GEO. G. MEADE
Major-General

It was all right. Phil could have the glory, if he and his army could have Robert E. Lee.

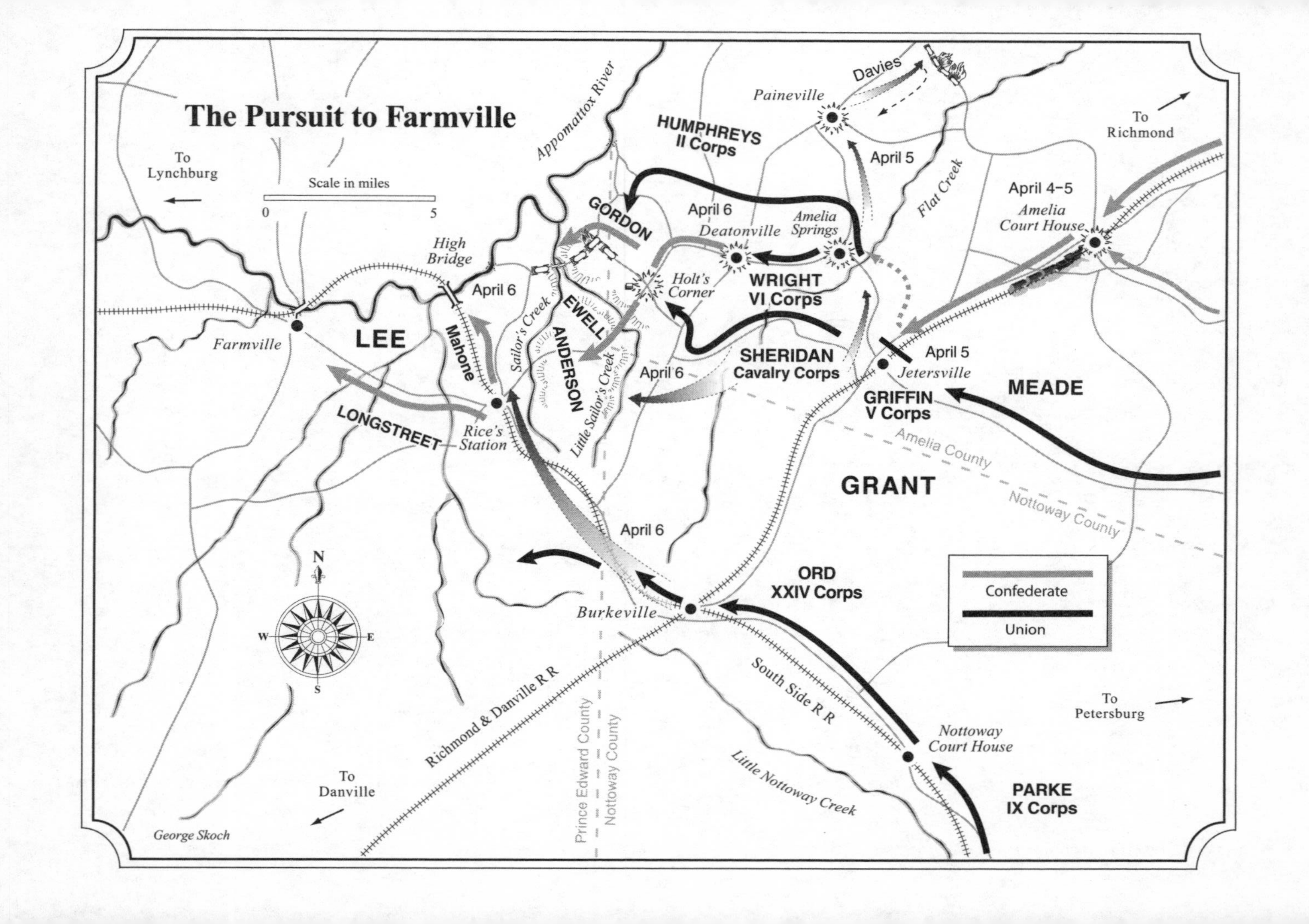
The Pursuit to Farmville
To Lynchburg
Scale in miles
0
5
Appomattox River
HUMPHREYS
II Corps
Paineville
Davies
April 5
To Richmond
Flat Creek
April 4–5
Amelia Court House
GORDON
April 6
Deatonville
Amelia Springs
High Bridge
April 6
Holt's Corner
WRIGHT
VI Corps
Farmville
LEE
Mahone
Sailor's Creek
EWELL
ANDERSON
SHERIDAN
Cavalry Corps
April 6
April 5
Jetersville
GRIFFIN
V Corps
MEADE
LONGSTREET
Rice's Station
Little Sailor's Creek
Amelia County
GRANT
Nottoway County
April 6
ORD
XXIV Corps
Confederate
Union
Burkeville
South Side R R
To Petersburg
Richmond & Danville R R
Prince Edward County
Nottoway County
Nottoway Court House
Little Nottoway Creek
PARKE
IX Corps
To Danville
George Skoch

ELEVEN

Ten a.m., April 5, 1865
Amelia Court House

The wagons came back empty. Almost all of them. And the few that delivered tithes to the Confederacy carried only dry corn, spoiling hay, and, rarely, a treasure of side meat and potatoes. Lee had waited, refusing to give up hope, as one line of wagons after another creaked past, their accompanying officers disconsolate and ashamed. With almost all of the foraging parties returned, there were barely enough provisions to feed a regiment, let alone a hungry army.

His immediate task was to keep up a resolute front. But it was hard. The weight of trusting thousands lay upon him.

Lieutenant Colonel Cole tried to explain: "Sir, the entire county's been picked over. What little they have, they hide. Richmond commissaries been combing those barns and smokehouses since last summer, folks can hardly feed themselves." Cole's left eyebrow always sagged; today it hung lower than ever. "Even those who gave didn't want the scrip."

They were right about the certificates, Lee knew. He did not believe the scrip or chits or his government's currency ever would be redeemed. But formalities had to be honored.

And now there were rumors—not yet reports—of Federal cavalry at Jetersville, worrisomely close to the line of march.

Put that aside for now, he told himself. Perhaps there was nothing to it, merely a scouting party that could be driven off. He did not believe the Federals could move so swiftly, not in force.

Another empty wagon passed. Lee turned from his commissary

chief, whose broken spirit felt all too contagious. It was a terrible thing for a man to learn that his best was inadequate.

He offered Cole no sympathy as they parted. It was not a time for softness, for indulgence. The army could not be nourished on excuses, men needed something to put in their mouths and chew. Cole had failed. He needed to bear his failure.

Longstreet appeared, a bear unchained, and together they walked back into the yard that hosted the headquarters tents.

"What shall we do, General?" Lee asked.

Longstreet grunted. "March."

"I meant the question in a larger sense."

"March harder."

Longstreet did not reproach him for the fruitless delay. He would not. He did not need to.

"I tell myself," Lee said, "that the men remaining to us are the finest. The weak have fallen away." It went unsaid what both men knew, that hunger weakens the strongest body, the greatest heart.

"They'll march, all right," Longstreet told him. "Done it before. Won't say they're not disappointed, though."

A mild way of expressing matters, Lee thought.

Marshall emerged from a tent to greet him.

Lee spoke first: "The army will march at one p.m."

"Yes, sir."

"You look doubtful, Colonel."

"No, sir. It's only that . . . General Ewell still hasn't closed. He doesn't expect his rear to reach us until late afternoon."

"The roads will be crowded until then. General Ewell can follow."

"Change of orders for General Gordon, sir? You said you might—"

"No. General Gordon's corps will continue to serve as the rear guard. It would only sow confusion to change the order of march. General Longstreet, screened by General Lee's cavalry, will keep the van. General Mahone will follow. The first increment of trains will move between Mahone and General Anderson. General Ewell's command will follow Anderson. The remainder of the trains moves in Ewell's rear, protected by General Gordon."

"Yes, sir."

"John Gordon's going to feel like we're feeding him to the lions." Longstreet wore a wry smile, almost invisible in his bearded face.

"I believe," Lee said, "that more than one lion may break a number of teeth."

Eleven a.m.
Paineville

Hank Davies beheld the greatest opportunity for mischief he had encountered since being asked to leave Harvard and forced to leave Williams before romping through Columbia with only minor scandals and admonishments. As a lawyer, he'd even played a few courtroom pranks. But the hell a fellow could raise with a general's stars on his shoulders and a brigade of horse was of a higher order than any mere stunt.

It had surprised his father halfway to apoplexy when the Union army made his reprobate offspring a brigadier and followed that up with a brevet to major general. It had emerged that Henry E. Davies, Esquire, and the cavalry were made for one another.

"God Almighty," his aide gasped, admiring their discovery.

"Thank the devil, I think." Davies drew out his field glasses, although they hardly were needed.

Before them, down a long slope still shy of greenery, hundreds of wagons wobbled along a farm road, interspersed with artillery sections either undermanned or not visibly crewed except for the drivers. Infantry details plodded along as escorts, slouching as though they were off to their own executions.

And they were.

The commander of his lead regiment, the 1st Pennsylvania Cavalry, clopped up beside Davies. At the sight spread before them, the colonel whistled.

"Lorelei, honey, tell me I'm not dreaming. . . ."

"Going to be a nightmare for those Johnnies," Davies told him.

As soon as the lead fours of Pennsylvanians crested the low ridge, the Confederates took notice. A lone gun crew's members leapt to unhitch their piece.

"He who hesitates," Davies said, "doesn't have half so much fun. Charge them. Now. As soon as the Twenty-fourth comes up, we'll join the party."

"Bless Robert E. Lee for this day's bounty," the colonel said.

In half a minute, a bugle sounded the charge. The Pennsylvanians went madcap for the wagon train, unfolding from column to lines as they dashed forward. Davies followed at a trot, letting the 24th New York overtake him. He dispatched a courier with orders for his trailing regiments each to guard a flank.

Confederate infantry scurried about to form firing lines as a double rank of horsemen descended upon them, hooting and howling. Davies noted that some of the Rebs moved much more crisply than others: veterans here, new recruits or invalids over there.

The attack swirled about the central wagons. The Johnnies did not get their fieldpiece into action, but concentrated rifle fire made it hot for a bit. The Pennsylvanians wheeled about and rode back to re-form, bugle sounding one call after another.

"All right," Davies said, to himself as much as to anyone, "they've preserved their damned honor. Now it's time for the reckoning." With the 24th New York almost on line, he had his own bugler sound the charge.

The New Yorkers joined the Pennsylvanians in a second attack. It was too much for all but a few small packs of Johnnies. Most threw down their weapons or ran for the brush.

None of the teamsters attempted to bring off their wagons. They stopped, leapt down, and fled.

All of his troopers were veterans. They knew how to rifle a wagon train as swiftly as skilled burglars went through a house.

Not a bad climax for a minor scouting mission, Davies thought. Crook and Sheridan would be delighted.

Reports came in quickly. Dozens of the wagons were filled with rations, while others held headquarters papers, officers' trunks, medical supplies, and loads of ammunition.

"What do you want us to do with them? Bring any off, sir?"

"Burn them," Davies said. "Shoot the lead horses and mules. Cull out any that look like they might last the day."

It didn't take long for his men, who had mastered such skills in the Shenandoah Valley, to begin torching the canvas tops of the wagons.

As other riders herded prisoners, Davies' aide rode up, breathless and bewildered.

"General Davies, sir . . . you've got . . . sir, you've got to see this for yourself." The captain seemed half overtaken by mirth and half fixed by astonishment.

"All right, Captain. Lead on."

Toward the rear of the long line of flaming wagons—Davies judged the count at more than two hundred—a large group of captives waited in smart new uniforms.

It was Davies' turn to be startled: The disarmed men in jaunty kepis and gray coats with still-gleaming buttons were Negroes, every one of them.

"They put up a fight," a major offered. "Just a little one."

"Well, I'll be damned," Davies told all and none, "the cow jumped over the moon." He rode closer to the oddest prisoners he'd yet taken in the war and halted his mount in front of one who wore sergeant's stripes.

He felt unsure of how to address the fellow, so, to the accompaniment of the shouts of cavalrymen playing vandals, he just asked the fellow:

"Are you . . . all of you . . . actually Confederate soldiers?"

"Not no more," the sergeant said.

Once the smoke began rising, Davies understood he was in for a fight. No wagon train of that size would be moving separately from its army. He had the recall sounded.

They'd take eleven flags, most of them found in the wagons and saved from the flames. He told the regimental commanders to distribute them to the best soldiers they had. Each flag was worth a Medal of Honor if "captured," plus a ninety-day furlough. Although he now doubted the war would last ninety days.

Take care of the men, and the men took care of you.

They'd gathered in six artillery pieces, too, and a quick count of the prisoners came to six hundred, half of them uniformed Negroes. He started his trophies on the way back to Jetersville, arraying his regiments for a fighting withdrawal.

And fight they did. It wasn't twenty minutes before the first Reb cavalry came at them screeching and slashing. As Davies fought from one rearward position to another, still more Rebs descended on his brigade. Some of the fighting was close, with the unforgettable clang of saber on saber marking private combats amid the scrambles. Just in time, Crook and Sheridan sent reinforcements. For a spatter of minutes, it looked as though a proper battle loomed. But the Johnnies quit. Before they even caught a glimpse of the first infantry skirmish line at Jetersville.

General Crook rode out to greet his brigade commander.

"Well, Davies . . . you've had yourself quite a morning. Rebs will never forgive that escapade."

The well-bred Davies, graduate of Columbia and erstwhile attorney-at-law, said:

"Fuck 'em. They're falling apart."

One p.m.
Amelia County

The delay grated on Gordon. If he could get his men back on the march, it would go easier. Better to drive them along than to leave them sitting and scowling and waiting with acid-raw stomachs, sulking because their daddy generals could not make rations appear by daddy magic. Men on the move thought first about their feet and the weight they carried. Men left idle began to think dangerous things. Idleness was blood-kin to defeat.

What was he to do? As they waited for the plodding army to pass? Drill them? Put them to work improving the roads for the Yankees hurrying their way?

Not long ago, he would have given his men rousing speeches, moving from one division to the next, inspiring them with rhetoric maybe half of them half understood, but that sounded fine and pleased Southern-born ears. He recalled the speech he'd given to his brigade that first morn in the Wilderness, just hours before they saved the army's left wing. Even after he'd climbed to division command, silver words had coated the losses in the Shenandoah. Now he had a corps and words were useless. The time for speeches was over. As was the hour of the Confederacy.

He meant to fight on, though, damned if he didn't. No hardship would change that. Hardships only tested a man's character. Those who lasted to the end were those who'd shape the future. He meant to be one of them.

His belly was empty, too. But he was not about to let a soldier see him sneaking so much as a cracker. Not while his men did without.

They couldn't see his thoughts, though. No man could. His plans and hopes and dreams belonged to him alone, and they were bounteous, even extravagant. The army might be defeated, but John Brown Gordon would not be broken.

Not all of the men were strong, though, and the air had quitting in it. As his corps sat waiting so he and his men could play the rear guard again, the Army of Northern Virginia suffered its death sentence, mile by mile. When soldiers from other commands strayed into his encampments, they were no longer searching for their regiments, but looking for Yankees to whom they might surrender. Mere days before, those men would have been relieved to come upon others in gray coats. Now they were disappointed and too hasty with explanations.

It wasn't a question anymore of whether the army would die, but whether it would die well.

He thought of his wife and the new infant back in Petersburg.

He was certain that Fanny would be treated decently. He had to believe that. If his kind had to lose the war, he did not want to lose his wife. Not that.

God, he loved that woman, though! When they got home, they'd send the children off and shut themselves in the bedroom for a week, let the servants snigger.

Would there still be servants?

There would always be servants. Most men and women were born to serve. Sometimes you just had to change the name of their servitude.

Well, of all the commandments he'd broken or scratched deep, he never did covet his neighbor's wife. He coveted his own.

What would peace bring them? He meant to astonish his woman, come what might.

Horse left in an orderly's care, Gordon walked down the lane dividing his regiments. Letting the men see him as he posed a two-legged challenge: *"Anyone have harsh words they want to share? Anyone have a complaint? Anybody here?"*

Dull-eyed and sour, the soldiers watched him go. Old veterans still called greetings, missing the old banter, the remembered ritual. He did what he could to oblige them, but no man's heart was in it.

He wished he could feed them. Just that.

His next call was on Kyd Douglas and his staff. As a brigade commander, the major had proved a hellion. All who knew him had hoped to see prompt action on his promotion to brigadier general, but promotions weren't a priority just now.

"Well, gentlemen," Gordon said, "care to venture a wager on my thoughts?"

A captain spoke up, in a tone a little too sharp. "Reckon you're wondering when we'll get up and march, sir. Or when Ewell's circus train might finally come up. Does seem to me that we're waiting on monkeys, not tigers."

Achilles, too, had sulked, Gordon reminded himself. These men would fight as well as ever, when the next shots were fired.

"No, boys," Gordon teased, "I was only pondering how pleasant it would be if I were confronted with a fine, big beefsteak. A little crusty at the corners, nice and pink inside. And hot bread, of course. Made with the best white flour. Slathered with so much butter it gets on your fingertips. Tall glass of porter for lubrication . . . though an abstemious man might take him a lemonade." He smiled wider. "Reckon you don't have much appetite, though."

"General, I always knew you were a hard man. But I never dreamed you were such a cruel man."

"What about you, Kyd?" Gordon asked. "Big fat beefsteak sound tempting?"

"Settle for half a sausage and a biscuit, sir. *Half* a biscuit." His handsome face wore a failed attempt at humor. "And no sausage."

Miles off, a mighty explosion sounded. Followed by another. And a third.

All of the men looked to Gordon.

He shook his head. "Blowing up the artillery stores at Amelia. Can't drag them with us."

Another huge blast shook the distance.

It was not a good sign. They all knew it. No one spoke.

It had been splendid, Gordon told himself, back when speeches counted, when men could be rallied with a word, when he could still envision himself as wise Ulysses tenting before Troy. He—all of them—had believed that war was glorious, even as the evidence mounted that war was a filthy slaughter, one vast corpse.

Now they knew.

As he parted with Douglas and his companions, Gordon turned back through the mass of bleary, hungry men, the best of whom used the time to clean their rifles. Tired and uncertain of the length of their stay, no one had bothered to mark off ground for latrines. A week past, he would have chastised any officer who let discipline falter so fundamentally, but now he figured they'd just leave the Yankees their visiting cards.

He stopped to see Clem Evans, who had been downcast the last time they spoke. Clem, who had believed above them all in the sacred destiny of the Confederacy, believing it with the same conviction he brought to his faith in the Lord and the Methodist Church.

"Going to have to keep the men closed up, once we do start marching," Gordon told Evans and his pared-down staff. "I expect we'll be going all night again, doubt we'll even get moving before dusk. And tired men do foolish things. Keep them closed up, just keep them all together."

Clem of the thousand hopes and prayers settled his murderer's eyes on Gordon and spoke with the soothing Georgia voice that would fit him for the pulpit of which he dreamed:

"I reckon the Yankees will keep us closed up, all right. Doubt they're far off."

The hint of despair in Clem's words was the first thing that had truly worried Gordon.

Two p.m.
Burkeville Road

His arm and shoulder bit him with pain at every step of his horse, but Lieutenant General James "Pete" Longstreet would not reveal his discomfort to any man. Bad enough that they had to see him struggle to make his disobedient right hand support his left well enough to do up his drawers.

He rode beside Robert E. Lee, a man who had mastered the art of quarreling without speech. Lee's silence had the force of an entire brigade of artillery. And Lee was silent now, but quickened, listening to the *snap-snap* of skirmishing close enough to annoy the best-made plan.

They rode with Field's Division, behind a cavalry screen led by Rooney Lee. The vanguard of the army was headed for Burkeville—in the face of rumors that Federals had reached Jetersville, smack on their way. Were it so, their presence would be a first-degree inconvenience.

His corps could brush away cavalry, but how long would it take? You could never really tell with Lee, but Longstreet feared they measured the hours differently. Yet he'd known Lee long enough to realize that the old man might be even more worried about their late start than he was. Lee just wouldn't show it, not until all that pent-up fermentation burst out in an irrelevant remark on an unrelated matter to an officer uninvolved.

Lee could be as private as a time-biding, dark-thinking woman. He would no more succumb to a lapse in rigor, in the artifice of his temperament, than he would choose to reveal the bodily ailments of which all around him knew but dared not speak. Lee might be suffering all the pains of Hell, or feeling as spry as a lamb, and you'd barely catch a faint change of expression. Then he would cut down a man with one icy sentence.

Men loved him.

The queer thing was that Lee reminded Longstreet of Grant in that narrow respect: You just never knew what Sam was thinking behind that agreeable front-porch expression of his. Different in almost every other way, Sam and Lee were as alike as two Chinamen in that regard. Just couldn't figure them. Even when you thought you knew them as well as any man could.

Hadn't they misread Grant, though? Longstreet had tried, within the conventions of Southern overconfidence, to warn his fellow generals not to dismiss Sam Grant. Yet even he, perhaps Grant's closest friend in better days, had not foreseen the heights to which happenstance and a steady, bulldog genius would lift Sam. All he had known for certain was that no man possessed more exasperating integrity or greater reserves of stoicism—not even Robert E. Lee. He saw his old friend so clearly in his memory, in the hard years after Grant resigned his commission, when Sam had been reduced to peddling cords of wood on the streets of St. Louis, dragging a laden sled down snow-covered streets, accepting a workingman's poverty as his lot. And still he had pressed that five-dollar gold piece on Longstreet to settle a debt. Longstreet had not wanted to take it from his comedown friend, but knew Grant well enough to understand that his pride hinged not on worldly success, but on a stubborn view of right and wrong. Ulysses S. Grant had been the least ambitious man that Longstreet had ever encountered. Now he led vast armies subduing a continent.

Longstreet tried to imagine Robert E. Lee in rags, hawking wood in the street. He could not do it.

"General Longstreet," Lee said in that savagely polite tone Virginians were born to, "if you have discovered a subject of mirth, do share it with me."

A schoolmaster chiding a schoolboy.

"Just reminiscing, sir."

"Oh? About what?"

"This and that. You know."

Did Lee know? Did Robert E. Lee ever daydream? Surely . . .

"I believe, General," Lee concluded, "that the matters at hand demand our full attention."

There were times when Pete Longstreet was tempted to drop a great, loud fart in Lee's presence.

And yet . . . Lee had worked miracles. Again and again. Whatever devils drove him, Lee had mastered them well enough to prolong the war at least into this year, checking Grant's every move. Longstreet knew of no other general, himself included, who could have done half so well against such numbers, against such remorselessness on the part of an enemy.

Grant was still there, though. And getting ever closer. None of them could quite understand how he'd done it, losing clash after clash, yet winning campaigns. Members of Lee's staff joked that he'd *defeated* Grant all the way from the Rappahannock to Hatcher's Run, just whipped him so badly that the Army of Northern Virginia had backed up a hundred miles.

They never told that joke in Lee's presence, of course. And now Hatcher's Run was behind them, too.

He'd warned them that the reports of Sam's drinking were heavily embellished, that if he'd gone to seed in the Oregon Territory, it was hard to find a sober officer out there. And then there was George Pickett with his squaw. Grant hadn't longed for the bottle, he'd longed for his wife. Maybe Sam should've taken a squaw of his own?

No, he wouldn't.

He recalled standing up for Grant, along with Cadmus Wilcox, at Grant's wedding. Sam had been the happiest man in the world. That day, at least.

Again and again, Virginia's nobility had brushed off Longstreet's warnings: gay and invincible, all of them, until there was suddenly no more cause for gaiety and "that drunkard Grant" taught them that they weren't invincible, after all.

Longstreet wasn't about to give in, though. If Sam could be stubborn, so could he. Just have to see who was tougher, who lasted best.

The skirmishing in the middle distance intensified. A horseman galloped ahead of a pack of riders, coming back down the road from the cavalry screen and kicking up sufficient dust to draw stupendous curses from the infantry.

No man would curse in Robert E. Lee's presence, of course.

The rider was Lee's son Rooney. The old man always treated his sons with such severe formality that Longstreet had to wonder about their boyhoods. Had they undergone formal inspections, morning and night?

Grant loved children, he rolled around on the floor with them crawling all over him. But, then, maybe Lee did, too. When no one could see. Perhaps there was a heart within that armor.

Robert E. Lee was a great man. But there were times when Longstreet wasn't convinced that he was a good one. Virtue carried to an extreme. . . .

Rooney drew up, panting. His horse shook foam from its mouth, spattering the father's trouser.

Lee declined to notice.

"Sir," Rooney panted, saluting, "Yankee cavalry. Confirmed. In strength. On the high ground below Jetersville. Digging in. Been digging in for a while."

"Infantry?" Lee demanded.

"One report. I sent out scouts to confirm it."

Lee appeared to shudder. For one instant. Then the armor closed around him again.

Rooney had spoken loudly and hurriedly. The soldiers stumping along must have overheard. He'd be lucky if the old man didn't chide him for it. Longstreet sympathized with the boy, ever so earnestly seeking to please his father, to gain one word of praise, a good general burdened by a greater name. Longstreet felt a kinship with him: the brotherhood of loss. Rooney's wife had died in the course of the war, her infants lost before her, while scarlet fever had taken Longstreet's children. Thousands dead on the battlefield had not forced tears from his eyes, but he had not been able to leave the house to attend his children's funeral. He, James Longstreet, had sat in the shrouded parlor with his wife until it was done. And Rooney Lee had worshipped his young wife.

To that, Longstreet believed, the cold, old man would have said, "We are not to worship earthly things."

Lee let the men worship him, though. He basked in it.

Don't be bitter, Longstreet cautioned himself. Don't be small. You've had the honor of serving a very great man. Be grateful. Be wise.

Turning to Longstreet, Lee said, "General, shall we ride forward and see for ourselves?"

Not just cavalry, but infantry, too. In force. Lee had not believed that those people could march so swiftly. On such poor roads.

They scented blood. His blood.

"I could turn my lead divisions," Longstreet said. "Push them back, keep the road clear."

Lee shook his head. Meaning only: *Wait.* He pressured Traveller with his knees. The horse ambled forward. Lee touched the reins lightly and Traveller stopped.

He raised his field glasses. Perhaps . . . perhaps Longstreet's corps *could* fight through them. But what would follow? If one

Union corps had arrived, others might be close behind. And if they had reached Jetersville, the odds were strong that they were already at Burkeville.

He didn't want a battle now, not with the army exhausted, hungry, and stretched for a dozen miles. He wished to choose his own ground, if the time came to give battle.

He would have to hasten a courier to the nearest telegraph stop still in operation, to warn the railroad not to forward those rations on to Burkeville.

Had it been a grave error to try to feed his men?

The army would have to march for Farmville now and turn south there. Lee saw no choice. It was not time to fight, not without more certainty of the Federal dispositions, not before his men were fed and rested. Rations could be held at Farmville for them.

A bad day. Another bad day. First, those empty wagons. Then word that Federal raiders had burned one of the army's wagon trains, a large one. Part of his own headquarters trains had gotten mixed in with Ewell's wagons, guarded by soldiers given the task by Custis. Those people had burned every vehicle, including the only wagons left to the army that carried rations, precious wagons shepherded forward by Ewell, enough to feed the Richmond men for a day or two, even if the rest of the army hungered.

That had been a small disaster. It must not be prelude to a greater one.

He turned his horse back to Longstreet and Rooney. He felt terribly proud of his son, very close to him now, but dared not show it.

The boy's wife had been lovely, a scented flower. But the flower had been cut down. He had wept for her. And for his son, as well. He had tried, too, to put his feelings into a letter to Rooney, but words were ever inadequate in such matters.

Why had he thought of her now?

"General Longstreet, you must reverse your march. We must seek a more northerly route, we must aim for Farmville." He turned to his son and his voice almost cracked, still another betrayal of flesh and spirit. "Have you local men to guide General Longstreet? Among your scouts, perhaps?"

"Yes, sir. I can have men ride back and clear the route, as well."

"My staff will see to that. Such is not your province." He tried to recall the details of the inadequate maps his engineers had made. As an old engineer himself, he'd been angered that his engineer officers had not used the winter lull to better effect. Armies needed maps. He did not know this poor side of Virginia. There *were* possibilities, though, of that he was certain. If the army could not move one way, it would move another.

"We dare not lose any time," he added. "We must steal a march again."

Longstreet nodded. He had returned from his convalescence more given to brooding than ever. But he was stout of heart. When other hearts failed.

No man would ever know it, but there were moments when Lee's heart failed him, too.

Seven p.m.
Petersburg

Yankees done come again, bring by more food. It for you, Miss Fanny, how they say. Come from some high general. Us can't eat it up, it be so much."

"Front door or back?" Mrs. Frances Gordon asked the servant.

"They comes round back this time."

Enlisted men on a detail, then. Not officers for once. Respectful, all of them. As if they had set out to prove that Northerners could out-gentleman the squires of the South. Nor had they been so indelicate as to expect her to receive them in her condition.

The servants and even the owners of the house had told all, of course. The Federal officers knew she'd been indisposed and had not intruded. But the plate in the hall had filled with visiting cards and notes bidding good wishes in handsome penmanship. Not a few of the writers praised John effusively.

What cared she, though, that chivalry wasn't dead? She just wanted John alive.

From all she could gather, the Yankees were in high spirits, the chase was on. They seemed to believe it would all be over soon.

Would it? She craved firm news. It would be fine by her if it ended now. As long as her marvelous John remained alive. Throughout the war, she had refused to contemplate life without him. She would not do so now.

The Sharpsburg wound had been the low point for her. But she had grown almost fond of the scar on his cheek. She could bear any scars on his body, as long as warm blood still flowed through its veins.

The servant saw to the bedcovers and left. Fanny Gordon picked up her newborn son, a child of war, who thus far had proven the best-tempered of her infants. She jogged the tiny man gently in her arms.

Perhaps she'd receive the next officers who called. She was well enough now to go down to the parlor. Well-placed visitors might have news of John.

Oh, it was all such a . . . a travesty. This war, all of it. She had given her heart to the Cause because it was John's cause. She had believed because he believed. She had scorned the North because it was his enemy. She had celebrated victories, especially when they were his. And she had believed that the South must triumph because she knew John would triumph.

But all of it had been such a waste, so needless. From the start she had seen the war for what it was, an epidemic of boyhood in grown men, a vast and gruesome repetition of fistfights behind the schoolhouse, the ultimate stupidity of the male.

A dozen women, North and South, could have resolved the war's causes in one afternoon, with time out for coffee and cake. But the men had *wanted* to fight. And when they died, the women they left behind were supposed to shut themselves off from life and mourn them eternally—never mind feeding a swoggle of children and paying the note at the bank. The dead were to be *cherished*.

Fanny Gordon wanted to cherish her living, breathing husband.

With the infant growing restless in her arms, she walked over to a window and stared through the twilight.

"He's out there, you hear?" she told her son. "Your daddy's out there, causing them all a fuss."

Nine thirty p.m.
Amelia County

Led by one of Sheridan's scouts, the party of horsemen cantered through the darkness, leaving the roads behind and risking the countryside, bold to the point of folly to trim the distance. Now and again they glimpsed campfires that had to belong to the Rebs, but their luck had held thus far and they'd never been challenged.

As they neared their destination, the danger was bound to increase by leaps and bounds, but no rider dared suggest a safer route.

Ulysses S. Grant was enjoying himself immensely.

The several hours required to ride from Nottoway Court House to Jetersville already had provided the longest stretch of pleasure he'd known since Julia went to New Jersey to see to the children.

He loved to ride, and Sheridan had delivered a grand excuse. Grant had been settling into the staff's evening review when Phil's unprepossessing scout—got up like the lowest Reb—had appeared with a note wrapped in foil concealed in a chaw. Among other things, Phil had written that he wished Grant were present at Jetersville, suggesting great possibilities with Lee's whole army before him.

Grant had understood immediately. Meade had caught up to Phil, and the two of them were at it again, with Meade determined to do things right and Phil determined to do things now. They would have been polite to each other's faces, saving their bile for when they returned to their corners. And Meade was sick. So it fell to Grant's lot to referee the match. He didn't mind much. And he relished the chance to leave his pony behind and swing up onto the back of Cincinnati, by far the finest horse he'd ever owned.

Wouldn't it be a marvelous life if a man could just ride a good horse for a living? Beat being a general.

The night was brisk and black, but the riders were cloaked and the scout had a feel for the ground. He was one of those uncanny men with a compass in his breast and a sense of the enemy just this side of eerie. Phil had a knack for matching men to purposes.

Grant had brushed off his staff's concerns, the worry that he might be killed or captured. Only John Rawlins had not bothered to protest—he knew Grant too well. And Grant had chosen the four best riders from among his officers and told the commander of his headquarters guard to select a dozen men with hardy mounts.

There had almost been an addition to the party. The recollection amused Grant. Frank Barlow, Meade's young fellow, had all but begged on his knees to come along. Just caught up from Petersburg, eager and impatient, Barlow had sensed that a fight was on the way. And a fight meant opportunity for a major general who wanted another division worse than any child ever wanted a pony.

Grant sympathized, but he didn't know Barlow's level of horsemanship, or whether he even had a decent mount, and Grant didn't mean to slow his pace for anyone. He'd told the fellow that he could come up first thing in the morning, riding along with the rest of the headquarters squadron. Barlow, a renowned savage, had been crushed.

The night air was brilliant, better than the finest Habana cigar. Grant longed to give his horse free rein, to gallop headlong, jump whatever obstacles got in the way, and drain every ounce of pleasure from his precious hours of freedom. He'd seldom been happier than he'd been at West Point setting jumping records that were said to stand to this day.

It wouldn't do to get ahead of the scout, though. Getting picked up by the Rebs would be a touch awkward.

Meade and Sheridan, Sheridan and Meade. He did have that to look forward to, no matter how late the hour of his arrival. His heart leaned to Phil, who always wanted to fight, but he respected Meade's greater understanding. Phil would not have considered the damage even a slight reverse might do just now: Even the smallest Reb victory would give Lee's army new life. For his part, Meade would want to have every corps up and ready to do things right, to leave Lee no chance of pulling off one of his tricks.

But neither Sheridan nor Meade would see things go as desired, Grant was certain. Lee would be a fool to hold still until morning. And Lee wasn't a fool. No, Robert E. Lee, the perfect officer, darling hero of the War with Mexico, would be slipping off to the west, veiled by the darkness.

Catch him tomorrow afternoon, Grant reckoned.

Midnight
Amelia Springs

Yankee cavalry!" someone screamed.

Jolted by shouts and stampeding hoofs, defrocked artillerymen dragged from the Richmond defenses—inexperienced soldiers with bleeding feet—struggled to cap their rifles. First shots pierced the night: quick, startling flames. More shots followed. Men fired toward the noise, in what they took for the enemy's direction, and then they reloaded, groping for ramrods and cartridges in the blackness, spilling the ammunition from their pouches. Grown men shrieked. Others, attempting to flee, slammed into each other. Muzzle blasts filled the night with giant fireflies.

"Cease fire! Cease firing! Just stop shooting, goddamnit!"

It took another few minutes to quell the panic.

When all was over and the column re-formed, a staff officer reported to Custis Lee that a horse had broken its tether and galloped along the line. There had been no Yankee cavalry, but several companies had fired on each other in the confusion. A major had been wounded, perhaps mortally.

Custis Lee's first thought was to hope that his father wouldn't hear about the incident. His second was to wonder how these weary, untested men would hold up in the face of veteran Yankees when run to ground. He had regiments of heavy artillerymen reduced to serve as infantry, a swiftly organized Navy battalion of sailors, marines, and officer cadets washed up on land, and various strays slapped together to form a division. It was his first true field command, the first time he had not been chained to an office or bound to fixed fortifications, and he knew it would be his last. The war was ending, any fool could see it.

He longed to make his father proud just once.

TWELVE

Six thirty a.m., April 6, 1865
Jetersville lines

Humphreys kicked over the field cot. His Second Division commander tumbled onto the floor, cursing before his eyes had opened properly.

Andrew Atkinson Humphreys, heir to old Philadelphia blood and career soldier by choice, booted the overturned cot again and barked:

"Get up, you sonofabitch. Get on your feet, get dressed. You're relieved of command. Clear out. Report to Meade."

Astonished, Bill Hays said, "But Humph . . ."

"Shut your mouth." Humphreys walked over to the frock coat draped over a chair. He tore off the general's shoulder boards and threw them at Hays, who had managed to get to his feet, a sorry sight in his discolored underclothes. "Sew them back on, if you like. But your brevet ranks won't be worth a pile of shit from this day on."

It required all of his self-discipline not to hurl the chamber pot at the man who seemed to think war was a holiday.

Hays remained bewildered, paralyzed. Humphreys was tempted to punch him. Miles' and Mott's divisions had stepped off promptly at six, and they were already prowling for a fight. When Hays' brigades had not come up to join them, Humphreys had ridden to the division headquarters. Through the rain. It did not help his temper.

Except for a handful of guards trying to stay dry, everyone encamped at Hays' headquarters had been asleep, sprawled on the farmhouse floor or curled in corners, as if a plague had struck and left them dead.

They had all come back to life now. Humphreys heard them blundering and scurrying.

"Sir . . . ," Hays tried again, "I don't know what happened. I didn't mean—"

"That's right. You goddamned well *don't* know. Any idea what time it is?"

Humphreys wheeled about and strode back through the doorway. The members of Hays' staff were on their feet, all right. Most had slept in their uniforms, but had taken off their boots. The corps commander was half minded to make a circuit and smash his heel down on their toes, one foot after the other. He could not remember a single time in all his service when he'd been so livid. They had a chance to smash Robert E. Lee and these lazy sonsofbitches would snore it away.

He'd known it would prove a mistake to let Hays come back from New York and take a division. But he'd had little say. Politics had decided the appointment.

Well, politics could go to hell and rot.

A lieutenant colonel inched toward him and said, "General Humphreys, everyone was exhausted, we've been on the march for—"

"You're relieved, too. Get out of here. Go with Hays." He turned on the entire room. "Jesus Christ, don't you think the buggering Rebs are tired? They're worse off than you, for God's sake. We're *all* goddamned tired. But I don't care how beaten down any man is, or how sick, or if he's a goddamned corpse—when I say you step off at six a.m., you damned well do it."

He whipped around to his aide, who was only a bit less cowed by the general's outburst. "Go down to his brigade and bring up Smyth. He's got temporary command. And send a courier off to Meade—" Humphreys broke off, still so furious he could barely speak.

"Yes, sir," his aide said. "The message? For General Meade?"

"Tell him I need Frank Barlow."

Nine thirty a.m.
Flat Creek

With Federal artillery already across the creek—that cursed creek—Gordon rode up to Clem Evans, whose division awaited the next Union advance. Brazen as could be, the Yankees weren't exactly trying to hide themselves. At least two divisions had crossed the stream, forcing Gordon from his first position. Now they formed a front a mile wide: harvesters wielding fiery scythes, looking to cut human grain.

A fine-looking man on an average day, Clem appeared haggard and hard-used, a youth turned into a grampus.

"Clem, pull off. That low ridge—" Gordon pointed westward. "Set your division in there. I'll jump Grimes behind you, soon as it gets too hot here. Standing order for the day: Hold 'em as long as you can without becoming decisively engaged. Then fall back behind whoever's in place and set up again."

"Something to see, is it not?" Clem asked, nodding toward the Yankees. The rain had ceased and the air had been washed clean. Wet they may have been, but from a distance, the Yankees appeared pristine, well drilled, and deadly. Plentiful, too.

"Second Corps," Gordon said. "I read their flags from Grimes' lines."

"Humphreys."

"I will admit there are men I'd sooner face. 'Least when I'm tuckered. He'll be out to show the world he sits better atop that corps than Hancock did. With time running out to do it. He'll be aggressive."

"Trip him up, if we can."

"Surely. Best get to it, Clem."

Evans saluted and turned to shout his orders. Gordon watched the Yankees a bit longer. Their artillery opened, firing long. Wouldn't take but a minute or so for them to correct the range. Bound to be a long day.

Drummers off toward the creek pulled the rain covers from their tubs and began to hammer them. The blue ranks filled and straightened. Flags rippled out and officers cantered parallel to their brigades.

Bound to be a long, hard day indeed. And the night had been wretched enough. No one had slept, no one had eaten, and no one had stayed dry. Matters had been fouled from the very start, with a bridge collapsed and hours lost. Units backed up like farm boys at a peep show. The trains had gotten jumbled and the wagons crawled along, throwing wheels and mules failing in harness. Tempers were short and men strained not to say things the like-born could not forgive. Instead of being miles to the west, well on the way to the next set of bridges over the Appomattox, Gordon's men had met the dawn just outside of Amelia Springs, the resort known across the South for its healing waters, with the last wagons he was pledged to protect still in view when the drizzle stopped and the Federals showed up east of the creek.

Evans' division pulled out by brigade, in good order, considering how beaten down each body was. Gordon was bleary and sore himself, despite having a horse to carry his bones.

It wasn't just the direct threat that troubled him, either. Intermittent firing off to the right, to the south and southwest, told him that the Yankees were pressing on parallel to the retreat, not just chasing the army from behind. They'd caught up.

He pictured their cavalry nibbling at the flank, hunting weak points along the sprawling column.

Wasn't promising. Not at all. Risk of his entire corps being cut off. But he did his best to smile for the soldiers trudging by, and one grizzled fellow called out to him, just as men had done in better times:

"Know what I hate about retreating, General?"

"Well . . ." Gordon played along, pierced by remembrance. "I dislike myriad aspects of it myself. But I'm ready to weigh your grievance."

"It's that leaving dead Yankees behind us is such a waste. Never do get to have a look through their haversacks, see what's for eatin'."

"Corporal, I disagree, although I grant you a measure of

profundity. Killing Yankees is *always* gratifying. And I do believe you share my opinion yourself."

"Dog-danged right," a sergeant put in.

These men loved lofty rhetoric and words rich to their ears, the music of language even without the meaning. They didn't need to understand, didn't hardly care to, but trusted black cravats and silver tongues. That was how secession had come about.

He, too, had trusted. Even as he'd spoken the words himself, drunk on vows and vocabulary. If the Yankees held trials after the war, not a man in the entire South would ever be arraigned for thinking clearly.

Easy to see it now. Impossible in that first intoxication. Richer than the finest whiskey made. *Insult! War! Freedom! Rights! Glory!*

How good it once had been, though, how very fine . . . when men could still be wantonly blind and hope with gross extravagance. Nor did he find killing Yankees "gratifying." It was merely something that had to be done, given the circumstances conjured by the South's infernal, exultant rashness. Oh, he'd found victories thrilling, when such were still to be had, but he never had reveled in the killing itself.

Not like the Greeks, not that way. The delight they took in besting and butchering the other fellow . . . he'd glimpsed it, *almost* felt it, but something in him always recoiled in the end. Maybe it was different with bronze weapons, with spears and short swords, perhaps grappling with death on such intimate terms transformed a man into another being, enriched by the blood he spilled, ennobled by gore, under conditions that differed from modern war. But Gordon had come to doubt it.

He'd loved the excitement. He welcomed the opportunities. He cherished the praise that trailed him. He had even discovered a gift for *la vie militaire.* But he could not love war. Loving war was as foolish as loving the wagon you found yourself riding in. The point was just to stay on board to the end, to get someplace worth the bother.

He'd known men who loved war—Jackson, above all—and

thought them mad, if useful. But he'd had to face new truths about himself. He was good at war, and war had been good to him, but, more and more, he was in it, but not of it. Of late, he'd even felt less drawn to the *Iliad,* that profane bible of his early manhood. He couldn't even say offhand where the copy of Cowper's translation—given to him by Fanny two Christmases back—had been packed away.

Say one thing for Homer's heroes, though: They didn't hide their jealousies. All of it out in the open, hooted and hollered. Humphreys, over there now in his blue suit—he'd never admit that he wanted to prove himself a better commander than Hancock, whose health had failed him just before he could squander his reputation, a queer stroke of luck. And, Lord knew, the Confederacy had been poisoned by more jealousies than a hundred high-bred gals could muster in competition for a single male. He himself desired to shine to the end. Especially at the end. That was what men would remember: who was still on board that wagon when it arrived, for better or worse.

The truth was that he was tired of it all.

Another Union battery went into action. Things were growing hot for Grimes' Division. Gordon started his horse toward the fight, waving up his colors and his staff.

The drumbeat across the long fields changed and the Union lines advanced.

Ten a.m.
Flat Creek

Barlow had nearly killed his horse, but horses could be replaced, while time could not. He found Humphreys atop a hillock, wreathed by his staff and field glasses pressed to his eyes, watching his men drive back the Rebel defenders. The splendid, familiar racket of war filled the morning.

He wanted to speak, to report and be invested with command, but Barlow knew Andrew Atkinson Humphreys sufficiently well not to interrupt his thoughts.

Except for an occasional nod of the head, Humphreys held himself inhumanly still, erect in the saddle and fierce-jawed under his old-Army mustaches. The members of his staff kept their mouths shut, even stilling their horses if they pawed.

A thousand yards to the west, the Second Corps lines swept over just abandoned Rebel defenses—no doubt the usual hasty-made wall of fence rails, branches, rocks, dirt, and debris.

Humphreys lowered his glasses. "*That's* the old trick he's going to play. Hold us up as long as he can, then run. With another position readied to the rear. Playing damned leapfrog."

"They're trying to delay us, sir," a major ventured.

Humphreys turned on him. "Of course they're out to delay us, you bloody fool. That's what rear guards *do*. And that's the rear guard for Lee's whole damned army."

He noticed Barlow.

"About time," Humphreys said. "You walk here?"

Barlow didn't reply, but sat as calmly as a sweat-covered, flush-faced, anxious New Englander could.

"Well, now that you've graced us with your presence, Barlow . . . you've got the Second Division. Smyth's in temporary command, he'll turn it over to you."

Poor Smyth, Barlow thought. They'd never gotten along. The Irishman hated him, had sought and fought for a transfer out of the First Division when Barlow had it. For his part, Barlow did not intend to hold it against the man. As long as Smyth performed well.

He was just delighted to have a command again.

Humphreys turned to a courier. "Guide General Barlow to his division. *When* he's ready."

"My orders, sir?" Barlow asked.

"Take *command*. That division's been slow every goddamned day. If you can't move it, I'll find somebody who can. All right, Frank. Your orders are to secure the right flank of this corps. You will move at echelon-right to Miles, with de Trobriand advancing on his left. You will *not* engage unless confronted or flanked. Or upon my order."

Barlow felt an eyebrow rise below his hat brim. Humphreys noticed. When Barlow had left the army the past August—carried off on a stretcher, an invalid—Humphreys had been the chief of staff to Meade. He hadn't missed anything then, either.

"Mott was hit this morning," Humphreys explained. "First thing. He'll survive, but de Trobriand has his division." His mouth wrinkled. "We'll see what our Frenchman can do."

The corps commander fixed a hard gaze on Barlow, who waited him out.

"So . . . I've got *two* new division commanders today," Humphreys went on. "And goddamned Gordon in front of me, if the prisoners aren't flinging shit. What do you think of that?"

"I *still* need to settle with Gordon for Gettysburg."

Humphreys' eyes cut him down. "You won't settle personal scores with *my* soldiers, Barlow." His face had the look of a man with a mouthful of vinegar. "You've been crying like a baby for a division, now you've got one again. Make a hash of it and you'll be crying because you lost your division the day you got it."

Below them, a battery limbered up to follow the advancing infantry. The battle noise had dropped to the crackle of skirmishing.

Resurrecting his droll battlefield voice, a tone that served as his private Harvard joke, Barlow asked:

"Anything else, sir? I should be remiss, if I didn't ask."

"Yes, goddamn it. Get yourself a fresh horse from the spares. The first thing you kill today should be a Confederate."

Don't you mind the general, sir," the courier confided, voice as Irish as unwashed bodies and rags. "He's ever like this until things boil up proper. Then he turns easy, he does."

"I don't mind General Humphreys in the least. He's quite the real thing."

"Ah, that he is, the very thing himself."

Barlow was amused at the man's effrontery: The Irish did love to gab.

"The soldiers have grown fond of himself, they have," the fellow went on. "Burns their ears, he does, enough to make a priest faint at the altar. But he never wastes their lives, if he can help it. Barks like His Lordship's mastiff, he does, but the men can tell that he's a regular sort."

Letting the fellow engage him, Barlow said, "I'm not sure General Hays would agree just now."

"Oh, Hays . . ." The fellow smoothed his mount's gait, an Irish horse thief born. "The lads call him 'Crazy Haysie,' you know. Not that the fellow was crazy, no, but the lads just liked the sound of it. Not a bad fellow, old Hays, as generals go. Begging your pardon."

"I heard he was caught napping."

"Snoring like Clancy on Sunday, would be more like."

" 'Care-charmer Sleep, son of the sable Night . . . ,' " Barlow recited.

The courier paused, then plunged. "Up from headquarters, are we, sir?"

"Indeed."

"And do they all believe we're near the end?"

"Don't you like the war?"

"Well, sir, I'm in it, whether I like it or not."

"I'd say that a confident atmosphere prevails. What do *you* think, Sergeant?"

"Well, sir . . . based on me own encounters with Bobby Lee now, I'd expect to see a few last punches thrown. Before the dram-shop shuts up for the night."

"Let's hope," Barlow said.

They arrived at his division, which Smyth had drawn up handsomely, waiting either for Barlow or just for orders. The staff officers gathered around Smyth looked utterly terrified. And not, Barlow suspected, of the Confederates.

He turned a last time to the courier. "You haven't been with the corps very long, I take it?"

"Me, sir? Not at all. I'm loaned out by the cavalry, like a spare tool from the shed. For the riding back and forth and suchlike things."

"When you return to your duties with General Humphreys . . . do ask your fellows their views of General Barlow. You'll find it of interest."

In front of Miles and de Trobriand, the artillery opened up again.

"Let's hope," Barlow repeated to himself.

Ten thirty a.m.
Rice's Depot

It's well that you have stopped," Lee said to Longstreet. The two men stared southward at the skirmishers' smoke and the gathering bluecoats. Closer to the generals, Longstreet's men improved their fortifications with all and any material they could scavenge.

"Wasn't by choice." Longstreet grimaced. "Never known the Yankees to move so fast."

"Or our men to move so slowly."

"They're all bone-tired."

"Yes. But they will have rest, when we have crossed the river. And plentiful rations. At Farmville."

Longstreet caught a faint hesitation, the lightest slur, in Lee's speech. They all had been worn down to the verge of uselessness. Lee maintained his posture in the saddle, but weariness scarred his face and his eyes were troubled.

"I've just left General Mahone," Lee continued. "He's concerned . . . as am I . . . that the first increment of trains has fallen behind. There's already a gap of at least two miles. So he asserts."

Longstreet was tempted to remark that a two-mile gap amounted to an improvement, compared to the nightmare of the night before. But Lee never cared for sarcasm.

"Well, sir, we've got to wait, I don't see a choice. See what develops. Move on now, and the gaps get longer still. According to the prisoners we've taken, those are Ord's people we're looking at, Army of the James. It's not just Meade."

"I cannot credit it. That must be a mistake."

Longstreet shrugged.

"But the bridges?" Lee asked. "They're safe?"

"Waiting to hear from the cavalry. About that raiding party headed for High Bridge."

"We *must* preserve High Bridge. And the wagon bridge."

"Yes, sir. I sent Rosser, first word I got. He had his bearings already. General Lee followed, as soon as his men could rally. Shouldn't be a problem."

"If they are in time."

Longstreet shrugged. He longed to say, "It's out of my hands, it's up to your son now." But he dared not.

He had been reluctant to part with the cavalry, given the unknowns he faced himself. But Lee was right about High Bridge. The one thing he did not want to see was heavy smoke rising on the northern horizon.

The only hope the army had now was to get across those northern bridges and the span at Farmville, then burn them immediately. The Appomattox was more than a mere creek and the Yankees would require time to bridge it, at least a day. Once the army got over, there'd be a space to breathe and feed the men.

"Word from General Ewell, sir?" Longstreet asked.

"His left's been annoyed all morning. Small attacks, cavalry probes. He believes the Federal Sixth Corps is closing up. While Gordon's occupied with their Second Corps."

"It's the wagons," Longstreet said. "They're strangling the army."

Of a sudden, Lee sagged. His voice became that of a man speaking to himself, a despairing man. "General Longstreet . . . I confess that I do not know what to do. It's . . . not a sensation to which I am accustomed. I cannot think how to move this army faster. . . ."

Startled by the display of weakness, Longstreet wanted to reach out and rest a reassuring hand on Lee's shoulder. But he feared the reaction to such a liberty, to such an intimacy. He just said:

"We'll get through this day, too."

Eleven thirty a.m.
Deatonville Road

Tom Custer went out on another gallop, joining his brother's lead regiment for a lark. It was all a child's game got up for grown men, playing peekaboo with the Rebel column, appearing out of the trees and riding hard for them, pulling back only after tricking them to halt and deploy their infantry. A few times they'd even gotten in among them, burning a wagon or two. And the Johnnies they brought in as prisoners were the dirtiest, sorriest lot he'd seen in the war.

Autie had been high-nerved all the morning, resentful of George Crook and his whiskers leading off as the cavalry divisions nagged the Rebs, seeking an opening for a crippling blow. At last, Crook had been ordered to make way for Merritt's command. Which meant that Autie's division took the lead and—if Tom knew his brother—would take the glory, too.

The New Yorkers with whom he rode re-formed and went for the Rebs again, bugle blaring. Wearied, the Rebs fired early, barely able to hold their rifles steady. The fighting turned into a melee, with horses swirling and riders slashing as bayonets rose and clubbed muskets swung at the horsemen. Tom emptied his pistol, one shot hitting a Reb as gray as Methuselah smack in the forehead. Then more Reb infantry trotted up and the bugle sounded the recall. And off they went, cavalry doing what it was meant to do, harrying the enemy in a pursuit, grinding them down. He'd read enough books to know that much.

When he found his brother again, Autie was in a powwow with his colonels. Pennington gesticulated broadly, like an actor in a traveling troop, declaiming that victory waited to be grabbed.

"No, *really,*" Pennington all but shouted, "there's a break in the column wide enough to put a division through. Their lead train's struggling, it's all but standing still."

Autie had a familiar grin on his face.

Noon
Deatonville

The blackhearted buggers needed killing worse than English lords in Irish manors. Uncommon steady they were, a spectacle, parading across the broken country, merciless as a machine, maintaining their ranks through miracles, passing through groves and hamlets, bogs and briars, without ever breaking the great blue front that stretched for an English mile.

Yet they were not the first object of his wrath, for the Yankees were only doing what Yankees did, holding up their side of the donnybrook. No, what angered Riordan beyond the power of speech, beyond a cheated harlot's powers of blasphemy, were those manacles clamped on the army's ankles and wrists, the wagon trains.

Deft the man had been, that Gordon, giving Billy Yank a taste of lead and then a second dose just for good measure, before pulling back again—and again—barely avoiding a fatal tangle many a time that morning, all of them, men of three mean-tempered divisions, fighting all but endlessly to protect the wagons that carried no food to feed them, only tents that would never be pitched again, and officers' baggage, and papers Riordan could not read but that he was certain had no value worth the life of the lowest man among them. For papers were what the powerful used to tame the poor and to break the man of spirit. No finely dressed fellow who sought you paper in hand ever meant you well.

A fool's indulgence those wagons were, and he wasn't of a mind to die for mules.

But he turned his anger around and aimed it blue-ward as the Federals came strutting up again, drums beating and flags proud, as if they'd been waiting for this day through all those months of rotting at Petersburg, this chance to show off their new shoes to the shoeless.

How could a man's nerves not be tight as a young girl's cunnie, when he heard the rumpus of battle not only before him, but miles behind him, too? Oh, the Yankees were devils this mournful day. Short of holy water, he'd sprinkle lead.

Weren't *they* weary? Were *their* bellies full? Oh, it pained his soul to hear them cheer so lustily. And not just his soul had a plague on it, but his crotch and thighs burned and itched, rubbed raw and festered and bedeviled by vermin. The worst marching of the war, this was, and he almost preferred the bouts of actual brawling.

Evans rode just behind the line, speaking in that voice of a Protestant preacher, the lower sort, calling out, "Steady, boys . . . we'll give them two volleys, then see."

A soldier unhappy with all the world declared, "I'm going to set fire to those wagons myself, I swear I will."

There was no Irish in the man's voice, but his promise was empty as a Galway shill's and Evans ignored him. Times there were when Riordan pondered Evans. If the priests of Ireland had been as willing to fight as the preachers of the South, the English would've gone swimming home long before Ned Cromwell had his day. But rare was the priest who'd ever stood up like a man.

Perhaps it was the denial of marriage, the lack of hot-breathed wives, that unmanned them under those skirts blacker than midnight. Clear it was why the English let the priests hold sway in Ireland, for the one true church got down on its knees to Caesar, rendering more than Caesar thought to ask.

Would Ireland ever be free? He could not believe it. A man had a better chance in Louisiana, shoveling mud. Or even at war. Ireland, that pitiful whoreless whorehouse. . . .

Evans, though . . .'twas known that on the Monocacy, a fight not fondly remembered, Evans had taken a ball in his side that exploded a pack of sewing pins in his pocket, breaking the pins into tiny bits and splashing them into his meat, just where the spear poked Christ. 'Twas further said that the surgeons failed to fish out the bits and left Evans in pain. Well, that was what a man got for the folly of carrying pins in his pocket like a woman.

The day had turned fair, the sweet air mocking what men were about.

Officers shouted unnecessary commands. Every man knew what he had to do by now. Riordan tensed as he felt the men around him tighten their muscles. No matter how many times a man fought, there was always that fretful moment. . . .

Cannon sounded behind them. No good sign.

At three hundred yards, they gave the Yankees an early volley. To make them think again about their business. A few fell away, but the blue lines were hardly nicked.

Usually, their drums would have stopped by now, they were only for stepping off and the first bit of marching. But today the drummers kept up their infernal racket, their boldness as shaming as a landlord's visit.

He reloaded as swiftly as he could, hoping that someone was fast at work to bring up a fresh lot of cartridges and caps.

At a hundred and fifty yards, every second regiment let loose a volley, then thinned the lines. Fifty yards more, and those still on the line fired. Then they ran for the rear on aching legs.

The Yankees gave chase with a howl and leapt the abandoned barricade.

But Evans had positioned the first regiments to withdraw in a second line just to the rear. They let loose well-aimed shots at the forward-most Yankees, opening some bellies and spilling enough brains to befuddle the buggers.

With the sharpshooter battalion—what remained of it—pausing to sting the Federals as skirmishers, the shrunken brigades moved back behind the cover provided by Walker's waiting division, the next lot to have a go.

"What happens when we run out of space to retreat to?" a cracker's voice wondered. There was no poetry in his language, no song to his tone.

"We stop, ye stupid bastard," Riordan told him.

One p.m.
Holt's Corner

Bending in the saddle, Dick Ewell tapped his wooden leg through the cloth. Rarely bothered him, but the damned thing wouldn't sit right today.

Nothing seemed to be sitting right.

"How long do you want my division to hold here?" Joe Kershaw asked him.

Bearing a moaning wreck of bloody meat, a litter passed.

"Until you see Gordon coming," Ewell told him. "Then catch up fast."

"Like to see just one thing move fast today. Other than the Yankees."

A few hundred yards off, rifles spat again. They'd held the crossroads for over an hour, fending off mounted and then dismounted cavalry in ever larger numbers. Kershaw's men were veterans and solid, as was their commander. But the South Carolinian was getting rambunctious now. Nerves were shorter than a canister fuse.

Behind the mounted party—flags high and spirits low—the wagon train shifted forward and stopped again.

"Jesus," Ewell said. Turning to a staff man, he added, "See what the problem is this time. And get it fixed."

"Be here until Doomsday," Kershaw said. He nodded at the Yankees flanking the column from the south. "On us like a pack of wolves. Cutting out the sheep, one after another."

"I don't see us as sheep," Ewell snapped. "Sheepdogs, more like."

Kershaw shrugged. "*Those* wolves got a taste for dog meat long ago."

Kershaw was bound to chafe under his command, Ewell understood. While Kershaw had a sterling combat record, he knew himself for a disappointing man. Oh, he'd done fine early on, commanding a brigade, then a division. Fit him like a well-cut uniform. But about the time he lost the leg at Groveton, he seemed to lose something else. He'd done the best he could as a corps commander, but men still blamed him for hesitating on that first, confusing day at Gettysburg. Lee had been gracious, giving him time to grow into his command. But he just hadn't sprouted. At Spotsylvania, Lee had finally lost faith in him. After that awful morning in the salient.

Some blamed the loss of the leg, others his late marriage, for his failures, but Dick Ewell believed that a man might be good at one thing but not another, and that he might shine for a time, then lose his luster. All a fellow could do was to soldier on.

The way he'd soldiered on through all those dusty decades in the Southwest, keeping the Indians in, the Mexicans out, and the garrisons sober enough to do their duty. The Mexican War had been a fruitful patch in a bone-dry field, the one time that the Army fulfilled the expectations of his cadet years. Yet he had come to love the other Army, the real one. And what a curious thing that was! To love something, truly love it, when it gave you little or nothing in return. He'd seen marriages like that, though his belated union was not among them.

Well, it was all a matter of duty now, of a duty that had robbed him of his first love, that Army of the deserts and the plains, of maddening boredom and sudden, brilliant excitements. The day on which he had resigned his commission to go with the South had been one of the saddest of his life. Worse than the day on which they sawed off his leg.

A fellow old soldier, Lee had treated him as delicately as he could after Spotsylvania, removing him from field command "due to ill health," not failure. He'd sent him to Richmond, to better organize the city's defenses. And Ewell had done his best, although it wasn't a true soldier's command, not with other generals fighting the battles out on the Richmond lines. He'd been placed in charge of the rear fortifications, of securing hospitals and seeing to general order, of training the militia, and of providing color guards for ceremonies. But the position let him keep some vestige of pride.

Lee had done his best by Jube Early, too. Though Early was a decidedly difficult man.

And now, to his surprise and with everything gone to hell, Ewell commanded a corps of sorts again, with Kershaw attached and Custis Lee's ungodly amalgamation of sailors, dethroned artillerymen, stray regiments, and disappearing coons. Lee had entrusted him with that much, one more time, even if only because there was no one else. He even had nominal control of Anderson's corps, by virtue of his seniority of rank, but he preferred not to exert it. Anderson had been fighting while he had been signing papers and answering inane questions from the War Department.

He did not want to fail Robert E. Lee again.

The wagons remained halted and a Yankee battery opened on the plum target. The initial salvo overshot the train, but fell close enough to worry the mules and drivers.

"Shit on my grave," Kershaw said. "That's all we need."

Ewell did not have a single gun on hand—the artillery left to his corps had been sent ahead.

Undeterred by their earlier repulses, the Yankee dismounts worked their way forward again, banging away with their repeating carbines. Kershaw's lines stood firm, but Ewell recognized that by doing so, by remaining in position to fend them off, he was playing into the enemy's hands, becoming one more drag on the rest of the army.

What else could he do? Abandon the wagons? And Gordon?

Things had gone awry from the beginning. His wing had been supposed to turn north toward High Bridge, but Anderson had sent back word that he meant to stay on the Deatonville–Rice's Depot road, marching to the sound of the guns, in case Longstreet needed aid at the head of the column. Did Ewell object?

What could he do but follow and attempt to hold things together?

He'd sent Custis Lee's division ahead, with orders to get across Little Sailor's Creek as quickly as possible and maintain contact with Anderson. If he couldn't move Kershaw soon, his command would break in two.

And there was nothing to be done about it.

Men were simply reaching the end of their tether. Word was that

Bushrod Johnson had broken down in front of his brigadiers, just lost his grip and went to pieces, giving orders that made no sense at all. Henry Wise had been about ready to shoot him. Fitz Lee had needed to step in and set things right. But Fitz had plenty of work of his own to do.

After an unexplained lull, the Yankee battery resumed firing on the wagons. This time, the shells fell snugly around their targets, with one direct hit.

The mules went mad. Drivers fell into the harnesses as they fought to control their animals, and Ewell saw one man crushed beneath a wheel. Teams lurched into the fields, upsetting their wagons. Canvas tops blazed. The teamsters who had had enough skedaddled, running in any direction that might take them away from the Yankees.

"Stay here," Ewell ordered Kershaw. "Just hold." And he galloped into the shelling, the braying and shouts and confusion.

Pistol out and cocked, he warned a driver whose team hadn't even rebelled: "Get back up there, or I'll shoot you myself."

His officers knew what to do, he had to credit them. Half were recent invalids and the rest had more experience with supply trains than with battle. Served them well at the moment, though.

With the fit of his leg still a bother, Ewell slapped the reins on his horse's neck and made his way deeper into the clutter and carnage. One driver still sat on his bench, dead but clutching the massive splinter pinning him in place. His mules were unconcerned and well behaved.

At last, Ewell found a lieutenant—the only officer along that stretch of trains.

"You in charge, boy? Of these here damned wagons?"

"Yes, sir. Yes, General. Some of them."

Desperate, Ewell made a decision. "Listen here. I need you to move them. Yours and all the rest." He pointed toward the crossroads he'd just left. "Get up there, son. And turn this line of wagons to the right. That's the road to High Bridge, the one we should've taken in the first place. If the worthless map's right this one time. You get the rest of the trains on that road and move quick. You understand me?"

"Yes, sir. That there's the Jamestown Road. I know it, we're Farmville people."

"And?"

"Reckon it's best, if a man intends to get on. Only place like to hold things up comes a pair of miles on. Two low bridges, bottom of a fall off. Both on the narrow side. Sit over Sailor's Creek, just a little separate." He chewed a thought. "They pass wagons all right."

"Well, get moving, Lieutenant. Any officer questions your authority, refer him to General Ewell. Only other man you're to heed is Robert E. Lee himself. Now you move quick."

"Sir . . . I can answer for the men, but these mules haven't got much quick in them."

"Just get some quick in yourself, boy. Damn the mules."

The lieutenant saluted and pulled his horse around. As Ewell turned to follow, he saw that Kershaw had soldiers clearing the road. They toppled broken wagons into the fields and tore away burning canvas.

Get things moving, just have to get things moving, Ewell told himself.

Time to ride ahead and see how things were going with young Lee, young Mr. Custis. Robert E. Lee's eldest son did look like a general, tall, broad of shoulder, and handsome, with grace and flawless manners, some English scribbler's idea of a planter. Unlike me, Ewell smiled, accepting that part of his fate, old and bald, with empty pockets and a wooden leg.

He paused to confer with Kershaw, whose men had driven the Yankees back again. In the almost-quiet between attacks, new sounds of a clash rose to the west, a few miles farther along the army's route.

Were they already hitting Anderson? Had they struck the forward trains?

In parting from Joe Kershaw, Ewell repeated, "See that those wagons keep moving, Joe. Turn the rest north, we can't have more delays. Any man tries to back-talk you, just place him under arrest. And the moment you see John Gordon coming up, your job here's done. Follow me, quick as you can." He gestured toward the rippling noise to the west. "Wouldn't be surprised one bit if the Yankees force us into a have-it-out fight. Need to be together, if they do."

The wagon train had begun to move with what seemed to Ewell to be remarkable speed. Compared to the grinding misery of the morning.

"Should've stayed with the plan, sent the trains north from the start," Ewell muttered. "Times are, I can't figure things out at all, the way men reason. Anderson wanted to get in on the fight, he didn't need to take his extra linen."

He led his staff west toward Sailor's Creek, wooden leg still a nuisance.

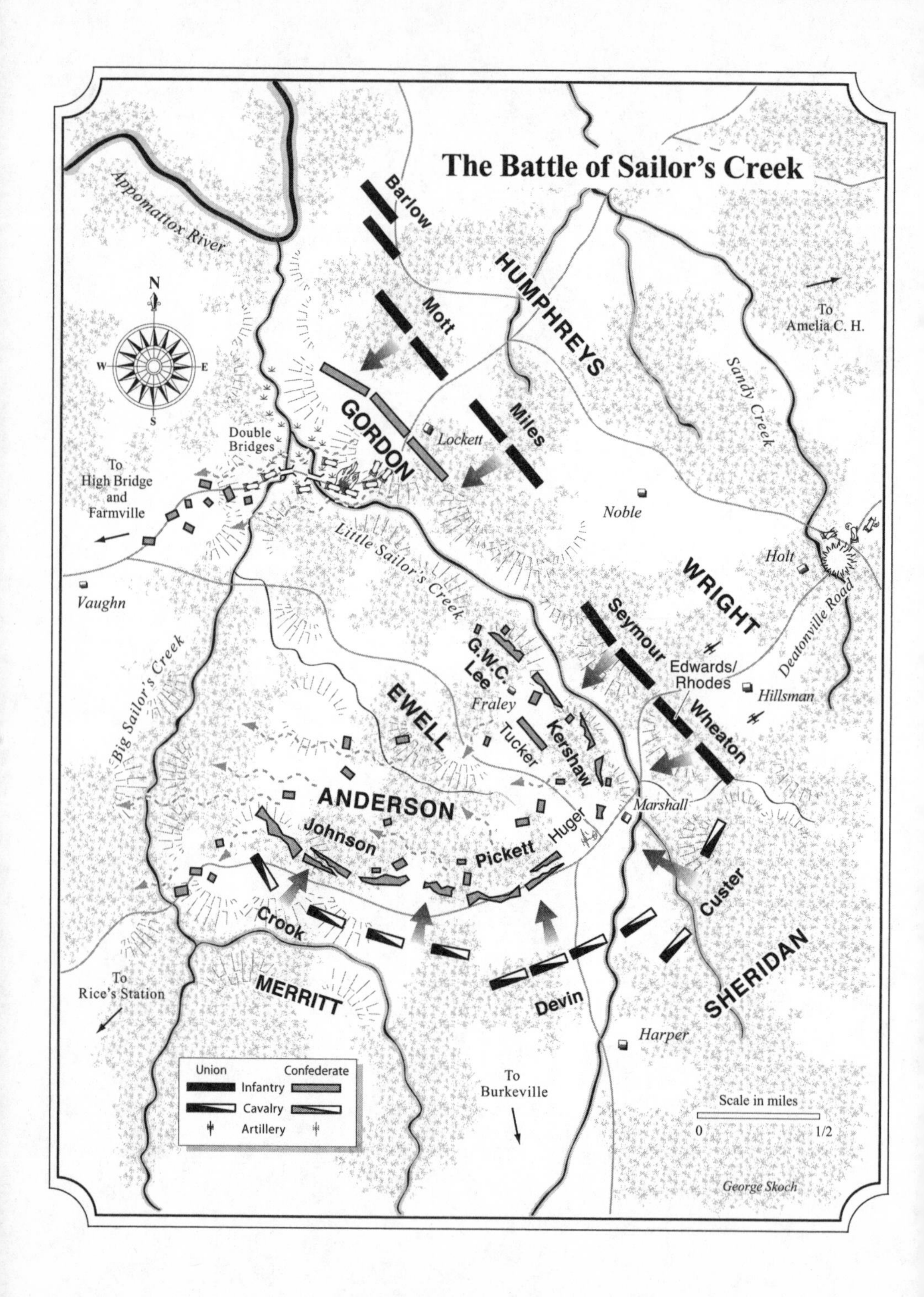

The Battle of Sailor's Creek
Appomattox River
Barlow
Mott
HUMPHREYS
Miles
GORDON
Lockett
To
Amelia C. H.
Sandy Creek
Double
Bridges
To
High Bridge
and
Farmville
Noble
Little Sailor's Creek
Holt
Vaughn
WRIGHT
Seymour
Edwards/
Rhodes
Deatonville Road
Hillsman
Wheaton
G.W.C.
Lee
Fraley
Tucker
Kershaw
EWELL
Big Sailor's Creek
ANDERSON
Marshall
Huger
Johnson
Pickett
Custer
Crook
SHERIDAN
To
Rice's Station
MERRITT
Devin
Harper
Union
Confederate
Infantry
Cavalry
Artillery
To
Burkeville
Scale in miles
0
1/2
George Skoch

THIRTEEN

One p.m., April 6, 1865
Sailor's Creek

With half the army bumbling about like damned fools, somebody somewhere had to make a decision. And Lieutenant Colonel Frank Huger, Confederate States of America, decided that he was the man destined to act.

Their dust already settled, the men of Mahone's Division had vanished toward Rice's Depot. Yet the lead trains still blocked the road above the creek, wagon brakes groaning, drivers as dull as their mules, and nobody present with the sense or authority to order them to continue. Behind the wagons, Anderson's infantry—the scarecrow remains of Johnson's and Pickett's Divisions—appeared equally flummoxed about what to do. Regiments lingered, sat, pissed, shat out what little they had left in their guts, fetched water from the creek, scratched indelicate parts, and chawed their last tobacco to kill the hunger. He'd never seen the army so broken down, never imagined it.

Huger's battalion of guns had been reduced at Amelia Court House, leaving him but twelve pieces. And even they were useless, halted down in a creek bed.

After his last caisson cleared the bridge, Huger ordered his battalion up the hill, determined to give things a shake and close the gap that had to have opened behind Mahone: The army had to close up or face dismemberment; couldn't the men with stars and wreaths on their collars see it?

Slowly, his limbers, guns, and caissons worked their way up the hillside, now on the road, now slopping through a field, the straining teams driven by whips and the men by profanity of a color rarely met in the Army of Northern Virginia: Blasphemy was Yankee manners.

The day excused it, though. Nothing had gone right. It was no secret the Yankees had overtaken them—every man could hear the scrap to their rear. Why had the column halted? No man knew.

Sergeants cursed stubborn teamsters, and the teamsters replied with invective startling and raw. Infantrymen brushed back from the road joined in, calling, "Redlegs a-runnin', piss-the-pants red-legs a-runnin'." But Huger's lead section made it to the hilltop.

To his chagrin, hundreds more halted wagons stretched as far as he could see, the column patrolled by a few lackadaisical foot soldiers. The only break in the line of wheels and canvas came at a stretch just beyond a crossroads.

He decided to fit his guns in there until he figured out what he could do next.

They had to *move*. They couldn't just sit still. Not with the Yankees nagging them. Couldn't anyone see it? Halting like this was no better than suicide.

A rider found him. It was questionable whether the man or the horse looked worse fed or in greater need of currying. And this fellow was a lieutenant, a brother officer.

"Compliments, sir," the messenger said, chasing his breath. "General Anderson says you're to halt right where you are. You're not to separate your command from the wing."

As soon as he felt he could check his temper, Huger pointed and told the lieutenant, "I'll fit my battalion in there, that stretch just past the crossroads. Tell General Anderson . . . just say I await his orders with great interest."

The lice chewed his armpits again.

One thirty p.m.
Marshall's Crossroads

Can't quite believe it myself," George Custer said. "But you were right, Al."

Leaning forward in the saddle, Colonel Pennington asked, "Shall I take them, sir?"

"Be discourteous not to, when a gentleman like Robert E. Lee sends the invitation. Take your whole brigade in. Grab those guns, burn the wagons, and just raise holy hell. Flush out their infantry, make them come out in the open."

"Honor and a pleasure, sir." Pennington saluted, grinned, and applied his spurs so fiercely that his mount lifted both front feet as it leapt into motion. The colonel waved at his flags and pennant to follow, shouting to his bugler, "Toot that horn, boy! Give the brigade the charge!"

With the 2nd Ohio riding in the lead, Pennington's horsemen swept over a low ridge and plunged into the next swale, aiming for the long line of wagons and parked artillery waiting barely a quarter mile off.

Pennington yanked his mount away from the charging column of fours to wave the other regiments to their places. He glimpsed Custer back on the ridge, personally emplacing the horse artillery.

What Pennington could see of the Rebs continued to astonish him. They weren't responding worth a lick. As if the noise and spectacle of a thousand horsemen weren't sufficient to wake them from their naps.

At last, a Reb artillery section leapt to unlimber two guns. A few increments of Reb infantry formed up.

Nothing to it, though.

Charging straight up the road, the 2nd Ohio jammed up where fences converged, creating a damnable muddle, but Pennington's roving staff men quickly directed the trailing regiments into the surrounding fields. With his troopers displaying veteran form, the charge regained momentum.

Crook's man Davies had made a great to-do over burning a wagon train. Well, this was a far richer prize. Pennington still could barely believe the gift he'd been given this day.

He kicked his horse to life again and followed his men in all their thunderous, saber-flashing magnificence, the broadening blue lines wild with hurrahs and hoofbeats.

Passing a last low crest, with those Rebs guns wheeling urgently into battery, he saw his New Jersey boys reach a line of still-limbered pieces that seemed to have been abandoned. Scattered rifle volleys tried to discourage them, but the effort was akin to trying to stop the ocean's waves with bare hands.

Those two well-handled Reb guns got off rounds of canister, but too late.

Pennington waved up his flags, his aides, and his escort.

"Let's join the party, lads."

One forty p.m.
Marshall's Crossroads

Where in the name of the Good Lord had they come from? A full brigade of Union horse was upon them. Caught dismounted, Huger drew his pistol and ran down his unready line, shouting orders to unlimber the guns and ram down canister, doubting all the while it could make a difference. Where had Fitz Lee's cavalry been? Weren't they supposed to screen the flanks and give warning?

He hadn't even time to get back to his horse.

Union artillery opened on the wagon train. The ground shook under thousands of pounding hooves. Before even a rough defense could be gathered, the first blue horsemen swirled around his guns, hacking anyone who would not surrender, swinging their sabers with glee.

Two of his pieces just made it into action, firing in quick succession before the crews were overwhelmed. The Florida regiment loitering by the wagons were stalks of wheat to a scythe. Worst of all, the Union riders all wore those bloodred scarves: George Custer's men.

Huger was not about to be taken by his West Point classmate: Custer had been so stupid that he'd probably mistaken algebra for the name of a tavern slut. No matter the reputation George Custer had since acquired, Huger would not succumb to a man that every one of his classmates thought a blockhead.

At the edge of his vision, Huger saw a Yankee horseman shoot O. B. Taylor dead, the best captain in the battalion.

With a shock, he realized he *had* no more battalion.

Then they were on him, too, calling for his surrender, greedy for a captive wearing rank. With perfect aim, he shot two men from their saddles then swung about to fire into the chest of a horse about to ride him down. The mount reared and threw a Yankee with corporal's stripes. The bluecoat landed hard.

"Surrender, you fool!" a major demanded, fighting to master his horse.

As the man worked his reins, Huger aimed for his head. The bullet tore through the Yankee's cheek. The major dropped his pistol and clutched his face.

Huger fired toward another rider and missed. He turned for the bushes and trees beyond the road. He would *not* surrender to Custer and be shamed.

A Yankee sergeant blocked his path, carbine extended across his horse's neck. The muzzle brushed Huger's skull.

"Quit, damn you! Or Jesus himself won't recognize you, after I blow off that pretty head of yours."

Huger made a faint motion with his pistol. The Yankee laughed.

"Reckon you shot yourself empty. Or you wouldn't be skedaddling. Drop it now, and behave yourself. Hate to have to shoot me such a lover-boy."

Huger dropped the revolver.

The Yankee herded him like a sheep. Driving him toward a collection of a few hundred other prisoners, more of his fellow Confederates than Huger had seen around this stretch of the wagon train.

Where had they been when needed?

If he could have shot down one more man, it would not have been his captor. It would have been General Anderson, with his idiot's order to halt.

The Yankee guards got them moving at the double-quick. When it was too late, Huger grasped why: Behind them a Rebel yell went up and rifles crackled. The Yankee bugler sounded the recall, but Huger, crush-hearted beyond endurance, saw some last, bold Yankees swinging axes at the wheel spokes of his abandoned guns, leaving them immovable and useless. The worst of it was that those had to be his axes, off his limbers.

As soon as the Yankees reached safe ground, a private seized his watch. Another tried on his hat and decided he fancied it. A third man took his toothbrush, and when Huger protested, the Yankee ground it underfoot.

"You lost, Johnny," the bluecoat told him. "We won."

Two p.m.
Marshall's Crossroads

Eppa Hunton's shrunken brigade rushed forward, spirits aroused despite hunger and exhaustion. He wasn't sure he'd ever been so proud of any command he'd been blessed to hold. Cresting the hill, wet-footed from the creek crossing, they swung from a quickstep to the double-quick, letting go a yell that seemed to conjure all the missing voices, all their dead, as reinforcements.

It was almost like the old days.

The Yankee cavalry didn't make much of a stand, just emptied their damned carbines and showed their horsetails. But they left behind burning wagons by the score and cannon with broken wheels.

"Come on, men! They're running!" Hunton hollered, throat hoarse and commands not quite reaching. It didn't matter. Every man present saw what had to be done. Nor would they be long alone. Corse and Terry were rushing up their flanking brigades.

It was a glorious feeling to be charging again, charging and driving the enemy, instead of waiting, robbed of hope, to get licked, just taking the beatings when the mood struck the Federals.

His wonderful, rag-clad, gap-toothed, brave-beyond-measure soldiers shouted, "Virginia! Virginia!" after the withdrawing Yankees. Proud men much reduced but still not broken, they'd found reserves of spunk they'd thought long gone. And there was Lieutenant Wilkinson, the senior officer left to the 18th Virginia, leading that company-sized regiment with indomitable spirit. How could such men be beaten?

By numbers. By incompetence. By fraud.

George Pickett, in Hunton's view, was no more fit to be the division commander over such men than Warrenton, Virginia, was Paris, France. Pickett, who had been gorging himself and drinking at Five Forks while Hunton's men fought desperately . . . the dastard was all Cologne water and moonshine. Thanks to Pickett, Hunton had lost half of his brigade and had to deem himself fortunate to have rallied the other half after the debacle.

His insides turned every time he saw the man.

At least Pickett had been on hand *this* day. And quick, for once, to order a counterattack on the Yankee cavalry: Custer's marauders, as their red scarves told.

His men drove Yankee dismounts through a grove and over a bump of ground, intoxicated by the prospect of one more victory, by this burst of redemption.

Careless of those repeating carbines, careless of all but his soldiers, *proud,* Hunton wasn't sure he was leading so much as following these good men made wild by circumstance, these heroes who smelled like mules and fought like archangels. . . .

A Yankee party with flags pulled off a hill in the nick of time. A gun section followed after, quick as it could.

His soldiers cheered again.

A courier from Pickett ordered Hunton's Brigade to stop its advance and withdraw to the crest of the hill. A battle line was forming.

The fire went out.

Two fifteen p.m.
Marshall's Crossroads

Custer grasped the situation the instant he saw their infantry crest the hill: Lee's army had broken in two. Reports put Longstreet's corps ahead, at Rice's Depot. But when the Rebel counterattack came, it came from the right, the east, with no response from the left. Those wagons stopped and helpless along the road—their canvas and hulls burning handsomely—marked a rupture in the Confederate march. Half of Lee's army had stopped.

The thing now was to make sure they stayed where they were.

He had his bugler sound the commander's call. While he waited for his colonels to gather, he watched through his field glasses as the Rebs formed up to defend the crossroads, tearing apart worm fences and searching out fallen limbs to pile up barricades. He counted nearly enough flags for a division, but only enough men to fill a brigade. The Johnnies had taken their beatings, one after another.

They'd shown spirit, though. That fearless charge and their ungodly screech.

High time to see that this particular batch of Rebs never raised that battle cry again.

Pennington came up first, sweat-greased from the hunt, followed in short order by Hank Capehart and Billy Wells.

Capehart said, "I hear you just had a West Point reunion, General."

Custer smiled charitably. "Poor Frank Huger. I cut him out of the prisoners, I'll see to him myself. He's not a bad egg, Frank ain't. We'll give him a feed and a pat."

"That brother of yours," Pennington said. "Best keep an eye on him, sir. He's taking lunatic chances. This close to the end . . ."

"High spirits," Custer said. "All right, gentlemen. We have but one clear duty. Fix the Rebs where they are, don't let them move an inch forward." He grew as serious as ever his colonels had seen him. "We can either end the war today, or come close. But we have to do whatever it takes to pin the buggers down." He looked at each of the weathered faces in turn. "It's not a day to count casualties. Only effects. We've got to hold them here till Crook and Devin come up on the left, cut them off completely. And give Phil time to bring the Sixth Corps up, get the infantry in it."

Al Pennington cast a look to the east. "Sounds like they're already in."

Custer shook his head. "If Wright was up, we'd hear guns." Again, he surveyed the faces. And he pointed a gloved finger at the Rebel infantry. "Attack those lines. We won't break them, I don't think, but we don't have to. Just go at them every time they make an attempt to move on." He smiled coldly and happily. " 'Entertain them,' gentlemen. As other men tell me the textbooks I didn't read describe the business."

"Let Crook get in their rear," Wells said, "and his boys get the glory."

When he replied, George Armstrong Custer astonished his subordinates:

"I don't care a fig about glory, just pin the Rebs."

Two thirty p.m.
Rice's Depot

Robert E. Lee said: "I regret this, General. It is bad news, indeed. And the wound is certainly mortal?"

"So they tell me," Longstreet answered. "Might linger a time, but there's no hope."

In the middle distance, the Federals continued to flirt with a serious action, only to withdraw when nearly embraced, coquettes of the battlefield. Still not enough strength up to make it stick, Longstreet decided.

"I pray the surgeons are wrong. I hold General Dearing in great esteem. We cannot afford to lose such generals now." Lee hesitated. "Of course, we shall feel the loss of Boston and Thomson. But Dearing, another general . . ."

"They saved High Bridge. They did what they set out to do. Likely saved this army." When Lee did not reply, Longstreet continued, "Yankees put up a fight. Madcap business. Desperate. A few troops of their cavalry charged an entire brigade. Trying to save their infantry. Got themselves cut to pieces. Breathed left his guns to charge right back at them, just about by himself. Lucky *he* got off with just a saber cut."

Lee nodded. "Today, those people sought to burn a bridge and brave men saved it. Tomorrow, we shall burn that bridge behind us. And those people will try to save it. We chose a curious profession, you and I." He sighed. "Any further word from General Ewell?"

"Thought you might have heard something."

Lee shook his head. "I have asked much of him. I hope I have not asked too much."

"He'll be along. We'll clear the river."

The scattered firing picked up, only to fade again.

Lee opened his mouth to speak, but his tongue faltered. As if speech demanded he muster additional energy. At last, he said:

"There are so few choices now. General Anderson . . . has been a disappointment. As have his present subordinates. Pickett is not fit for his command, and Johnson is of little use. But what shall I do? I'd hoped that placing Ewell between you and Gordon might prop them up, that we might bring them along to some effect." He gazed into the distance, the future, at nothing. "I fear I have erred."

"As you said, sir. No choice. Dick Ewell will do his best."

"Yes," Lee said. "That is the tragedy of it."

Three p.m.
Marshall's Crossroads

Redemption. That's what the afternoon looked like to George Pickett. No matter how many times Custer's pack came at them, mounted or dismounted, they were repulsed. If only the bones of his division remained, they were strong bones. If he could hold the road and open a path for the column to catch up with Pete Longstreet, he'd be the army's savior, not its goat.

He needed that redemption. He didn't have to overhear the words men spoke against him, he only needed to meet the rebukes in their looks. The blame for Five Forks had fallen on him unfairly: It wasn't his fault alone. What about Fitz Lee? He'd gobbled down his share of the shad, all right. Worse, what about Anderson? Worthless, he'd done nothing to help out, he'd let his corps sit idle a few miles off while Sheridan overwhelmed better men than his.

Pickett had avoided Robert E. Lee. He feared him, his distaste. But this day might bring salvation. The next time they met, Pickett might be greeted with praise, or at least forgiveness—and not with Lee's freeze-you-dead look and that refined, eloquent, quiet, merciless voice.

He didn't want to end the war in shame. He didn't want to face Sallie in disgrace.

The Yankees came on again, clumsy and foolish, riding straight for his division and Johnson's on the flank. Villains on good horses, they charged boldly. And shattered by canister, they barely made it into volley range. In minutes, the latest charge had failed, leaving men quivering on the ground or twisted and death-still, their tormented horses careening, blood streaming in their wake like crimson ribbons. A fine chestnut mare limped on three legs, its fourth mangled and dangling.

His men cheered.

When Yankee dismounts finally worked their way close to Johnson's Division, Wise charged them, the spindly old former governor leading his brigade himself, his queer white beard wrapped around his neck like a ruff in some old painting. Wise had been especially hard in his comments after Five Forks and hadn't minded that word got back to Pickett. Not a likable man, Henry Wise. But he did make a fine charge.

Pickett wished that his own men had made it.

Enough that they were bloodying Georgie Custer, beating back every effort that he made.

Pickett wondered how things were faring elsewhere.

Three fifteen p.m.
Sailor's Creek

Ewell hesitated. He felt they were being trapped. It wasn't enough for Anderson to block the Yankees at the crossroads—the Yankees were blocking him at the same time. The column had to start moving again, Anderson had to open the road to Rice's. Before it was too late.

It all seemed brutally clear.

But Ewell was reluctant to dictate to Anderson, who had been entrusted with a fighting corps by Lee. He didn't want to appear a sour old man. Or a meddling fool.

And a peg-legged fool, at that. He'd got down off his horse to rest his buttocks, but the leg was no better on the ground than it had been in the saddle. Damned traitor, that leg. Betray a man at the most inconvenient time.

The shooting and hooting up at the crossroads, back there around the bend, livened up again. Never seemed to come to very much, though. With his two divisions, Anderson could attack and drive off the Yankees while they only had cavalry on the field.

Perhaps Anderson had his reasons. . . .

Dick Ewell would have liked to see for himself, but he had to wait on Kershaw, to give Joe his orders to fill out the line, in case the Yankees outpaced them and came up in strength.

Why couldn't Anderson get the wagons moving? Those that hadn't been ravaged?

Black smoke rose above the trees to Ewell's rear.

Custis Lee walked up, wearing neither sword nor sidearm but fortified with his father's perfect posture. Brawny of build, young Lee still exuded refinement. And his uniform was clean.

Lee saluted. "Beg to report, sir. My men are in position. We command the left of the heights and the crossing."

"But? I hear a 'but' in your voice, General." Even now and despite his seniority, Ewell could not bring himself to call Lee "Custis." As if the old man stood at his son's shoulder.

"Sir, my men will fight. I do believe it. They're itching to prove themselves. After all the taunts." He nodded beyond the bare patch where they stood, back across the unsoldiered space that stretched toward the crossroads. "But the gap, between us and Anderson . . . I'm not sure they understand it."

Which meant, to Ewell, that the gap worried Custis Lee.

"Kershaw's going to fill it. Soon as he gets up." Ewell turned toward the creek valley and the farmhouse on the far hill, a mile off. "I expect him momentarily."

"Yes, sir." Doubt remained in young Lee's eyes.

"General Lee, I reckon your boys feel lonely, but the position's sound." Ewell chose not to add that he saw no alternative.

"I wasn't questioning—"

"Hellation, son, I realize the distance twixt you and whatever Anderson's got going on makes for some discomfort. But Kershaw's going to fill that gap, he'll stretch." Ewell smiled, straining at confidence. "Yankees come up on us here, they'll have them a stream to cross and a hill to climb."

"Be a fine thing to have more artillery, sir."

"Colonel Huger's found himself indisposed."

Ewell had one artillery piece on the hill. He'd called for more, but none had arrived. Huger had made a bad situation worse.

"I trust, sir . . . ," Lee said in a lowered voice, "that I haven't led you to think I'm growing alarmed?"

Ewell hooted one syllable. "General Lee, if you *weren't* alarmed, you'd be a useless fool. Plenty to get alarmed about today. But you go on now, see to your men."

To the east, the noise of combat erupted again. Loud enough to overwhelm the nearer noise of Anderson's fight to the west.

"Kershaw?" Lee asked.

Ewell shook his head. "Kershaw's on his way, he sent a messenger. Must be Gordon. He'll hold them up a while. Yankees won't come rushing down *that* road."

As he spoke, the lead brigade of Kershaw's Division trudged into view, filling the road that passed the distant farmhouse.

"See there?" Ewell asked. "We'll make this hill impregnable, just you wait. When Gordon catches up, we'll even have enough men for a reserve. Go on now. Days like this, soldiers want to see their generals strutting around like roosters."

Lee smiled. More warmly than his father tended to do. "What about sailors? Or marines? I suppose I should have brought an admiral's uniform."

"You just go on. Entire army's counting on you today." Ewell had tried to make his voice jovial and light, but it came out stilted and awkward, stiff as that wooden leg.

As Lee marched off, Ewell wondered, again, if he shouldn't order Anderson to attack and open the road. He had the authority, after all. . . .

There were days, plenty of them, when Lieutenant General Richard Stoddert Ewell just wished that he could be home with his wife.

Three fifteen p.m.
Northeast of Holt's Corner

John Brown Gordon was confused. Hours before, a message had reached him that the entire column had been diverted from the direct road to High Bridge and onto the Rice's Depot road to the south, Longstreet's route. But as his men beat off yet another Federal thrust, he'd looked behind himself, only to see two things that upturned matters.

First, the trains he'd been ordered to protect not only weren't on the Deatonville–Rice's Depot road, but the last, lumbering wagons in view had followed the northerly road closer to High Bridge.

The second and more alarming development was the appearance of Yankees all but behind him, passing the crossroads given as Holt's Corner on the map. Wasn't just a handful of Yankees, either. They were coming up in force, not a mile from those last wagons rolling off. The situation put the Federals smack between his corps and the rest of the army.

Hadn't anyone seen fit to tell him what was going on?

He made his decision, felt it forced upon him. Tangling with Humphreys and his Second Corps was work enough, keeping them off what remained of the trains. If the few reports that had reached him were correct, that might well be their Sixth Corps at Holt's Corner. That was simply more than he could handle: He didn't care to get caught between Humphreys to his front and Wright to his rear. And Lee had ordered him to protect the trains, that was his charge. . . .

He waved up his staff yet again. Some men were missing, others were bloodied, still more wore powder-burned faces and rode upon blood-streaked mounts. As concisely as he could, he sent orders to his three hard-fought divisions, directing them to oblique to the northwest and follow the Jamestown Road toward High Bridge, to keep on protecting the trains.

With his surviving staff, Gordon set out for a key bend in the road the last wagons had taken. His little band of horsemen didn't amount to much, but a bluff was the best he could offer until his brigades reorganized their withdrawal and followed after. He ordered his flags displayed to impress any watching Yankees that the wagons they'd glimpsed would not go undefended.

After putting a finely judged distance between himself and the infested crossroads, Gordon took out his field glasses again. One of the lenses had cracked, but the glasses served.

And Gordon saw endless regiments in blue coursing along the Rice's Depot road, obviously chasing the rest of his army. Remaining in march formations, they clearly were unopposed by any force.

How had that happened? Had he been abandoned?

Well, he'd keep on protecting the wagons and do his duty. Any Yankees he met would face a fight.

At the blue-swept crossroads, an assembly of mounted officers watched their regiments pass. The flags behind the mounted party were bunched and couldn't be read, but Gordon was certain he recognized one man from past encounters.

A brute little plug on a great big horse, Sheridan did stand out.

Three thirty p.m.
Holt's Corner

The lead Sixth Corps division surprised Sheridan. Weary as those men had to be, they were marching with *élan,* as if they truly wanted to get at the Rebs.

"That's it, boys. We've got 'em now. We'll whip those sonsofbitches till they shit blood. That's it, step lively, we've got 'em by the stones and we're going to squeeze."

A scattering of dead Rebels marked the crossroads, unlucky members of a rear detachment otherwise taken prisoner. The corpses had been kicked to the roadside by hard boys who weren't impressed by superstitions.

He turned to Horatio Wright. "Damn it, Wright. I can't give you orders, you're back under Meade again. But you know what to do. My 'advice' is to pitch right into them, as soon as you think you've got sufficient strength up. You saw the note from Custer. He's got them stopped dead and they don't feel strong enough to push him aside. Tells me they've lost their nerve or their wits or both." He leaned his barrel chest over the saddle. "Work with my cavalry, just as you did in the Valley. And you'll end this day with stories to tell your grandchildren."

"Getting late in the day for a major fight, sir."

Sheridan grunted. "Move faster. And bring up artillery."

Wright nodded. He'd do what needed doing, Sheridan felt confident of that. But the damned formalities had to be observed. Wright, God help him, still had a touch of the West Point martinet. The man was probably wondering, even now, if he shouldn't get a written order from Meade. Who was dragging along in an ambulance, all but whinnying, "Won't you wait for me?"

A just arrived regiment cheered at the sight of Sheridan. These were men who'd served with him in the Valley, when Wright had been under his command and Sheridan gave them victories.

Nodding to the north, Wright asked, "Shouldn't I send a detachment after those wagons? Regiment or two? Naught but a handful of horsemen to their rear, not much of a guard."

"Fuck the wagons. Let Humphreys worry about the cracker barrels. We're going to wipe out half of Bobby Lee's army."

FOURTEEN

Four fifteen p.m., April 6, 1865
Marshall's Crossroads

"Not yet," Major General Wesley Merritt said.

Custer prickled. "Wes, we've *got* them. Crook's in solid behind them, Devin's up, you've got Stagg in reserve . . . if we don't strike now, there's no telling how many of them might escape."

A thin smile cut Merritt's face below faint mustaches. Ever a step ahead in promotions, he alternately rankled Custer and passed for a decent fellow. Custer believed that he himself had Sheridan's affection, but Phil trusted Wes the more when it came to decisions.

"They're not going to get away," Merritt told him. "For God's sake, calm down, George." He shook his Puritan parson's head, slightly senior in age but grandly the elder in attitude. "Look, you did fine work this afternoon, just the right thing. Bully for you, George. But Phil wants all this to meld into one piece, this fight and the rest. He's driving the Sixth Corps as fast as he can move Wright."

"We could do this without the Sixth Corps, we don't need—"

"Not a time to go headlong, George. Cavalry against infantry's not the best odds. Even now."

"They're ready to break, they're tired."

"And they'll be all the readier, when they're struck from three sides at once." Still the condescending upperclassman, Merritt added, "As soon as we hear Wright's artillery, we'll count fifteen minutes, then hit them."

For a moment, the two youthful generals listened to the *snap-snap* of carbines from the left, Crook's share of the fight. Every shot was a nail fixing the Rebs, Merritt was right. But *he'd* held back so long, and with three mounted divisions ready to charge . . . Wes was playing it safe when the hour wanted dash.

George Custer longed to get at the Rebs, to seize the glory he'd dutifully postponed. To get the thing *done*. He'd been patient, limiting his actions to minor attacks and feints, forcing the Rebs to dally while a blue avalanche approached just out of view. Now he feared he'd done himself out of a splendid chance. He felt . . . panicked at the thought of opportunity passing him by, at stolen laurels. He couldn't keep his hands still, or his arms. In his stirrups, he tapped the air with the toes of his boots.

He wished he could have made his case directly to Phil Sheridan. But Merritt was Phil's deputy on the field, in command of all the cavalry that was up. Wes had the say. And though he was certainly brave enough, Wes liked to think things through, to put things in order, a shopkeeper with his eye on all the goods. He hardly seemed a cavalryman at all.

As if reading Custer's thoughts, Merritt said, "We've all run our share of risks these last four years. But never take one you don't have to, George. Sooner or later, every man's luck runs out."

Four thirty p.m.
Sailor's Creek

Oh, no," Dick Ewell said.

Kershaw whipped around to follow his stare.

Yankees. All of a sudden. On the opposing height, by that board farmhouse.

It made no sense. It should've been Gordon's men coming over that hill.

Yet there the Yankees were, undeniable, bristling, commanding. With skirmishers pressing forward and flankers out. Their lead regiment had not troubled itself to deploy for battle, though, it merely came on in column behind its flags, officers mounted and busy on all sides, an array of confident huntsmen running their quarry to ground.

"They must've . . . Gordon . . ." Kershaw, too, was stunned. He pulled out his glasses and studied the display.

Dropping his lenses down toward the creek, Ewell saw stray Confederates fleeing madly. Desperate to save some regiment's honor, one man carried a flag furled around its staff.

Ewell tried to listen beyond the scrap to his rear, quizzing the distance about John Gordon's whereabouts, his fate. But the racket from Anderson's action back by the crossroads made it difficult—Ewell's hearing had weakened since the war's beginning.

He'd ridden over to Anderson at last, suggesting he *attack* and open the road. Before the Yankees could muster a crushing force. But Anderson had sunk himself in the sparring match under way, he met Ewell with a disheartening mix of bad temper and apathy. And Pickett had stood there, silent for once, doing the mathematics of reputation. Ewell had never disliked the man so fiercely, nor thought so poorly of Anderson. He had turned and ridden back to his patchwork corps, his last responsibility.

Wasn't it all his responsibility, though?

Raising a hand to hush those gathered near, Ewell believed that he heard what he'd strained to discover. He told Kershaw:

"Gordon's still fighting, he's out there. Ways northeast, it sounds like. Must have followed the wagons up that road, goddamn the luck." He looked down at the veteran commander, caught on foot emplacing tired brigades. "Didn't you make contact? Before you pulled back?"

"I *saw* him. Mile or so off. That's when I pulled back. As you ordered, sir." Kershaw shook his head and half lifted his glasses again. "Left a small rear guard of my own. Expected them to fold in with Gordon's boys."

Ewell kept his temper. He tried to remember the wording of his orders to Joe Kershaw, but the specifics eluded him. Sleep-in-the-saddle weary, he'd expected some form of contact between Kershaw and Gordon, an exchange of information, at the least.

But he had not spelled it out, he didn't think. He'd assumed . . .

His fault, then. He'd ignored that basic lesson from West Point: *Never assume.*

And Kershaw was no West Pointer, just a fighter born. He wasn't to blame. Joe had done his best on a very bad day.

No point in recriminations. Especially if they did a man an injustice. The Confederacy had known arguments enough, sufficient discord between the men who had taken up arms to defend it. He had never liked that bickering much. But he, too, had indulged. At times, with relish.

Had they argued the Confederacy to death?

As the gray-coated generals and their staffs looked on, the Federals left the road to deploy for battle. Shortly after cresting the far hill, they'd turned from the road to line the still-brown fields, a gorgeous spectacle bathed in golden light.

"Looks like we're in for a bust-up," Kershaw said. He looked up at Ewell. "I'd best get these boys into position, see how far I can stretch out toward Anderson. Without making all this here a gift to the Yankees."

Never enough men now. Not enough time. Or food. Or sleep. Or hope.

Ewell nodded: *Go on.*

At least his wooden leg had stopped annoying him.

Raccoon-eyed, slump-shouldered soldiers piled up barricades, acting from habit, not conscious decision, like the automaton figures he'd seen in Manhattan.

So long ago.

The Yankees kept coming, filling the far hillside with long blue lines, the dropping sun mad for their bayonets. Their first artillery battery jounced up, leaving the road for a field near the little farmhouse. The gun crews unlimbered with splendid discipline, reminding Ewell of drill fields from his past, of canvas covers to keep the sand from muzzles on frontier posts, of hard-fisted, broken-toothed sergeants with gleaming leathers and narrow pride, of minor infractions magnified by boredom and the barren land's immensity.

He rode toward Custis Lee's lines, where the Navy battalion held the key position in his corps. He grasped the irony and smiled bitterly. All those years he'd served in blue, a professional soldier by choice, for life, a man of the Regular Army, only to finish in a different uniform, depending at the last on sailors marooned on dry land, on marines and half-weaned cadets, on volunteer artillerymen robbed of their guns and bearing rifles they'd never fired in combat, on the strays of the once grand, shouting-proud Confederacy.

Whatever might happen . . . what he *knew* was going to happen . . . those men would not bear the blame. He would. He had no excuses to offer, not this day, no charges to bring against others for dereliction. Spite and spleen might return, the quarrelsome smallness of which he and so many others had been guilty. If he lived until morning, anger might devour him, he might take the ignoble path and shift the blame, he might lie to himself as scorned men did. He could too readily see himself blaming Robert E. Lee for not giving up once things became utterly hopeless, for his selfish stubbornness, for putting all of them through this ordeal for nothing but an aristocrat's gory dignity. But not yet.

He saw now what a small man he had been, a view that, even in his lowest spirits, had never afflicted him. Did his wife see his smallness, too? Had she married him from pity? A peg-legged bankrupt serving a futile cause?

These past days, this day . . . had he done all that he could, had he shown real courage? The answer was "No."

Pausing again to watch the Yankees paint the horizon blue, Dick Ewell saw not only the spectacle before him, but his life marching in review. Everything he had learned, done, tried, believed in, hoped for, fought for . . . it all came down to this brisk afternoon. And he had failed. He had failed Robert E. Lee again, whatever Lee's flaws might be, but there was more than that: His entire life had pointed toward this hilltop, and that entire life had summed to failure.

Wasn't about to quit, though. Not just yet.

Ewell tapped his wooden leg for luck, smiled like a damned fool, and spurred his mount with his remaining foot: Nothing left to do but fight it out.

Four thirty p.m.
Sailor's Creek

Amid the discarded Reb blankets, rifles, and haversacks, Elisha Hunt Rhodes spied tiny wildflowers. They seemed to have sprung up overnight, pinks and whites, blues and yellows, to wake the world with color, weeks ahead of Rhode Island's sluggish spring. Perhaps Virginia had its virtues, after all.

As he rode along at the head of his men, Rhodes thought of Pawtuxet, of the old Broad Street house and the garden to its rear, two-thirds given to vegetables of necessity, but the remainder reserved for the flowers his mother loved.

Would he see her again soon? Would the Lord guide him through these last days of destruction? Might Carrie Hunt greet him as a man still whole, a suitor without impediment?

"Sounds like more than one fuss going on," Frank Halliday noted.

"When you hear cannon, you'll know it's a proper fuss," the regimental commander told his adjutant.

"Just you set that there lieutenant straight," a good-natured voice called from the marching ranks.

Rhodes *knew* his men, these proud survivors of the 2nd Rhode Island, men with whom he had shared four years of war. It still felt strange to have become their father, a lieutenant colonel commanding at age twenty-three—and recommended for a brevet colonelcy. He could not have dreamed of such a thing that bright morning back in Providence when, puny of chest and slight of frame, he'd had to beg to be allowed to enlist.

So many men had died to lift him up. The dead seemed as many as those roadside flowers.

More Reb trash lay strewn along their route. For days, they'd followed a trail of meager leavings, discarded equipment and personal possessions. It beggared belief that such an impoverished army had more to abandon.

Castaway letters flirted with the breeze. Missives from home were the last things men threw away.

Rebs must have it hard. Awfully hard.

Why didn't they just quit? They couldn't win. Why go on bleeding?

He guided his straying horse back to the center of the road and straightened his posture, warning the color guard to look lively now. A cluster of ranking officers waited ahead: Oliver Edwards, his brigade commander and in for a brevet; General Wheaton, who had the division; big, burly General Wright; and—drawing every eye—"Little Phil" Sheridan. Trotting through the fields, the generals had dared to ride ahead of their troops, protected only by a cavalry escort.

That did strike Rhodes as confident.

He wanted to feel confident himself. He knew the end was near. The Johnnies were falling apart. But he also reckoned on a last fight or two, it was just the Johnnies' nature, the stubbornness of old mules. And he was certain that his men felt exactly as he did himself, ready to pitch in and get it over with, but hardly desirous of being the last to die. Since the Petersburg breakthrough, they'd been at their most spirited, if footsore. His men would fight. But only to a point.

Probably just as true of the Rebs, he judged. Two tuckered-out armies thumping on each other. And his job was to hold his men together, to see to it that they handed out more thumps than they received. Really, that was all that war came down to. . . .

It was an honor to have been selected to lead the corps' column on such a day. But the honor had whittled his regiment by half, as he was obliged not only to pause and fight time and again, but to post guards at houses that needed protection and in the hamlets the army would coat with dust. Not least, details had been needed to escort prisoners—scrawny Rebs dejected or merely relieved—back to the provost guards. If a battle lay ahead—the last?—he'd take barely two hundred men into the fight, the strength of two companies before they'd seen the elephant.

As Rhodes and his men neared the covey of commanders, Colonel Edwards signaled for him to halt his regiment and join the group. As he rode up and saluted, Rhodes felt surrounded by all the stars in the firmament.

"Well, here's your schoolboy colonel," Wright teased Edwards. "We're all safe now." But the corps commander smiled. He'd always treated Rhodes kindly.

"How-dee-do, Rhodes?" Sheridan asked. "Ready to win the war?"

There was just something about Sheridan . . . Rhodes could never figure it. Even a quip from the little fellow could mold a man into an arrow, ready to fly at the enemy. He left men jolly about the prospect of death.

"All right, Elisha," Edwards began, grown serious, "as soon as you reach the crest, you'll see the Rebs. Some of them, anyway. They're drawn up on a hillside, across a creek, not a mile off. Follow this road a hundred yards past the crest, or as far down the slope as you need to go to clear supporting fires, and make a column-left into the field. Second Rhode Island will make up my third line, the brigade will fill in forward of your position. Understand?"

"Yes, sir."

"You give 'em a taste of the strap, Rhodes," Sheridan added to see him off.

His own officers had gathered ahead of his regiment, expecting their orders in turn. As Rhodes came up, Captain Gleason asked, "We fighting again, Colonel?"

"Looks that way, Charlie. We'll be in the third line, though."

Gleason looked down but mastered himself and smiled. "Well, this should be the last one, don't you think, sir? Win this one and we go home."

The other officers murmured similar sentiments. Rhodes gave his orders and hurried them back to their companies.

Before he returned to the column, Gleason said, "God bless you, Colonel."

"And you, Captain."

When Gleason was out of earshot, Lieutenant Halliday, something of a confidant for Rhodes, whispered, "Charlie's got the willies."

"Who doesn't?" Rhodes said. But he called up a confident smile, one more of the dishonesties of command.

He ordered his regiment forward, starting the entire corps on its way into battle.

Might this be the last face-off? The last men lost? The last letters that he would need to write to bereaved wives or broken parents?

As they crested the hill, the terrain revealed itself: The declining field met a thicket masking a stream. On the far bank, a slope climbed from bottom brush up through raw fields to a grove. That was where the Johnnies had tucked themselves in, some in plain view, others no doubt lurking in the trees. Too much open ground to cross for Rhodes' taste, but he didn't get to pick.

He ordered his men off the road into the field, judged his distance, then halted and right-faced the regiment. Company commanders collapsed four ranks into two. And they waited for the next regiments to fill out the lines of battle that would precede them.

The standard confusion followed. Rhodes had been relieved at the prospect of being in the third line, which meant the regiment might not even have to fight. But as the brigade deployed across the slope, an order came down to extend the left of the second line. No sooner was that done than the 2nd Rhode Island was ordered up again to fill in the first line.

"Oh, damn it to hell," a soldier declared in a voice of New England flint.

"Michaels," Rhodes said sharply, "you wouldn't want profanity to be the last words from your lips. Would you?"

"Colonel, I don't want *any* words to be my last."

The men got a laugh from that and Rhodes let it go. He knew they thought him a puff on religious matters, but prayer had gotten them this far. . . .

Wary of the ground to be crossed, Rhodes sent a trusted man to look at the creek, telling him to hurry. The division was largely in place, the order to advance could be moments away.

Federal artillery opened on the Rebs across the valley, but no guns seemed dedicated to his brigade. He could turn his head and see the fieldpieces meant to back their advance, but those cannon remained silent, one more of war's manifold mysteries.

The Rebs hadn't put out skirmishers, which was unusual. They all looked to be tucked in atop that hill. Waiting.

His scout burrowed into the thickets guarding the streambed.

How wet were they going to get this time? How bad would it be? He was glad to be on horseback himself, but he felt for his men with a chill evening coming on.

The scout reemerged from the brambles, but too late. The drums started up and the order rang out to go forward.

Well, he'd tried.

Didn't like it at all, just didn't like it. But he had to put up a good show for his men.

Toward the bottom of the field, his horse slipped in the mud and couldn't find purchase again. Rhodes got down and sent the mount back with an orderly—who didn't mind heading for the rear one bit. After scurrying to catch up and nearly slipping, he resumed his place just as his forward rank reached the undergrowth.

The Rebs opened fire with their rifles, despite the distance. And it seemed they had pushed out skirmishers, after all.

"Forward!" Rhodes shouted, seconded by his subordinates. Lieutenant Peck shoved reluctant men deep into the thicket. Other officers shouted and slashed the brambles with swords.

Thorns tore wool and found skin. Men cursed. The stream's bank had flooded into the undergrowth, drowning shoes and trouser legs.

"Forward!"

Mud gripped Rhodes' boots and spurs, but he thrust forward. Men dropped suddenly into water that reached their waists, even chests. Frantically, they rescued their cartridge boxes, looping them over rifles held overhead.

"Come on, come on!"

The creek bottom felt like quicksand, reluctant to let men proceed. As Rhodes struggled, the water leapt up to his sword belt. Just in time, he freed his pistol from its sinking holster, keeping the cartridges dry but very nearly losing his balance. Bullets ripped past, plunking water and punching mud.

Captain Gleason was driving, shoving, all but hurling men to the opposite bank, while sergeants blasphemed at privates, their imprecations at least as frightening as the waiting Rebs.

Grasping a handful of brush, Rhodes hoisted himself, slid, coated his knees with mud, and tried again. He made it out of the stream, but the ground remained a morass. He wanted to empty his boots, but there was no time.

"Second Rhode Island! Rally to your colors!"

Lieutenants and captains called out their company letters.

The Reb fire grew heavier, but it seemed inexpert, with most rounds whistling high. Rhodes didn't see anyone fall.

Not yet.

Wet, angry men emerged from the brambles and formed ranks under fire. Only then did Rhodes realize—and he was not the only man to see it—that their sister regiments had spun hard to the right as they crossed the creek, leaving an ugly gap between Rhode Island and the remainder of the Union.

Just get them organized, Rhodes told himself. Somehow, he did.

As the regiment prepared to step off again, to close to the right and climb the forbidding hill, the brigade's supporting battery opened at last. The first ranging shot landed in the mud *behind* the 2nd Rhode Island, splashing the backsides of Company G with muck.

It was a day of bountiful profanity.

The second shot just cleared their heads, drawing condemnations of every artillery officer who'd ever commanded a gun. But the next round climbed the hillside and soon the guns were pounding the woods on the crest.

"Right shoulder shift . . . at the right oblique . . . forward . . . *march!*"

The Reb skirmishers pulled back but paused to fire. Captain Gleason's hat flew off and he crumpled with a bullet through his head.

Rhodes shifted his revolver to his left hand, drew his sword and pointed. "Forward!"

Please God, not today. Don't take me today. Let us finish this. Jesus, protect us. . . .

Only the responsibility he felt—duty—drove him forward.

A gap of fifty yards remained between his regiment and the next, but the ground dictated that he turn straight uphill. Where he couldn't see the Rebs for the hump of the slope, though they had to be waiting.

"Regiment!"

"Company!"

"Half-left . . ."

"Half-left . . ."

"March!"

The men bent into the slope, and calves felt the strain. Rhodes about-faced and marched backward for a few paces, inspecting his lines as they climbed. He hated marching backward on a battlefield, but it had to be done.

His ranks were far from perfect, but they'd do.

The Federal batteries tore open the sky now, their rounds shrilling overhead in search of targets.

He saw a man fall. The rank closed up. Rhodes turned to face the enemy again.

He could see a string of Rebs now, but there had to be more. A storm of sound had broken out around them, as if the battle had spread, a bloody contagion. Yet his men were barely afflicted.

A hundred years below the crest, he halted the regiment and unleashed a volley.

"Reload!"

Veterans, the men dropped to the earth, fingering cartridges and working ramrods, while their officers crouched in their midst.

Not much firing in return—what were the Rebs up to?

Shells screamed and burst. Men taunted invisible foes or gasped for breath. A corporal rose to his feet, spurting blood from his neck. Bewildered, he sought salvation with burning eyes.

The officers got the men back to their feet.

"Bayonets!"

The familiar metal scrape, a grim and determined sound. All faces solemn.

"Trail arms . . . forward!"

The bite of the slope moved to thighs now, an intense awareness of life.

No flowers here.

Alone now, the Rhode Islanders pressed forward.

When the regiment was but fifty yards from the tree line, a gray-clad officer stepped forth and hollered, "Rise up! Fire!" Rebs swelled from the earth like spooks, shrieking that yell of theirs, and quick-fired a volley in his soldiers' faces. Men dropped, at least a half dozen. Before Rhodes could mouth another order, the Rebs—in wild disorder—leapt over their works and charged straight for his men. And the queerest mix the Rebs were, some with red artillery piping, others dressed . . . like sailors.

It was too much and they were too many. When Rhodes managed to get out the start of an order, he found his regiment halfway down the hill again, with Johnnies already among them. Worse, Rebs had come from nowhere to get behind them, trying to take them all prisoner.

What the devil had happened?

Down by the underbrush, personal combats ruled, with bayonets jabbing and rifle butts in play. Some men came to grips with their bare hands, brawling in the mud.

Rhodes worked his revolver as he descended, calling his men to re-form. Frank Halliday clutched his hip and dropped to his knees. A Reb grabbed the state colors. Lieutenant Perry had his skull crushed with a rifle butt.

A bearded Reb near Rhodes responded, "Aye-aye, sir!" to a command.

"Get the flag!" Rhodes shouted. "Charge through them, cross the creek!"

What men he could rally joined him in the dash. More followed after. They gained enough weight and drive to punch through the enveloping Rebs, dodging dead and wounded men in a mad assortment of uniforms.

"Through the creek!" Rhodes shouted. "Re-form on the other side!"

A flying battery came to their aid, galloping recklessly down to a shelf on the eastern slope and laying into the flanking Rebs with canister. Under the cover of their fire, Rhodes led . . . or followed . . . the survivors of his regiment through the creek.

It wasn't over, that was clear. Already hoarse, he began the work of re-forming the regiment. He judged that he'd left a good quarter of his command on the field. Someone told him that Captain Jeffrey and Lieutenant Peck had suffered serious wounds.

He couldn't think about that now. He had to turn the regiment back into a body that could fight again.

He turned to give orders to Frank Halliday, only to recall that his friend had been shot.

As Rhodes bellowed in the best command voice he possessed, General Wheaton cantered across the slope, trailed by his flags.

"Rhodes! I don't know what the devil's become of Edwards. You're the ranking officer now, you've got the brigade. Get them back into some semblance of order. We're going to take that hill and hammer those bastards." He literally growled, then added, "Understand me?"

If the battle had paused to their front, it had reached a crescendo elsewhere. Rhodes sent for his horse again. A mount was essential if he was to span an entire brigade. And he went straight to work, issuing orders that had become second nature, alternately bossing and cajoling, taking command of thousands of men, of their fates.

They went back in. Angry. Bayonets thirsty. Again, they splashed through the stream, with Rhodes' mount almost floundering. Again, they re-formed and pushed up the slope, grimly passing comrades writhing with wounds or stilled by death. And something had happened elsewhere on the field. There were cavalrymen on their left now, some of them riding hard at an oblique. With a howl, his men surged through a last ragged volley from the Rebs and then it all became absurdly easy. Johnnies emerged from the trees, throwing down their rifles and raising their hands, some of their shouts of surrender almost craven.

There were masses of them. And officers by the dozen. Giving up in an instant.

On the crest of the hill, looking out for any last Rebs determined to fight, Rhodes found himself in possession of at least a thousand prisoners, with more coming in each minute. And that was merely the haul for his command.

The brigade adjutant reported that a sergeant from the 5th Wisconsin had just captured a passel of Reb generals.

The battle had collapsed into a victory, the oddest affair, with cavalrymen and foot soldiers arguing over who had taken which prisoners or who was entitled to lay claim to which flags.

Small, sharp fights continued to sound to the west, which seemed to be the cavalry's domain, and a proper fight was booming to the north, but close by only one Reb unit still held out in the trees.

Rhodes ordered his men to see to it.

Five forty-five p.m.
Sailor's Creek

Commodore Tucker's disgust went a hundred fathoms deep. On all sides of his battalion—and that's what it was, not a damned brigade anymore, just four hundred souls—Confederate units had given up while they still had the means to fight. It was as if a ship of war had surrendered while its masts were still intact. Or, nowadays, before its propellers fouled.

He'd shown them, though. After all those taunts his men had borne . . . who was still standing and fighting? His sailors and marines, and his too-young-to-shave cadets. They might have blistered feet, but they'd done more than bluster. Unlike the mouthy landlubbers, they'd *fought.*

They'd hit those Yankees below the waterline, sent them reeling back down that hill crying out for their mammies' teats. They'd been pissing fire so hot they'd broken discipline and chased the Federals right down to that creek, letting them taste real Southern hospitality. He'd just about had to tie them up and drag his men back up the slope to their position.

And when the Yankees came back, when the other units ran or folded up, one after another, and even when cowards dashed through their ranks wailing that the Yankee cavalry had gotten in behind them, not one man had panicked. Shipboard discipline prevailed, with all hands still on deck.

Forced back into the grove, they made their stand, with more and more Federals crowding them on all sides, a fleet bearing down on a single determined frigate.

"Weight your marines to starboard, Mr. Kyle," Tucker commanded.

The marines snapped to, quick as could be, with their carbines held breast high, trotting to reinforce the beleaguered cadets.

Commodore John R. Tucker of the Confederate States Navy had not had the war he'd hoped, although he'd fought well, from Charleston to Wilmington and, at last, at Richmond, where he'd commanded a battery and a flotilla that had been bottled up on the James, sourly awaiting the order to scuttle. He'd fought when he could and delivered a few surprises, not least in Charleston Bay, but now he was far from the sea with his last command, as Yankee bullets ripped the green shoots from the trees.

He could have told them what would become of their country,

eager and stillborn. Walter Raleigh had been right a quarter of a millennium before the Confederate ensign ever flew: He who ruled the waters ruled the world. And the Navy had always been a Yankee affair, his own Alexandria birth a curiosity. Those cold-faced New Englanders were the country's mariners, born to blockade their former countrymen and to starve their families.

He'd done his duty, though, and never complained, even as Raph Semmes connived at fame.

Tucker did find himself in a dudgeon today, though. Plain disgusted. With cowards to port and starboard, men with no tradition of going down with their ship.

The Yankees came at them again, crashing through the brush and firing as they advanced.

"Mr. Martin, to the support of Mr. Nightingale, if you please. That's it, lads. Give them a proper broadside."

Once again, the Yankees pulled back, leaving corpses and the moaning wounded.

His own men were paying a price, though. The circle grew ever smaller, the flaunted jacks ever fewer above their shoulders. Like the English fleet caught by that Dutchman in the Downs, that's how it was. Didn't matter how well you fought, if you didn't have position *and* the numbers.

Well, he'd give the Yankees one last action, one they wouldn't forget.

How young and proud he once had been, in his first sea duds at fourteen years of age, and then on those countless port calls in Navy blue, or during the sad little war with the hapless Mexicans.

The firing had fallen off: The Yankees were licking their wounds. But Tucker felt their lines thickening around him, tightening like a great constricting serpent.

Instead of launching another attack, a Yankee waving a handkerchief stepped forward.

"Don't pot him, Brooks," Tucker told an eager marine.

The Yankee halted at a respectful distance.

"You fellows," the Federal called, "whoever the devil you are . . .

General Ewell has surrendered his command. If you're under Ewell, you're violating the articles of war."

"Really, I could pot him proper, sir," Brooks, an Englishman born, told his commodore.

"I think not."

"Just knick him, maybe? Touch 'is arm, for a lesson?"

"Be quiet, man." Tucker set his ears against this unaccustomed world. There was still a mighty to-do off to the north, but that was a good league away, if his ears were honest. Nor had all of the engagements stopped to the west, to the fore that was now the aft. But the space surrounding his hard little force had gone quiet except for the bark of Yankee officers and the rustle and rasp of thousands of men in uniform.

"How do I know that General Ewell has surrendered?"

"They've *all* surrendered, all your generals. We've got more on our hands than we can count." The officer hesitated. "Your men are set to die for nothing at all."

"We could try to break out," Lieutenant Gunderson whispered.

But the trap had closed. The Yankees were so thick around them that further resistance was hopeless. The ship was holed and sinking.

Tucker wanted to fight. His every instinct said, "Give them a volley." But he looked about at the half-starved men who had outfought those who had mocked them for their uniforms, disdaining their manners and doubting their utility. He could not sentence them all to death for his vanity.

"Oh, hell," the commodore said. He turned to his ranking lieutenant and said, "Strike the colors, Mr. Sanderson."

Five forty-five p.m.
Marshall's Crossroads

Following closely behind the fight, Custer was engrossed in giving the *coup de grâce* to his enemies when a monstrous sight made him stop in drop-jawed silence.

Lofting yet another Rebel banner, his brother Tom trotted up. The boy was doused with blood, he pulsed with it. He'd been slashed across the cheek and jaw and neck. Pumping blood at each hoofbeat, soaking his chest, Tom was even bleeding onto his horse. Unaware or uncaring, he grinned madly, his expression—his eyes—ecstatic and entranced, as if he'd just gobbled the flesh of his foe, drunk his blood, and gone into a spell.

Tom reined in so close that Custer smelled his brother's bloody stink over all the blown powder. What Custer could see of the wound nearly touched the jugular vein: He'd become a connoisseur of wounds, and Tom's threatened to turn mortal, if untended.

"Tom, for God's sake! Drop the damned flag, report straight to the surgeon. Go to the rear right now!"

Intoxicated by whatever he'd done, Tom spoke, but the words were muddled by the clots of blood that swelled from his mouth.

"Go to the rear! Drop that flag!"

Tom tossed the staff to a corporal, but spit out, ". . . get another one . . . killed him . . . shot me . . . killed him . . . go back in . . ."

And Tom, otherworldly and gloriously insane, turned his horse to return to the sputtering fight.

"Arrest that man!" Custer ordered the first sergeant of his escort. "Arrest that man and escort him to the surgeon."

Eyes crazed, Tom grinned again. Blood slimed from his mouth. ". . . killed him . . ."

Six p.m.
Marshall's Crossroads

George Pickett intended to be stalwart and rally his men, but as he was about to regale the line, a body of Yankee cavalry leapt the last barricade, pounding straight toward him.

Gaping, he flailed about for any aid. Shouting to Corse's nearest company, he ordered, "Get them! Yankees! Stop them!" Unsure whether he could be heard over the din, he quickly turned his horse toward the rear.

The Yankees were almost upon him, threatening and calling for his surrender.

Corse's boys were quick enough, whether they'd heard him or not. They spun to the rear and put a volley into the dozen Yankees, dropping men from atop their shrieking horses.

Pickett raised his hat to his savior-soldiers. Then he bent low along his mount's neck, applying the spurs and steering away from the fight. His adjutant and his medical director—paltry remains of his staff—followed after, but Pickett didn't care about them now.

Something had happened, something had broken inside him. Fear overpowered him, sudden, ice-cold terror. Cast beyond orderly thought, he dug in the spurs again. He couldn't be taken, the Yankees mustn't have him. He knew they wouldn't kill him, once made a prisoner, but knowing meant nothing. In a shell-burst of emotion, dread had conquered him, the sort of fright a child feels in the dark. He knew only that he had to get away.

It was . . . his duty to escape. His men could follow after. They'd rally to him again, as they had after Five Forks. He'd redeem himself. Lee would forgive him. Sallie would be proud and she would reward him. He daren't be taken, not now. Escaping was only sensible . . . the best thing. He could portray it as loyalty to the army, the refusal to take the easy path of surrender. There might even be tales of a breathless escape. . . .

Leaving the wrecked battle to his rear, Major General George Pickett abandoned his division for the last time.

Six thirty p.m.
Rice's Depot Road

My God . . . has the army dissolved?" Robert E. Lee begged of Billy Mahone.

Major General William Mahone was as shocked and irate as anyone, but the break in Lee's voice alarmed him more than the unfolding disaster. In haste, he told the older man:

"No, General. *No.*" Mahone gestured at his own men rushing

past them. Headed *toward* the fight. "Here are troops who are ready to do their duty. The army . . . isn't finished, sir. Far from it."

"Yes," Lee allowed, voice frail and lacking authority. "Yes, General . . . we have . . . there are some true men left. Will you please keep those people back?"

At Rice's Depot, Lee had ordered Mahone to take his division back to Sailor's Creek. Reports had come in of a sprawling and difficult fight. And the reports kept coming and worsening, some of them contradictory, others barely coherent. Lee had decided to ride back with the division, to judge the situation for himself.

Gaining the heights to the west of Sailor's Creek, they'd beheld a tragedy: men fleeing in untold numbers, their weapons discarded and all their equipment gone. Many of them had even lost their hats along with their pride, and a hurrying boy wore his left shoe but not the right. It was the worst behavior by Confederate soldiers Mahone had ever seen.

On the far hill, wagons flamed hugely in the twilight, torches to light the Yankees on their way.

"Stop your division," Lee said, his voice a study in desperate will. "Halt them here, General. It does no good to go forward, we must hold those people right here. And collect these . . . these discouraged men."

These goddamned, ill-led cowards, Mahone thought. But he just said, "Yes, sir," and got down to it.

When he returned, Lee was holding a battle flag, stiff as a statue, facing the thickening Yankees on the next height. Watching their cavalry sweep up prisoners halfway to his position, General Robert Edward Lee remained fearless to the great world's eyes, but he was unable to look at the battered men crowding nearby, these weaponless and hopeless, useless and leaderless, utterly broken men. Mahone believed that it wasn't merely anger or disappointment that fixed Lee's gaze on the horizon, no, Mahone sensed Lee struggling with all his strength to avoid collapsing in tears.

"If I may have the flag, sir? I'll put it to good use."

Lee gave up the flag, as absently as if he'd forgotten that he held it.

The flood of quitters only grew. Few regiments—what remained of regiments—had retained their flags. The soldiers who passed near the pair of generals either avoided looking toward them at all or turned upon them sheepish eyes that grew prayerful the closer they came to Robert E. Lee.

Mahone wanted to shout at them: "We're out of goddamned miracles, can't you tell? What do you want from us, from him? The magic's all used up. . . ."

Instead, he just passed the flag to a sergeant who still held on to his rifle, telling him, "You stand over there, behind my men. And you gather these sonsofbitches, haul them in. I won't have this army shaming itself while General Lee is watching, understand?"

That moment, he spotted Dick Anderson, still mounted in the midst of his fleeing men. Not doing one damned thing to put them in order. Lee had wondered aloud about Anderson earlier, so Mahone trotted forward, snagged the man who outranked him, and led him to Lee.

But Lee, still staring blindly Yankee-ward, would not even look at the failed corps commander's face. He only pointed behind himself and said:

"General Anderson, take charge of those stragglers and go to the rear."

Lee's lips quivered as he spoke.

As the light drained from the landscape and shadows blackened, Lee spoke abruptly. "What shall we do? What shall we do now?"

Mahone, who knew the country well from his days as a railroad man, had given the matter plenty of thought.

"General Longstreet needs to move, take the river road past Farmville. Burn the bridge at the edge of town behind him, don't wait for anyone." He gestured northward at the continuing ruckus. "Has to be Gordon up there. God bless John. If he can break away after dark, he should cross at High Bridge, save what he can. As for my boys, we'll hold here until the Yankees quiet down. Then I can take them through the woods to High Bridge, cover Gordon as he withdraws."

"You must burn it down, too," Lee said. "We need time now. More than ever, General Mahone. Those people must not have that bridge, nor any other. We need *time*."

When the devil didn't they need more time? Chased across southern Virginia like a three-legged rat by a pack of Yankee terriers. But Mahone was an engineer and a railroad man, and he thought beyond the war, beyond the conclusion that any man could predict.

"High Bridge is quite a structure, sir. Crucial for the economy down here, locals raised the money to put it up. Burning one span will do as well as burning it all. It's near a mile long, and its name speaks to its height, it's a true marvel." He drew breath before he concluded, afraid he'd seem soft, even fatalistic, to Lee. "One day, folks are going to have to repair it. No need to make their work harder than it has to be."

When Lee didn't reply, Mahone continued, "Call up Colonel Talcott, the engineer. Give him instructions for his pioneers, they'll get the job done right."

Lee nodded. Still more weaponless men trudged by. But the fight to the north continued unabated. If anything, it had grown even more desperate.

A rider came up. Without hesitation or awe, he approached Lee, extending a shred of paper and calling, "From General Gordon, sir."

Silhouetted against a purple sky, Lee seemed to awaken, to reinhabit himself. He took the message, thanking the courier, but his eyes betrayed him. Mahone knew Lee wore glasses to read, everyone knew it, but even now he would not reveal that weakness to the men. He extended the message to Mahone.

"If you please, General . . ."

Mahone, too, had to strain to read the scrawl: Even the light was deserting them.

"Says he's closely pressed, sir. His force is reduced and much of the train will be lost, unless he's strengthened." Mahone smiled.

"Typical Gordon, though—he adds that the enemy's loss has been very heavy. And there's nothing about retreating."

"I must go to General Gordon, I must look to him," Lee said. Turning unsteady lips and wounded eyes to Billy Mahone, he asked, "General, have you a guide who might assist me?"

Six thirty p.m.
Five Forks

Splendid," Sheridan said. "Splendid, splendid, *splendid.* Well done, all of you. Well *done*!"

" 'A thing of beauty is a joy forever,' " Merritt commented, showing his cut of a smile.

Sheridan gave Merritt a baffled look.

"Ain't it grand, though, Phil? Wasn't it grand?" Custer asked.

George Crook, all whiskers, nodded in satisfaction.

Lines of ragged prisoners tramped past the generals. They were silent, mostly, the Rebs, downcast and played out.

"Wright believes he bagged at least four thousand," Sheridan told his subordinates.

"We took that many easily," Merritt responded. "Grabbed so many Reb generals I've lost count." His cold smile returned. "A sergeant took old Ewell."

"Won't be much left of the Rebs but Lee and a nigger bootblack," Custer put in. His merry mood was tinged with a wistful sadness: The war was ending, there wouldn't be many more days as grand as this. To the good, though, a surgeon had seen to Tom immediately. If he didn't do anything foolish, Tom would be fine. With a souvenir gouged in his cheek and a second Medal of Honor headed his way. It was almost enough to make a brother jealous.

He'd have to write Libbie, of course, tell her all about it. But first he intended to treat a clutch of Reb officers to supper and buck them up, poor devils. Wouldn't be a curmudgeon like old Crook. All brethren of the military calling. . . .

"Pretty well smashed, that they are," Crook said at last. "Sons-ofbitches got what they deserved."

But Sheridan nodded to the north, where the racket of battle still shook the middle distance. Artillery flashes pierced the thickening twilight, and hidden flames scorched the sky beyond the trees.

"Once Humphreys wraps things up . . ." Sheridan's smile toughened. "Got his teeth into Gordon, so he claims. I'd love to shove that bastard's face in the mud."

Six forty p.m.
Lockett's farm

The Death Coach was come for many a lad, at the busy Banshee's summons. The sun had followed a downward slope to doom, and now, in the gloaming, in the cold grip of black shadows, flames shot from muzzles to ward off darkened forms come close, too close, great lines of rushing shadows as Yankees made demons by a queer come-hither sought to push them off the last high ground. And the Irishmen left to Louisiana stood their ground like the scrunty fools they were.

Riordan had taken a chill, he had, not of the lungs but of the heart. Never before had the dread come over him, not like this, but he'd no more flee from Billy Yank than from the Banshee itself, no, he swore he'd stand up to God himself and to every priest in Christendom before he'd turn tail and run. For what was life worth?

A great deal, perhaps. A great deal, if not for him.

And yet the old terror was on him, Old Night, the fear that came on the winter winds in Galway, when the gusts spoke to the priests before the priests, the old ones, *them*.

He shivered and shot and knew his bowels for traitors.

Dark-hearted Yankees dying in the dark, or screaming short of death, oh, that was merriment. Maddened they were, the blue-bellies who had always quit when it grew so hot as this, reluctant to die and pricing their lives in silver.

Now they just came on.

Velvet-tongued officer boys with nothing to do but die from fool behavior tramped the line, exhorting the men to stand, to save the trains, their flags, their army, the Southland. But wasn't every man fighting to save himself now, glory be damned? Riordan fired, reloaded, and fired again, as his line inched backward, ever so slowly, not willing it but driven by leaden gales. Men spilled the stinking contents of their bellies, intestines torn open, and—one time—long guts trailed the man who owned them, face white in the last glow before night. Leaping into the Coach Devour, with Death his only comfort.

A shoulder burst apart a foot from Riordan, slapping him with mush, cutting him with bone.

Wiping his eyes clear, he finished loading.

Out of percussion caps and low on cartridges. With the infernal Yankees pressing them like a landlord's vigilantes after poachers. He stepped backward into the meat of a man, and the fellow—his voice a stranger's—pleaded for Riordan's help. But Riordan only bent to help himself to the fellow's supply of ammunition.

Why should he have a heart, when the world had never had a heart for him?

To live, that was the business. To kill and kill and kill so he might live. Animals, weren't they all? Gordon, Evans, the lot of them—what had they to teach him on this earth? Fine manners for a massacre? Prayers to an empty sky? He'd have none of it, not Danny Riordan.

The Yankees replaced a battery they'd withdrawn from the field beyond the contested house. And they fired madly into the glowing darkness, careless of their own wounded between the lines.

They had to hold, the officers cried it until their voices broke. And Riordan could picture the sorry why of it, he'd served long enough to know they bled clinging to the last level ground before the hillside dropped down into the shadows. For where the ground fell off like that, there'd be a stream at the bottom. And the stream would have a bridge. And the bridge would prove too narrow for the wagons, or the wagons would be too heavy for the bridge, and the ramshackle span would break, or the wagons would topple, or both at once, and the officers who'd studied their maps and made their perfect plans would scratch their heads and their nether parts and wonder what to do next.

And while they wondered, many a man would bleed.

The Yankees seemed to have had their fill of charging, though. They only inched forward as his kind inched their way back, the Federals relentless, if slowed to a creeping, shoving the entire Confederacy toward the precipice and whatever waited below. He could hear their shouts and curses, their demands that his people surrender, and, too, the reckless, hooted replies, the dares and mockery, from men whose uniforms still showed a shade paler than the night, ghostly in gray.

If he should die? If the Death Coach had marked him down for its passenger—singling him out among the abundant choices—would he regret much?

Oh, many things. And now, in this madness, he wondered if he should not have taken that girl, should not have pressed himself on her and stolen her prize, the one time in his life when such a woman was fully at his command? What a fool a man was, tricking himself into virtue when he was no more than a dupe. He should have knocked her to the floor and filled her.

He recalled her terrified eyes and wanted to vomit. Whether from the confusion of his innards or because another man's slop crept to his lips.

The Yankees rolled their guns forward, manhandling them over the field, the crews drunk with blood and eager to swill more.

They unleashed canister. A stretch of line near Riordan disappeared in splashes and screams, bodies and body parts flying off like witches surprised at their sabbath.

Despite all he'd known of war, this slaughter's nearness, *this* gore, gripped him as no other had done. His impulse was to run, and to run madly.

Still he did not, would not. Instead, he aimed at the phantoms working those guns, at the outline of the cannon themselves, wanting to punish men he'd never met and never would and didn't care if he did.

At last, the order came to withdraw by regiment. But the Yankees soon felt the weakness of it and on the buggers came. 'Twas then the wildness came out in men: The last, clinging regiments folded and fell to bits. Soldiers plunged down through the darkness, colliding with trees and each other, seeking that stream as if it were the Jordan, falling and tripping and tumbling and breaking bones that the day of battle had spared, discharging weapons by accident as they blundered, threatening the horror of a bullet from a messmate's rifle come sudden to steal your life. After all this.

Riordan muscled his way along, unwilling to be taken—not again—and refusing the open door of that coach descended from no living man knew where.

"Open the gate," his mother had warned, "and the coach will pass you by, for death only comes unbidden."

There were no gates here.

But the marsh on the edge of the stream held a jumble of wagons, their teamsters long gone and many of them burning, revealing panicked men to Yankee sharpshooters. Riordan veered well away from the flames, scrambling down to the dark-on-dark line of the creek. And in he leapt.

He felt the sudden insult of cold water and the promised scourge of wet wool on raw flesh. And the worst of it was that the water would do nothing to rid him of lice or the burn of his crotch.

Up he climbed, on the far bank, pushing straight up the hill past slower men. And he still had his rifle, the one charm in his life, though many another man had lost his own. The crackle of flames and the pleading bleats of officers competed with pecking volleys and the blind blasts of his own sorry side's artillery, their shells searching the heights his brigade and division had left, seeking to halt the Yankees short of the stream.

He doubted the Yankees meant to cross that night. They didn't need to get themselves wet and suffer. For they'd done all the damage the buggers needed to do.

He heard shouts of "Louisiana! Louisiana, over here!" They were calling to him, those living men, for he'd slipped past the Coach Devour, the carriage of death.

But he wasn't ready to rejoin his regiment. Not yet, not yet, not yet.

Riordan sat down and clutched himself and shook like a frightened child.

Eight thirty p.m.
Vaughn farm

Would to God I had never seen this day," John Gordon said.

The reports from his subordinate commanders had yanked the words from his mouth. Behind a splintered barn, they spoke by a lantern's light, their faces hard and glum.

"Bad day, awful day, indeed," Jim Walker remarked. Walker had saved most of his division, though, herding the last of his men across the creek, then making a daring escape from the pursuing Yankees.

They all had tales to tell. Earlier, as the last light fought the smoke, Gordon had looked across that cursed creek and seen Kyd Douglas topple from his horse—only to watch the lad rise again like Lazarus, after a terrible minute. A spent round striking a button on his coat had carried just enough force to knock him out of the saddle, yet it hadn't broken his skin. Kyd surely would be sore by morning, though.

As for Gordon, he'd saved most of his corps. He still had three divisions, if somewhat depleted. But the army's other losses . . . what he'd heard . . .

"Give Lee credit," Clem Evans said, "he doesn't fall to pieces. Taking the news of his son like that. And all the rest of it, too."

Clem always saw what he needed to see, but Gordon was no longer convinced of Lee's imperturbability. When the army's commander had arrived at sunset, his face had been stoic, but his eyes were burdened. And when news arrived that Custis Lee had been captured along with a crowd of other generals, the old man's expression had not changed, but those eyes . . . Gordon had been close enough, cold-blooded enough, to judge, and his verdict was that Lee was nearing an end of one sort or another.

And then there was the matter of his health.

The odd thing was that this suggestion of weakness warmed him to Robert E. Lee. He'd always respected and admired Lee, and he'd served him with alacrity. But, always, there had been ambition in it. Loyalty, yes. But a healthy measure of calculation, too.

That day his heart had gone out to the careworn commander and worried father. Who proved to be human, after all. In that ravaged hour, John Brown Gordon had realized that he'd stick by Lee to the last, not merely from self-interest and because of his postwar ambitions, but because he had felt, at last, the love—that unreasonable love—men felt for Lee.

"Past a point," Jim Walker said, "more bad news don't really amount to much. Just more gravy on a full man's plate."

"But a man's son . . . ," Evans said, unwilling to relinquish his belief in the all-ruling power of paternal bonds, perhaps thinking of Abraham and Isaac and that cruelest test the Lord ever forced on a man. Clem, with his young family and his ardent Methodist wife.

"Well," Gordon declared, "better captured than dead. Far as family goes."

"Plenty of company that boy's got, he won't lack for partners at cards. Christ Almighty," Walker said, "Ewell, Kershaw, Corse, DuBose, Custis Lee, half a dozen others just swept up, if the telling's true. Johnson gone willy-nilly and no word of Pickett. Two corps' worth of generals, gone in a snap. . . ."

Gordon almost quipped that Pickett was no great loss, but he held his tongue. Never knew whether you might need a fellow's good word ten or twenty years on. Life wobbled this way and that, and there was no point in making a needless enemy. He did believe George Pickett was worthless, though.

Unlike Jim Walker. The Virginian had a colorful past, expelled from the Virginia Military Institute in his senior year—at the behest of Stonewall Jackson, who wasn't "Stonewall" yet, just Professor Jackson. Young Walker had challenged the world's sternest Presbyterian to a duel, which had not come off. Then, a decade after their classroom collision, Jackson had recommended Walker for a brigadier general's star and had given him command of the Stonewall Brigade.

And the dead had even more stories than the living.

Feeling the press of the hour, Gordon rallied, summoning his Roman senator's voice. "*Well*, gentlemen, *this* corps hasn't been captured. No, sir. Nor did it run. Every single one of you can be proud. Your men fought like devils, like demons."

"And got ourselves plain whupped," Jim Walker said. "Just grates, it does. It does grate upon me, damn it all to Hell."

Clem Evans gave Walker a hard look. Clem was a forgiving man when it came to men's misdeeds, but he took a hard position on their language. Said nothing, though.

Regretting his moment of weakness, that ultimately insincere declaration, "Would to God I had never seen this day," Gordon told them all:

"We did our part. And all of you did it well, not a man here I'd fault, not in the least. Numbers do tell, though. As they did at Thermopylae and Roncevaux. But the Second Corps will stand back up tomorrow, a fighting concern still. And we'll get ourselves another chance at the Yankees."

Proud and licked but not ill-humored, Walker responded, "Reckon they'll have another go at us, too, Leonidas. Cuts both ways." Then he grew serious. "Think we're all right tonight? Think they'll hold still long enough for us to get ourselves off?"

The day's climax had faded to stray shots, medical orderlies seeking out the wounded, and wagons still aflame across the creek.

"They've got to be as disorganized as we are," Gordon said. "And they'll be slower to put themselves to rights. But Humphreys now, he's a hard one. He'll come after us soon as he can, he'll have it all planned out."

"Which means?"

"Which means, gentlemen, that you'd best return to your commands and step lively for High Bridge. Little Billy sent word he'll hold it for us, and we wouldn't want to be tardy for General Mahone."

Marching off in defeat again meant many things, from leaving the wounded behind to another sleepless night of numb legs and hunger. But not a man present was inclined to surrender, Gordon knew that much.

"Order of march, sir?" Kyd Douglas asked.

"Thus speaks my onetime adjutant," Gordon said. "Who left his work to me."

They all were fond of Kyd Douglas, who'd fought like Mars and lost much of his brigade. Clem Evans said:

"What you get, John, for trying to make this Lion of Judah a house cat. Kyd here wasn't meant to shuffle papers."

"Order of march, sir?" the young major—unlikely ever to see that promised general's rank—all but demanded. A clergyman's son, Kyd Douglas liked things orderly, and he had no inkling that Gordon knew of his taste for prissy novels written for womenfolk: no *Iliad* or *Odyssey* for him.

Gordon thought for a moment. They all were exhausted, and he couldn't afford a mistake. At last, he said:

"Jim, take your division off first, get going soon as you can. Provost will see to the stragglers. Corps trains and artillery follow, then Grimes' Division." He turned. "Clem, your boys will have to bring up the rear, can't promise you pleasure." Regarding every weary, dirty face a final time, he added, "See you gents at dawn, across the river."

Nine p.m.
Lockett's farm

Barlow couldn't stand it any longer. As the last fighting sputtered out, he left his division in search of his corps commander—and found Humphreys at a field desk, writing orders by lamplight amid the dead.

By way of greeting, Humphreys snapped, "Did I send for you, Barlow? I don't recall doing so."

"Sir . . . my division's still fresh, we've hardly been engaged. I'd say we *haven't* been engaged. And I'm in position to cross that creek and cut off their retreat."

"Or stroll into a great big nest of rattlers. In the dark. And get yourself snakebit where it hurts, with your pants around your ankles." Humphreys let his studied grumpiness soften. "Oh, hell, Frank. You're a goddamned disappointment, you know that? The Barlow I knew last year would've figured things out by now, seen what was afoot."

"I want to get in on the fighting. My division is—"

"In on a school yard brawl? Or a battle of some use? Which would you prefer?" As always, Humphreys looked primed to grind bones in his jaws. Even the set of his eyebrows threatened ferocity. Yet, as Barlow knew, the man could be a charming, erudite, even witty guide for the grand ladies of the North during their visits. "Have you even looked at a map of the area, Frank? Allowing that I have yet to see one truly accurate map of Virginia south of the goddamned James. . . ."

"Yes, sir. I've studied it."

"And where will Gordon's corps go next? Along with half of Lee's other raggle-taggles?"

"He'll make for High Bridge. He has to. That's why I suggested—"

"And that's why I've held you back. Didn't need your division today, would've just crowded things up. And now I've got a fresh division ready. And Gordon doesn't, Lee doesn't."

"Yes, sir."

"And whose division do you think is going to be on the road at dawn, marching for High Bridge? To seize it and the wagon bridge before the Johnnies put them to the torch?"

"Mine."

Humphreys nodded. "Harvard wasn't entirely worthless, I gather." Again, he softened. "Frank, it's not about rounding up prisoners right now. We've got more than we can handle, from what I hear, Sheridan and Wright took seven or eight thousand, and I haven't counted our haul. Lee's army is breaking to bits. What matters now are those bridges, to get *this* army across, force Lee to keep moving. Or surrender."

"And . . . you think he may be ready to surrender, sir?"

Humphreys smiled knowingly. "Don't worry. He'll see that you get a last fight before he quits."

Eleven thirty p.m.
Burkeville

Grant considered writing a message of his own to Lincoln, introducing the day's results as reported by Sheridan. But he soon gave up. Sheridan's succinct account better suited the hour than his summation could do, so he simply forwarded Phil's single paragraph through the secretary of war to the president. Knowing that Lincoln would leap at the last line:

"If the thing is pressed I think that Lee will surrender."

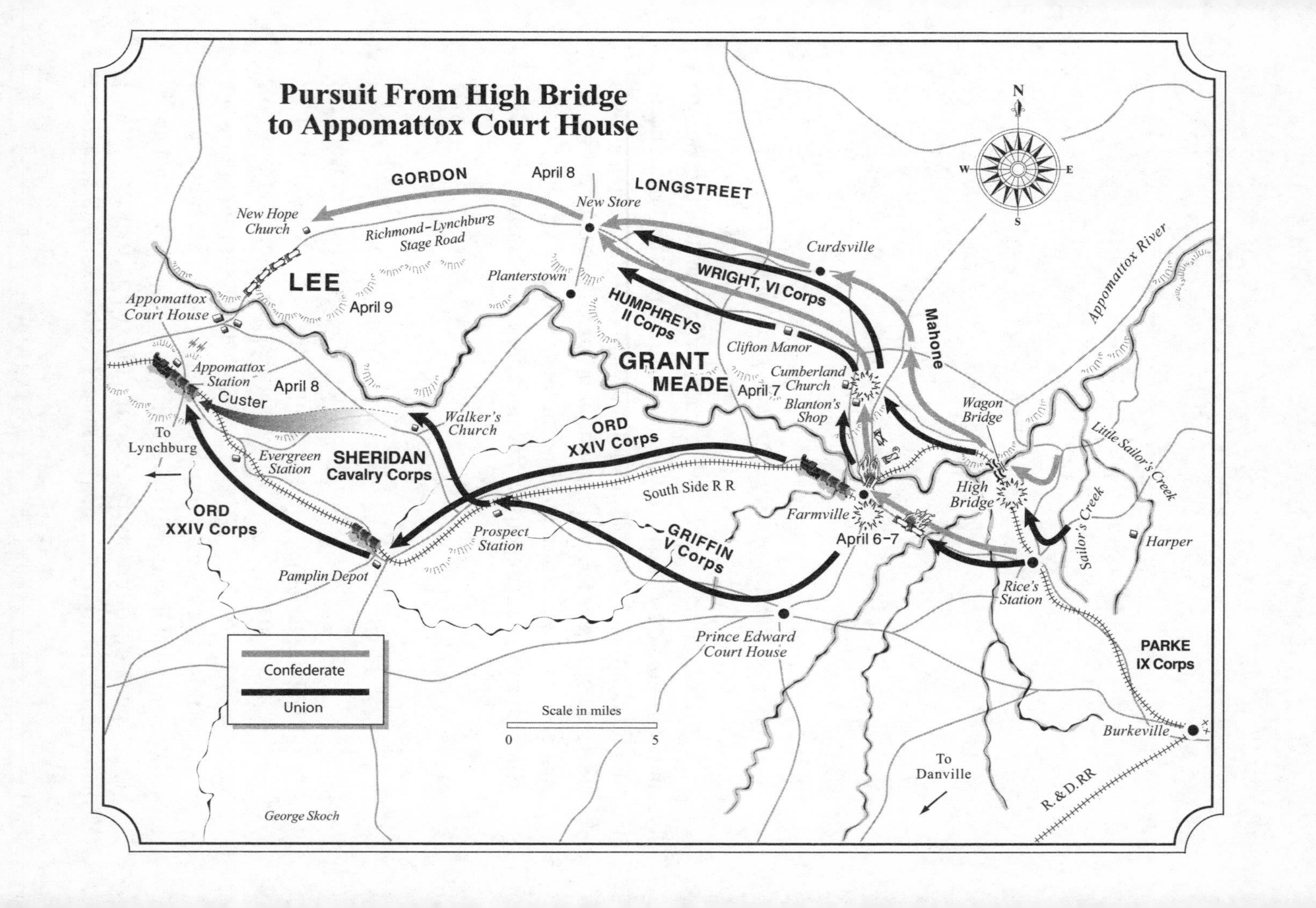
Pursuit From High Bridge
to Appomattox Court House
N
W
E
S
GORDON
April 8
LONGSTREET
New Store
New Hope
Church
Richmond–Lynchburg
Stage Road
Curdsville
Appomattox River
LEE
April 9
Planterstown
WRIGHT, VI Corps
HUMPHREYS
II Corps
Mahone
Appomattox
Court House
Clifton Manor
GRANT
MEADE
April 7
Cumberland
Church
Blanton's
Shop
Appomattox
Station
April 8
Custer
Wagon
Bridge
Walker's
Church
ORD
XXIV Corps
Little Sailor's Creek
To
Lynchburg
Evergreen
Station
SHERIDAN
Cavalry Corps
South Side R R
High
Bridge
Farmville
Sailor's Creek
Harper
ORD
XXIV Corps
Prospect
Station
GRIFFIN
V Corps
April 6–7
Pamplin Depot
Rice's
Station
Prince Edward
Court House
PARKE
IX Corps
Confederate
Union
Scale in miles
0
5
Burkeville
To
Danville
R. & D. RR
George Skoch

FIFTEEN

Six thirty a.m., April 7, 1865
Sailor's Creek

Custer had an idea he couldn't resist. Devin's division had set off early, leading the Cavalry Corps, with his band tooting "Rally 'Round the Flag" and the like. Custer remained at the Harper house, issuing orders and sharing coffee with the Reb generals and colonels he'd favored with a feast the night before, a soldier's delicacies spread over a tent flap, blue and gray mingling and talking long after the meal was done. Then he'd shared his blanket with Joe Kershaw, a venerable Reb and a perfect gentleman. It had all been fine, the gallant way a war was supposed to be after a battle waged between honest foes.

But the morning sun only rose for the victorious. At dawn, the Confederate prisoners took their mood from the gray clouds on the horizon. Kershaw was polite, but grave. Perhaps weighing all they'd left and lost, the Johnnies with stars on their collars were somber and mournful.

And when Devin's departing bandsmen played "The Battle Hymn of the Republic," poor Kershaw had looked like a man contemplating suicide.

Custer decided they all needed cheering up.

Having made his courtesies to his favored captives—and to General Ewell, who'd stumped up for a slosh of Army coffee—Custer sought out his division's provost marshal, who'd been assigned to transfer the senior Confederates. He ordered the captain to gather the dejected officers out along the road.

"Good as done, sir," the burly captain assured him.

"And ask Major Bailey if he'd be so kind as to bring up the nearest enlisted prisoners, too. If he lays down his I-answer-only-to-Sheridan card, remind him that he owes me a *personal* favor. He'll come around." Attention stolen, Custer paused. "Those are plum blossoms, ain't they? My wife loves plums, you know."

Swiftly, he spoke with his brigade commanders, confirming their orders for the day and adding a little twist. Last, he gave instructions to his senior bandsman.

The scheme meant a slight delay, but Custer believed he could overtake Tom Devin with little effort.

He watched from a distance as the provost marshal herded the ranking Rebs—with every courtesy—to the appointed spot along the road, facing a great field where his division had mustered. No sooner were the Rebs settled than his men began parade-ground evolutions in their honor, a grand display, with his band playing "Yankee Doodle" and "Garryowen," the carefully chosen tunes setting up the trick.

He waited until the brigades had closed back up, ready to follow the road in a column of fours, before he rode to their head, visible to all and followed by a special escort flying thirty-one captured Rebel flags. Leading his division in person now, he swung the column around the edge of the field, extending the spectacle, before cantering up along the road to where the Reb generals and their colonels waited, surrounded by hundreds of ragged prisoners.

His band struck up "Bonnie Dundee." With his best mount shot from under him the day before, Custer spurred the magnificent black he'd borrowed for this show and galloped ahead, rearing the horse in front of Ewell, Kershaw, and the rest and doffing his hat, sweeping it low.

At the signal, his band burst into "The Bonnie Blue Flag."

The mob of enlisted Confederates couldn't restrain a Rebel yell, briefly alarming the horses, but the generals in gray just removed their hats, returning his courtesy.

Custer slapped his own hat back on his curls and made his horse prance as his color guard caught up. Drawing his sword to let it catch the sun, he saluted the captives as the captured flags dipped in their honor.

The band played "Dixie."

The first notes broke strong men. As Custer rode away, yesterday's enemies, hard men wearing stars, wept like children and cheered him.

Seven a.m.
High Bridge

Your men are lagging, Starbird," Barlow said, his voice far colder than the morning air.

"Sir . . . ," the colonel of the 19th Maine began, "they're marching fast as any regiment ever—"

"*Not* fast enough," Barlow told him.

He scanned the western horizon again. Still no sign of a misplaced dawn of flames, no pinking of the bellies of the clouds. Surely the Johnnies would apply their torches at any moment. They couldn't be such fools as to leave those bridges intact.

Riding at the head of his lead regiment, protected only by skirmishers a mere hundred yards forward, Barlow had never been more resolute. He intended to seize those bridges, if the task lay within human possibility. And war had taught him that human possibilities were greater by far than rude biology allowed: Men had to have the will to win, to triumph.

So much of what he had learned at Harvard seemed asinine. If he might claim to have learned anything at all.

This was real. *This* was life.

Nor did he intend to bear the blame for the self-indulgence, the false mercies, of other men. In war, the only "mercy" was to win and conclude the business. It was a disgrace that the conflict had lasted four years.

Even Humphreys, for all his Spartan pretensions, was too soft. He'd wanted to rest the corps longer after the fighting and had issued orders to move out at five thirty. Barlow had gotten his lead brigade out on the byways by four.

He only hoped that the road his division had followed was the correct one. He'd set their route according to the map, but let discarded Reb effects guide his course afterward, following a sorry trail of cast-off rifles and skeletal mules dead in harness, of corpses that turned out to be slumbering Johnnies dropped by exhaustion, his judgment confirmed by dozens of gaunt deserters desperate not to be shot in the easing dark.

Now it was light and, ahead, his skirmishers waved.

He saw the smoke before he could see the bridge.

He kicked his horse and rode between a pair of abandoned redoubts, turning onto the rail bed. And there it was. High Bridge, aptly named. It lorded over the river valley below.

The farthest spans were ablaze, the fire abrupt and spreading.

He turned to his division engineer and ordered the man to get to work, to put out the flames at any cost in lives. But the order wasn't necessary: Pioneers scrambled forward, armed with axes and picks, grapples and ropes, racing to protect the bridge as if it were their own property.

Riding forward after them, Barlow peered into the valley. The wagon bridge down below hadn't yet been torched. But Rebs were scurrying over the planks, piling branches and slopping them with tar.

Halting beside him, Colonel Starbird asked, "Should I seize that bridge, sir?"

Astonished by the idiocy of the question, Barlow trimmed his voice to a club-room cut:

"I think that would be a good idea, don't you?"

Awakened by the mocking tone, Starbird—who did look exhausted—shouted back to his regimental officers, and blue-clad soldiers dashed pell-mell down the hillside, finding reserves of energy they did not believe they had.

To his credit, Starbird went with them, leading from the front, doing it properly. Or perhaps, Barlow mused, he was merely anxious to escape his new master.

Barlow remained on the high ground to direct the arriving regiments and brigades. As a rule, he despised the falsity of rhetoric, but he found it useful now.

"Come on, lads! Take that bridge, don't let them burn it. The war ends on the other side, just get across that bridge and we'll finish the business."

Shots pricked the morning, a few and then many more. The Rebs appeared to have been surprised, which made no sense at all. Had they expected Grant to take a holiday?

Bill Olmstead, commanding the First Brigade, galloped up, rushing to the sound of the guns as a proper soldier should. Humphreys appeared to have schooled his officers properly. Better than struggling old Hancock had done in his last days commanding the corps, when the erstwhile lion had gone lame and suffered. Poor Win, reduced now to a signature on Army requisitions that hardly mattered.

Of course, he'd been in a bad way himself. War used up men without bothering to kill them.

But he was back, and Win wasn't.

"Olmstead, get your brigade across that bridge. Get up on those heights over there, don't waste a moment. Unless they're complete fools, the Johnnies will counterattack." He smirked and almost spoke his mind aloud: Clearly, the Rebs had bungled things, for whatever reason. It was sweetly reassuring to confirm that blunders weren't native only to his side.

Below, the men of the 19th Maine hurled themselves onto the bridge, swarming over it, forgoing formation or discipline, just doing what had to be done. Some halted to shoot at withdrawing Rebs, while others beat the flames with their unrolled blankets or emptied their canteens on the creeping flames.

To his credit, Isaac Starbird was smack in among them, dismounted and doing his part.

It looked as though the wagon bridge would be saved.

The great railroad bridge was another matter. Soaring above massive pillars, it was dizzying merely to contemplate, but his engineers scrambled over the spans, leaping like monkeys and struggling to save what they could of the mighty structure, clumsy, determined acrobats wielding axes.

A great cracking sound demanded Barlow's attention. He looked back up and a blazing span of High Bridge dropped into the valley, smashing earth and splashing water.

And that was that.

But he had a bridge, if not the grand prize. One of his regiments after another double-quicked down to cross the wagon bridge, with Olmstead on the near shore waving his men along. And Smyth's Third Brigade came up at a dogtrot, with the irredeemably Irish Smyth parading at their head. The fellow was good for a brawl, though. Barlow sent him straight into the fray.

He longed to join the fight himself but wasn't about to repeat his Gettysburg error. He needed to maintain control, to issue orders and see that they were executed, to suit his actions to the greater purpose, not to indulge in ill-suited heroics. And he had to dash off a note to Humphreys, urging him to rush up the rest of the corps.

Waving up an orderly, Barlow took a last look across the wagon bridge before getting down to work with pencil and paper.

He saw Colonel Starbird crumple. Men rushed to his aid, including Olmstead, the fellow's brigade commander, who leapt from his horse as if his own brother had fallen.

Barlow was unmoved.

The division had a bridge. Nothing else mattered.

Seven thirty a.m.

Jackson home, Beech Street, Farmville

Lee had allowed himself two hours of sleep after he reached Farmville. When Colonel Marshall woke him, his body—perhaps his soul—had been reluctant to rejoin the world. His rheumatism pained him and his heart concerned him, nor were his innards as disciplined as desired. But he rose. Stiffly.

The rations waited at the depot, a splendid trainload of them. Longstreet's corps would arrive shortly and his men would be fed. The commissary general already had begun to load wagons with rations for Gordon's men and the others on the march north of the town. With the town bridges primed to burn after Longstreet crossed, the soldiers would gain some hours of needed respite, perhaps a full day to replenish their haversacks and cartridge pouches. Should the Lord grant them his favor.

Still, there was endless work to be done, dozens of fateful decisions had to be made. And he owed a call to an officer's widow residing in the town, a courtesy that must not be neglected.

He hoped his eldest son was in good health, that Custis had not been harmed before falling captive. Again, he remembered the previous day's debacle—and the murmuring from his own officers that surrender was inevitable.

When he came downstairs, leaving the beauty and sweetness of the featherbed provided by Mr. Jackson, Colonel Marshall guided him to the back porch, where a basin of warm water and a towel awaited his *toilette.*

Lee closed his eyes and bent and doused his face, truly waking. The warmth of the water made the world seem less cruel.

Shots sounded in the distance, their direction unclear. It did not sound significant, though.

He splashed his face and beard again, worked up a lather with a sliver of soap, and cleansed himself. He wished he might remain on that porch, to rest and savor the bracing morning air.

A rumpus announced an arrival as Lee toweled himself. Barely outpacing the visitor, Marshall announced:

"Brigadier General Wise, sir."

And the former governor of Virginia, a year older than Lee himself and a good deal stormier, burst onto the porch with his lean face mud-striped. Combined with his grizzled ruff of a beard and pale, ferocious eyes, the discoloration of the old fellow's cheeks and forehead gave him the look of a madhouse inmate.

But Wise was sane, if angry. He'd saved most of his brigade after yesterday's battle, refusing to surrender when others quit, fighting as long as he could, then escaping afoot to report for duty again. Lee wondered if he should not have promoted Henry Wise to division command, but there had always been arguments against it.

Lee felt the weight of yet another error, another misjudgment.

Discarding ceremony, this subordinate who seemed to be made of wire charged with lightning paused in the doorway to make his declaration:

"My poor men are back on yonder hill, turn around and you can just about see them. More dead than alive, I swear to God. Fighting day and night for a week, with not a bite for their bellies through all that." Wise drew himself up, a rooster prepared for a cockfight. "By God, sir, they shan't move another step, not before somebody gives them something to eat."

"Come in, General," Lee said mildly. "Your men deserve to eat, and they shall be fed. The rations are here, and plentiful. Now you must share my breakfast."

But the former governor chose to dine on spleen. "Cowards, that's what they were, all of them. Bushrod Johnson, you call him a leader? Damned coward. Goes for Anderson, too. And Pickett. The lot of them. Run off so fast yesterday they soiled the trousers of the men *behind* them. But Johnson, he was the worst." He bore down on Lee, as if about to lay hands on him. "Got any idea what it's like to serve under such a worthless, no-good . . ." Wise paused at the edge of profanity.

Lee knew it was the truth, but could not bear it. Not yet. Nor might he tolerate it. Gently, he replied:

"General Wise, are you aware that you're liable to a court-martial? That execution is the punishment for insubordination toward your commanding officer on campaign?"

Wise would not be deflected. "Well, a damned commanding officer ought to be giving out commands, not running off the way

Johnson and Anderson did." He stepped closer, enraged by the injustice of the world, and snorted like a hog. "Shoot me? You can't afford to shoot the men who fight. Shoot me? I wish you would, sir. I say I wish you would. Save the Yankees the trouble and me the bother."

Lee tried another tack. "General Wise, let us set such issues aside. I would value your judgment of our situation."

" 'Situation'?" Wise pawed the stain on his cheek. "There is no 'situation.' It's past time for you to do the right thing and put your poor men on their poor mules and send them home in time for the spring planting. Burns like gall, but we've lost. Look at yesterday. What did we gain? What high purpose did any of those boys die for? This army's hopelessly whipped and growing downright demoralized. Those men have endured more than flesh and blood can bear, and they've stuck it out for *you,* not for some highfalutin fairy tale of the Confederacy." The hard old man grabbed breath. "I say to you, sir . . . I say to you, emphatically, that to prolong this struggle is murder. And the blood of every man killed from this day forth is on your head, General Lee."

The bluntness staggered Lee. Others had approached him to cautiously raise the prospect of surrender. But no man had dared to speak to him so directly.

Waving his hand in annoyance, Lee said, "Don't talk so wildly. I bear burdens enough." He grasped for words. "What would the country think of me? If I did what you suggest?"

Wise spat. "Country be damned. Ain't no country. Hasn't been, not for a year or more. *You're* the country to these men. They've fought for *you*. No pay, no clothes, no food. Their faith in *you* held this busted army together, nothing else." He spluttered, his fury outracing the tongue's capabilities. "Even now, you ask them to die for you and, by God, they will. As will I, sir, fool that I am. But *you* know the game is up. You *know* it, General. And if you stop this now, no man—no decent man—will ever gainsay you. So I repeat: The blood of every man killed hereafter is on your head alone."

For a time, Lee could not respond. Wise stood there waiting, unmercifully, his eyes those of a prophet confronting idolaters. The silence between them endured until the arrival of Longstreet's troops, at which Lee said:

"I shall excuse myself. I have pressing affairs."

Nine a.m.
Northwest of High Bridge

Billy Mahone had experienced war aplenty, but he never had faced such a blasted combination of incompetence, confusion, and outright cowardice. The engineers left behind to burn the bridges had fiddled away the hours, letting the Yankees grab the wagon crossing. By the time he'd been informed and mounted a counterattack—*two* counterattacks—the Federals had crowded onto the western heights, the north bank of the river, with Humphreys' machinelike Second Corps funneling over the bridge, just throbbing over it. In his rage and frustration—next of kin to grief—Mahone lacked a single gun to shell the crossing site and so much as annoy the Federals, since his last battery had been ordered ahead by the corps' chief of artillery.

Then he'd had to suffer the proximity of Bushrod Johnson and Anderson, those two skedaddlers issuing witless orders, as if they still had a division and a corps, when all they commanded were torn-hearted, weaponless, half-starved, shaking survivors of their folly. Pickett, too, had been slinking about, doom-laden as the albatross in that poem Otelia liked. Only one of the previous day's battlefield commanders possessed a lick of anything worthwhile, in Mahone's view, and that was Gordon.

His own men had been promised a feast of rations when they reached Farmville. Trouble was that they weren't going to get to Farmville. Not now, with the Yankees across the river and on the move. He knew the terrain from railroad surveys done before the war, and Farmville would prove a trap, if Longstreet and Lee didn't leave the town immediately. The only fair ground for defense lay to the northwest, by Cumberland Church.

The way Mahone saw the matter, he had two tasks on his hands:

Delay Humphreys for as long as possible, then hold the high ground by Cumberland Church until the army could gather itself again.

And Gordon . . . he'd been hammered hard the day before, but John would have to hold back any force Humphreys pushed down the South Side Rail Road toward Farmville, he'd have to buy time for Lee to withdraw again. Mahone couldn't risk splitting off a brigade to defend the rail route when all he had was a bled-white division with which to stand up to a full-blooded, well-led corps.

He scribbled off another report—another warning—to Robert E. Lee. Who had not yet replied to his earlier messages.

The whole sorry business frustrated Mahone, this shabby workmanship of careless men. It insulted the engineer in him, his love of precision and reliability.

His wife could've done a better job than half of his fellow generals, Mahone told himself. And at the thought of Otelia in command, he felt an exhausted grin crack open his face. Oh, wouldn't she be something, though, up on a horse giving orders? Probably do a better job than he had done himself, that wicked woman. . . .

His none-too-sweet, sharp-clawed, superb Otelia. She never had been completely convinced that men were to be entrusted with great affairs, and the present situation did appear to confirm her worst suspicions.

Well, he'd do what he could to redeem things. And to make that woman proud, though she'd only mock him for it, that tongue of hers sharper than any saber in any scabbard anywhere. He'd see if he couldn't give Humphreys a bloody nose.

Billy Mahone was a small man, but not a little one. Let the big, husky fellows like Bushrod Johnson show the white feather. No upright man would ever say that William Mahone quit the fight.

Otelia would call him a damned fool for that, too. Had a scrape to her, that woman did, peel the skin right off a weaker man. Suited him just fine, though.

He did believe he'd see her before too long. If Grant didn't lock up all the Confederate generals, court-martial them, and hang them as an example.

About what they deserved, for being plain stupid, Mahone reckoned, one hundred percent certain Otelia would agree.

Ten a.m.
Farmville

The locomotives and railcars loaded with rations were gone again, shunted westward in great haste at the commissary general's insistence. St. John had assured Lee they'd be waiting at Appomattox Station, though, thirty-eight miles to the west.

Then Longstreet's chief of artillery had informed Lee that "really, sir, we should have stayed south of the river. Grant has the direct road now, just thirty miles to Appomattox Station."

Lee had somehow controlled himself, face stoic though his heart pounded. Bleak and black-bearded, Longstreet had been in a fury. Less than half of his soldiers had drawn rations when the boxcar doors slammed shut again in the face of the waiting supply wagons. Outraged soldiers had helped themselves from the wagons meant for Gordon's corps—vehicles bearing a fraction of what was needed. Barely a third of the army had been fed, but all had to move on now, hungry or not.

When the first bad news arrived, Lee had been writing a message to President Davis, who wanted to know what the army's "object" was now. Restraining himself, Lee had replied that he would have to adjust his purposes each day, based on developments. Interrupting his flight at Danville, Davis had shown no sense of the army's condition, nor did he seem to want to know the reality. Nor had that morning's meeting with John Breckinridge, secretary of war and the president's emissary, provided Lee with encouragement. A good man, if a weary one, Breckinridge stood to his duties, but hopelessness clung to the fellow like a smell.

As Lee tried to find the words to instruct the president, Marshall had rushed in, abandoning his usual show of aplomb.

That firing in the distance? It had been serious, after all. Marshall held two messages from Mahone, both of them warning that those people had seized the bridge below High Bridge and were crossing the river in force.

The day of respite lost, another retreat began. Campfires were extinguished. Soldiers swallowed uncooked dough and gobbled cuts of raw bacon, resigned to even this humiliation. And they were the lucky ones who'd been issued rations.

Men cursed the locomotives as they carried off the food of which men dreamed.

It began to rain.

Before Lee left Farmville, he stole the time to dictate to his military secretary. Anderson, Johnson, and Pickett were relieved of their commands and were released to their homes to await orders. Lee kept his language formal and coldly proper, although he wanted to scorn aloud the men who had failed the army so disastrously. As for the handfuls of soldiers that remained of the former commands of those disgraced, Mahone would take Pickett's survivors and the rest would report to Gordon.

Anderson's corps, once mighty, ceased to exist.

Abandoning Farmville with its bridges aflame and its people dejected, Lee had ridden but half a mile when he suffered a seizure of a sort that led him to stop his horse by the roadside and sit there, in the saddle, in the rain. He felt utterly unable to go on, constricted and bound. His thoughts blurred, it was as if . . . as if the world were ending, the rattle of nearby engagements a sign of Doomsday. He could not speak, could not . . . it was as if he saw but could not see.

Longstreet saved him. Simply by riding up, judging the moment, and grunting, "We'll get through this mess, too, see if we don't."

Eleven a.m.
South Side Rail Road,
between High Bridge and Farmville

When he saw Tom Smyth carried rearward, shot through the face and neck and paralyzed, Barlow felt the briefest of pangs, then nothing. The colonel's fate was inherent in his profession.

"He was too far forward, sir," an officer riding beside the litter told Barlow. "Within fifty yards of the Rebs, out with our skirmish line."

Nobody said the Irish weren't brave, of course. But Barlow hadn't time for praise or sentiment. The rain threatened to retard his division's progress.

He would have none of it.

"Return to your brigade," Barlow told the captain. "You can't help Smyth. Go back and inform Colonel Woodall he's in command. Tell him to press on, I'll have no lulls."

Humphreys had split off Barlow's division to press down the tracks toward Farmville, while the rest of the corps nipped the heels of Mahone's lot. As near as Barlow could make out from the prisoners already taken, his division faced Gordon's corps—or its prickly remains—and a loose assortment of other battered commands. North Carolinians seem to have done for Smyth.

Rather a bad stroke for a man to be paralyzed. But one glimpse had convinced Barlow that Smyth likely would die, after some lingering. It did seem preferable. He'd been laid up sufficiently in his own term of service to dread the thought of a mewling life as a cripple. His mother's ministrations would be dreadful, and Nellie Shaw would blight her life from a fool's sense of obligation.

Better just to be dead and have it over. Men's lives were overvalued.

Barlow rode closer to the line of contact, ignoring bullets and his staff's concern. To his disgust, he learned that a counterattack had taken a hundred of Olmstead's skirmishers prisoner, trapping them in a rail cut, another blunder.

When he found Olmstead, he simply said, "I expect you've sent out another lot of skirmishers? A more robust force this time? And better led?"

The rain stopped, leaving the day misted but warming.

When Barlow's division neared Farmville at last, he met a phenomenon recently grown familiar: burning wagons. The difference was that this time the Rebs had set their own wagons afire as they fled.

"Bloody well done for," Barlow said aloud. "They're bloody well done for."

It seemed a shame that what might be his last battle had been such a paltry affair with so little result.

Noon
South of Farmville

A courier caught up with Grant and delivered a telegraphic message from Lincoln. It said: *"Let the thing be pressed."*

Six thirty p.m.
Cumberland Church

Well, you're not the holy goddamned trinity, are you?" Humphreys teased his subordinates, unexpectedly amiable after their latest repulse. "I suppose I have to be content with wonders and bugger the miracles."

His tone raised Barlow's eyebrow and left a puzzled look on de Trobriand's face. As for Miles, he'd been in a grump since Barlow reappeared.

Not one of them grasped how much they had achieved, even though each attack on the Rebs had failed. But Humphreys saw it: Tactical disappointments had done the strategic trick.

Didn't do to dole out too much praise, though. Not yet.

The day's intermittent drizzle had paused again, but the sodden atmosphere still dampened spirits. His division commanders had expected to *win*. Now they drank bad coffee under dripping limbs, as a campfire smoked and flared to paint their faces.

Thick night neared.

"We could go in again," Nelson Miles said. Humphreys knew that the red-haired boy was determined to show up Barlow, the benefactor who'd lifted him through the ranks as the war dragged on.

"Too dark," Humphreys told him. And that was that.

"Devil of a position, what I've seen of it," Barlow said. His men had just come up to fill out the lines. "Somebody over there is a judge of ground."

Hat tilted and beard prim, de Trobriand shrugged.

"Listen," Humphreys said, voice stern again. "When you go back to your divisions, just stay active. Keep your skirmishers busy. Keep the Johnnies worried about what we might do to them, instead of thinking what they might do to us. Keep them on their guard and fixed in place."

In his languid, affected way, Barlow said, "We still might flank them, I rather think."

"Tried it," Humphreys snapped. "More than once. While you and Gordon were comparing peckers. Took some guns, and lost them again." He rubbed the day's whiskers. "Their reinforcements got here, ours didn't. Now *we're* outnumbered, and by more than I like. We're lucky the Rebs are too blown to figure it out."

"Or *un*lucky Wright never showed," Miles put in. "I'd like that explained to me, why the devil everybody's dawdling. We could've ended the war today, right here."

"Had they their old *élan,* the Johnnies," de Trobriand announced, "they would have attacked *us.*" He smiled. "My compliments, *cher Général.* You have made of them fools, I think."

De Trobriand had begun to see it. The Frenchman kept a sharp eye on the world.

The corps *was* outnumbered. But it hadn't been so early on, and Mahone had put up an admirable defense, Humphreys had to credit him. Now, though, they faced all the remnants of Bobby Lee's army, which remained deadly. His last attack had failed because the Sixth Corps was supposed to appear on his left, but hadn't shown up. That botch-up might have proved fatal, had the Rebs been in higher spirits. Instead, Humphreys had sustained his bluff, conducting himself as if he still held the advantage, displaying a confidence he didn't feel, and nailing the Rebs to the spot. It had cost him lives, but it would cost Lee his army. The old turncoat might continue to run, but he'd never escape them now.

"They haven't slept, they're in worse shape than we are," Humphreys said, downplaying the day's achievement. "Mahone's men haven't seen rations since they started, deserters are coming over for a cracker. Tenacious sonsofbitches, though, what's left of them."

"Really wouldn't mind knocking on their door a final time," Barlow persisted. "They'll slip off in the night again, if we don't."

"And make another night march," Humphreys told him. "How many days have they gone now without sleep?" He shook his head. "Another night of marching will hurt them far worse than another attack would. And if they're fool enough to stay till morning, Wright will be up by then and we'll finish them off."

"They'll be gone," Barlow said.

Humphreys smiled at the younger man's incorrigibility. He wished he'd had Barlow with him earlier, when they'd first struck Mahone. But Barlow had been the obvious choice to send off on an independent mission.

Another shower pattered through the grove.

"Go back to your divisions. Make some noise. Rest your men, but don't give the Rebs any peace."

Andrew Atkinson Humphreys folded his arms and watched his lions prowl off. Rain stung his eyes, but he ignored it. Men made too much of rain; soldiers didn't rust.

He wished he could've smashed Mahone. He wished he could have done more. But he'd forced Lee to concentrate and stop, when the old fox should have been racing ahead of the hounds. With Sheridan pressing westward to close the trap.

Humphreys smiled again, sourly this time. *Sheridan*. Ought to label him "Sheridan the Shameless." He'd already heard that Phil had claimed yesterday's victory for himself, as if Wright and he and their two corps hadn't been there. But that was Phil to perfection, wasn't it just?

Well, he'd never been in it for the glory. He'd been taken in by the lure of soldiering young and had never escaped it. Recognition was welcome, all men had vanity, but soldiering well was its own reward in a way that no civilian could comprehend.

He did feel for George Meade, though. Meade had made the victory yesterday possible. Sick as a poisoned dog and riding along in an ambulance, Meade had shaped the movements of the army, pushing ferociously from behind to let Phil plunge ahead, doing his *duty.* While everyone—even Meade himself—saw that Sheridan meant to cut him out.

Well, let them settle it any way they wanted. After the war, he'd be content to revert to a colonelcy and go back to a little empire called a garrison, if not to the engineers and useful work.

The skirmishing picked up, as he'd directed. The Rebs wouldn't attack. The bluff would hold. Lee's only thought would be to slip off in the night.

As he turned to bark for coffee, a rider slopped up on a foaming horse, his rain cape gleaming wet. A sergeant in his wake held a soaked white flag.

By the cast of the rain-bitten campfire, Humphreys recognized Williams, now of Grant's staff.

Williams did not dismount, but saluted and called, "Message from General Grant for General Lee. Can you have your men hold their fire, Humph? The Rebs are trouble enough." The man did look used up. "Already tried getting through from the south, but the fire was just too hot. I need to try again."

"Better thee than me, Seth," Humphreys said in his best Philadelphia-Quaker intonation. He called for his horse to accompany Williams and pass him through his lines. As for dealing with the Reb skirmish line, Grant's emissary could go out on his own. Almost too dark to make out a white flag . . . let Seth Williams see what it was like for fighting men.

"Call for Lee to surrender, I take it?" Humphreys asked as they cantered, ducking wet branches.

"The contents . . . the commanding general's message is privileged, sir."

"Get off your high horse, Seth. I'm not a fool."

Was this it?

Seven thirty p.m.
Farmville

Grant stood on the porch of the Randolph house, forcing a smile and nursing a worsening headache. The brass bands, fervent and jolly, were unbearable.

Crook's cavalry had long since passed to the west, followed by the Army of the James going into camp. Now Wright and his Sixth Corps had overcome the problem of the burned bridges above the town and were moving at last to join Humphreys—who'd gotten his bulldog's bite into Lee's leg.

As darkness fell and the rain passed on, a burst of elation had filled the marching soldiers. Bonfires had flared along the street and Wright's men improvised torches to turn their progress into a parade, honoring the general who'd brought the army so far. Wood smoke sweetened the damp air, and the spectacle was as grand as it was embarrassing.

Grant wasn't one to display himself, but Rawlins had convinced him to step out onto the porch and acknowledge the tribute—a victory celebration, if premature.

He'd been met with cheers that moved him, headache or not. The bands blared and thumped and the men straightened their backs and sang "John Brown's Body." He would not have recognized the song had it not been for those piercing, implacable words—he never could make sense of any melody. "Tone-deaf," they called it. He always joked that he only knew two tunes—one was "Yankee Doodle," the other wasn't.

On the endless columns went, uniform coats and blouses black in the firelight. Men's eyes shone, wet steel gleamed, and confidence filled the streets with a force irresistible. Flags dipped in his honor as they passed, men raised their hats and offered still more cheers. They sang more songs, their voices raw and manly. Torches held high crackled. And Grant's head pulsed and pounded.

His headaches didn't come often, but when they did they were brutal.

As he'd felt the pain coming on late that afternoon, he'd sat down alone to write a message to Lee, suggesting that he surrender his army to prevent further loss of life in a hopeless contest. He hoped Lee would agree, but suspected the Virginian would require more wooing than a single note.

Lee had seemed to be Mars himself, a peerless god of war, to every junior officer in Mexico. He'd been their flawless idol afterward, too, in the desolate peacetime Army that broke Grant: a god of war incarnate, with flawless diction and a gentleman's manners. Set above the common run of humanity, the erect, elegant officer appeared unapproachable; his very grace struck lesser men as forbidding.

Grant intended to approach him now.

There was no way Lee could win. He was all but cornered. The question was how long that towering pride would prevent him from accepting that it was over.

With a cough, Rawlins joined his old friend on the porch. The campaign, the night air, the wet, was hard on John's lungs.

The chief of staff gestured toward the exuberant soldiers parading past, their faces bronzed by the torchlight.

"We've come a long way, Sam," Rawlins said. "*You've* come a long way."

"Not done yet."

Nine fifteen p.m.
Blanton's Shop

Drained of spirit and vigor, Lee had to read Grant's message twice. Then he read it a third time, bending closer to the parlor lamp.

Without a word, he extended it to Longstreet. And he waited, afraid to close his eyes, afraid that doing so would precipitate a collapse into unconsciousness. Earlier, with the Federal cavalry raiding the army's remaining wagons below Cumberland Church, he'd tried to lead a counterattack himself, a part of him yearning to perish in a last battle; but once again his soldiers had dissuaded him, clinging to his bridle and promising to do the work at hand. And they had done it, driving off those people and capturing General Gregg, who was much embarrassed.

Now those men faced another night's march, more than half with empty bellies burning.

How could he ask his men to go on if he could not? He longed for rest. The fleabites on his legs itched and his bowels stewed. His temper had grown cranky, patience ravaged. Even his heart lacked steadiness, its beating leaping ahead, a flopping fish.

How much longer could it go on like this?

Grant's message was concise and all too clear:

General:

The result of the last week must convince you of the hopelessness of further resistance on the part of the Army of Northern Virginia in this struggle. I feel that it is so, and regard it as my duty to shift from myself the responsibility of any further effusion of blood, by asking of you the surrender of that portion of the C.S. Army known as the Army of Northern Virginia.

Very respectfully,
your obedient servant,
U.S. Grant
Lieutenant-General
Commanding Armies of the United States.

Longstreet's war-hardened face had no expression as he reviewed the call to surrender, but after studying the words a second and third time himself, he raised his eyes to Lee and said:

"Not yet."

SIXTEEN

Seven a.m., April 8, 1865
Farmville

Grant refused to succumb to his headache, which broken sleep had worsened. He would have preferred to go back upstairs to the hotel room and lie down with his eyes shut and the shutters closed. But finishing matters with Lee was a sight more important than any man's discomfort.

He believed there was a fair chance that Lee would surrender. That very day.

Even the chatter of officers breakfasting punished him, though. Each laugh stabbed into his brain.

Lee's response to his note had arrived with surprising speed, in the early hours. Equivocal, the answer insisted that Lee didn't "entertain" Grant's view of the hopelessness of his army's plight, but Lee nonetheless inquired about the terms of surrender on offer.

Grant overlooked the show of pride and welcomed the evident opening to peace. Already that morning, he had dispatched an answer, sending copies in care of four separate couriers to ensure that it reached Lee as swiftly as possible. The heart of the message had read:

> *. . . peace being my great desire, there is but one condition I would insist upon, namely, that the men and officers surrendered shall be disqualified for taking up arms again against the Government of the United States until properly exchanged. I will meet you, or will designate officers to meet any officers you may name for the same purpose, at any point agreeable to you, for the pur-*

pose of arranging definitely the terms upon which the surrender of the Army of Northern Virginia will be received.

Regarding the terms of surrender, Grant meant to be generous. Lincoln was right. All the demands to punish the South were folly. The challenge now was to knit the bones back together, not worsen the break. Nor did he feel much personal animosity. How could he hate Pete Longstreet? Or Cad Wilcox? Other old friends and comrades? He'd read enough history to know that quarrels were best patched up once the last blows landed. Made no sense at all to worsen the hurt.

Sitting there signing papers on which he struggled to focus, he wished he could take his fists to the hurt in his head. After reading a few lines, he'd have to stop and gather his wits again. A cascade of decisions had to be made, orders issued or corrected, queries from Washington answered. He told himself that he could endure it all, since he had no choice. Just had to last a little while longer.

A Reb colonel, looking a wreck, strode up to Grant, unimpeded, to surrender himself. He claimed that his regiment had just faded away, local boys who'd had themselves enough, and that he owned the hotel in which Grant sat.

Grant told him to go home.

George Meade was due to arrive, all coughs and sneezes and conscientiousness. If Meade could bear what appeared to be pneumonia and still command the Army of the Potomac, Grant reckoned he could push on with a headache.

A door slammed and sent needles through his brain.

He decided to travel along with Meade for the day. Probably best to take the same route as Humphreys, stay close to the Rebs. Had to be where he could easily be found. Didn't want Lee's response to go astray.

Wouldn't it be grand to end it, though? To finish it *today*? With no more blood?

They called him a butcher, wounding him and mortifying Julia. And he supposed there was something to the charge. But everything he had done had been for one purpose, to end the war. He'd done it the only way that had seemed possible.

Now here they were, at last. John Rawlins was right, he had come a long way. From the hideous tanyard of his boyhood, all stink and blood and hides, from the loneliness that had crushed the juice from his soul in the Northwest, from all his subsequent failures, from that storefront in Galena, the humble vantage point from which he'd watched his country crumble. And all he'd wanted before the world took to shaking itself half to death was to care for his family and, maybe, make his wife proud of him, after all the humiliations she'd faced.

Out in the street, an endless line of wagons creaked along, interspersed with artillery trains so abundant these reserve battalions were superfluous, the long tail of the greatest army the United States had ever fielded, all of it his to command. And still more armies stood in his charge, from the Carolinas to the Trans-Mississippi and parts west. He had reached heights he never would have imagined, a power none of his countrymen had foreseen: The might of a Union renewed marched at his word.

Didn't make his headache any better.

Ten a.m.
The road to New Store

Keegan, give us a tune on your pipe," Riordan teased, "in thanks for the joy of the day."

"Bugger yourself, Daniel Riordan," the former chief musician told his comrade. "And it's still '*Sergeant* Keegan' to you."

"Is that all the spirit they learn a man in Mayo, then? Ah, look at the darling spring come all around us. And you begrudge the boys a blow on the tin?"

"Shut up, Riordan," a fellow—no Irishman—told him.

"I'll shut me gab when I've eats to fill it up, go piss yourself."

"I'm too dry to piss my pants 'way you micks do."

But they'd marched all night and the morning through and hadn't the will or the strength to turn to fists. They just tramped on as mountains rose on the horizon, as distant as Galway. The truth of it was that the day herself was sweet, but men were sour. Riordan had thought his feet the equal of any march, but now they ached as though the bones were breaking.

At dawn, a frost had whitened the westering hilltops, thrilled by the sun. Come light, trees flowered pale and new green summoned color to the world, more than a hint. Men had no eyes to see, yet Riordan felt it. The queerest thing it was, to bear such misery and, just for a moment, to know the joy of a fresh draft of air in the lungs, to feel a vague and, perhaps, traitorous promise.

A half mile onward, Keegan said, "I couldn't get up a jig to save me life. I've not the spit for it." His voice sounded broken, bereft, and shamefully honest. No man should ever be as honest as that, Riordan was certain.

"At least the buggering Yankees aren't upon us," Riordan told his fellow survivor, another relic of their ravaged Louisiana Brigade, which hardly mustered the men to see to a slops pail.

Ghosts they all were, the living and the dead.

"You have to wonder at them," he continued. "Why they're not on to bothering us. When they were hugging us to death but yesterday."

"Maybe they done give up," a born-South voice heckled both of them. The mockery drew laughter. Every man knew the Yankees would never give up. Not now.

Riordan, who had grown ever quieter over the days—gone dark and deep and inward—could only marvel at the change in himself. He wished to speak to others again, as every good Irishman did, and were he not dry unto death himself he might have told them tales. Starved to the edge of dizziness, to a place beyond conscious hunger, he felt the *need* of others as never before. It unsettled him.

If Ireland had not taught him to look out for himself and damn the rest, Yankee prisons had finished his education. He killed with satisfaction and trusted no one, man nor woman. And yet, this day, he wished to live and rub against his fellows.

Of late, there had been demons in his dreams. He closed his eyes with reluctance and woke with relief. Sometimes he shook in the darkness or sat up gasping. No, marching all night was not the most hateful of doings, not to him.

Give him a good feed and he'd march forever. Broken feet no matter.

"Old Lee's going to surrender," a cracker voice said abruptly. "That's why they ain't all over us. Don't need to bother. We're just giving up."

"Never going to happen, not this army."

"What army? Any man here see anything looks like an army?"

"Done heard it. We're going quits."

"That's malarkey, that is," a scrunty mick scorned the argument. "If we were all to be given up, why would they have us marching off again?"

"Bobby Lee ain't never going to give up."

"An't that a wonderful comfort?" Riordan asked. "Knowing he'll fight till the last of us is dead. And not just the Irish." He laughed, scrape-throated. "Now there's your 'equality' for you. A bullet for every man, born high or low. Oh, I'm glad and gay I made my way to Americkee."

"Left to my druthers," a new voice called from the rank behind, "I'd give every officer *two* bullets."

"Before or after you finished licking his ass? Rivers, you've got more brag in you than any half-dozen generals. And you're just as useless."

"Didn't run how you did at Fisher's Hill."

"Only 'cause them feet are slow as your brain."

"Jesus, would you save it for the Yankees?" Keegan begged.

"I'm saving it for the first gal I get my hands on," another man said. "Been saving it up for months, mean to flood her over."

And Riordan thought, again, of the cowering girl, left on the floor of her kitchen, and he shamed himself with imagining what might have been.

A soldier tried to start a song, but it didn't catch. When they halted by a well, they found it dry.

Ten thirty a.m.
Prospect Station

Where are my goddamned scouts?" Sheridan demanded.

He'd breakfasted earlier on a proper cutlet and felt fortified. Strong. Ready to fight. But first he had to locate the damned Rebs.

No one attempted to answer him. Not Merritt, mounted at his side, nor any of his staff men.

"Goddamned worthless," he continued. "All of them."

But the scouts weren't worthless, and Sheridan knew it. He needed them to find the Johnnies *now*, though. He needed to hit the Rebs and hit them again until they begged for pity. Then he'd finish them off.

A message from Grant had ignited him. Grant believed Lee might surrender; they'd exchanged notes. And that was too soon for Sheridan. The Army of Northern Virginia couldn't be let off. Its remnants had to be slaughtered.

The South had to learn it could never get back up.

And he, Philip Sheridan, needed to win the last victory of the war in the eastern theater, the one that mattered. He had to complete the work he had begun at Sailor's Creek, to eradicate Lee's army and prove himself the indisputable victor, rival to Sherman and second only to Grant. It was no longer about what had been done, but about what *would* be done after the war. And by whom.

He was the man to put the final arrow in Lee's heart, to kill the myth. He had under his command the entire Cavalry Corps, as well as Charlie Griffin and the Fifth Corps, which had been subordinated to him again, and Griffin was marching up at whiplash speed, driving his men. Ord and his corps, sandwiched in between the cavalry and Griffin, would do as bid, too. Ord was ever unsure of himself, despite his mouth and swagger, and he secretly longed to be given instructions absolving him of the need to make decisions. Ord would fight, as long as he needn't think.

Three corps would be enough to smash Lee's vagabonds.

Oh, he was the man to do it, all right, but he had to act before Grant called off the game. So the scouts had been roused in the dead of night, to don their Reb disguises and head off, to find the exact location of Lee's army.

And that army was close, he knew it. At dawn, Crook's division had seized a locomotive and cars evacuated from Farmville the day before, the rail wagons loaded with feasts of rations as good as any his own army could provide. But there was more, far more. Ranging afar, his scouts had tapped the Reb telegraph lines, bringing him the intelligence that multiple trains with rations and arms had been dispatched to Lee.

But where were they headed? Where were they now? The options had narrowed, but Sheridan needed definite information. He had not an hour to lose. Sam Grant wanted peace a sight too badly.

Sheridan itched to ride forward, but Prospect Station had been appointed as the spot where he would wait on the scouts and a firm report. So he sat high on Rienzi, with the horse, too, growing restless, reading his master's mood. For his part, Merritt just watched his divisions move westward at a walk, leaving a trail of droppings, dust, and hoofprints along another neglected Virginia road.

Normally, the sight of his men in column excited Sheridan. He loved the display of it all, the animal power waiting to be unleashed. But today he worried their movement might be errant: They couldn't just wander the countryside, trusting to luck to guide them.

His escort tensed as hooves thumped up behind them.

Two riders approached at a gallop, outfitted as down-at-the-heels cavaliers, the man to the fore in a flopping planter's hat, the other with a straw topper feathered and frayed.

How the devil had they avoided the pickets?

The officers and men gathered round relaxed: just Sheridan's pet scouts.

The horsemen were glossed with sweat, and their stink preceded them. As Rebs, they were convincing.

The senior man, a sergeant Sheridan recognized, pulled his mount about, saluted, and called, "Appomattox Station, General. They're at Appomattox Station. Counted four locomotives myself, but others say there's eight." As breathless as an asthmatic, he gasped, "Appomattox Station. That's where they'll be, them trains you want. No sign of their army yet, though. Nothing."

"Good work. Fine work. Get yourselves some rations, boys. Nigger won't stop his cook wagon, shoot him dead."

And it *was* fine work. If he didn't know exactly where Lee was, he knew where he'd be, which was a good deal better. Those trains, four locomotives and maybe more, would be the magnets to draw Lee's shattered metal. Lee was heading for Appomattox Station, no doubt about it.

He had to do his duty and send Grant a message, but first he turned to Merritt.

"You heard him, Wes. Kill the horses if you have to. But get there before Lee." He thought for a moment. "Put Custer in the lead."

Three p.m.
Richmond–Lynchburg stage road
Northeast of Appomattox Court House

Gordon shook himself up and down, ridding flesh and bone of the saddle stiffness. Sometimes it was just grand to plant your toes anywhere but a stirrup. They'd been on the march for almost eighteen hours, with the usual misdirections and delays. At the rear of the army for days on end, they now were in the vanguard. At least there was less dust for a man to swallow.

Beside him, Clem Evans soothed his chestnut gelding. Turning to Gordon with that almost-smile he wore even in repose, Clem said, "Glad we stopped, John. Men do need a rest." He gentled the back of a hand down the horse's neck.

Clem, the eager killer and martial Methodist, was a kindly man when he took his ease with friends. Gordon just about loved him as a brother, not least for his blood-soaked innocence.

"I'd as soon push on," Gordon told him. "Lee wants the army to close up, I understand. After what transpired day before yesterday. But I don't like stopping, not now, when we're this far."

"Men are bone-worn, John. Those still by the colors."

"Thought the Lord was on our side, Clem?" Gordon teased his subordinate. "Shouldn't he get busy? Help us out? Put some git in our legs? Far as those railcars?"

Evans regarded him patiently. "He tests us sometimes, the Lord does."

"Well, doesn't the Scripture say 'I can do all things through Him who strengthens me'?"

Clem's look turned quizzical. "Indeed, it does. Philippians four: thirteen, as I recall."

"Well, mightn't he gird our loins for a few more miles? That must fall under the doing of all things."

" 'He removes kings and establishes kings.' Daniel two: twenty-one. But his hand doesn't necessarily—"

"We're not talking kings here. Just about moving this corps on along to Appomattox Station."

"John . . . I've got men who've marched all through this war without falling out. Now their feet are bleeding through their shoes. Their bellies are empty and have been."

"The loaves and fishes are waiting at that station, Clem. And they're not going to come to us." He watched Clem's hand touch his side. "Those pins still ailing you, Clem?"

"Not substantially. Can't say I won't remember Monocacy, though."

With that, the two generals let the matter rest. Their horses nibbled the spring grass. Overhead, a good sun shone, warming their shoulders. At last, Gordon said:

"Oh, hell. I guess it doesn't matter now. It's just my way, to want to push along, to get things done. Reckon I need my Fanny to soothe me some. Ulysses must return to his Penelope. And hope that Ithaca isn't a total shambles." He removed his hat and swept a palm across his forehead. "It's over, and that's the truth."

To his wonderment, Evans seemed shocked. And not by his minor blasphemy.

"It true, then?" Evans asked. "They're in correspondence?"

Gordon shrugged. "So I hear tell. Grant sent Lee a *billet-doux* and it seems there was an answer. As for the state of the romance, I'm uninformed."

"I can't believe it," Clem said.

"Well, no need to credit rumors, I suppose. Not yet, anyway."

"I can't believe it. We're not whipped. We're *not*."

It was Gordon's turn to be startled. He knew Clem was a born innocent, that his faith in victory had always been unbounded, but surely . . .

"Clem, for the love of . . . this army's not a third of what it was. Barely a quarter. We've fought as hard as men can fight, but . . ."

" 'One of your men puts to flight a thousand, for the Lord your God is He who fights for you.' Joshua twenty-three: ten."

"Joshua wasn't fighting Ulysses S. Grant." Gordon looked down at the earth, as if the right words might be written upon it. "Aren't we supposed to accept God's will with grace? Come on now, Clem. Wouldn't you like to go on home to Georgia, see Allie again? The children? Take to the pulpit, the way you always planned? Leave all this behind? And praise God that you're alive and mostly whole?"

"After what we've been through . . ."

"After all we've been through, we got whupped. Truth is we were finished after Stedman. Isn't fair, but there it is." He gripped his friend's upper arm, meaning to comfort, unsure how. "Bible's not a chronicle of fairness, as I recall. Trials and tribulations, Clem. We have to bear them, isn't that what it says?"

Clem looked just about broken. As faithful and unsuspecting as a child, shocked by a cruel and unexpected betrayal. How on earth could he not have expected this? Was he utterly blind?

The division commander turned away, hiding his emotions.

Of all the heroes in Homer and cherished by Gordon, only Hector neared Clem Evans in character, in his innate sense of nobility and obligation. Hector, too, had been a magnificent killer.

Not all things on earth lent themselves to reason.

As for Gordon, he was damned sorry they'd lost. But he preferred to ponder the future now. And he would have a future, because he'd make one. Not least, he looked forward to merry fussing under Fanny's nightdress. *They* would have a future, and a fine one.

Clem surprised him. Instead of speaking of the Cause, or of the sacrifices of his men, or of his cherished family, he said:

"Know who I feel sorriest for? If it really is the end? The Children of Ham, the coloreds. Imagine what'll become of them, once they're all turned loose with no guiding hand. It's unchristian, it's positively unchristian, John, to abandon them to a false messiah's promises, to tempt them with lies of manna, milk, and honey. Given their proclivities . . ." He stared through the earth to the future. "I . . . fear for the Negro race."

Gordon felt on firmer ground with that topic.

"We'll see to the niggers, all right," he assured his friend.

Four thirty p.m.
Appomattox Station

By the time Custer caught up with the head of his column, the men of the 2nd New York were having a grand time. Before the rest of Al Pennington's bunch had closed, an advance party of the New Yorkers, a handful of men selected for railroad experience, had captured three trains with over fifty railcars.

Now they were tooting the whistles and shuttling the trains up and down the track, a few hundred yards each way, greeting Custer with a jolly pageant. Leaning from a locomotive's cab, a sergeant waved his red scarf and hollered against the engine noise, unintelligible but thrilled at Custer's arrival. Blackened by oil and engine soot, the fellow grinned like a painted coon in a minstrel show.

Pennington rode up and gave his report.

"Got 'em, sir, we took 'em just like that. Rebs didn't even try to put up a fight. And every one of those cars is packed to the roof. Rations, blankets, uniforms, rifles . . . enough to furnish Lee's army and build another."

"There were supposed to be four trains. Or more. I count three, Al."

"One got away, sir. Must've had a warning. We saw the smoke receding, off to the west. Wouldn't know about any others, though."

"Well . . . splendid. Grand. Capehart should be up in half an hour and we'll resume the hunt. Meanwhile, put out pickets, in case our Southern brethren want their dinner back."

"Already have, sir. And if I may—"

The familiar whistle of an artillery shell plunged toward the depot. It burst in an open lot behind the water tank.

A speck of dirt stung Custer.

"What the devil?"

More shells followed.

"They're trying to hit the trains, they know we've taken them," Custer shouted, pulling up the nag he'd been forced to ride. His best horse had been shot from under him back at Sailor's Creek and another went lame. "Al, have those railroad men of yours move the trains off east."

He scanned the horizon, his view interrupted by stands of poor timber and a sprawl of undergrowth.

Another explosive shell made his horse shy.

"Think I've got a sense of them," Pennington told him. "Over that way. Not a half mile off, I'd say. Judging by the arcs."

"Well, return their greeting, old fellow."

"Damned poor ground for cavalry."

"Worse for artillery."

Pennington waved up his bugler to sound the assembly and sent a captain to order the trains shuttled eastward. The command proved unnecessary, since the soldiers on the throttles had judged the situation for themselves. Before the order reached the first cab, steam was up and driving wheels were turning.

The trains pulled off, whistling defiantly. Pennington dismounted three of his regiments and led them into the undergrowth himself, with Custer watching and waiting on his next brigade.

With the captured trains already to his credit, he figured that grabbing a few Reb guns would put cherries atop the cake.

Wouldn't Phil be pleased?

The attack failed. Bleeding cavalrymen wandered out of the thickets or staggered down rutted wagon tracks, helped along by messmates. The lightly wounded cursed bitterly, while the worst hit muttered women's names or stared blindly.

"It's worse than a damned jungle," Pennington explained. He'd lost his hat and his forehead had been scratched open. "Bastards hit us with canister. Couple batteries' worth. Before we could even see them." He sighed, then blasphemed mightily. "Let me round the boys up and we'll try again."

"Wait for Capehart. Scout them for now. Sounds like there may be more out there than we thought. Push out a skirmish line and snatch me a prisoner. I need to know who we're facing, I need to know if they've got infantry with them. We've had enough surprises."

A lone drop of blood traced down into Pennington's eyebrow. "They can see us, that's the thing. They ranged the depot fast enough. And they knew we were coming after them. But I couldn't see them at all, it's the queerest thing."

"Either they know the ground, or they're good at guessing. Just bring me a prisoner, we'll set things straight soon enough."

The Confederate guns shifted back to shelling the station. But the day's first shots had been mostly luck, and they never got the range that close again. Instead of improving, their accuracy worsened, although they did hit a horse holder and four mounts.

The Rebs couldn't see everything, but his men were as good as blind. It promised to be an interesting squabble.

It's their entire artillery reserve," Pennington reported. "Got ahead of their army somehow. There's a wagon train, too, bunched up along the stage road. And cavalry, a regiment or more. Fighting dismounted. They've got surplus artillerymen fighting with rifles, too."

Surprised, Custer asked, "A Reb told you all that? So fast?" His features tightened. "You didn't—"

Pennington smiled. "Better than a Reb. Snapped up a darkey teamster who'd run off. Scared as a rabbit when we brought him in. Seemed to think Yankees are cannibals. Guess he hasn't heard it's the Jubilee."

"Anything else?"

"They got here late this morning. They're waiting for Lee to catch up." Pennington chewed his mustache. "They had no idea we were anywhere close. Which explains why the trains weren't guarded."

The head of Capehart's column appeared down along the rail bed. With flags flying.

Methodical this time, Custer had Capehart dismount all of his regiments but one and move forward cautiously, with Pennington ready to move to his support.

The fighting soon bogged down. Capehart's men stuck to it, though, playing hide-and-seek with the Confederates. Custer rode into the fray himself, following dirt tracks forward, the brambles forbidding entry to his horse. Once leaves sprouted fully, the tangles would be impenetrable even on foot. He didn't intend to stay that long, of course. But it truly was an ugly piece of ground.

Afternoon light slanted through the trees, nature's timepiece.

Custer couldn't see much, but his men saw him. It stirred them up and kept them moving forward.

Bullets zipped past, snapping twigs and thunking tree trunks. A soldier jerked, cried, "Mother!" and toppled forward.

Custer found Hank Capehart on foot, slashing at the briars with his saber.

"Thinking of taking up gardening after the war?" Custer asked.

"Not in goddamned Virginia. This sorry place . . ."

A dozen cannon blasts sounded in quick succession. Men screamed. Howled. Clutching their carbines, soldiers—good men—ran blindly rearward past Custer and Capehart.

A dazed lieutenant emerged from the undergrowth, clutching an arm attached only by a few tendons. Belatedly, the presence of his superiors registered on him.

"Canister," he muttered. "Waiting for us. Canister."

Custer offered the boy his horse, but the lieutenant just said, "Can't," and staggered rearward.

"Sound the recall," Custer told Capehart.

"My bugler's dead."

When Wells' brigade completed the division, Custer sketched out his plan for his three colonels.

"We're going to make it stick this time," he told them. "One regiment per brigade will remain mounted for a pursuit, but everybody else goes in on foot. We feint toward the center and get their attention. Then we envelop both flanks." He examined the faces, each colonel's expression serious in the gloaming. "I want to see *spirit* this time. I know what the men are thinking. 'Why should I be the last to fall?' I won't have it. The war's not over yet. And I will not have this division shamed by a pack of cast-off Reb artillerymen and cavalrymen who've been dining off their horses."

"Wonder if they haven't been reinforced?" Pennington said. "Been at it over three hours, quite a rumpus. If Lee's anywhere close, he'd be pushing men forward."

"No, Al, I don't think so," Custer told him. "If reinforcements had come up, we would've heard cheers. Just how it works, you know that."

"Night attacks are bad enough," said Bill Wells, the latecomer, "but from what I've seen of the terrain . . ."

"Just keep your men tight. You'll have plenty of moonlight."

"And that canister? Hell on tight formations."

"Keep the men tight. But stay on the flanks."

"About the bugles," Capehart said, "I'd just as soon go in quiet. See if we can't surprise them."

"No. They'd hear us coming, anyway. Thrashing through that brush. Just do what I said. Spread out the regimental buglers. Make it sound as if the entire Cavalry Corps is after them, not just one division. I want them jumping out of their skins before they hear one carbine."

The commanders set their pocket watches, straining to read the faces.

"All right," Custer said. "Step off at eight thirty. That means everybody. Keep the men shoulder to shoulder. And go as fast as you can." He drew himself up straight and added, "I want this finished before Devin gets up. I won't have anyone else stealing our credit."

The Rebs were played out. Custer's men burst over them. Some Rebs fought, particularly the gun crews defending their pieces, but most ran away or surrendered, begging, "Don't shoot, Yank! Done thrown down my gun, don't shoot me, Yank!"

A few of Pennington's men remembered the blasts of canister and ignored the pleas. But the savagery was brief.

Soon wagons were blazing, with prisoners herded rearward and Reb fieldpieces hitched to captured limbers. Even in the dark, Custer's men were appalled by the condition of the Reb horses and mules.

A sergeant reported, "Got us a Reb general. Sick in the back of a wagon, puking sick. Near burned him alive, but his coon-boy stopped us."

As regiments regrouped and adjutants counted heads, Custer said,

"All right. Good work. Just splendid." He turned to Wells, whose men had seen the least action. "Who did you hold in reserve, Bill?"

"Fifteenth New York. Augie Root's desperadoes."

"Send them on to the Court House. See if they can scare up any more Rebs. Or spot campfires. Phil's going to want to know if Lee's about."

"If he was, he would've done something for these poor bastards," Pennington said with a gesture toward their prisoners.

"Can't just reason it out, Al. You know that. Bill, you tell Colonel Root to find the Rebs."

"*If* they're out there," Pennington said. Tired and stubborn and just how he got sometimes.

"They're out there," Custer told him.

The 15th New York returned from their scout without their commanding officer, who had been shot from his horse in the village street. The acting commander, a major, reported to Custer and Wells:

"They're out there, all right. Might be Lee's whole army, judged by the campfires. See 'em spread out soon as you cross the ridge." Catching his breath, the major added, "I told the colonel we were too far forward, sir. We'd already been fired on twice. But he wanted to locate their skirmish line, he was set on it."

"Well, he did what he set out to do," Sheridan commented. Recently arrived, he had been suffering Custer's account of the day's heroics when the 15th New York returned. "Thank you, Major. Brave work. See to your men."

"Handsome way to go, I daresay," Custer commented. "Augie Root has covered himself in glory."

"And we'll cover him with dirt." Sheridan was weary and saddle-sore. And hungry, although he'd had a pleasant repast that afternoon. "Anything worth eating? That cook of yours catch up?"

"No cook, Phil. But carloads of bacon and all the trimmings besides. Didn't dream the South had all those vittles left."

Sheridan grunted. He'd had something better than fried fatback in mind. "I wonder what Bobby Lee's been eating tonight."

"Crow," Custer said.

Ten p.m.

One mile northeast of Appomattox Court House

Gordon watched Lee rise—with some difficulty—from the blanket under his rump. Turning from the good warmth of the fire, Lee stared again at the campfires to the south and spreading westward, beyond his lines and blocking the army's path. Gordon did not get up. Didn't need to. He'd had all the looking he needed. From the high field that served as Lee's headquarters this night, a man could see additional Yankee campfires, many more, to the northeast, crowding Longstreet's lines and the army's rear.

They were all but surrounded.

Longstreet heaved his big form up on his pins and stepped to Lee's side. They made a somber pair.

"Only cavalry," Longstreet said, following Lee's gaze southward. "No reports of infantry ahead."

Lee's proud shoulders sagged, but his voice sought firmness. "I do not believe their infantry march with sufficient vigor. They have not the steel of our men, the force of character. They could not be there so soon."

Gordon thought of the scarecrow bodies of his remaining soldiers, of their sunken eyes and caved-in bellies, the new bend in their backs and mouths hanging open because men lacked the strength needed to close them. Perhaps some scraps of steel remained in their hearts, but their bodies were flesh and blood.

Still, he'd wanted to push them harder himself. He always did. Clem had tried to talk sense to him. Wasn't a man a tangle of contradictions, though? Homer understood.

Sprawled on his blanket, nearest to the fire, Fitz Lee said, "If it's only cavalry, my boys can see to them, push them aside. If that's what you want. Infantry, though . . ."

"There will not be infantry," Lee said adamantly. "I do not believe their infantry will be up, not in our front. Not if we move briskly."

"But if . . . ," Fitz Lee said.

Gordon had soured on Lee's nephew. If Fitz's performance had been poor at Five Forks, it hadn't shown much improvement at Sailor's Creek. Just wasn't the man to command the Cavalry Corps. He'd been sound enough in command of a division, but leading the entire cavalry was too much for him. The mounted arm just had not been the same since Wade Hampton left. Weren't all that mounted, either, at this point.

Nothing delighted the heart of an infantry soldier like the sight of a cavalryman forced to go on foot.

Returning to the fire, Lee warmed his hands. "I have asked Grant to state his terms, but he has not done so. Not with adequate clarity. He has offered a meeting."

The three generals looked at him, not one willing to ask the question all wished answered.

"I am not unwilling," Lee said. "But I fear punitive terms. He writes of paroling the soldiers, but my concern must be with our officers."

"Grant's not a cruel man," Longstreet said. "No fool, either. If I know Sam, the terms he'll offer won't shame us."

Anger colored Lee's face. Or perhaps it was the fire's cast. "Not cruel? The man dares speak of ending the 'effusion of blood.' To me! Grant!"

Gordon understood the outburst well enough. Lee still hadn't cottoned to being whipped. It was hard for all of them, not least for the fervent spirits like Clem Evans, but Gordon suspected it was harder by far for Lee. He was much the elder of all present, a generation senior even to Longstreet. And his staff men had barely settled into their britches. Every other man around the campfire could look ahead to a future, if not necessarily an easy one. But what lay ahead for Lee?

Gordon was aware of the camp talk among the old Regulars, the suspicion that the Yankee government would imprison all the

Confederate officers who'd turned their arms against the United States, in violation of their commissioning oaths. The Northern press had deemed them "traitors" many a time.

Might just sweep up *all* the Southern generals, West Point or not. Couldn't rule it out. But Gordon reckoned the fuss would blow over quickly for men like him, men who'd worn no uniforms until the war, who'd never pledged to serve the Constitution. They'd be too much bother to prosecute. Even a country lawyer could make a spectacle of it, comparing them to George Washington, as men of conscience rebelling against oppression. Might take away their franchise and ban them from office, but there would be ways around such inconveniences.

As for the old Regulars . . . the Union might feel a thirst for bloody vengeance, but it would be tempered by practical concerns. If the Yankees treated Southern officers barbarously, the outcry from abroad would set things right. The Europeans hadn't been willing to fight for the South, but they'd be glad to dent the North's rival economy. No, the Yankees needed trade, it was their lifeblood. They wouldn't hang men in droves if it meant a drop in shares on the New York Exchange.

Might they be fool enough to imprison Lee, though? Even hang him, as an example? They'd wreck any hope of reconciliation, they'd spark enough hatred to last a generation.

But men did foolish things. . . .

As if reading Gordon's mind, Lee said, "I fear not for myself, but for the South. What shall become of us, gentlemen? What will be left us? Those people speak of liberty for all, but one hears echoes of tyranny in their voices. I fear some among them wish to destroy the South. Not merely our armies, not only the institution of Negro servitude, but . . . everything."

"Not Grant," Longstreet said stubbornly.

"But Grant is not the president, General Longstreet. Nor is he a minister of government. It is . . . it is not those who've fought us on the battlefield whom I dread. It is those who have stayed at home, baying for blood."

"Yankees *have* shown a talent for tearing things down," Fitz Lee put in. Fitz had survived grave wounds from Comanches and Yankees, only to send many good men to their graves.

Gordon knew how things would play out in the future, though. Thanks to that last name, to its magic spell, Fitz would come out fine, despite his failures. So he only said:

"We'll find our way forward, all right. There's always a way. We're not going to disappear, we'll still be here."

"If a sight fewer in number," Longstreet said wryly. Gordon found him a dark and brooding man, ferocious and conditioned to disappointment. Over the past hour Longstreet had veered between apologizing for Grant, his prewar friend, and evincing an appetite for slaughter worthy of the Old Testament.

Gordon could hardly tell from one moment to the next whether Longstreet intended to influence Lee to fight on or surrender. They were hardly exemplars of courage, any of them, each waiting for the other to speak up and press Lee to a decision, one way or the other. For his part, Gordon believed that further resistance was hopeless. As he'd told Clem that afternoon, they'd been finished after Fort Stedman.

He looked at Lee again. The fire crackled and flared, lighting a worn face.

Longstreet sat back down on his blanket, joining the others in awkward repose. Formality had broken down along with the army—in the past they would not have sat while Lee remained standing.

But Lee stood alone now. Struggling with his old-fashioned ideas of rectitude as plainly as a woman laughed or cried. After four years, the fate of a world would turn on his decision. Davis was impotent, Johnston's army doomed, Forrest and all of the others out there useless. Whatever the formalities that might drag on for months, the Confederacy would die if Lee surrendered.

Gordon believed Lee's eyes were growing wet. It shocked him and he found the sight intolerable.

Gripped by unreason, he rose and spoke from the far side of the campfire, no longer scheming Ulysses but Achilles, full of passion.

"By God, sir, we have to *try*. If the Federals only have cavalry in our path, we can sweep them away." His voice rang out, or so it seemed to him. "My corps is good for it, we can open that road. And hold it open."

All the while he spoke, he doubted his own veracity. All day—for days—surrender had seemed inevitable. He didn't believe for a moment that one more attack could alter the course of the war. And yet, looking at Lee standing there, shouldering that incalculable weight, Gordon had found himself compelled to rush to his aid once more. He simply could not help himself.

An attack would spill more blood, to no good purpose. But it was fated, written.

And yet . . . what if they *could* open the road? And then push on toward Lynchburg and turn south? What if they reached Johnston, after all?

Fitz Lee, too, had risen. "My boys can lick their cavalry. Now, or anytime. If that's all they have in our way, we'll see to them smartly."

"Have to hit them early, while it's still dark," Longstreet said, coming back to life. "I can hold off Meade and Humphreys, all of them."

Renewed and suddenly eager, they fell to planning the details, how Gordon would punch through and swing to the left, holding open the Lynchburg road while the stripped-down wagon train and artillery passed. Longstreet would follow, relieving Gordon and serving as the rear guard. Once they were in the clear, they would turn south and march to join Joe Johnston. . . .

Their hope was the hope of children.

Two a.m., April 9
Clifton manor

Grant lay awake, head pounding. Sleep was impossible, lying awake unbearable. The mustard plasters the surgeon applied had been useless. Downstairs, staff men, exuberant and gay despite their weariness, had thumped a parlor piano until midnight, when Grant finally sent an orderly to hush them. He hated to spoil their revelry, but couldn't bear the racket any longer.

His head felt ready to crack into pieces, his brain about to bust out of his skull. The headache was the worst he could remember, and he'd known fierce ones.

He couldn't even fit a cigar to his mouth.

Lee had disappointed him. He'd expected an answer, even if it only announced another step in their dance. But none had arrived. He'd begun the past day optimistic that it might see the last hour of war, at least in Virginia. He'd written as much to Sheridan.

Hadn't worked out.

Struggling with the pain was trial enough, but he had to fight against self-pity, too. He'd learned to fear the weakness, the indulgence, hidden inside him. Let a man pity himself for just one instant and good sense fled. Pain passed, but the consequences of folly dogged a man. He'd learned that lesson.

In all his life, the only pain he'd been unable to bear had been that crushing separation from Julia, when the Army sent him alone to the raw Northwest. He'd taken to drink and made the decisions that cost him his shoulder straps. But this headache, this new and startling level of torment, threatened to unman him.

He breathed in gasps, a substitute for tears.

Damn Lee. *Damn* him. The war needed to end, it was bloody filth. Lee knew it as well as he did.

Lightly, warily, knuckles tapped his door.

"Come in," Grant called. He struggled to put his mind, his features, in order.

John Rawlins stood in the door frame, thin as a shadow. He held a lamp and a paper.

"Come in," Grant repeated. "Can't sleep, anyway." He recoiled. "Easy with that light."

"Still that bad?"

"Half wish somebody'd blow my head off my shoulders." Grant eyed the paper.

"From Lee," Rawlins told him. "His Royal fucking Highness, Robert E. Lee. The old pisser. Wait till you read it."

"Read it to me. Not sure my eyes can point in the same direction."

Rawlins shoved aside doilies and china dogs, settling the lamp on a dresser. Bending to the light, he read:

Lieutenant-General Grant,
Commanding Armies of the United States:

General: I received at a late hour your note of to-day. In mine of yesterday I did not intend to propose the surrender of the Army of Northern Virginia, but to ask the terms of your proposition. To be frank, I do not think the emergency has arisen to call for the surrender of this army; but as the restoration of peace should be the sole object of all, I desired to know whether your proposals would lead to that end. I cannot, therefore, meet you with a view to surrender the Army of Northern Virginia; but as far as your proposal may affect the C.S. forces under my command, and tend to the restoration of peace, I should be pleased to meet you at 10 a.m. to-morrow, on the old stage road to Richmond, between the picket-lines of the two armies.

Very respectfully, your obedient servant,

R. E. Lee
General

"The high-toned sonofabitch," Rawlins said, inflamed anew by the words he had read aloud. "It's infamous, intolerable. He's playing with us."

Grant rested his face in his hands for a moment longer. Then he said:

"No, John. No, he's letting himself down easy. Must be the hardest thing he's had to do in his entire life, this surrender business. Hard enough for two lifetimes, for a man of his sort and breeding."

Grant closed his eyes to shut out the pain, but only locked it in. "Things have always gone his way, more or less. Now they aren't going his way anymore. It's a shock that requires adjustment."

"He's a scoundrel. Nothing but a high-flown scoundrel. You're too damned soft."

"Haven't been charged with that in quite a while."

"Really, we need to pound him. Phil's right, at least about that much. The only way to make Lee see reason—if it can be done—is to destroy that army, smash it once and for all. Teach every goddamned Reb a lesson they'll never forget. Grind them to dust."

Grant took a drink of water from the bedside carafe, too wanton in his pain to use the glass. "And then what? Then what, John? You might befriend a man you've whipped, given time. But not a fellow you've humiliated."

"You're going to just accept it? This insult?"

Grant tried closing his eyes again. Didn't help this time, either. "There's no insult. Except to common sense. Or to his own soldiers."

"And . . . this peace nonsense. *You* can't negotiate a general peace, he has to know that. That's for Lincoln, the politicians. He's trying to pull a fast one, get you to commit to something that'll drag you down, that would outrage every political hack in Washington."

Grant shook his head. "You're thinking like a politician yourself, John." He almost smiled. "Soldiers are simpler folk. Even Robert E. Lee."

"You know you can't treat of peace. You can only take the surrender of his army."

"I know it." He was beginning to find Rawlins as exasperating as Lee. "Maybe my own words misled him. Lee . . . isn't a dishonest man, I don't believe." He scratched his leg through underclothes gone gray. "Think there's one fine house in all Virginia doesn't have bedbugs?"

Impatient, fuming, oblivious, Rawlins asked, "You're going to reply?"

"Of course I'm going to reply. But I won't agree to meet him;

that offer's revoked until he starts talking sense. I'm not going to haggle and let this thing drag on." Blue lightning shot through his skull again, but he mastered himself and continued: "Don't worry. I won't get too big for my boots, not about to let the president down. If any man knows his place . . ."

"You'll let me see the message, though? Before you send it? Your future—"

"My future isn't the issue."

"Somebody has to think about it. If you won't."

Agitated and sleepless himself, Rawlins fell into one of his coughing fits. He shook out a blood-pinked handkerchief and shut it over his mouth.

When his friend, his true and trusted friend, recovered, Grant added:

"Lee can wait until morning, though. He made us wait long enough. Don't want to write while I'm out of sorts myself, let spleen seep in."

"He's playing for time, Sam. You know it as well as I do. You need to bring him up short."

"Like I said, he's just playing out his pride. I believe . . . I think I've come to understand the man. To some degree."

Lee. The great, the grand Robert E. Lee. Every lieutenant's idol, hero to all.

Grant pondered things a bit longer, striving to think clearly. "Tell you, John . . . I wouldn't be surprised if he comes at us one more time, one last attack in the morning. One final gesture of pride. Then he'll fold his hand."

Whittled sharp by consumption, Rawlins' features became those of an inquisitor judging an unrepentant heretic.

"Well, if he does . . . if Lee *does* attack again, we'll be ready for the sonofabitch."

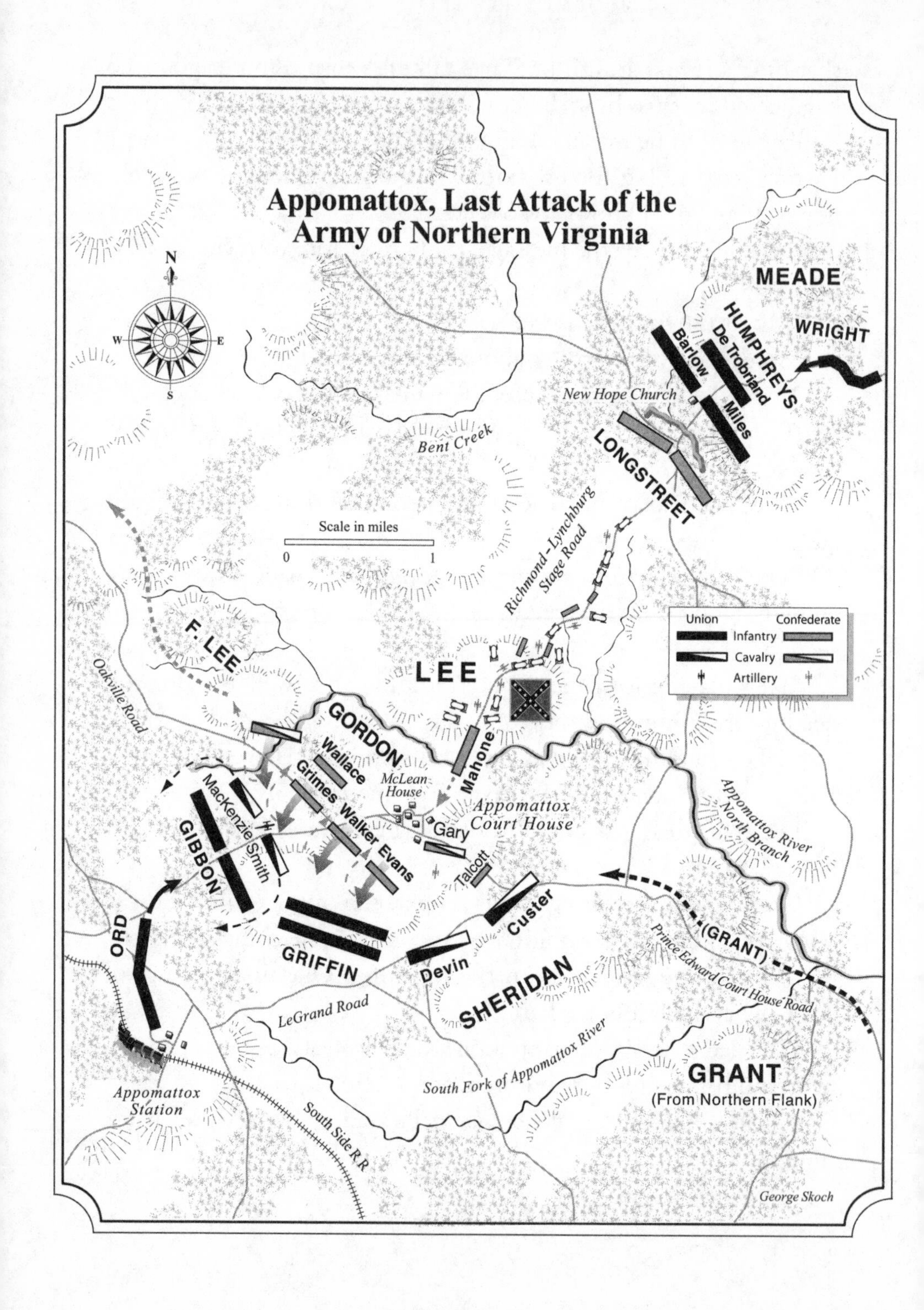
Appomattox, Last Attack of the Army of Northern Virginia
N
W
E
S
MEADE
HUMPHREYS
De Trobriand
Barlow
Miles
WRIGHT
New Hope Church
LONGSTREET
Bent Creek
Scale in miles
0
1
Richmond - Lynchburg Stage Road
Union
Confederate
Infantry
Cavalry
Artillery
F. LEE
LEE
Oakville Road
GORDON
Wallace
Grimes
Walker
Evans
Mahone
McLean House
Appomattox Court House
Gary
Talcott
MacKenzie
Smith
GIBBON
ORD
GRIFFIN
Devin
Custer
SHERIDAN
(GRANT)
Appomattox River North Branch
Prince Edward Court House Road
LeGrand Road
South Fork of Appomattox River
Appomattox Station
South Side R R
GRANT
(From Northern Flank)
George Skoch

SEVENTEEN

Five twenty a.m., April 9, 1865, Palm Sunday
Appomattox Court House

That's infantry up there," Fitz Lee insisted, delaying again. "I'm telling you, the Yankees brought up infantry during the night."

Minutes short of sunrise, the conclave of generals peered toward the ridge in the paling light. White-breathed, those without riding gloves rubbed their hands together. The division commanders present appeared worn out and willing to let their superiors argue.

Gordon felt betrayed. The night before, in front of his uncle, Fitz Lee had been full of fight. Now he didn't want to attack, it was plain. It had been agreed that should they find themselves faced with Federal infantry, the attack would be called off. But Gordon had sent his scouts to prowl the enemy line and each had reported only cavalry present. Might well be infantry somewhere back behind them—and the Yankees would be marching hard, at the very least—but Gordon believed, just plain *felt,* that the Yankees a quarter mile off were dismounted horse soldiers. Even the hasty defenses they'd thrown up lacked the quality of those erected by infantrymen. Any man could see it, despite the mist and poor light.

"Cavalry," Gordon contradicted Fitz Lee. "No doubt in my mind."

The horse soldier seemed to have a case of the jumps. At the campfire back-and-forth, Fitz had carved out an agreement that if they couldn't break through the Yankees to free the army, his command would be allowed to slip off, to take to the byways and forest trails to avoid surrendering—if it could be done without dishonor, before any surrender became official.

Gordon believed that Fitz just wanted to go.

Men had different spirits on different days; he'd witnessed the phenomenon many a time. Even Homer's heroes had been unsteady. Whatever other failings he possessed, Fitz Lee had never shown a taint of yellow. But this morning he was as agitated as Gordon had ever seen him. Fitz no more wanted to attack than he longed to kiss a rattlesnake on the lips.

The space between the armies remained still. For the slight noise the Yankees made up on that ridge, they might have been slumbering. But they weren't. They were waiting. Horse soldiers or foot soldiers, they were waiting for their opponents to make up their minds.

In Fitz's defense, Gordon didn't feel as confident himself as he had by that campfire. At least, not so enamored of gallant gestures. Whether or not the army escaped to fight another day, that fateful day would come, and soon enough. They'd been defeated beyond hope of redemption, and every man with stars on his collar knew it. Except, perhaps, Clem Evans.

But Gordon had made a promise to Robert E. Lee, and he would not break his word. A man talked big, he had to live up to his brag. But Gordon would have been quietly glad if he could have believed Fitz Lee that the Yankees settled atop the ridge were infantry, up in strength. But he could not believe it, just didn't. And so he was bound to attack, to lead his corps—his withered corps—in what he suspected would be its last advance.

And yet . . . it surely would be a fine thing to trounce the Yankees one last time, to bust the odds, to rescue the army. . . .

Trouble was that Fitz Lee was supposed to lead the assault, that was the plan. Plunge down the stage road and sweep west as Gordon's infantry came up in echelon and widened the corridor to the east, blocking Yankee counterattacks.

"Fitz," Gordon tried again, "it's getting light. We have to go now, or we're just throwing lives away."

"I don't see it," Lee said. "Not against infantry. John, I just don't see it."

They'd gathered behind Grimes' stretch of the line and the division commander, elder in years and junior in rank, had kept his views to himself up to that point. Now Grimes said:

"Damn it, I'll go in. Then we'll see who's right." He glared at Fitz with a dismissive mien. "Not inclined to keep my boys out here shivering for nothing."

Lee came to himself. "All right. Of course. Mercy, I suppose we need to try. I'll get my boys moving."

A crimson streak of sunrise cut the gray.

Five forty a.m.
Appomattox Court House

Forward they went with a Rebel yell to wake the dead and terrify the living. Dirty gray and mud brown in their rags, they lifted themselves to a fury and thrust themselves up the long and mild slope, frightful devils not to be resisted. The fierceness was upon him, it was, all the rage of his long-tormented people, cruelty even, for in the glum dark, in the scrap of time he'd stepped off for a hard squat, a dastard had stolen his blanket and haversack—though leaving his rifle—and, seething, he'd lain himself back upon the clutch-a-man cold ground, not sleeping but livid, for if any man had been born to do the stealing of such, it was him, and to be done unto was a humiliation not to be borne. So the Yankees would pay for his loss, in place of the culprit.

The short, wet grass damped trousers worn thin as thousands of feet tramped forward at the quick and then, with shouts, more shouts, and flags unfurled, at the double-quick, running toward the intolerable Yankees, toward the flashes offending the eye and the sharp cracks piercing the ear. On with heart pounding Riordan went, fueled by outrage at every injustice on earth, all done to him. A bullet met flesh beside him with a *thup,* but the next man's misfortune didn't cost Riordan a step, for he was Cain in search of a thousand Abels.

Where his comrades found the strength to holler must go unanswered, for mysteries abounded in his world: how it could take so long to cross so short a patch of ground, yet let a man arrive at his goal in a blink, as quick and easy as death. Riordan vaulted over the sorry battlements, the low wall of fence rails and branches the Yankees had built, and when a bluecoat turned on him—ah, too slowly, boyo!—he knocked away the barrel of the carbine and thrust his own rifle under a bearded chin and pulled the trigger, blowing brains skyward, the kick of the weapon nearly undoing his thumb.

"Ireland! Ireland!" Keegan screamed steps off, a madman misbegotten, the fool crying out for their horrid homeland, as if they'd never left that sorry place, as if it merited loyalty and blood and would not relinquish its children even now, the children it had starved until they fled. And Keegan had never been a Fenian sort, nor aught but a musician in hard times.

"Are ye praising the place, or cursing it?" Riordan mocked. "Your bloody Ireland?"

Keegan, wild, heard nothing, but took to smashing down a fallen Yankee, a lad who begged as he struggled to fend off the blows, only to take such a beating that bones snapped in protesting forearms. The lad tried to roll away, but Keegan, far from a hard boy in days past, brought down the butt of his rifle toward the lad's head. The first blow caught only a shoulder. Keegan kicked him groin-ward and brought down the butt again, a smash to the ear, and Riordan felt the briefest urge to stop him—the boy was begging broken-mouthed—but Keegan smashed down the butt over and over, until the boy was beyond merely dead, his body desecrated and the scrambled eggs of his brain distributed over a yard or more of undergrowth.

Keegan looked up at Riordan, eyes aflame with madness. So terrible was his look that Riordan stepped back and left his comrade gasping.

Adept hands searched the possessions and pockets of prisoners, even as the regiment made of a dozen regiments re-formed and moved on from the starveling grove, with men reloading on the move, gobbling bites of purloined cracker or biscuit between clatter-thrusts of the ramrod, oh, they knew their business, those lads did.

"Riordan, you're all bloodied up," a fellow called.

And when he felt himself, he found that something had opened up his temple. He felt warm blood on his fingers, but no pain.

He had no idea what had happened to him. Nor did he care. Revenge was the Irishman's sweet-cakes and his milk.

Onward they went. Across a field, Yankee horsemen rode up and dismounted in a hurry, yanking carbines from saddle holsters and hurling themselves to the ground. They knelt to fire.

No Rebel yell this time. Instead, a growl.

The Yankees poured on their lead, from carbines begotten by Satan, firing without cease. Men crumpled, or staggered, or dropped on their backsides, stunned by what had happened to their bodies. Hands searched for wounds, frantic as if vicious animals had gotten under their rags. And the dead, oh, you could always tell the dead, their artless postures unmistakable.

Orders halted their rugged line to return a volley and then let off another. With oaths unholy, they went forward again, hot in the chill.

Keegan caught up with the forward line. Blood and brains adorned him. He'd vomited down his shirt.

This time, the Yankees fell back before one gray-garbed warrior reached them.

Riordan's comrades howled in triumph, their wild tribe victorious.

Six fifteen a.m.
Appomattox Court House

Elated, Gordon scribbled a message to Robert E. Lee. Fitz had reported that the way was clear, the stage road lay open in the direction of Lynchburg. The army would indeed live another day.

They'd done it. He'd done it. And wasn't it cause for astonishment?

He'd been right: The Yankees had nothing in front of them but cavalry. His men had rushed over their lines with a spirit that recalled the years of victory.

Had his own weariness and endless calculations blinded him to what his men could achieve?

He wrote the message in sober terms, but his spirit was jubilant. He hadn't let Lee down.

Six forty a.m.
Confederate left flank

Brigadier General Clement Anselm Evans hadn't had his best night's rest. The pin splinters blasted into his side at Monocacy had decided to devil him again, biting his flesh no matter which way he turned. It had been—almost—a relief to rise again.

And now this glory.

Never had he been prouder of his men. He rode among them with no thought of danger, urging them onward with praise. These men whom he had not been able to feed, men for whom he had petitioned the Lord, begging his mercy and a short ration of bacon, his men had risen from their misery, a mortal resurrection, to sweep over the Yankees one more time. They'd not only taken prisoners aplenty, but several fine strings of horses to add to the prize.

He waved them on, his Virginians, his fellow Georgians, his Louisianans, waving his hat and beaming, crying, "Praise the Lord! Thank the Lord! Close on your flags, keep your order!"

For another hundred marvelous yards there was no resistance to speak of, only stray shots fired in hatred and rue.

Beyond a fringe of trees and some bad brush the ground swelled again, another mild roll in the terrain, the low crest unoccupied in mist-filtered light.

The strength of one truly was as the strength of thousands, if the Lord willed it.

Looking about for Colonel Waggaman, anxious that he tighten his brigade line, Evans let his tattered, filthy, exultant soldiers pass him.

Couldn't see Waggaman. Hoped he hadn't been hit.

Something changed. The weight of the world, the air itself, grew heavy in an instant. Colder. Enough to give a man a mortal chill.

When he turned his horse about, he found that his soldiers had stopped on the low crest. Just stopped, without a command.

Spurring lightly, he cantered up, calling, "Who gave the order to halt?"

As he neared the top of the ripple in the earth, the sealed book opened before him: Long lines of Yankee infantry had formed to advance toward them.

Seven a.m.
South of Appomattox Court House

Angry and embarrassed, Gordon tried to still his horse so he could write legibly without dismounting. Fitz Lee, damn him, had retracted his report. The road to the west was *not* open. Yankee infantry were astride it and preparing to attack.

He regretted his haste, his credulous delight, in sending off the message just minutes before, claiming the road was open and they were saved. It was that same impetuosity that he'd displayed at Fort Stedman repeating itself, another premature claim of improbable victory.

John Brown Gordon realized that for all his imagined wiles, the one man he fooled consistently was himself.

He wrote, painfully and quickly, to tell Lee that Federal infantry were on his right.

Before he could hand the message to the courier, he received a verbal report from one of Clem's staff men.

Yankee infantry were on his left as well.

He corrected the message to Lee, then ordered his soldiers to halt and defend their ground.

Seven a.m.
Confederate left

Jesus, Mary, and Joseph, where had they come from? There were more Yankees to their front and flank than whores in the French Quarter. More than there were priests and nuns in Ireland. More than . . .

A painful, ugly thing it was to see them in their glory and their pride, unfolding from the line of march, one regiment after another, some already advancing over the broken ground—now hidden, now plain again—to pay back the debt of the morning.

"Christ Jesus," a cracker complained. "How many of those suckers does a feller have to kill? Just how many folks they got up North?"

Well, if they were in for a proper fight, Riordan was ready and willing. But a man had to die presentable. He turned to Keegan and said:

"Would ye just do me the pleasure of wiping that lad's brains off your snout and shoulders? And tell me if I got any on meself."

Seven thirty a.m.
South of Appomattox

Doing his best to keep his head, Gordon felt caught in a whirlwind. Bryan Grimes reported repelling a Yankee brigade that had advanced unsupported, but Federal infantry kept appearing in greater numbers, threatening both flanks and now his center. Evans believed he could make out the flags of the Union Fifth Corps. And Fitz Lee claimed to have spotted at least one brigade with black faces, which not only promised ugliness to come, but meant a second Union corps had arrived on the field, since their Fifth Corps had never fielded colored troops.

Initial reports of an enemy's strength often were exaggerated, Gordon knew, but when he tried to put together a picture of what his men faced, it seemed incontestable that the Yankees had somehow managed to march up two full corps behind their cavalry screen. Were that so, there was no hope remaining.

His men had taken two cannon from the Yankees. And the Federals had replied with two fresh corps. Hardly seemed sporting.

He'd sent his corps engineer to look over the terrain to their rear and identify the best ground to make a stand, a position where he could contract his lines and hold, but the answer came back that the only spot that was suited for defense lay back through the courthouse hamlet, across the creek and almost in Lee's lap.

Gordon was about to ride forward again, to have another look with his own eyes, when heavy firing erupted along his line and a rider came up from the rear at a full gallop. It was Charlie Venable, one of Lee's staff intimates.

"General Gordon, sir . . . General Lee's compliments and he wants to know the exact details of your situation."

Gordon almost snapped at the younger man. Exact situation? Damned if he knew. Yankees, and plenty of them. There was no "exact" once bullets started flying. He suspected that the choice of language was Venable's, not Lee's.

Guts churning, Gordon said, "Tell General Lee I've fought my corps to a frazzle, and I fear I can do nothing . . . unless I'm heavily supported by Longstreet's corps. That exact enough, Charlie?"

"Longstreet can't help, sir. Humphreys has advanced skirmishers in our rear. Looks like an attack from that side, too."

"Didn't expect him to be of help. But you asked. That's my situation, plain as Aunt Sally."

"General Lee . . . will be disappointed, sir."

Gordon wondered if Venable had ever had his face slapped.

Seven thirty a.m.
South of Appomattox

Sheridan rode up to Charlie Griffin, whose corps was on the attack.

"Smash 'em up, goddamn it. Wipe those bastards out. Crush the buggers."

Affronted, Griffin said, “I think I know what to do, Sheridan. If you think you can fight this corps better than I can, welcome to it.”

Sheridan simmered but softened his tone. Never had found a chink in Griffin’s armor. Should have replaced Warren long before. Sound man, Charlie Griffin. Heartless in a fight. As a soldier should be.

Not one for proper respect, though.

“Ord’s been at them for almost an hour,” Sheridan added.

“Looks to me more like they’ve been at him. I’ll sort it out.”

Almost defensively, Sheridan said, “My cavalry held them as long as could be expected. Fine delaying action. Waiting for you.”

Griffin looked at him, face firm as an Indian’s. “My men marched thirty-five miles to wipe your ass, Phil. Bad form to shit on them.”

Apart from Grant himself, there were only two men in the entire army whom Sheridan couldn’t back down. The other was Humphreys.

“All right,” Sheridan said. “Just don’t delay. I don’t want some goddamned truce to interfere. Just kill them. Kill them all.”

Griffin’s features closed and his lips narrowed. “You want me to kill men surrendering, Phil?” His voice was acid.

“No. No, of course not. I didn’t mean—”

“Then watch your mouth when you’re around my officers. Until you or someone else relieves me, I give the orders in this corps. And now I’ve got orders to give.”

Griffin turned his horse back toward his staff.

Eight thirty a.m.
Gordon’s right flank

Bryan Grimes’ men fought stubbornly, withdrawing under pressure, with Grimes amid the storm of Yankee bullets, stiffening his line where his presence was needed.

Never had he been so angry in his life. Fitz Lee’s cavalry were leaving, exposing his flank. Just up and riding off, looking after themselves. With more Yankees coming his way than a full-strength division could have fended off in the best of times.

Coon troops out there, too, though not committed. Grimes hoped the Yankees would show sense and hold them back. He couldn't be responsible for the behavior of his men, for maintaining discipline, if a line of Negroes advanced in their direction. He doubted they'd obey orders to withdraw. Not if they saw black faces coming their way.

Damn it, though. He should've just kept his mouth shut, let Gordon and Fitz Lee talk themselves to death.

Wouldn't give a Confederate dollar for Fitz Lee. Not after this. Taking himself off like that.

Well, Gordon would stay. Gordon always stayed. John might be a sly one and full of hot air sometimes, but he was a fighter.

Grimes meant to stay, too.

The Yankees reinforced their attack. To Grimes' relief, the assaulting troops were white.

That meant normal killing.

Ten fifteen a.m.
Appomattox

Gordon had tightened his lines as best he could, conducting a fighting withdrawal over the hours, riding back and forth watching good men die. For his last, valiant, unnecessary attack.

Few men ran. The soldiers who remained by their colors were the hardest of all the hard men who'd filled the ranks of the Army of Northern Virginia. They still had a healthy taste for killing Yankees. Driven all the way back through the village, they'd dug in their heels again.

And Gordon found himself in a quandary. He knew it was over, but couldn't save his men. The Yankees wouldn't let him; he could see them beyond the houses, readying another attack. He had to keep fighting, even though every last body knew the army was finished. The Yankees wouldn't quit, so he couldn't quit.

He damned well wouldn't be the first to surrender.

He needed Lee to ask for a truce, to accept things.

The Yankees had brought up artillery, too. A bad situation was getting worse by the minute.

He'd stopped visiting Clem's division on the left. He couldn't bear to witness Clem's desperation, his fanatical effort to work an earthly miracle. Nor would Clem move back from the forward line and show some sense. Gordon had the stomach for a great deal, but he didn't want to see Clem fall, didn't want to be there.

Billy Mahone was over there, too. He'd come up to bolster the folly. Hardly the size of a house cat, Little Billy was a tiger.

The message came at last. A cease-fire had been agreed in the army's rear and would apply everywhere.

The end, then. This was the end. Despite himself, Gordon felt a moment's shock, an irrational disappointment.

He shouted to his ranking officer present, "Colonel Peyton. Come here. *Now.*"

Peyton didn't dawdle. His face looked as much like a question mark as ever a man's face could.

"Get a truce flag. Ride out. Do it yourself. Ask to speak to the nearest Union general with any weight to him. Might be Ord, maybe Sheridan. Tell him—listen to what I say now, listen close—you tell him that General Gordon has received notice from General Lee, stopping the battle. And you don't say anything else, any parleying to be done is way above your position in this army. Understand?"

"Sir . . . we haven't got us a truce flag. Not sure we ever did. But with the wagons gone . . ."

The racket of renewed fighting primed Gordon's temper. "Then you get out your handkerchief and—"

"Haven't got a handkerchief, sir." Peyton brushed his hands over his pockets, testing their emptiness.

"Then tear your damned shirt, man. Tie it to a stick and *go.*"

"General . . . all I got's my flannel shirt, same as you. I don't believe there's a white shirt left in this army."

Gordon burst into his worst rage of the war. "Get *some*thing, man. Soldiers are dying for nothing now. While you . . ." Turning away in fury, he just said, "Get something and *go*!"

Ten fifty a.m.
Stage road, northeast of Appomattox

Meade sniffled. Not yet himself again, but much improved, he found it rather a treat to sit on a horse instead of jarring and jerking along in the back of that ambulance. Beastly time to be ill. Well, he'd done his best.

And here were the fruits of his efforts. Of years of efforts, really. To his immediate front, the guns were silent, with only scattered riflery in the distance. Took time to pass the word to all, of course.

This was set to be the greatest of days, his ultimate vindication, even grander than that third day at Gettysburg. Only the formalities remained. He couldn't see Lee backing out, at this point—trapped and on the verge of complete destruction. The old fellow had ridden out from the Rebel rear, expecting to find Grant waiting. But messages had crossed, and Grant had gone off on a cross-country jaunt to Sheridan's wing of the army, certain that Lee would be near the Confederate vanguard. At Meade's relayed suggestion, Lee had written duplicate notes to be sent after Grant from both sides.

Somewhere, Meade was certain, the two would meet. After the morning's farce had been resolved.

"I suppose I should be pleased," Humphreys said with a grunt.

"Aren't you?" Meade asked, wiping his raw nose with sodden linen.

"In the logical sense, I suppose. But when you suspended the attack . . . George, I could have swept Longstreet's men from this earth." With his enthusiasm for battle not yet ebbed, Humphreys went on: "The effect would have been salutary on the whole goddamned South. No lesson could be too hard for those sonsofbitches."

Meade's chief of staff, Al Webb, put in, "I felt a bit sorry for Lee.

Seeing him like that, alone and got up in his finery. You should have come out to see him. It was . . . I don't know . . . funereal."

"The old traitor," Humphreys said, all but spitting. "Wouldn't mind if it *was* his funeral. Broke his oath. Killed thousands. Tens of thousands. And you want me to pity him, Al? Not a whore's chance in hell. . . ."

"I've always believed," Meade said, "that Lee was convinced his actions—his choices—were honorable."

"This isn't the damned Middle Ages, George. Honor doesn't excuse a country's destruction, this . . . this slaughter, this continental massacre." He shook his head bitterly, intractably. "This was an unnecessary war. It wasn't caused, it was manufactured. By loudmouths and traitors."

Webb said: "Had our share of bigmouths in the North, Humph."

"I don't excuse them, either. Christ. How many of them came anywhere near a battlefield? Anybody see Greeley lead a charge? Otis Howard's the only one of the bunch who has any principles."

Meade looked at his fellow Philadelphian, his protégé and former chief of staff. In a gentle, uncharacteristic voice, he said, "It's over, Humph. It's done."

He believed he understood, though. After four years, men had so much pent-up rage in their hearts that their minds couldn't reason half of it away. It would take time. They all had seen too much, learned too much about their fellow man. Meade smiled ever so faintly, feeling the irony of his assessment of Humphreys.

For himself, he'd seen too much of Sheridan. The newspapers that had caught up with the army were one long homage to Phil, with perfunctory mentions of Grant. No one by the name of "Meade" seemed to be on the campaign.

It grated, but he saw that he'd have to get over it. Phil was a man of the future, he supposed. Treating the newspapermen to champagne and oysters, regaling the wretches with tales of his own glory . . . part of their grasping, seedy, graceless milieu, of the rising class.

Well, it was a changed world, no longer the one he knew. Perhaps this would be a better one, though Meade doubted it. The living, lofty values he had cherished had been slain as surely as had the legions of soldiers. The war had unleashed great energies and opened new positions to ruthless men. And men without conscience, men such as Phil Sheridan, would reap the harvest fertilized by blood.

He wiped his nose again. He supposed he was as sour as Humph, if not worse. The war was as good as over, men should rejoice. He should welcome the prospect of going home to Margaret.

Instead, Meade felt only drab relief, a peculiar sorrow, and insistent envy.

When he next looked at Humphreys, Meade was shocked to see tears on his weathered cheeks.

Eleven a.m.
Union lines, northeast of Appomattox

Barlow saw the difference in their shoulders, the way the rank and file relaxed their postures. Already, their uniforms no longer fit, too large by half. It was as if the shedding of blue coats would reveal a fraud, the smallness of these men who'd done great things.

He dreaded the mediocrity of peace.

He'd noted the change in their faces, too, the mixture of relief and lingering wariness, the urge to shout for joy and the fear of doing so, the superstitions of soldiers restraining their voices until they knew for certain. When the order came down from Humphreys suspending the attack, the atmosphere had changed palpably. The men had sensed, as he had himself, that the suspension was, in fact, a cancellation. Perhaps Teddy Lyman could explain the collective awareness in scientific terms.

Soon after the order reached the division, word had spread that Lee himself had appeared between the lines, dolled up like a prince and looking for Grant.

And so, on this indifferent spring morning, the soldiers marveled that their lives had been spared, when so many comrades known by name, habit of speech, and even odor had fallen away. Every man in the army faced a rebirth, and the world before them held a wealth of promises, many false but all of them enthralling.

As the men waited for him to offer them definite news, to assure them that a surrender had transpired and was irrevocable, Barlow's feelings passed his understanding. He didn't know precisely what he felt, beyond impatience and a vague foreboding—not about war, but, rather, about its absence. War might be immoral and grim, an inexcusable waste and a crime, but he knew in that moment that his true life—this acute sense of being *alive*—would never return.

He saw what lay before him all too clearly, the dreariness of success, the predictability to which he was now condemned. He would return to his Manhattan law practice. He would submit himself for public service. His reputation, forged in war, would be an advantage should he run for office. He would marry again, whether Ellen Shaw or another. There would be children, to whom he would seem remote and, at last, a bore. He might grow rich and would certainly live well. But he would never again be as truly alive as he had been only an hour before, waiting to lead his men into the attack.

War was life. The rest was dull amusement.

Eleven fifteen a.m.
Appomattox

A blue-coated officer—unmistakably an officer—rode ahead of an orderly bearing a white flag. The fellow was a magnificent horseman, all but a centaur, as Gordon could judge even from a squinting distance. He rode a poor mount and made it seem a charger.

Met at the line and escorted back to Gordon, the rider announced his identity by his appearance—the gaudy outfit, the velvet jacket and stars of ludicrous size, the cavalier's hat with flowing locks under its brim—no mistaking that one. He made the late J. E. B. Stuart seem modest in choice of attire.

The visitor slipped from the saddle with a circus rider's grace.

"I'm General Custer and I demand your unconditional surrender."

Gordon felt both affronted and amused. He folded his arms to avoid offering his hand, got up a skeptical smile, and didn't answer, letting Custer bear the weight of his own words.

Unable to still himself, Custer resumed, "I speak for General Sheridan! He demands your unconditional and immediate surrender!"

"Does he?" Gordon asked, softening his Georgia drawl in mockery. "You will, please, return my compliments to General Sheridan and tell him I shall *not* surrender my command. Not until ordered to do so."

Reddening, Custer insisted, "He directs me to say to you that . . . if there's the least hesitation about your surrender . . . that he has you surrounded and can annihilate your command in an hour."

"Can he? I believe I have grounds to dispute the case. And I know my situation as well as he does, young man." He smiled at Custer's wince. "I have nothing to add to my note. Should General Sheridan choose to resume fighting during a truce, the responsibility for the bloodshed will be his."

Custer glared.

"I hope," Gordon said with a refreshed smile, "that I have not inconvenienced you?"

Spluttering, Custer said, "This isn't the last word on this. It isn't. You *have* to surrender."

Gordon shrugged. "I don't see why."

It struck him, though, that Custer's behavior didn't augur well. If all of the Union officers were so obnoxious . . .

"I demand to see General Longstreet," Custer said, voice wavering.

Imagining how Pete Longstreet, with his pride and his cottonmouth's temper, would react to Custer's impertinence, Gordon agreed at once to provide an escort.

It wasn't twenty minutes before Sheridan rode out from his lines in person, followed by a retinue that might have passed for a regiment. Gordon walked forward and met him at his front line—barely in time to stop a well-meaning, none-too-intelligent sharpshooter from putting a bullet into Sheridan's head.

Immediately, firing broke out on the left.

"What the devil's that?" Sheridan demanded. "That your goddamned truce?"

Alone and embarrassed of staff, Gordon had to entrust a message to one of Sheridan's officers to ride off under a white flag to stop the fighting.

Sheridan dismounted. "We've met before, I believe," he announced to Gordon. "At Winchester and Cedar Creek, in the Valley."

Gordon refrained from noting the Union general's atrocious behavior toward civilians and property in that campaign, although it still rankled. Determined to remain a gentleman, Gordon said:

"I was there. I recall our encounters as impersonal, though."

"I had the pleasure," Sheridan continued, "of receiving some artillery from your government, consigned to me through General Early, your commander."

"Indeed, General. And this morning I received artillery from your government, consigned to me through General Sheridan."

"That's not true!" Sheridan declared, as petulant as a child. "That's impossible!"

"Ah, I see that your officers failed to inform you. But, then, I believe my men have kept them occupied."

Gordon was tired of the exchange, of the role he had to play, of putting up a front with nothing behind it. He resented Sheridan's boorishness, his bullying sense of triumph. Maybe surrender wasn't the best idea?

He would not let the Yankees see him chastened, though. He would not let his soldiers see him despondent.

The interview ended when Sheridan received a note from Grant. He did not share its contents but rode off.

Clem Evans appeared. Crestfallen. But still in one piece.

"Lord, Clem . . . was that your division firing? Making me send a Yankee to tamp you down?"

"Hadn't gotten the word, sir. Didn't know y'all had got up a truce. I was trying to work things out and the boys got feisty."

Gordon shook his head. "I do suspect that Brigadier General Evans got feisty, too."

"Sorry, John. I truly didn't know."

With a smile that cost a great effort, Gordon said, "Just won't quit, will you? Trying to start the war back up by yourself."

Clem looked down at Gordon's boots, in no temper for joshing. Crushed. As dispirited as a man of spirit could be.

Gordon patted his living, breathing, unvanquished friend on the shoulder.

"You know, Clem . . . your boys fired the last shots of the Army of Northern Virginia? That's something to claim, a story to tell."

Invincibly despondent, Clem shook his head.

"I'm done," he said. "I'm done with the pride of man and things of this earth. I'm just plain finished."

"Reckon your wife may think different," Gordon told him.

One p.m.
Appomattox

Lee sat beneath an apple tree and waited for Grant's response. He felt immensely tired. And as he sat, pondering the likely terms of surrender, his mind tricked him into remembrance.

He thought, as he sometimes did, of that enchanted day—no, merely a wondrous moment—when he and his child companions had been let loose to amuse themselves in the mowed fields. He believed that he had been a serious child. How could he have been otherwise, given his circumstances? But on that day, in that unforgettable instant of gilded light, he had not yet been old enough to understand he was the poor relation, more tolerated than welcome. Nor could he say which plantation his mother had descended upon that time, with her silent claim to blood-kin charity. No, all he could recall, all he ever recalled, was that sublime moment and the elation he felt at play in the sun.

Perhaps that had been the best day of his life.

A Union rider approached, coming from the village and through Gordon's lines. Lofting yet another truce flag.

The fellow, Babcock, delivered the fateful message. It was a relief, in a sense. Now he could not renege, could not change his mind and renew the fight without dishonor. All that remained were the details and the question of Grant's intentions.

"Perhaps," he said to the Union officer, pointing, "we shall find a suitable place to meet in the village."

"I'll see to it, sir," the officer told him. There was no arrogance in his voice, giving Lee frail hope. "If you'd appoint an officer to accompany me?"

When they were gone, Lee waited again, sitting on a folded blanket to save his finest uniform, which he wore to honor the day and avoid any hint of insult toward Grant. The army had gone silent, almost eerily so, and the nearest soldiers only eyed him furtively. Their faces showed that they wished to speak and dared not.

The morning had been all humiliation, if incidentally so. When Gordon's attack had been blunted and no hope remained, he had ridden out through Longstreet's corps, accompanied by a white flag, all but alone, expecting to meet Grant.

But Grant, it emerged, had gone elsewhere, to the other end of the line. And those people—their Second Corps—stood ready to attack. Humphreys, brusque and Northern, had declined to receive him and sent a cold-faced colonel as go-between. Dismissing Lee's request for a longer truce, Humphreys had claimed he had no authority to delay the assault. Only when Lee's supplication was passed to Meade had a truce been extended to allow time to reach Grant. Nor had Meade himself deigned to ride out and meet him, sending a careful deputy instead.

He had steeled himself to surrender his army, if the terms were not barbaric, only to find himself riding back again, passing mournful, suspecting, knowing faces, to wait like a servant on the master's summons.

Whatever penalties might be imposed on his person, he hoped they would not bring too much shame on his family or inflict wanton pain on those he loved. He was resigned to all a vengeful Union might exact from him. But he wished to protect his sons, his nephew, his officers.

He did not believe the soldiers would suffer excessively. No more than they already had. They would bear all that came, as common people did.

Should he have stopped all this sooner? In his mind, if not in his heart, he had known it was over, if not after the debacle at Fort Stedman, then when Petersburg and Richmond fell. He had been seduced by the sin of pride, an all too mortal sin for those who followed him.

He could not pray, not now. A public display would have been too ostentatious and his petition to the Lord belated. He faced man's judgment, without the Good Lord's mercy.

But that lost day, that moment, the ineffable, wondrous sweetness of that single instant in childhood . . . he carried that with him, the last light in his heart.

He had been innocent then. None were innocent now.

And when word was brought to him that a suitable house had been found, he summoned his staff men to him, young men whom he cherished, and he asked them to accompany him to meet Grant. To his dismay, Taylor refused outright, unwilling to offer a reason, opaque. Venable did not bother to appear. Only Marshall agreed to come along. As military secretary, it was his duty.

And Lee rode into the valley, through men robbed of so much by their failed Cause. Now and then a burdened voice called, "No! No, General!" But the tone was soft, a plea and not a demand. Traveller's hooves clapped on a wagon bridge. Ahead, up one last slope, the village waited.

They had never demanded anything of him, those men. And he had asked so very much of them.

It mattered not, in the end, how those people judged him. Perhaps he deserved to be humbled, clothed in some Northern version of sackcloth and ashes. He only feared the judgment of the Lord.

The Union officer, Babcock, waited for him by a yard gate. The house at his back was much the finest the village had to offer, brick and sound, suited to the merchant class.

Lee dismounted and tied his horse to a post. A half-dozen Union officers and orderlies gawked but said nothing. Belatedly, men saluted. He returned the gesture.

The stairs to the front porch seemed formidably steep. He climbed them more slowly than he might have wished, but with resolve. His spurs jangled. Upon gaining the porch, he wanted to pause but forced himself through the front door without slowing.

Babcock and Marshall followed him. The home's owner, a nervous-handed man, gestured toward the parlor. The room was decently furnished, in common taste.

Lee sat down, with Marshall near. Babcock went back to the hall to watch for Grant. And Robert E. Lee waited for the victor whose face he could not recall.

One thirty p.m.
The road to Appomattox

Grant warned himself not to be smug. He *commanded* himself to be flawlessly polite. Not one breath would embarrass Lee, let alone humiliate him. He'd already formulated the surrender terms in his head, striving to be a Lincoln man, to fit military requirements to the president's intentions. If Lee was not unreasonable, they'd finish things without further ill feeling.

The instant he'd read Lee's message, his headache had disappeared.

Cantering up the road, past the waste of a last fight, he worried his soiled uniform might seem an insult to Lee. Wasn't meant as such. Headquarters wagons hadn't caught up, or he would have put on the dress getup he reserved for Lincoln's visits and members of Congress.

Muddy business, riding a steeplechase through Virginia in April. His single act of celebration after receiving the give-up note from Lee had been to lead his staff and escort on a merry chase, cutting away from the roads to ride directly, relying on his sense of direction and the lure of gunfire, to reach Sheridan.

He'd almost galloped into a nest of Rebs. Which would have caused a measure of embarrassment. But he'd swerved in time, and, under him, Cincinnatti's broad back had pulsed with equine strength, unmatchable. A horse was a marvelous thing.

He'd done it, though! He'd whipped Robert E. Lee! He'd defeated the paragon of paragons, the man they all had worshipped.

Couldn't show it, of course. Wouldn't show it. But he had to admit to a bushel of gratification.

He, Ulysses S. Grant, had defeated Lee.

Topping a crest, Grant found a hamlet before him. Not much to it, but he supposed it would do. A cluster of men in blue and their horses had gathered before the yard of a brick house.

By God, he'd done it! He'd whipped him after all! Lee, the dashing gallant, the flawless officer, pride of the old Army, Lee the Invincible. . . .

He didn't let his feelings show to anyone. Wouldn't even smile, forbade himself the least curl of the lips. Didn't want to encourage gloating on anyone's part.

Just glad it was coming to an end. Sherman would finish with Johnston. What remained of the Confederate States Army after that wouldn't amount to the dandelions on a rich man's lawn.

Well, he could honestly claim that much: He'd forced the great calamity to an end. With plenty of help, he reminded himself.

Don't get too big for your britches, boy.

It repelled him, though, whenever a man, be he general or congressman, blustered about a "noble endeavor" or "sacred cause." There had been nothing noble about the war, and certainly nothing sacred. Just four years of murder.

Be a good man, the man to make Julia proud. Show Lee that a fellow can be a gentleman, even if not born into grand society.

Sheridan waited, a slight distance from the gate. Phil wouldn't miss this, of course. No sign of George Meade, though.

Just as well. Didn't want George blowing his nose like a foghorn.

Yet Meade had earned the right to be present. As much as any of them, and more than most. For a moment, Grant hesitated.

But Meade wasn't there, and that was that. It wouldn't do to humiliate Lee by keeping him waiting longer.

Grant dismounted, passing the reins to an orderly. He paused to brush off what dried mud he could and straightened his coat.

"Lee in there?"

Smiling, Phil said, "He's waiting."

Officers crowded around, from generals down to captains.

"How many with him?"

"Just one. A colonel. Nobody else. Babcock's in there, keeping an eye on the bugger."

Grant looked around at the eager faces. "Everybody stay here. I'll send for you when it's time."

Grant crossed the yard and took the porch stairs two at a time.

This was it. At last.

His life had come to something, after all.

Babcock opened the front door with his usual smirk.

In the gloom of the hallway, Grant froze. Overcome, he felt himself shrink. Stricken by the dread of a schoolboy called to the headmaster's office. Or a failing cadet called before the superintendent. As if Lee might admonish him and dismiss him even now. Making him small again, the failure men spoke of with mirth, all of his triumphs a fraud, a great illusion. . . .

"Sir?" Babcock asked.

"Nothing. It's nothing. Where is he?"

Babcock led the way and Grant followed, straightening his posture and gathering all the dignity he could muster.

He passed through the parlor doorway and saw an old man.

EPILOGUE

When Lee finished reading Grant's terms of surrender, he looked up and said:

"This will have a very happy effect upon my army."

He was glad he had spent a lifetime controlling his features. Grant had proved extraordinarily generous.

No officer or man faced a Northern prison. All would be paroled to return to their homes and remain unmolested, forbidden only from taking up arms again until "properly exchanged." Artillery, small arms, and public property must be surrendered, but officers would retain their personal weapons, mounts, and baggage.

Such generosity compelled Lee to ask for more. He explained to Grant that Confederate service differed from that in the United States Army. Enlisted cavalrymen and many artillerymen owned their horses or mules, having brought them from home. Most were farmers who needed the beasts for spring planting.

Grant declined to change the written terms, but told Lee he would instruct his officers to allow any soldier who claimed a horse or mule to take it with him.

And still Lee asked for more. He explained that his soldiers had nothing to eat.

Grant asked how many rations Lee needed and promised to deliver them.

The meeting between the generals ended with dignity and relief. As Lee left the house, the Union officers gathered in the yard removed their hats and Lee reciprocated, but no one presumed to approach him. Lee avoided their eyes.

When Lee had gone to inform his men of their fate, Grant forbade triumphant celebrations. There would be no brass bands or artillery salutes. The Confederates would not be shamed.

Then he, too, left. And the pillaging began. Union generals and colonels ransacked the parlor in which the surrender had been signed, flaunting greenbacks for tables, chairs, and lesser souvenirs, leaving the owner, Mr. McLean, stripped bare.

Sheridan bought a table for Custer's wife.

Appointed as a commissioner to work out the surrender's details, Gordon found his Union counterparts, Generals Gibbon, Griffin, and Merritt, gentlemanly and fair. Outstanding questions were resolved with goodwill, from the geographic radius within which the terms applied to the order in which the branches would stack arms.

Weighing the challenge of disbanding Lee's army, Grant authorized free transportation on Federal rail lines and vessels for all paroled Confederates going home. And they received more rations. Gordon recognized the gestures as clever and wise.

The weather soured, dousing the armies with rain, but within two days the formal surrenders began. First, the artillery turned over its guns, vehicles, and ammunition reserves, along with any animals that were property of the Confederacy, many of them lamed or dying in harness. The same day, April 11, the cavalry that had not ridden off with Fitz Lee piled arms and laid down its banners. But the great, the awful, ceremony remained, the parade and surrender of the Army of Northern Virginia's infantry, scheduled for Wednesday morning, April 12.

Lee declined to lead the men in person. He remained with the army that final day, but shut himself in his tent. And Longstreet, the senior corps commander, refused to participate. Stubborn, Dutch, and black of temper, Lee's "Old War Horse" stalked off.

Gordon understood. No one wanted the responsibility. Of all the ways a man might be remembered in coming years, to be pegged first and foremost as the man who led the surrender parade would count with the worst. And Gordon had great, if inexact, plans that centered on public ambitions.

The war was over. Leading a shaming parade would help no one at all. Why throw away the credit a fellow had built up on dozens of battlefields, why squander the investment he had in his scars?

It rained again.

And as John Brown Gordon watched his men shiver under their blankets and torn rain capes, waiting to be released to begin their journeys home to burned farms and hungry families, to lives in pieces and the silent reproach of neighborhood widows, as he watched them endure this last, sodden detention, he knew he could not leave them leaderless, cost what it may. He told Lee he would be honored to oversee the formal surrender of the infantry.

The morning dawned as gray as his dress uniform. Clouds blundered across the sky. It was cold and he'd lost his gloves again.

He took his position at the head of the column, with Henry Kyd Douglas returned to his role as adjutant and the Stonewall Brigade in the place of honor behind them. He would have liked to brace up his subordinates with some drollery, as he had done in countless desperate moments, but he could not construct a smile or find words of encouragement.

It was all so . . . empty now.

When the procession could no longer be delayed, he nudged his horse onto the road. No drums beat, no bugles called. There was only the sound of men slopping through the mud.

When he looked back over the depleted ranks, he seemed to see more regimental flags than men beneath them. He led more ghosts than soldiers.

They crossed the splintering bridge and climbed the hillside toward the village, reluctant but bound to this last, humbling duty.

It was just a thing that had to be gotten through, Gordon told himself. Like having a bothersome tooth removed. It would soon be over.

But it was worse, far worse, than having a tooth yanked.

Cresting the hill, he spotted mounted Federals by the roadside, a dozen of them, waiting in the officious posture and loose order of a staff. Beyond them, long ranks of Yankee infantry lined both sides of a gauntlet.

The one hard term on which Grant had insisted was this surrender ceremony, a public stacking of arms.

Well, let them gloat. He'd put this day behind himself soon enough. They all would.

Despite his oaths and promises to himself, Gordon felt as low as he had ever felt in his life. Damned fool decision, to expose himself to this public degradation and become the one forever tarred with capitulation, given that no one would ever blame Robert E. Lee.

His mood was as black as his mount as he traveled the endless hundred yards to the Union officers. One of them, heavily mustached, sat on his horse ahead of the others, clearly the man in command.

Gordon didn't recognize the officer. He didn't know whom the Yankees had appointed to take the surrender. And he didn't care.

Just get it done.

A speck of rain struck his hand.

As Gordon neared the Federal in charge, the fellow drew his sword sharply and lowered it in a salute.

A bugle sounded.

Orders echoed in flinty Northern voices.

One after the other, the Union regiments snapped to "carry arms" in a grand salute. The blue lines executed the gesture with a precision, with a *respect,* that moved Gordon almost unbearably.

He straightened his posture, drew his sword, and returned the Yankees' acknowledgment, making his gelding prance as it had in better days. Turning his head, he called back an order to the Stonewall Brigade: "Carry arms!"

The order passed on to the next brigade, and to the next, growing fainter. He could feel his soldiers grow taller behind him, proud once more, ready for this or any other ordeal. Even their footfalls in the mud seemed brisker, newly resolved.

Erect and determined not to weep, Gordon led his last command past the Union ranks and into an uncertain future.

In a boardinghouse in Washington, an actor prepared for his defining role.

THE END

Author's Note

After studying our Civil War and visiting its battlefields since my centennial-era childhood, I've spent the better part of a decade attempting to portray the war in the eastern theater, from Gettysburg to Appomattox, with realism, fidelity, and humanity. I sought to free the famous from their prisons of bronze and marble, to let them live again as the complex, imperfect, challenging, and ultimately inspiring individuals they were. The best known demanded a soldier's appreciation; the half forgotten clamored to be acknowledged; and the common soldier had to be redeemed from cold statistics to be seen again as a being of flesh and blood: heroic, fearful, selfless, selfish, homesick, loyal, murderous, merciful, hot, hungry, bored, terrified, humorous, devout, and profane. Above all, I wanted to be just, to shun today's pernicious habit of judging the past by our own self-righteous standards. Whether they wore Federal blue or Confederate gray, I tried to *understand* these men on their terms, to appreciate the values for which they fought so long and hard.

I failed, of course. As a planned three books turned into five, I still could not engage all the men and events wanting resurrection. And no book, or film, or techno-reality can do more than suggest—faintly—what those men experienced. They are beyond our knowing. The best I could do was to rub the facts together and hope to spark the reader's imagination.

This cycle of books sought to grip the feel of our country as it was then, as an agrarian age passed beyond recall and another era—that of the modern state—rose from the destruction. In a blink, we moved from the rule of the plow to forms filled out in triplicate. I wanted each novel to stand on its own, but if all five are read in order, from *Cain at Gettysburg* to *Judgment at Appomattox,* they're meant to provide a deep immersion, a unified two-thousand-plus-page American epic. As characters wove in and out; as armies moved and the seasons passed (few things are more vivid to soldiers than the weather); and as a sobered country changed irrevocably, I wanted to give the reader a glimpse of the war's terrible grandeur—a vision not of false romance and sanitized gallantry, but of the haunting reality, the great devouring.

Here and abroad, the 1860s formed a revolutionary decade. These books cover the two years that saw the birth of modern industrial warfare played out on battlefields an army commander could no longer survey from a well-chosen hilltop. From Gettysburg, the last Napoleonic battle, to the final months on the Petersburg front (a war of telegraph stations, steam power, rapid-fire weapons, and vast trench lines—and, for the North, a stunning logistics performance), warfare changed more profoundly than it had in the century and a half from the Duke of Marlborough's victories to that fateful morning when Harry Heth's soldiers encountered dismounted cavalry outside a country town in Pennsylvania.

It remains our greatest and most tragic war, the central event of our history. It forged the nation we know and echoes today. If we do not understand it, we won't understand ourselves.

Abundant thanks to all the readers who joined me on this journey. I'll invite you on a briefer trip to Chancellorsville in a few years, through a "prequel." My editor challenged me to take on Stonewall Jackson, the only other general in that war as unique and ineffable as Grant. I also fancy writing about Reconstruction, an era reduced to clichés in the popular memory, but whether that will come to pass I cannot say with confidence. Often, authors are kidnapped by marauding subjects that descend unexpectedly, demanding a ransom of several hundred pages. And a publisher must be convinced of a book's appeal.

As for *this* book, my repeated thanks to the wonderful team at Forge (and Macmillan); to George Skoch, whose maps are superb and vital; to Sona Vogel, who, despite my obsession with accuracy, always discovers a factual error that's just plain embarrassing; and to Jack Mountcastle, retired U.S. Army brigadier general and stalwart mentor.

Not least, my gratitude goes to Ricarda Huch, an early and courageous opponent of Adolf Hitler whose unique books taught me how to dramatize history.

As always in these books, I must acknowledge key historical works that proved of particular value as I researched and wrote. I also continue the practice of not listing books cited in the previous author's notes in this series, simply because the list would grow too long. So you won't see many of the best-known sources for the Richmond-Petersburg front or the Overland Campaign listed here—they've already been credited in the author's note to *The Damned of Petersburg* or elsewhere.

Of course, the *Official Records of the War of the Rebellion* are fundamental, followed closely by the letters home, diaries, private papers, and memoirs. But on these concluding pages I need to concentrate on the debt I owe to contemporary and earlier historians. Reputations ebb and flow: revisiting Bruce Catton after decades of neglect, I was startled by how well he wrote and how wisely. He was the model of a popular historian. Douglas Southall Freeman, by contrast, seems the last of the Lost Cause propagandists, his marvelous research and fluid prose undercut by blithe adulation of his gray-clad subjects. He diminished great men by perfecting them.

Setting those giants aside, many Civil War historians, whether professionals or dedicated amateurs, deserve far more attention than they receive—book sales are Darwinian in the worst way—so please consider the works cited below (fellow authors, forgive me if your books are not listed here—a lifetime is literally insufficient to read everything that's been published on our Civil War).

The Final Battles of the Petersburg Campaign, by A. Wilson Greene, is simply first-rate: finely detailed and clearly presented. Briefer takes on aspects of those fights can be found in *The Battle of Fort Stedman,* by William Henry Hodgkins, who served on Hartranft's staff; and in the well-illustrated and succinct *Dawn of Victory: Breakthrough at Petersburg, March 25–April 2, 1865,* by Edward S. Alexander. *The Confederate Alamo: Bloodbath at Petersburg's Fort Gregg on April 2, 1865,* by John J. Fox III, is a vivid, peerless account of the horrid fight that let Lee's army survive that fateful day.

The great historian and battlefield preservationist Chris M. Calkins authored *The Appomattox Campaign: March 29–April 9, 1865,* which provides the best and most readable overview of the subject. It's the key book battlefield visitors should read before they retrace the campaign in person (presumably in greater comfort than "Lee's miserables" did).

For the chaotic "black day of the Confederacy," Colonel Greg Eanes' *Sailor's Creek* is indispensable. As I wrote the chapters on that multilayered battle, I turned to Eanes again and again for corroboration—and his historical writing uses much the same technique as my dramatization does, switching back and forth between opposing viewpoints. To a remarkable extent, Eanes tells the story in the recovered words of the participants.

Whenever the eyewitness accounts and history texts conflicted (eyewitnesses didn't always get everything right; they saw only their sliver of the field), I did what I always do and relied on my own military experience filtered through common sense: "What would Private Snuffy do?"

This time around, the unit histories I found most useful were *Red Clay to Richmond: Trail of the 35th Georgia Infantry Regiment, C.S.A.,* also by John J. Fox III, and *Irish Rebels, Confederate Tigers: A History of the 6th Louisiana Volunteers, 1861–1865,* a wonderful book and a labor of love by retired journalist and defender of the printed word James P. Gannon (please note that Mr. Gannon bears no blame for my interpretation of Private Daniel Riordan).

Another evident labor of love is *Major-General John Frederick Hartranft: Citizen Soldier and Pennsylvania Statesman,* by A. M. Gambone. Thank the Lord for dedicated historians such as Mr. Gambone who do the grinding research and produce books that honor the lesser-known heroes of the war—knowing that the audience for such books will be painfully limited. Such works contribute far more to our understanding of the Civil War than yet another academic bundle of naïve misjudgments about Gettysburg.

"Happiness Is Not My Companion": The Life of General G. K. Warren, by David M. Jordan, is a handsomely written testament to the complexity and qualities of a fine soldier who is remembered by most—if at all—only as a savior of the Union left on July 2, 1863. Jordan brings an earnest, talented man back to center stage, an officer who, to his misfortune, fits the cliché of being his own worst enemy (having Phil Sheridan out for his scalp didn't help, either).

Fighting for General Lee: Confederate General Rufus Barringer and the North Carolina Cavalry Brigade, by Sheridan R. Barringer, and *From Blue to Gray: The Life of Confederate General Cadmus M. Wilcox,* by Gerard A. Patterson, are both valuable not only for filling in the lives of two gifted leaders and hard-luck souls, but for the way they fill in our sense of command relationships in the Army of Northern Virginia.

Inevitably, I turned to the magnificent and definitive biography *Richard S. Ewell: A Soldier's Life,* by the irreproachable historian Donald C. Pfanz. Read it if you want the military backstory of the Confederacy.

Among the memoirs and original sources I haven't mentioned previously, *All for the Union: The Civil War Diary and Letters of Elisha Hunt Rhodes,* edited by Robert Hunt Rhodes, is just plain wonderful as an account of a young man's unexpected rise through the ranks. Rhodes' depictions of his regiment's participation in the Petersburg Breakthrough and at Sailor's Creek decisively shaped my portrayal of those fights.

Henry Kyd Douglas' classic *I Rode with Stonewall* didn't end when Stonewall was no longer riding. His account of the closing years of the war—and his basic decency—makes this a must-read for students of the war. As for insight into Robert E. Lee and the staff work of the Army of Northern Virginia, two valuable works are *Lee's Adjutant: The Wartime Letters of Colonel Walter Herron Taylor, 1862–1865,* edited by R. Lockwood Tower, and Taylor's memoir, *Four Years with General Lee.* One only wishes that, at some point, Taylor had really let himself go and given full vent to his feelings. Of course, his careful temperament made him well suited to work closely with Lee.

I will forever be grateful to the U.S. Army on many counts, but in this case for exposing me to every American dialect and giving me the voices from the vastness. And I owe a debt to the 1st Battalion of the 46th Infantry for teaching me that, indeed, soldiers do not rust. I can still feel the German winter rain and recall the bleak landscape as Lieutenant Colonel Ralph Hagler, a true soldier's soldier, grinned and dismissed our discomfort with a favorite quip: "I've never seen a rusty soldier." Plenty of wet ones, though.

My compliments to the Commonwealth of Virginia (and to Chris Calkins again) for the redemption and preservation of the Sailor's Creek battlefield as a state park. Some of the key terrain remains to be recaptured and the park deserves unstinting public support.

Finally, my thanks to the National Park Service for all the splendid work its rangers and historians do. I've been on many "staff rides" and battlefield explorations in my life, but the three-day "walk" historian Pat Schroeder put together for the Appomattox Campaign ranked with the finest. I shut my mouth and did my best to learn from Pat and his colleagues.

My thanks to all.

Ralph Peters
November 17, 2016